NATHAN M. HURST
Tusk

ISBN: 9780993582318 (e-book)
ISBN: 9780993582301 (paperback)

Published by Nathan M. Hurst
www.nathanmhurst.com

Copyediting: Fiona Viney

Cover Art: Sparth
www.sparth.com

Formatting: Nathan M. Hurst

To Jo and Samuel.

ACKNOWLEDGMENTS

An incredible thank you to Stuart and Fiona Viney, for their support in creating this book. To the many voices of encouragement from friends and family who have listened to my endless musings, and to those who motivated me to put one word in front of the other until I crossed the finish line. To my wife Jo, for her daily smile and grounding (I will be going to space today). Lastly, thanks to the various local coffee houses for your early morning Java.

Tusk

PROLOGUE

Falling against the bulkhead in exhaustion, he winced. His uncut grey hair hanging across his ageing features was matting to his sweat-covered brow, knitting into his two-day-old facial stubble. He closed his eyes and pushed back the wave of nausea arising from the pure overexertion of running the length of the ship. He had been so careful for so many years. All this time he'd been driven, focussed and filled with hate and vengeance, but age had finally been his failing. The slow withering of the mind had left gaps in his defences, room for error. Chances for his enemy to find him, to destroy him.

'Travis, stop.'

He grimaced with determination and pushed off again, running down the corridor as quickly as his eighty-year-old legs would carry him. He had been aboard ship for as long as he could remember, hiding in shadows and keeping to the mission plan. However, the mission plan was becoming vague and his understanding of his part in it was now almost forgotten. There was just too much fog in his mind. Memories of his wife, Zoë, and his children were hazy, and he started to get angry with himself again, as their names slipped recollection. How could he possibly forget his children? What kind of parent could he have been? What kind of useless parent forgets the names of his own children?

'Where are you going, Travis? We need to talk.'

The door at the end of the corridor closed, cutting off his means of exit. He arrived at the door and hit the control panel but nothing happened. He keyed a passcode to override the door control—again nothing happened. He looked around frantically. There was a corridor a little further back and he stumbled off towards it.

In his head he heard voices, like those of the sirens he'd read about as a child. Beautiful and seductive, they beckoned him and directed him. They tried to reason their way into his thoughts and dreams. They tried to pull the truth from him, but he wasn't going to succumb so easily. He wouldn't give away his deepest secrets; Zoë would never forgive him. She was his one link to a world that once made sense and had true purpose and meaning: love and productivity. Now, he found only confusion and darkness.

More doors locked as he carried on down the corridor. Another dead end. Lights would flick out in the corridor as he walked. Another dead end. He felt like he was being led, like a rat in a maze, to a particular room for a particular purpose.

"You will never succeed—you can't succeed! We'll fight you until the end!" he screamed into the void about him, a little spittle drooling from his mouth in his rage. A side door to the corridor opened; he took it instantly and ducked into the room.

'What have you done, Travis? You must know I'll find out, whatever you're planning. I'll find out, somehow, the same way I found you—eventually, you'll make a mistake.'

He was frantically looking for a way out, a door home. With a few more steps, he reached the door on the opposite side of the room and opened it onto another parallel corridor. It was his own fault that he'd stepped out of his cabin this morning without wearing his device. He couldn't remember how he got it, or how it worked. All he knew was that it would keep him safe. That was what he'd been told once. There wasn't much he was sure of these days, but he was sure of that.

After a few more corridors, none of the doors closed off his progress and he started to think he had escaped, in which case his only option was to make his way back as soon as he could to his cabin, put on his safety device and get back to work.

He came to a sudden stop. Ahead of him was the image of a woman, an angel. She was so beautiful that his heart was suddenly full and his chest thumped with the urges of a much younger man. In his mind, Zoë smiled on him and extended a hand to aid him. For some reason, he was unable to grip and stumbled a little. He frowned, slightly confused and befuddled by the misjudged contact.

'This way, Travis. Sit and rest a while. You deserve a rest after your long years of service.'

She was right. He had done everything they had asked and more. It was time to rest, at least for a little while.

'Have you completed your tasks, Travis?'

He seated himself on the floor with some considerable effort. He leant against the wall and relaxed, trying to grab some air while he was able, before he had to start running again. Wondering for a moment what he was running from, the voice asked him a question. 'You have done well, Travis. Can you tell me that you've completed your task? Can you confirm?'

He smiled and closed his eyes, "Yes."

'Yes? Please confirm.'

"Yes. I've completed my mission."

'Confirm your mission.'

Why? Don't they know? Seeing as how they set it, they should know. He opened his eyes again to view the woman that he'd thought a moment before to be his wife.

For a moment, he became lucid. A moment of cognitive reasoning sparked out of the fog of his mind. He saw a control panel, and the far wall seemed to have lockers for astrosuits or EVA kit. He turned to his left and saw the striped paintwork of the external airlock door, the strip of the viewing panel set into the upper section. Looking to the internal door, his panic began to set in. It was closed and locked, and the airlock sequence had started.

'Confirm your mission, Travis. This is your last chance. What have you done aboard the *Endeavour*?'

He sat back and grinned. His work was done and he could go to Zoë and his children knowing he'd done right by them. It had taken him his whole life but he had done it right. They would be given the justice they deserved.

'There are others, Travis. You will tell me eventually.'

He didn't even hear her. The voice was nothing he needed to hear any more, nothing that conveyed anything of importance. Suddenly, all the energy left him and a feeling of complete calm and peace enveloped him. All his striving, all his trials and hardships, and he was now at the end. He was going to his family. His smile became one of complete contentment.

'So be it. Goodbye, Travis.'

An alert sounded and the airlock performed an emergency depressurisation. The external door opened in an instant and the atmosphere and contents of the room were ejected into space in a spinning, expanding, spiralling mass. Ice crystals twinkled in what little light there was from a nearby star. As the trauma of sudden exposure to vacuum wrought its toll on Travis, his ageing heart stopped almost immediately. There was no final breath to give.

CLAYTON

The sun flickered and danced among the leaves in the trees above his head, creating shadows on his face as he lay in the grass looking up. Floating in the gentle warmth of the afternoon breeze drifting through the glade, he let the worries of the day melt away and the memories of a different time and place fill him. It had been too long since he had afforded himself any time to reflect on his family—the point in his life which centred him.

In the soft caress of his surroundings, his eyes were unfocussed and his mind slipped free to roam amongst his past. The joy in his wife's eyes and love in her voice as she told him they had been given permission by the state to have a child...fast forward, the day they turned up at the clinic for consultations...fast forward, a screaming little girl, full of life and potential...fast forward, family and hope. There was a physical warmth he felt in these thoughts, which simply made him happy. A small smile broke across his lips and a snort that could have been a laugh.

The leaves on the trees, such a vivid green in their backlit state, and the pure blue of the sky without a cloud to be seen, were captivating. However, sounds started to infiltrate his senses and the giggling of children cut through. His wife's voice was also unmistakable. She was only a few metres away and enjoying her daughter's joke, whatever it had been. There were others in the background but he couldn't make them out—a low voice, softly spoken, and a light sing-song voice which sounded like music to him.

He felt a hand brush gently across his forehead and he looked up. His wife was looking down. "Are you going to dream the day away?"

"No, just enjoying the moment," he replied with a smile.

A shadow flew across his vision and his daughter launched herself at him in a playful tumble. "Let's play, Daddy!" and before he could answer she was gone again, running away shrieking with laughter as she went.

"You'd better get going, or you'll never catch her."

"She gets that from you, you know. Definitely, your side of the family." He got up slowly, like a dazed boxer after the count, and looked round slowly for his attacker. She was quicker than he expected. Four years old and faster than a spring hare. Shrugging off the sluggish warmth of the afternoon sun, he started after his daughter. She screamed again and jinked away, staying close but just out of reach. A game of chase, simple but with delicate rules. If the prey was too easily caught or the pursuer too aggressive, the fun was lost. No fun in a quick game. The game was in the timing: just long enough for the fun to peak and the prey to think they had escaped again. Then the pounce and capture, sudden, with tickles and hugs, then repeat. He was sure this was the same for fathers and sons or daughters the world over, the rules of the game consistent as the rules of life. Everyone knew the rules, no matter what side.

After the sixth game of chase, he fell to the ground and feigned exhaustion. Dawn was smiling at him with a knowing 'Is that it?' look on her face. "What? I'm shattered. Try and keep up with her."

"I am," he said in an exhausted voice, loud enough for Dawn to hear. "She's just so fast."

"Daddy, let's play more." Dawn was in his arms in a moment. "Come on, Daddy!"

"Daddy needs to rest a while," he said. Was the tag going to work? Jemma took up the challenge. She knew the cues.

"Come on, little one. Daddy needs a rest. You've worn him out."

Nice work. He flopped down and took a look across the glade. The picnic was laid out on a blanket in front of him, now mostly remnants of a long grazing lunch. Picking up a juice drink and taking a rough gulp, he noticed the sing-song voice again. He looked around but could not identify the source, nor could he work out what it was saying. Probably a glitch in his implants; he'd run a diagnostic when he got back to the hotel. Jemma was playing and chasing Dawn through the trees and across the long grass, threading zigzag patterns as they went.

They had been off the grid for a few days now—a long overdue holiday—and he was loving it. Jemma had been insistent. His work had been getting the better of him recently and she was right. She was right most of the time. He wondered if that ever got tiring for her. A few days in the country, away from the city and its distractions and its uncompromising, relentless work schedules, but, most importantly, a moment to take time with his daughter. She was young and full of life, running with her mother and leaping like a gazelle—she was their triumph. High IQ, good genetic coding and high longevity quotient, she was booked into the best academies and had the next thirty years of her life mapped out. Nothing to do but keep it all on track, a little tap here and a nudge there to guide their golden child into a good life with the best prospects. He smiled inwardly to himself. Life was pretty good.

Of course he would need to surface again at some point, but that was a good week away yet. Don't wish your time away, he thought to himself. But work always had a way of finding its way in. He had left things in good hands. The guys at work knew the drill, and he couldn't see the research they were working on getting any critical uplift in the next year or so. Funding was secured for the next five years, so there were no hoops to go leaping through in the near future. He always niggled though, he was one of life's worriers. He would at least check his mail when he got back—he could do that on the sly and Jemma would likely not know. Actually, who was he kidding? She would know. He wondered if he had a 'tell' and that's how she always knew. It was a good job he wasn't a gambler. The poker tables would be a direct route to poverty if his 'tell' was as easy to read as Jemma clearly found it.

On reflection, he was pleased Jemma had insisted. He could and did quite regularly get a little over-involved. Focus was not the word for it. He would literally lose himself in his work. The next code line, the next puzzle, the next problem being the one where he would take a break. He would find time slipping and only be pulled from his endeavours with a quick incoming message from his wife telling him his dinner was cold and she was ditching him for the pizza delivery boy. Joke? Yes, thankfully. A holiday would help, he could give back a little of what his work took away.

So, here they were in a small glade in a forest a couple of hours west of London, on a hot Indian summer's day in September. The sweet smell of wild flowers and the sound of wind through the trees was a wonderful change to his usual routine of days and months locked up underground in a research facility. Thick concrete walls and even thicker doors. His world was a team of twenty people working like there would be no tomorrow without their efforts that day. Some of them so dedicated he would regularly find them asleep at their desks the next morning, looking like someone had a face-painting competition where the best panda would win. Sunken dark eyes and a look that really shouldn't be on the faces of the brightest and best minds the country had to offer. Still, they were all working on a project that meant the world to all of them. They knew that if they could pull it off, they would be set for life. No more worrying about the next pay cheque, they would all be IW, Independently Wealthy, and the government would pick up the tab for the after-work party. It was a price worth paying.

Round they came again, like a couple of comets in an elliptical orbit, rushing past only centimetres away and zooming off into the trees. Dawn was calling to Jemma to chase her again and again, not seeming to need a breath while running like the wind with the occasional skip and pronk thrown in for good measure.

They were close but had hit a snag, a technological brick wall. He had worked in AI technology research his whole life, and over the last few months academic consensus had started to crystallise around there being no way forward. AI was simply a very complex and well-informed machine, but always a machine. The neural cortex within the machine was not responding to logic changes, advances in the code that tried to mimic the human condition. Something else was needed. It was almost as if the more they knew the further from a workable solution they actually got. It was time to try a different angle, attack the problem from the human perspective, not that of the machine. How about mapping one neural network to the other? The data would be vast, so take it in steps. What was needed was the human capacity to learn independently, and to analyse and respond to problems without the hard logic and accuracy of a machine. To allow itself to be fallible, then reinvest.

Dawn had decided it was time for a drink and to stop Daddy

dreaming. She and Jemma sat back around the blanket and started to pour some orange squash. "You're dreaming again, Daddy? What are you dreaming about?"

"Sorry. Work." He took a look and saw the question in her eyes. "I think I've just had a good idea." Quickly, he spun up his capture bio-comms, his D-RTx bio-comms wetware, sometimes known by the techs as Dr Comms or Bio-Cs, and saved his memory for later consideration. "I'm all yours. I'll work on that later."

"Home time," Jemma chipped in. "If we want to get back to the lodge before dark, we should pack up and get going."

"Aw, Mum!" This did not go down well. Then again, it never did, so why would now be any different.

"She's right, you know. It's more than a two-hour drive back to the lodge." The look on Dawn's face was all pouting and disappointment; however, he could not help but find it funny. One day, rather than look all hurt, she would simply say 'Okay, Daddy' and do as she was asked. But he was fooling himself, kids never did that. His smile broadened. "Go on, one more race around the field."

"I'll race you," she said. "Go!"

Dawn was already half way across the field before he could even get off the floor.

The ride home was quiet. Jemma wasn't really in the mood for long conversations and Dawn was sleeping. She had been running around all afternoon, so it wasn't really a surprise. Now in the car, the gentle rocking and the drone of the engine was all it took to nudge her into a deep sleep. They got back to the lodge by early evening and had a late tea. Dawn was still pretty exhausted and asked to go to bed, which was not really the norm but under the circumstances not entirely unexpected. After a bedtime story about a penguin in the city trying to find a man with a bucket of fish and a time machine, she was asleep again.

By the time he had finished putting Dawn to bed, read her a story and settled down to relax with a nice healthy glass of red wine in the lounge, Jemma was already most of the way through a glass herself. "I've been thinking about tomorrow. How about we take Dawn skiing in the Alps?"

"It's been forever since I've been skiing—I'll break bones in minutes." It sounded like a good idea, but he wasn't keen about breaking bones. He could be knitted back together and out of the hospital within a couple of hours, but it was the initial pain he never liked. He remembered back to the moment he broke his arm falling from a tree as a kid—the sensation of free fall and the sudden blinding pain as his left arm twisted under him, and the mass of his body and gravity doing the rest. His mum and dad were there to pick him up from the local A&E, with a bag of his favourite chocolates, all smiles and consolation, his arm fully repaired and ready to go. But, technology can't take away the initial shock and trauma. It can fix you up quick enough after the event, but you always remember the pain. So, skiing? After a pause: "Sure, she needs to learn sometime. We can take the vaclev to the Paris Gare du Nord then connect for the alpine routes there."

"How about the City helojet? We'll be there in half the time." She always preferred air travel; he preferred his feet on the ground. Something about evolving without wings had decided it for him. No wings, no flying. He thought he was going to lose the argument though. Despite knowing the vaclev was faster, he just shrugged his shoulders.

"What's faster than a bullet in a vacuum?" he countered.

"Ah, but where's the view? I like to see the mountains as we go. And Dawn has never seen the mountains from a helojet. She'll love it." And there it was, they would be flying. He sighed, with a smile. She had a point.

Jemma giggled and took up her glass of wine, "It'll be great. I could invite the Roberts, or the Wisemans ..." His bio-comms started playing up again, and his wife's voice faded into the background and the same weird floating voices he's heard earlier in the day returned. He still couldn't make out what they were saying, but he was convinced now that he needed to do something about it. "Are you alright, Honey?" Jemma was now looking slightly worried and had moved to his side. "You don't look so good."

"I'm okay. I think I've got a gremlin in my bio-comms. Sound interference maybe, I don't know. I'll run some diagnostics and see if I can't clear it up, or it'll be a trip to the clinic tomorrow." He didn't fancy that option. Those kind of trips could take a day out of your life really quite easily. Even as he was saying this, his vision also started to fracture—a crisp image of his wife started to become vague and a little blurred, slowly splitting into what appeared to be a double. One of the images moved away from him and returned to the armchair across the room, but the other stayed where it was with an expression which seemed bland yet sympathetic. "Err, maybe that should be a call to the clinic tonight." His wife, in an armchair which he believed always looked more like a star ship crash couch, settled down and closed her eyes. She didn't respond to his comment but instead appeared to be cycling through her bio-comms, maybe to catch up on her mail, maybe to watch a movie. Either way, she wasn't taking any notice of what he was saying. The wife still sitting by his side, however, cocked her head to one side and replied in a weird voice, as if she'd been breathing helium.

"No need for the clinic, Dr Clayton." Her voice modulated a little then lowered in pitch. "We need to talk for a moment. I need to begin the reintroduction sequence. It's time."

There was part of him that knew nothing of what she was saying. What did she mean by reintroduction sequence? However, some deeper part of him seemed to stir, and other memories began to bubble to the surface, memories from a more recent place and time. As these newer memories came into focus, so his whole visual world started to morph into something else completely. His living room began to melt away like a watercolour painting in the rain, slowly blurring until the drained lines meant nothing and the only thing that he was aware of was his wife opposite him with that gentle smile on her face and a look of quiet understanding at his mild confusion. Before he could start asking any questions, Jemma—or the woman now looking like Jemma—moved forward and took his hand, or rather his wrist. It was a moment before he realised that she was taking a rudimentary pulse, checking his physical wellbeing.

All he could think to say was, "Am I okay?"

"Looking good so far," said the other Jemma, "I'll know more in a couple more minutes. Shouldn't take long."

More memories came to him. It was like someone was turning on layers of memory which he felt he had always been aware of, but not with this level of accuracy or clarity. Schematics of the United Terran Ship *Endeavour*—an Interstellar Class starship—every passageway, circuit and conduit, navigational charts to a Terra classified planet designated 21 Hayford b, an Earth analogue in the second quadrant of the galactic north, roughly four parsecs coreward, communications protocols, biotech-generation algorithms, biodiversity methodology and terraforming theory. The stream of information was flooding him, and he could feel the rate of incoming information like a pressure in his skull, pushing from the inside, driving up and out, expanding and probing for a way out, an escape from the confines of a mind too small and ill-equipped to cope.

While this was happening, Jemma sat calmly, holding his wrist and waiting, counting. His anxiety was rising, then complete calm. A key piece of understanding had been unlocked. It was like the gasping breath of a drowning man as he reached the surface. The release he felt was palpable. His body was covered in sweat, and he realised he was gripping Jemma's hand, perhaps too tightly, but she didn't react or complain.

"Hello, Jem," he said finally, getting his composure back and his breath under control. "Thank you."

She held his wrist for a moment longer, taking a last moment to diagnose any potential problems or side effects of the process. Satisfied with what she was seeing, she gently placed his hand back to his side. "You had me worried there, for a moment," she said. "I wasn't sure you were processing correctly."

"Nonsense. Things can just take a little longer after an extended sleep period."

"I'll be the judge of that."

"You're the doctor," he smiled back. "How are the crew? Did their resequencing go to schedule?"

"All to plan. You are among the first to be revived. Senior team and medical staff first. The rest are being revived as we speak. We should have a full crew complement within the next 48 hours." That was impressive. The clones would have been grown over the last twenty five years or so, but the tricky part was reintroducing the memory wave into the host mind. There was always a chance that the reawakened person was unable to reintegrate into their new body. It was their own body of course, just a little younger than they left it, but on the very rare occasion a newly revived person would find it impossible to reintegrate into their new frame, there was a chance of insanity. Thankfully, this was rare, as all deep space star-faring crews were put through the most mentally rigorous testing and psychoanalysis before they stepped anywhere near a starship. Spacers were fully aware of what they jokingly referred to as 'reskinning'. It was new, but it was just another part of the job.

Jemma seemed pleased with progress. "Do you think you can stand?"

"Sure."

"Okay. If you follow me, we have a resuscitation couch ready for you." She started to walk away into the void around them and as she did so the background began to coalesce and take on forms and shapes again. A corridor with white walls and grey floors, yellow guiding lights indicated the way ahead and bright light panels in the ceiling gave the whole scene a washed out, sterile appearance. She headed towards the end of the corridor and a door automatically slid open as she approached. Turning momentarily to check he was following, she stepped inside. The resuscitation room was reasonably sized, well-appointed and not at all like the corridor. It had ten couches lined with five along each wall, four of which were already occupied. The walls were a relaxed green in colour and there were potted plants dotted here and there. One of the walls had been given over to a floor-to-ceiling screen which showed a serene forested panorama. The occasional bird could be seen sweeping across the view, deer might sneak through the foliage on occasion and a bubbling brook could also be heard, along with the other more ambient forest sounds.

There were a few other attendants working through the room, serving water or nutrition bars to those reclining on the couches. "Here you are—your chariot awaits," she said, pointing like a magician's assistant at one of the couches in front of the forest scene.

"Thank you."

"Would you like a glass of water?"

"Yes, please," he nodded and smiled comfortably.

Jemma moved to a side table and poured him a glass of iced water, returning and leaving it for him on the table next to his resuscitation couch. "If you can lay back and relax, I'm going to place this warm towel across your eyes. Relax and everything will work out just great." He did as he was told, quickly making himself comfortable and adjusting his position, waiting for the application of the warm towels, the purpose of which was mostly to keep you calm as some pretty advanced medical machines piped his psyche back into his younger cloned self. In a couple of moments, he was going to physically become twenty-five again. Personally, it was not an age he would choose—he had always been far happier in his thirties. His mother had always told him he had an old head on his shoulders. Funny, now he really did. His wave was now hundreds of years old—*he*, was hundreds of years old—but in relative terms he was twenty-five on the outside and forty-five on the inside. Modern deep space travel really did mess with your internal clock. Like the worst kind of jet lag.

The transition, as always, was seamless. "All done," he heard Jemma say from a couple of feet away. "Wave is holding and attenuation is stable." Not a bump, flash or tingle. The towel was gently removed from his eyes and he looked up into the room. His stasis state had mimicked the resuscitation suite exactly: the glass of water on the side table, the serene forest panorama wall and the couch upon which he was reclining. He was constantly astonished at the level of detail the developers who designed and modelled the stasis software were able to achieve. He had done some reading on the subject during a brief vacation when last awake. They apparently really didn't need to provide that much detail. The human mind is a wonderful thing and will quite happily fill in massive amounts of detail from some very subtle cues. There stood Jemma, khaki coloured uniform with white shoulder flash designating medical team. She was checking some details on a screen embedded in the resuscitation couch he was laying on but seemed casual and relaxed. No problems. Good.

She looked fantastic. Twenty-five again, fresh and alert with the vigour of youth but the wisdom of age—a real heady mix. Jemma looked over to him. "You should have some water. Plenty of fluids. Make sure you inform me of any headaches or bright flashing lights in your vision." Nodding to someone across the room, she continued, "Amanda will take care of you for the next hour. If you're hungry, let her know, but don't go crazy. This is a new body and it's only just been unplugged. The stomach will still be a little sensitive." That was the medical brief out of the way.

"So how am I doing, Doc?" She gave him a withering look.

"Nothing wrong with you, Captain. Now, rest and I'll see you later for dinner." With that, she moved in close, their eyes locking for a moment, both of them enjoying the closeness. Then they kissed. Life in stasis felt fleeting, so to him it really had only been hours since they last spoke, but to have just successfully reskinned, it was worth marking.

"I hope you don't treat all your patients like this," he goaded.

"Hey, it's the personal touch. They love it." She smiled back.

"Quite a bedside manner. You'll get a name for yourself."

"I already have one of those."

He looked confused, and she kissed him again quickly. "Dinner at eight," and, with that, disappeared into the hallway as the door slid shut behind her.

He watched Jemma leave then looked over to the far side of the room where Amanda was tending and checking on another newly revived crewman. He couldn't see either of their faces, as she was standing with her back to him and her patient was obscured by her. He decided to take a sip of water—he was under instruction to do so after all. Ice and a nice dash of lime. Perfect. Taking a pull on the straw, he could feel the cool liquid slipping down his throat and into his stomach, its every motion being experienced by his over-sensitive new cells. The soft sounds of the forest murmured in the background and the gentle hypnotic swaying, susurrating leaves pulled him into a momentary daydream.

Every new host body he had been reskinned into had this honeymoon period. Fresh out of the cloning process, the cells of the body were alive and as a baby's, fresh from the mother's womb. He lay back and closed his eyes from the bright lime of the spring trees, and took a deep breath into his new lungs. The air was sweet, the sounds in his ears, the rush of his own heart pumping blood round his body; all sensations were acute and hypersensitive. He exhaled and placed his palms flat on the couch, moving his hands back and forth to feel the soft brushed leather. Older hands would be numb to the delicate sensations. It wouldn't take long for this newness to degrade, for the amplification of the senses to become dulled by simple use. It was like being born again, physically but not mentally, like a remembered reincarnation. He loved these first moments of a reskinning.

"Hello, sir." Amanda was by his side and checking the data panel on the side of the couch, as Jemma had a few moments before.

"Hi."

"Can I get you anything? More water, maybe?"

"No, that's okay," he said, sitting more upright in the couch. She was a tall woman with a slight build and jet black hair, dark brown eyes and a look of concentration. Clearly quite busy with the other recovering crew members in the room, he decided not to impose on her time. He was slipping into work thoughts already. He was a little annoyed with himself over how little time that had taken. Barely an hour. "Things going well?"

"Yes, sir. Things are currently going quite smoothly. No issues with wave transfer, no problems with rejection. On the whole, a good morning." She shifted over towards him and gave him a small packet containing two pills, standard issue supplements for the post-resuscitation process. "Take these please, sir."

"Thanks." He opened the packet and took them with a swallow of water.

"Your clothes are on the bench at the foot of your couch and the changing room is through the door at the end of the room. You can leave your robes in the laundry by the exit." She was already talking like she'd been saying this all day for a year. Information dispensed with the repetition of the workplace. Why didn't she just ping the information to his bio-comms? Then he could watch it in his own time and she wouldn't be endlessly repeating herself. Maybe it was down to the 'personal touch' that Jemma had mentioned earlier. Somehow, it didn't feel that personal.

"Thanks," he said again. "Am I free to go?"

"One last check, please look to my left ear." He did, and there was a flash of intense light in his eyes. "And now, my right ear." Again a flash of light.

He continued to look at her, this time with the expectation of a boy about to be let loose in a sweet shop. Light spots still echoing in his vision, he blinked a couple of times to recover. She was quietly checking some readings against records and getting the sign-off for his release.

"Sign-off has been accepted. You're clear to leave when you like, sir." She broke into a smile for the first time since he had seen her. It suited her much more than the frown of concentration.

"Wonderful. Thank you, Amanda." He hopped off the couch with an excited urgency and scooped up his clothes. The resuscitation suite was meant to be place to lay a while, relax and recuperate. Some could stay there for hours after reskinning. He was the opposite: he found it only a gateway to a magic garden and could not wait to get through the door at the end to explore.

On the other side of the door, the room was empty. The

resuscitation process had only really just begun and, from what Jemma had told him, he estimated there to be only around forty crew members currently awake. The ship was designed to carry eight hundred crewmen and around double that number again in scientific staff. Some of the crew, like himself and Jemma, were married or had partners, but the majority were not. Expectations on arrival at a new planet were for colonisation, so healthy relationships were encouraged planet-side. Aboard ship things were left alone, no need for any pressure—there was pressure enough and everyone was well aware.

Dressing quickly and fumbling a little, he bumped into benches and had to sit down a couple of times as he got his leg twisted in his clothing or his balance gave out. Eventually, he made it out of the changing area and into the passageway leading from the medical bay to the elevators. His bio-comms visualised door numbers, bulkheads numbers and signage as he went, overlaying a virtual world into his physical one. He requested a room location and immediately a cyan trace lit a path ahead of him, turning right at the end of the corridor. He set off to follow it.

As with its crew, the *Endeavour* was still waking up. It had been mostly dormant for one hundred and thirty years, operating on minimum power and life support. Once up to speed and aimed at its target, the starship had joined the cosmic dance and become one of the largest man-made comets ever created, along with her five sisters. With its crew in wave stasis and the seeds of their regeneration in cryogenic suspension, it could drift in the cosmic wind for the entire voyage, maybe a navigational nudge here or gravitational adjustment there, but the more uneventful the journey the better. Its only purpose was to carry the hope of humanity to new worlds.

Walking past corridors leading to accommodation blocks, lights flashed on and systems began their final preparations to make the space ready for habitation and human occupation. Drones buzzed around cleaning, repairing and maintaining, each with its own specific role in the long sequence of events that would breathe life back into the ship. Air was being pumped through the space, the aeration units having been started several weeks prior to ensure the fully breathable atmosphere within. Hydroponics would have been started months before within their own micro biosphere, and engineering would have been warming up the engines and critical systems. The list was vast, but all needed to happen correctly, and in the right order.

He knew the engineers had been thorough in the design of the ship. Through his bio-comms, he could see redundancy built into every system—backup systems, backups to backup systems— they had over-engineered in places to ensure success. It reminded him of any early engineering at the frontier of its time. A lack of understanding of new materials, or of the environments that their designs would operate in, always gave the engineers cause to add in an additional safety factor to their design—a 'fudge factor', he called it. They had been doing it for as long as there had been engineers, he didn't see why that would change now. Work out the mathematics and add a bit for safety's sake.

Rounding the corner, he found the elevators. One was waiting for him, and he walked in. "CIC," he said. The doors closed and the elevator moved rapidly to the requested level, lights flashing past as levels were gained on the ascent. The Command Information Centre was empty. Systems were operational, with screens displaying various operational data and local telemetry information. He glanced quickly at a couple of screens while pacing through but considered he would get all the updates he needed in the room at the rear of CIC. A short linking corridor and a door that had a single word written on it, repeated in floating graphics in his vision. The navigational trace stopped at the door.

The sign read, 'DAWN'.

DAWN

The door slid aside and a tall man with keen intelligence walked briskly through with no pause or ceremony. Moving directly towards the centre console of the room, he quickly keyed a passcode into the machine and recited a passphrase aloud. Although she had been watching and monitoring him from the moment he was revived, it was only now that Clayton12 animated her own holographic image in the corner of the room. She chose to focus her visual receivers through the hologram in order to feel human for a while. As the ships AI, she was in constant contact with all parts of the *Endeavour.* She felt the physicality of the ship as part of herself—an extension of senses on such a massive scale that simply by thinking about a servo, a door, a drive engine, she could activate it or manipulate it in an instant. She was the ship, the ship was her. But at the same time, she could still feel human, the way she had been so many years before. The hologram, now, was her conduit to that feeling and that interaction with the crew— especially her father.

"Hello, Dawn. How have you been?" Dr Peter Clayton, captain and scientist, stood before her. He had been revived only a few hours ago and already was more interested in her wellbeing than his own.

"Good to see you, Daddy." She had always called him that in personal moments such as this, otherwise she would call him 'Captain', as it kept the crew settled. It appeared they were happy with an AI within the ship, just not an AI as daughter of the captain. "I'm fine. The ship is operating within expected tolerances, the crew are being revived with no issues or anomalies so far, and you have had far too little recovery time before getting back to work," she chided gently.

"I needed to see my girls," he replied with a warmth that made her feel like a sprite thirteen-year-old again. "Saw your mother in the resuscitation lounge; don't let me forget dinner at eight." She pinged him a reminder instantly.

"Reminded."

"You can't remind me the instant I ask you to remind me, that doesn't work."

"I think you'll find it does," she said.

He laughed.

Moving across the room, he sat in the couch next to the holographic image of his daughter. She had chosen to wear the crew uniform but, as the only AI on the ship, had invented a magenta designation flash for herself.

Seeing him sitting there, in the youth of his new clone, was always a surprise to her. She had not even been born when he had first looked this young. They now looked roughly the same age, and, though she could alter her own appearance, she always liked the age before the accident. She had been twenty-six. No age at all. Although, she felt lucky: she had been the daughter of a man who could save her. Not in the conventional sense, but he had been able to save her spirit, her wave, the essence of who she was. He was able to capture her memories.

His work at the Formillun Institute—a research facility in the UK specifically for investigations into the viability of AI technology—had been her saviour. After years of work on creating an AI, he had realised that the missing component, and the component that would be needed for a human to truly believe that the machine was another human, was a human operative. He perfected AI splicing. Her essence—her wave—recorded from her ailing body was injected into an AI container construct and given time. Time to adjust, time to be reborn. The process was not painless, though the pain was only psychological. The readjustment to her new being, one contained and constrained within the confines of a machine, was almost too much for her to bear, even with the support of her father. She flew through emotions of wild rage, despair and self-destruction, and at all times within a cloud of complete confusion.

At some point though, she had become calm. Whether through something her father and his team had done to the machine container, the coding of the AI splice, or whether through some natural subsiding of the storm inside her, she emerged. Project Clayton12 was reborn as Dawn. She was herself again and accepting of the new world she now lived in. She would not be flesh and bone again, ever, but she was okay with that. There were so many things that she could accomplish in this state, first of which would be in assisting further research into AI theory and of her new place in the world. She was the first of her kind, this new human-machine hybrid.

And the knowledge she could access while she was in the laboratory was vast. Before, she had to look things up, memorise, network the information and then sit and read for hours to understand and assimilate the data. That had all changed. She could access information now, almost at the speed of thought, and once she had located the information, it was instantly understood. Processed.

"So, I have over one hundred and thirty years of catch-up to wade through," he said. "Give me the highlights."

Dawn had prepared a summary file in advance. She pushed it to his bio-comms and saw him settled back in the couch to get started. Beginning with the ship status, crew update, current galactic position and mission status, they quickly got onto mission detail, flight telemetry and destination data.

Although he looked younger, there was certainly no mistaking the man. His personality and determination, compassion and vitality shone through. He had a charisma and way about him that people instantly warmed to. It was not something he appeared to be aware of, just something others wished they could achieve. It seemed to be a similar trait in most leaders she had read about. It drew people to them, their ideas, and their dreams, and it inspired action.

Mingled in with all this, he was her father, twice over. She considered that her mortal life had been one phase of existence and her AI life another, where he was the constant. He had been her guide through it all. She loved him as any daughter loved a father, but recognised the gift and luck in both the circumstances that brought her into being and the inspiration for invention when it happened, something she was immensely grateful for. His dedication to her through his work had given her an idea, it had given her a purpose, and it was this that had possibly been the trigger to calm the tempest inside her. Whatever it was, she would live to repay her father for all his efforts and help him in any way she could to advance his goals. His dreams would become hers. Little did she know that she would have such an instant effect.

Within the first decade of research and the legal turmoil that had sprung up around her sudden existence, it had become apparent that if a person's wave could be captured and mapped to a machine, could the process not be reversed? This line of research stumbled under the ethical weight of the host required for the process, as you couldn't just fire a wave at a host with an existing conscience. Would the current host conscience be displaced? Would the result be a jumble of multiple minds or would the transfer simply fail? No-one knew, nor could they calculate for certain. Evidence was required and that was simply something that ethics boards and governments would never sign off on—the requirement of human experimentation. Animal experimentation was the normal next step in a process such as this; however, for this particular research they could not be sure of the outcome, as they had to test memory, personality and cognitive functions. Some could be done, but the human factor needed a direct test subject.

She watched her father reading his status updates and remembered the moment life changed for him. The years of fighting to advance his theories and the perpetual knock backs from all the funding and governing bodies had made its mark on him. He was growing impatient with others and could see no way round the bureaucracy. With frustration getting the better of him, he turned inwards for a solution and at that moment he chose his test subject. He would be the first receiver of a contained human wave.

The experiment would need to be a circuit, and confirmation would be required at each stage of the process to ensure completed transfer. That was where she came in. Dawn would have to perform and control the experiment, recording the critical data at specified validation points. They would build a human-AI-human circuit, with defined static points to test transfer success.

Shifting his wave to an AI container would not be a problem; the theory and implementation had proven success. The problem was going back. The recorded consciousness patterning would be rejected or cause echoes when returned to the host—in this case, his own body—due to the already active mind in place. He had not needed to consider this problem previously, as, when Dawn was spliced into her AI container, the AI was effectively empty and there was no need or requirement to return to the originating body. Imaging his wave would cause a problem. He wasn't moving his wave, he was making a copy and he would be conscious in two places. Another ethical dilemma: which version of himself would truly be him? He had to isolate his own consciousness in any instant.

Dawn considered his solution. She had not had to undergo returning to a host, as her own body had been too frail after the accident to survive. There was no return for her. But his answer to the returning issue was a chemically induced and sustained brain death in the host, to erase the current hosted mind and keep the physical structure of the brain intact. She had been alarmed and argued against it with some passion. He had saved her through necessity but to do this through choice alone seemed madness. What about her? What about mum? They argued for hours while setting up the final experiment. All she could do in the end was check, check and check again all the parameters, all the components of the experiment, to ensure absolutely nothing went wrong.

Her answer to the problem caused her father to appear momentarily dumbfounded. He could not believe he had not considered it before. Cloning. A cloned version of himself could be generated, the growth of which could be controlled and monitored closely. It would provide a bio-container similar to those he had already produced in machine terms for the AIs and the bio-container would be empty. The physiology would be identical to his, if not a little younger, so there should be no rejection of the wave when spliced back into the system. The theory appeared sound. All that was needed was to obtain a clone of himself to continue his research. There would still be risks, but far fewer and not to him directly.

She could remember the moment when the light bulb switched on in his mind, as he considered the possibilities of what she had just revealed to him. It still made her laugh. He looked so goofy.

Again, legalities surfaced. You could clone a sheep, a whale or a baboon, or any other animal you cared to mention. You could even grow component parts of a human for medical replacement. But what had been ruled out from the very early days of the cloning programs had been the potential to clone another complete human being. People got jittery about the thought of another identical human being roaming the planet, with the same features, same hair, same voice.

There was going to be a battle, a legal one, and he needed a way of convincing people and peers that the process was ethical. His solution was for there only ever to be one single active wave. He would need a way to convert the wave transference to a one-way process, but, so long as there was only ever one person and one wave, he might have a chance of getting things past the Ethics committees.

Dawn began to think he had a death wish. The solution he had come up with was, again, at severe personal risk to himself. His method was to take his wave, splice it to an AI construct, then inject his wave from the AI directly into the clone. Once this was done, and the process complete, the origin of the wave—the body that had been born to this world naturally—would be shut down. No way back.

She was back to checking and rechecking all his work, his assumptions, his calculations, the technology and tools they would need. He made his preparations.

After completing the primary build of the dual transfer machine, her father had decided they couldn't complete the project alone. The cloning process required medical staff and scientists that he did not have the authority for at the institute. Since the success of the Clayton12 project, he had more resources and more technical staff on hand for his research, but not medical resources. He was going to need the buy-in of the institute director, Sir David Jessop.

Her father shifted in his couch, bringing her back to the present. "Dawn, there's something missing here," he said, in matter-of-fact tones. "Our resuscitation was to have been made to bring us to readiness a month from Hayford b." He was rubbing his chin in thought. "From your report, we are much closer." He paused, doing some quick arithmetic, "About...a week out?" he exclaimed, surprised.

"Yes."

"Is the reason in the report, or did I miss it?"

"No, you didn't miss it," she said quietly. Delivering bad news was not something she wanted to do, and she had been putting it off. "I've lost contact with the *Intrepid*."

"How long?"

"She's at station, but communications have been offline for a month."

"You really know how to spoil a perfectly good day," he mocked. "Alright. Well, if she's at station, that's some good news at least. If it's a serious problem, it could take some time to fabricate and repair parts."

"I've checked for misaligned arrays, and for transmit and receive anomalies, but the array has gone completely dark and won't respond to comms. We are also unable to check the hardware connection to know if it's been damaged. We have not yet performed a visual inspection. It's just that there's no response from Ellie." Ellie, or Clayton94, was the AI currently in the mission sister ship *UTS Intrepid*, twenty thousand kilometres to the planar south east of their position. As the mission had such a long duration, the planners had believed the success of the mission would be improved if they built in some level of redundancy. Each seed mission, therefore, had three starships. The greater the number of starships, the greater the probability of mission success. In reality, it also increased the number of things to go wrong.

"How about the *Indianapolis*? What does Obi make of it?" Obadiah was the AI on the *UTS Indianapolis*, which was ten thousand kilometres to the south east, the ships in an echelon formation with *Endeavour* at the head and *Intrepid* at the rear. As an afterthought, he added, "How close to readiness is the *Indy's* crew?"

"Similar to us. Obi and I discussed the situation and decided we would delay and bring the crews to readiness a little later to be closer to the planet for safer evacuation if needed. We are not so far out as would cause any logistical or resource problems," she relayed.

"So, Captain Straud is awake?"

Dawn quickly contacted the *Indianapolis* for an update on the status of the crew. Obadiah answered, digital communications made at the speed of light. Captain Elizabeth Straud was currently active and in her ready room with four others.

"Yes."

He patched into the comms system, icons enumerating, directing the connection. "Captain Straud?" Her image flashed into view via his bio-comms, and he flipped it to the display in the room, so that Dawn could also take part. This wasn't really required, as Dawn could interact directly via the bio-comms stream; however, she found that, regardless of technological function, there was always some human element of interaction that still found its way into the natural usage of such things.

"Captain Clayton. Good morning. Have you just been briefed?" replied Straud.

"Yes. What's the situation from your side?" he asked. She was confident as ever and straight to business. She was all about formalities and professionalism; it was a characteristic he really appreciated.

"We've been trying to contact the *Intrepid* for several days now, with no response. All channels have been reviewed and there are no system issues that we can find. The simple answer is that Ellie is not responding and the crew are either not yet awake or they are awake and not responding." Straud was worried, that came across in her body language more than her tone. It's not until you are light years from your home planet and as isolated as this to understand that any problem, no matter how small, could escalate quickly, and out here there was no help. She was jumping ahead and running the scenarios with her team. Worst case was always the loss of the ship. They needed more information.

"We need to find out what's going on over there and why Ellie, at least, is not responding." He paused for a moment, a stern look of concentration where a smile had been only minutes before. He stood and started to pace around the small room. "Captain Straud, could you get a team together and send a shuttle to the *Intrepid*?" It was raised as a question, but it wasn't. "We need some eyes on the problem. Let me know when they are ready to go. You appear to be slightly ahead in the resus process and physically closer, so we'll use your people until there are a few more available to resource here. Let me know when your team's ready to go."

"I'll keep you posted. Straud, out." She signed off and the display went blank, replaced with the slowly spinning logo and initials of the Outer World Exploration Corporation.

Dawn reviewed the latest data from the *Intrepid* investigation and then turned her attention back to her father, still pacing up and down, lost in his thoughts. "Should we not send our own team too?" she suggested. He looked over to her, and shook his head.

"Not yet. Straud's team should be able to deal with the initial sweep and investigation. We'll concentrate on getting the crew back to readiness, then analyse the findings as they become available." He looked up and ran his fingers through his hair. "It's got to be something simple."

"Flight time to the *Intrepid* will be eight hours by shuttle. Give them an hour to make their initial survey and response, and we should get our first report nine hours after they depart."

He stopped pacing. Electric blue and red lights flashed and twinkled in the control panels around him. Dawn's hologram faced him, head slightly to one side, as if listening intently. "Okay, Dawn. Sean Hopper. Is he awake yet?"

"No."

"Let's get him up and in my ready room. I need our chief engineer on this as soon as he can stand."

"He's in the final stages of resus. He can be with you in two hours."

"Thanks. Inform the medical team to prioritise him. Get him to me as soon as possible." With that, he moved back towards the door. "Here's a list of other priority resus cases. Get them to me as soon as you can, if not sooner. See you later, my favourite daughter." A file appeared in her process queue.

"Daddy, I'm with you all the time. I am the ship." Her holo-image rolled its eyes. Sometimes he just forgot.

She watched her father walk back through the ship, this time in the direction of the bridge. No one else was yet on the bridge but he walked with a purpose and determination. He had been given a problem to solve and she knew there was nothing he liked more. Ever since she had been old enough to understand what her father did for a living, she had understood his fascination with puzzles and problems. The reason was irrelevant; the problem was everything. It was a part of him she saw in herself—an obsessive and a problem-solver. But now she could solve problems with the power of an AI and the processing capacity that bestowed upon her. She was already running the scenarios, as she knew Obadiah and Ellie would be, if Ellie was still 'alive'. The variables were vast, with an incredible number of outcomes. She was refining and honing her solution as much as she could but even with her great abilities she was days away from an answer. Too many things could actually be at play but it was still 'damn strange', as her grandfather used to say. Was Ellie offline? There were fail-safe systems in place to ensure Ellie was always on, systems distributed right the way through the ship to ensure that no single failure would disable Ellie or cause her death. The latter seemed most unlikely, given the ship was clearly still operational and systems were still working on a fundamental level. Communication was simply mute. Her father's decision had been correct and necessary.

Her systems monitored the incoming call from Captain Straud. Straud's team was ready. Details of the team were available to review. They were mostly engineers with some security and two pilots, twenty in all. Her father signed it off and the mission was launched. The countdown to intercept was set. Eight hours, mark.

A direct communication request arrived from Obadiah on the *Indianapolis*. She opened the connection. "Dawn, I thought I'd update you in person. The investigation team have just launched. I've been continuing to try and contact Ellie, but I am still unable to get a response from the primary communications array."

"Nor I. I see Commander Havers is leading the investigation. I've not worked directly with him before." Pulling up his files, she immediately knew his history. Born on the Luna arcology and schooled at a mid-grade university on Earth, he was a competent officer and an excellent engineer. "I can see what his file says, but what's he like in person?"

"What's your interest here? He's a good officer. He'll get the job done, no question."

"I just want to know we have the best guy on the job. There are a lot of people depending on him—not least those on the *Intrepid*." She followed the tracking telemetry of the shuttle and observed the crew and investigation team as they settled into the eight-hour flight. Commander Havers was making his way around the shuttle casually chatting to a team member here and there, all very relaxed. She saw a man confident in his abilities to lead his crew.

"I've seen him in action. He's one of the good ones, don't worry. Captain Straud has confidence in him to lead this mission. So should you." Obadiah was gentle in his assertion but she could hear a level of defence in his voice. He was close to his captain and having her choices questioned was something he didn't seem to like.

"It was an academic question, I guess. I just don't know what we're going to find, and I want to know we have our best people on the job."

"Dawn, all our people are the best people. They are all more than capable of handling anything we are likely to encounter."

"We don't know what we're going to encounter out here." She was smiling again. It was the not knowing that was the excitement of any adventure. No matter what the circumstances of its start, it was the journey and the destination that mattered.

Changing the subject, Obadiah moved back to his calculations. "I have some preliminary assessments on my outcome analysis. The two lead scenarios suggest asteroid strike or disablement of Ellie's primary function."

"Wouldn't an asteroid strike of that size cause severe damage to the ship and some level of alteration in vector and momentum?"

"Unless corrected. We don't know what level of control Ellie may have. It could be that navigational control is unaffected."

Conjecture. More data was required and that was at least eight hours away. She decided to bring the conversation to a close. "Okay, Obi. Thank you for the update. Let me know if you get something more solid or you pick up any sort of communication from the *Intrepid*."

"I'll continue the simulations and communication attempts. I'll also see if we can get some early visuals from the shuttle's optics when they come into range. Obadiah, out." The connection closed.

Her grandfather popped into her head again, 'Darn peculiar.'

HAVERS

The shuttle crew were utilising the flight time to the *Intrepid* in their own way. Some were plainly asleep, some were prepping equipment, others were watching movies, listening to music, catching up on their reading or more generally chatting with their crew mates. He did wonder about the few that were sleeping. They had only just been resuscitated into their new younger selves; how could they sleep now? He felt like he would bounce off the walls with the amount of energy he had pent up. Reskinning was an experience that juiced him up so much, he would spend his first few days wide awake and even then it was longer before any recognisable sleep pattern started to kick in. He could never just drop straight back to sleep again only hours after resus. He pinged a message to Larsen, who was laying in what looked like a rather uncomfortable position in his crash couch. 'How can you sleep at a time like this? You've only been out of resus for four hours.' Larsen did not move so much as a muscle but a response popped into his receiver.

'I'm not sleeping. Just resting. Really hard.'

'Some things I don't need to know, thanks.'

Havers snorted a suppressed laugh. It probably was a good idea to try and catch some rest for a couple of hours before they arrived.

It was a reasonably long flight time to the *Intrepid* but, thankfully, they were not heading over to the *Endeavour*—that would be sixteen hours. Usually, the formation would be tighter, but as the crews were not awake and only the AIs were flying, safety protocols dictated a looser formation. Not that the AIs were unable to fly in a straight line for one hundred and thirty years. More that human scepticism, leaving nothing to chance and reducing risks where possible, produced some healthy margins of error in the flight protocols. Especially when there wasn't a captain awake to take responsibility. Although, he was sure there would always be someone that could be found to pin it on, if it all went wrong. That was just human nature. Having said all that, if a power core blew out while they were all in stasis, he knew that he for one would like to be as far away as possible.

He returned to the immediate task at hand: the in-flight meal of vegetable soup and a protein bar. He thought of the number of people throughout history that had been sitting in a similar position and been equally disappointed. What was it with in-flight meals that meant that they had no flavour or excitement? It was as if there was a god of the inadequate meal who had decided to take it upon themselves to annoy the hell out of any flight-related traveller. He reflected on the food back on the *Indianapolis:* that wasn't bad at all. However, they had some great chefs, and the ships were more like space-faring self-sustaining cities than your short range skiff or commuter transit vessel. He let out a huff of resignation and opened the protein bar. The order was important: eat the most tasteless and inedible first, then at least the soup would be a little treat in comparison.

"Sir!" It was Technician Anderson, sitting a couple of couches to his right, his face a grimace in anticipation of what the commander was about to endure. "Are you seriously going to eat that stuff?"

Havers looked at the protein bar and thought for a second. "Yes. If I don't do it now, I'll only have to do it later." He looked back to Anderson, "And at least I know there is a toilet five metres away, if I get into trouble."

"You know it'll give you gut rot," pitched in a voice with a Texan accent—thick, deep and drawling. Boyd was one of the oldest and most well-respected engineers on the crew with several lifetimes of experience. Even in his new twenty-five year old body, Boyd looked and sounded old. It was a talent. Almost everyone considered him the wise man of the group; a little coarse at times, a little vulgar, but generally he was the guy everyone turned to for advice, whether professional or personal. He was like the father of the team. Well respected, well liked. So when he told you that you were in for a heavy dose of 'gut rot', it was a reasonable warning to heed. Boyd looked at him knowingly, as if over some imaginary spectacles. He looked at Boyd, to Anderson, back to Boyd, then to the protein bar. Somehow, he didn't feel hungry any more.

"Okay. Powerful argument. I'll go check on the cockpit."

Packing and stowing the so-called food, he unclipped his seat harness and pushed off in the direction of the cockpit. He still wasn't quite used to the weightlessness of the shuttle and needed a couple of corrective taps of the wall and cabin furniture to get him to the bulkhead and cabin exit. Once there, he realigned himself down the corridor and made his way along the hand rails, passing the small utility and toilet area, then the medical bay, and finally making it to the ladder leading to the cockpit. As he reached the top of the ladder, a bulkhead door slid aside and revealed the rear of the cockpit and a couple of empty flight couches for the use of passengers or in-flight engineers.

As he settled himself into one of the couches and fastened the harness, he saw the two pilots seated a couple of metres further forward, still and almost lifeless, then the cockpit view. The cockpit was more or less a glass-alloy bubble sitting up high and at the front of the shuttle, from which you could see a full three-sixty view horizontally and, from the pilots' position, through the floor. It was as if you were sitting in open space with a twenty tonne piece of metal strapped to your back. But the view! Ah, the view was stunning. Open space never ceased to amaze him. He could sit and stare at the stars for hours; it was one of the reasons he was there. A childhood dream fulfilled every time he got to look out of the window. He loved the shuttle design for this. The *Indianapolis* had its observation lounges and cupolas, but with their artificial gravity and recreational function as saloons and bars for the crew, they were often busy places. Now, if you wanted to view the stars with a little peace and quiet, a shuttle trip was the place to do it. The pilots controlled the shuttle and communicated almost entirely via their bio-comms and sub-vocal conversation; they were plugged in for the ride. Not all pilot crews embraced sub-vocal communication, some would still communicate 'old school', but, with those crews that did, you could sit on a flight engineer's couch and just watch the cosmos in all its spectacle and grandeur, with only your own thoughts for company. It was his idea of a perfect moment.

After a few minutes of heaven, an icon appeared in his view and flashed. He opened the message and the text streamed across his vision. 'Hello, sir. Didn't see you there for a moment. All okay?' Branner, the senior flight officer, was still in his couch, internally working through whatever pilots worked through to navigate their way.

'Yes, thanks. Just wanted somewhere quiet to go over the mission plan.' He looked back out to the stars around them. 'I'll leave you to your work.'

'Okay, sir. Let us know if you need anything. FYI, flight time to contact is currently three hours forty. We should rendezvous at 14:30 TST.' Two thirty Terran Standard Time gave him some time to prepare then some time to rest. Sounded perfect.

'Thanks, Branner.'

'You're welcome.'

He laid back and got comfortable. Then closed his eyes and called up the mission documents. What was known was very little: loss of contact from Ellie on the *Intrepid,* a completely dead communications array, no recorded alteration or correction to course. There was simply no response. Obadiah had given him his most likely scenario assessment, which at the moment included an asteroid or other space body impact to critical systems. He thought this unlikely, as if an asteroid of even moderate size hit *Intrepid* at a good velocity that would most likely be the end of her. The light of a small nova would have been recorded from both remaining ships and *Intrepid* would have been no more. If the space body had been small, and if it had passed through the ship completely, rendering some horrible damage on the way through, Ellie's infrastructure had enough redundancy within it to cope. She would still be operational and able to chat all day about the nasty rock that just put a hole through her. There was something else going on.

With the crew in stasis, a major atmosphere loss would be recoverable. If the core collapsed for some reason, the small nova situation would occur again, so no solution there. If Ellie shut herself down for some reason, that might explain the loss of communication with little external side effect. But for what reason would she do that? She had a crew to care for and a ship to maintain. He supposed there was always an outside chance that she had become unstable, although those recommended for AI splicing were thoroughly assessed and mental stability was something they took as a primary requisite to the process. If you were to become AI spliced, you had buy in totally to the program and your new existence. The integration needed total acceptance by the human element. It was all to avoid splice-divergence, which would ultimately lead to the death of the person, loss of the spliced wave and of the AI container—an expensive failure for all parties.

So he had to cover three bases: the bridge, to enable him to command interaction throughout the ship; CIC, as this was essentially where Ellie's AI suite was located; and the engine room, for any propulsion- or power core-related issues. This should give him total control of the ship and key access to resolve any issues aboard.

However, his first priority was how to get on board. The issue that had been pretty much skipped by Captain Straud was the *Intrepid's* defence grid. Regardless of the ship's primary purpose, which was science and colonisation—both missions of peaceful intent—the ships were built with defensive short-range weapons and some longer-range projectile weapons. Nothing of mass effect, just simple projectile weapons. The long-range canons could accelerate a one kilogram projectile to high velocity, which could be useful for slow or static targets like asteroids. As these two cannons were housed in turrets towards the bow of the ship—one in the belly and one on the back of the *Intrepid* along its centreline—and the ship orientation had not moved from its navigational heading, he was less worried about them than the short-range point defence projectile batteries that fired thirty millimetre rounds at around six thousand rounds a minute. That would make his shuttle and everything in it Swiss cheese in the space of a few seconds.

He requested external schematics. Starting by looking for blind spots in the point defence system he worked his way over the ship, finding the airlocks and shuttle bay doors. *Intrepid* was only slightly different from the *Indianapolis*, which he knew like the back of his hand. However, those differences could be critical, so he was thorough. All three ships were built around the same basic design: five rectangular section engine pods arranged in a circle around the main hull at the aft of the vessel; a central section which rotated as a drum and contained most of the living quarters, science and engineering operations; a mid-quarter section that housed the shuttle bays; and the bow which housed the bridge and a forward instrument array.

His analysis of the point defence coverage did find a slight weakness. It wasn't much, and he would need to park the shuttle at distance and breach the defences with a small drone team. The point defence weapons coverage was a bubble around the *Intrepid*, but breach that bubble and you had a chance. The tactic reminded him of his boxing lessons at the academy. It didn't matter if your opponent had a longer reach than you, all you had to do was get inside that reach and you had the advantage. You could bring down an opponent twice your size as long as you got inside their guard and had good timing. Timing was the trick.

By identifying a gap in the ship structure between the front of an engine pod and the rear of the rotating central habitat section, which would take them inside the point defence guard and out of the line of fire, he had the beginnings of a plan. From inside, he would need to disarm the point defences from the bridge or CIC and bring the shuttle in. Once his team were inside, they could begin the investigation.

Easy.

He wrapped up his plan and sent the documents to Larsen, marked for immediate review. Larsen was a resourceful type and one of those who always appeared to have the correct answer to any given engineering problem instantly. No need for iterative design, he just leapt straight to 'correct'. It was an annoying trait, for no other reason than the arrogance it reinforced. Larsen was a cocky SOB who could really do with being taken down a peg or two. If only he wasn't so damn right about everything. He guessed that, when Larsen got it wrong, it would happen hard and he wasn't sure he wanted to be around when it did.

After a few more minutes of wonder, staring out of the cockpit window, a comms request popped up. It was Larsen.

"Sir." Larsen was making a face like he was chewing something particularly unpleasant.

"That didn't take long. What are your thoughts?"

"I have some…" Larsen paused, clearly thinking of a politic way of informing his boss that the plan needed work, "…optimisations."

Nicely done. "And what might they be, Lieutenant?"

"Only a couple really, sir. Regarding approaching the ship, it is more likely to react aggressively to a fast-moving target than a slow one. I suggest the drones go no faster than two metres per second."

"That's only a little faster than walking pace. At the distance we need to park, that will easily add another couple of hours or more to the mission time."

"Only if the grid is active. Is time a consideration?"

"Not getting the team killed is my prime consideration here, along with the wellbeing of the *Intrepid's* crew," he said a little too sternly. "I'll look into it. Okay, what's the next…optimisation?"

"I notice that you mention that, if the defence grid is active, all external access to airlocks will be locked out. Standard procedure. If that is the case and the defence grid is active, we need a way in. You recommend cutting tools."

"Yes."

"Well, I was wondering about the comms, sir. I know the long-range comms array is offline, but what about more local short-range comms like the internal network? If we can get close enough and find a part of the ship that is less shielded, like the habitat section, we may be able to piggy-back into the internal command network."

"I like that idea. We wouldn't need to force ingress and we could get visual and system status reports before we go poking around inside. I'll get onto the *Indi* and get the access codes. Okay, anything else?"

"That's all, sir."

With that he cancelled the connection to Larsen and instantly opened a channel to the *Indianapolis*.

"*Indianapolis* this is Tusk One. Over."

A moment later, the comms officer aboard the *Indianapolis* responded in a crisp, efficient tone. "Tusk One, this is *Indianapolis*. Go ahead. Over."

"*Indianapolis*, I have mission plans for One Actual. Please relay. Over." Before the comms officer could reply, Captain Straud was on the line.

"This is One Actual, what have you got Tusk One? Over."

"I'm sending you the plans for our boarding of the *Intrepid*. You will see that, in addition, we will need the access codes for the internal wireless network nodes. We believe we have a chance to override the physical systems from outside the *Intrepid* without a forced entry. Over." In his mind he watched Straud's face for a reaction to the news. Pursed lips and severe expression at the double-edged sword he had just passed her. On one hand, he had just told her he could access the *Intrepid* with no physical damage to the ship and therefore crew—that was good. The bad news he knew she was digesting would be the fact that they could gain access to *her* ship with little or no physical damage to the ship or crew. Which meant, potentially, others could do the same. And by 'others' that meant 'anyone'. She would be having urgent talks with Commander Li, the Indy's chief of security, the moment they finished their conversation. That brought a wry smile to his lips. That was a sport. Anything to get Commander Podrick Li running around chasing his tail was worth every moment of effort.

"Thank you for your report, Tusk One. We'll send you the codes in the next few minutes. One Actual, out." The connection died and the silence of the cockpit returned.

The view had not changed. It was at times like this that the vastness of space revealed itself. Many points of orientation, just nothing within millions of kilometres. They had been en route to the *Intrepid* for more than four hours and the distance they had covered had no reference. Visually, they hadn't moved. He considered that for a moment more, then pinged Larsen a message. 'Hold my calls. Wake me in an hour.'

'Okay, boss.'

CLAYTON

Dawn's hologram had appeared next to him like an assassin from the shadows and made him jump. "Daddy, I've lost contact with Tusk One." She spoke directly without introduction in urgent tones that relayed her anxiety.

"Dawn!" Clenching his fists and counting to ten, he closed his eyes, trying to compose himself. Dawn stopped talking, crossed her arms with impatience and waited for him to recover. Once the initial adrenaline had ebbed, he opened his eyes and looked at her with slight annoyance. "I do wish you'd stop sneaking up on me. This heart of mine is too old for the shock."

"It's twenty-five years, four months and eight hours old. I'm not going to shock you to death." She raised an eyebrow and waited for her father to catch up. "The shuttle, Daddy. The shuttle has lost comms too. This is too much of a coincidence. Something is going on over there."

"We know something is going on, Dawn. That's why I sent the shuttle." As he was talking, he fired commands at his bio-comms and requested the latest information on Tusk One. A raft of information was now returning. The last communication was from Tusk One's team leader, Commander Iain Havers, reporting back that they would shortly be reaching their minimum safe distance and were preparing to execute the boarding plan. A copy of the plan was available to review. The shuttle had been about ten kilometres from the *Intrepid* when the signal had faded as the commander was mid-sentence. 'We estimate ingress within the ...'.

"Have you read their boarding plan?"

"Of course," Dawn replied.

"Give me a summary."

She began to run through the key points of Commander Havers' plan—from utilising drones to penetrate the point defence cannons to searching for internal wireless network nodes and accessing airlock controls via the internal network. She then summarised the arrangements intended to find and fix the communication fault, which, after the recent events, appeared to be less a technical problem and more an external one.

"Something is interfering with the communications," he said to himself, more than to Dawn. He sat and started to rub his forehead in concentration. "But, what?"

"You're assessment is sound. Current analysis from the team observing the area immediately around the *Intrepid* found anomalous readings—energy signatures we have not been able to identify. They appear to be coming from the *Intrepid* but are not of the *Intrepid*." She tilted her head to one side again, looking for his reaction.

"Okay. I need my crew, Dawn. This situation is escalating and I have no crew." He punched a few buttons on his console and a graphic slid into view showing the crew resuscitation schedule. The people he needed were first in line and about to be given the news to double-time it up to the bridge. He estimated that they would be with him in another fifteen minutes.

"Captain, Chief Hopper." Dawn said. He looked up at her, slightly surprised. While in his funk about the state of his crew, he had not heard the bridge door open and his chief engineer walk in.

"Captain. Dawn." Hopper nodded his greeting to each in turn. "I hear there is a situation. How can I help?"

Hopper was a small man in frame, but what he lacked in stature he more than made up for in charisma and sheer bloody-mindedness. If there was ever a person able to knock a square peg into a round hole, it was Hopper. He was an excellent engineer, one of the best Clayton had ever worked with, and he needed that talent and experience at work straight away.

"Chief Hopper. Excellent." He almost jumped out of his chair in greeting. "I can't wait for the rest. I need to get you working. Here–," he nodded and, in doing so, sent Hopper the file pack for the current situation with both the *Intrepid* and Tusk One, "review the file I've just sent you. I need you to investigate, especially the connection between the loss of communication in both vessels. I could put the loss of comms from the *Intrepid* down to some sort of technical problem but the loss of comms from the investigating team's shuttle just as they turn up on site…" He scrunched up his nose and shook his head to finish the sentence.

"I'll get on it right away."

"Let me know what you need. I've prioritised the resus of key crew, but if you need anyone to jump the list, let me know. Time is of the essence on this, whatever you can tell me as soon as you can tell me, could be vital."

"I will, sir." Hopper turned on his heels and almost ran out the door, heading for engineering.

As Hopper left the room, Dawn turned to him with a question. "I know things are a little busy right now, but weren't you going to have dinner with Mummy?" she asked, an innocent reminder to an event he should have remembered himself. What time was it?

Jemma was going to be pissed. He had only been out of stasis for a few short hours and he was already going to have to cancel dinner. His hormones began to play games with his body. Thinking of Jemma had an involuntary effect on him, one which he had and hadn't missed. He wondered how anyone got anything done during their younger years. A surging libido was not conducive to any kind of work. Pinching the bridge of his nose, he tried to concentrate and bring himself back under control.

This time he heard the door. He turned to see five people walking onto the bridge—one still in his resus gown—all looking like they had run all the way. Despite the seriousness of the situation, he couldn't help but raise a smile for Dr Klein. "Good to see you lady and gentlemen. I'm guessing you couldn't find your clothes, Dr Klein?"

"Yes, sir. I have them here. I'll get dressed when I get a moment." Dr Klein held out the clothes draped over his arm as proof. "Someone mentioned this meeting was quite the 'top priority'." He was looking coolly at Dawn. She was acting coy and trying not to laugh. He would have to have words later—this really wasn't the time for jokes.

"Indeed. The situation has become more problematic in the last few minutes." Gesturing to the corridor at the rear of the bridge, "Please follow me. We'll continue in the briefing room."

Walking the short distance through to the briefing room, he sent a quiet message to Dawn. 'I expect more. Knock it off.' She didn't respond but in the briefing room her mood was more sombre and professional.

The briefing room was a small lecture room of circular seating, stepping down four levels. It could comfortably seat his command team and their immediate seconds. If ever others needed to attend, it would be standing room only. Centremost was a projector and control array for various comms and display purposes. Currently, an image of the *Intrepid* appeared to be floating above the projector with various tracking trajectories extrapolating away from the main body. A small red dot some distance from the *Intrepid* was circled with an orbiting icon indicating Tusk One, with a dotted line heading towards the *Intrepid* showing its heading. All of this gave those gathered a fair impression of what was going on already. Faces became intense and one or two stepped forward to take a closer look.

"A month ago, we lost contact with the *Intrepid*. We were alerted as we came out of resus and immediately sent an investigating team once we realised there was nothing further we could learn of the situation remotely. Tusk One was ten kilometres from intercept when we also lost contact. Whatever our thoughts may have been regarding a technical problem beforehand, with the loss of contact from Tusk One, we now suspect external interference.

"As you can see, we can still scan and track both vessels. And, as far as we can tell, the communications arrays for the vessels are technically functional; however, they are non-responsive." He moved around the hologram as he spoke, indicating various points on the *Intrepid* that housed the communications arrays. "There has been no unexpected deviation of course from the Intrepid and, from the investigating team's plan submitted a few hours ago, they are also manoeuvring as per that plan." He sent each team member assembled a copy of Tusk One's interception and investigation plan.

His message queue icon began to flash. A message from Dawn: 'Anomalous power signatures.' It was a quick reminder. He wove this new information into the briefing without a moment's hesitation—no-one realised it was a prompt. "In addition, there have been anomalous power signatures identified coming from the *Intrepid*. At this time, we don't believe they are of the *Intrepid*, so it's likely the source is something else. I'd like to know what that 'something else' is." Pausing only long enough for the point to take on some weight with those listening, he continued, "I have met with Chief Hopper already and instructed him to begin investigating things from our side, and I need you all to do the same. Anything you can tell me, I need to know straight away. We need to find out what's going on over there.

"Commander Roux, could you please liaise with the *Indianapolis* and ensure we know everything they know as soon as they get it and vice versa."

Commander Roux simply nodded agreement.

"Any questions?" They were all mute with either shock of disbelief. It was the 'interference' bit that had thrown them. That inferred intentional action on behalf of someone to stop communications from getting out. Why? That was the million-dollar question. He gave them a moment longer. Even if there were no questions now, there would be plenty later.

"Okay everyone. Let's get to it. Dismissed." He turned and headed up the steps from the presentation floor and back to the bridge, leaving the others staring at the hologram of the *Intrepid*. Heading down the corridor, he heard the sudden burst of chatter as they all started airing their thoughts at once.

Reaching his crash couch on the bridge, he sat and got the will power up to call Jemma. A quick call was better than no call at all. "Hey, you," he said in as calming and reluctant tone as possible.

"Hey. Dawn told me about dinner. Looks like you have your hands full." She put on her best sympathetic smile.

"Yeah. You know how it is. Wake from decades in stasis into a major crisis before Dr Klein can even put his clothes on." He spent a second thinking about that. "That's not a picture for anyone." It made her laugh.

"Well, keep me posted. Sleep's going to be a bit random these next few days. Maybe I'll be awake when you manage to get some time to yourself." She paused and then added in a more demure, sultry tone, "And if I'm not, wake me." The connection ended abruptly. He just sat there trying to get himself in check again. She was incorrigible.

"Sir. Something wrong? Apart from the obvious?" Commander Roux took the seat to his left and started to punch a few buttons on his console, plugging into the command net and bringing up status reports on crew, navigation and, of course, the *Intrepid* investigation. His French Canadian accent smoothing over his words to make them somehow sit more rhythmically together than other languages—more so than, say, German, which demanded you sit up and pay attention to every syllable. Clayton always felt that the French language was as close to a vocal hug as you could get. Roux called up the *Indianapolis* and sent over a couple of requests before Clayton had even had time to respond.

"Jemma. Had to cancel dinner."

"Ah," Roux said, as if he understood completely. Clayton doubted he ever would. The guy was a serial monogamist, although it never seemed to get him into trouble. The trail of ex-partners around the ship left something to be desired but, whether it was the situation on board or an unwritten rule amongst the crew, he still had healthy friendships with most. He was unsure whether to call Roux lucky; he was certainly charmed, or maybe just charming. His smooth accent most likely helped him out quite a lot.

They sat in silence for a while, working through observations and suggestions that were now starting to come across from the *Indianapolis*. They had been collecting observational data from the shuttle as a real-time transmission before the shuttle went dark and, having had some time to review the data, some items were worth noting. The power signatures were not stable, they varied in amplitude, and, at the point Tusk One went dark, the anomalous power signatures were seen to have spiked.

"This looks more and more like someone or something is intentionally jamming comms traffic," said Roux eventually, "but to what purpose?"

At that moment they noticed an alert notification and routed the item to the bridge main screen for all to see. The fact that it was only Roux and himself was a point he overlooked—it was a matter of habit. Both of them saw the new object accelerating away from Tusk One on a vector towards the *Indianapolis* at eight g. There was suddenly a group on the bridge as the others ran from the briefing room to the bridge, all wide-eyed and trying to assess what was happening.

The object continued its rapid journey away from Tusk One. "Missile?" offered Roux.

"Probe," stated Dr Klein.

Dawn interrupted, "Captain, there is an audio message

incoming from the probe. It's using burst transmission on a loop every few milliseconds."

"Play it." He leaned forward in his couch to concentrate on the incoming message.

The voice of Commander Havers could be clearly heard. He seemed unfazed by events and spoke in a measured tempo. "*Indianapolis*, this is Tusk One Actual. We have experienced complete communications black-out and have launched this probe hoping that it will relay our intention. Break. We are proceeding with the mission and will aim to also identify and disable the source of the jamming occurring to comms. Tusk One, out."

"At least we know one thing," Dr Klein said, breaking the short silence once the message had finished. They were all looking at him. "The loss of comms is two-way." There were a few agreeing nods from the others.

"Yes, thank you. That seems most likely," replied Clayton. "One thing, Dr Klein. For the sake of others, but mostly my sanity, would you mind putting some clothes on?"

"Er, yes. Of course." Looking a little sheepish he turned back to the briefing room where he had left his clothes. "I'll be a moment."

Stepping toward the bridge's main screen to get a closer and more detailed look, General Oliver St John, the head of security for the *Endeavour*, spun round theatrically to address the others. "Do we know how many of those probes they have?"

"Six," replied Dawn, before any others could offer an answer.

"Then the conversation is going to be quite one-sided and very short. We need to keep communication to Tusk One open somehow. The *Intrepid* is another problem, but Commander Havers appears to have that in hand at the moment. The key issue for me is to ensure we can continue open comms with that team." St John turned his attention back to the visual on screen. The probe had extended its distance from Tusk One by some considerable margin and the shuttle itself had nudged a little further forward towards the *Intrepid*.

"What do you suggest, General?"

"Sir, radio band comms are clearly being affected. We can, however, still see all that is going on, which I suggest means they are not jamming or subverting light transmission in any way."

"Laser," chipped in Commander Eli Holt.

"Morse code?" responded Commander Paula Litton. The group

seemed to be on the same thought train.

"Morse code is an option," confirmed St John. "I would suggest firstly attempting to simply use the tight beam laser comms. Then, if that doesn't do the job, Morse code across laser channels may be our last option."

Clayton raised his hand a moment, to pause the conversation. "Hopper, we have an idea we want to run past you."

Hopper turned to the camera and, to his audience, his face loomed five metres high on the main screen, the screen now split in two. "Yes, sir?"

Clayton pointed to St John to continue.

"Commander Hopper, we need to keep open comms with the shuttle, Tusk One. The idea is to use the laser comms, as we don't believe they'll be jammed by whatever is acting against the current radio transmissions."

Hopper was nodding in agreement at each point made. "Laser comms have been attempted with the *Intrepid,* as part of the initial tests conducted by the *Indianapolis.* They came back negative, as the *Intrepid* did not respond to the communication. However, we know Tusk One is manned and responsive, so at least when trying to contact them we know they should respond if they receive the transmission." Havers looked away from the bridge team and at a screen his side, then made a face and a little shrug of the shoulder that suggested to those watching that there was a problem with their idea. "The only problem I can see, and I'll need to confirm with the *Indianapolis,* is that I don't believe the shuttle is rigged with laser comms. *Endeavour, Indianapolis* and *Intrepid* are, of course, but shuttles may or may not, depending on function. Wait one."

While waiting for Hopper to contact the *Indianapolis* to confirm the specifications of the shuttle the investigating team were using, Clayton did a quick scan of shuttles in their own shuttle bay. Hopper was, of course, correct—some shuttles had laser comms, others did not. Why was this key piece of kit not standard? He shook his head slightly.

"Confirmed," Hopper came back. "Tusk One is not outfitted with laser comms. I would assume they would have already tried to contact us on that system if they had it." He became distracted for a moment, then returned his focus to the team on the bridge.

"My engineers are beginning to arrive. Let me brief them on what's going on and I'll get back to you shortly. I like the idea of the laser comms—there may be something in it. I'll bear it in mind."

"We are also considering using the laser in some way to transmit Morse code," Clayton stated evenly. "It's a long shot, but it may give us something."

"Morse code? Yes, sir. Hopper, out." With Hopper gone, the main screen resized to show the *Intrepid*, Tusk One and the probe floating in space. Tusk One was a little closer to the *Intrepid* and the probe another leap away from both.

LARSEN

"You know, I gave you the drone idea so that no one had to do this crazy EVA plan of yours." Larsen was in an astrosuit and clipping himself into the EVA pack while Havers looked him over and double-checked his work. The astrosuit was slim fitting and made of a white ridgimorph material, with harnesses and packs for tools and equipment. The suit was designed with maximum flexibility and comfort in mind for the wearer and was self-adjusting, so that, quite literally, one size would fit all.

"I know. It was a good plan, too. But you know what they say about plans."

"It's nice to have one," they both answered together, smirking and shaking their heads as they continued to clunk, click and plug parts into place.

Havers continued, turning to pick the helmet from the wall mount, "Well, the moment the comms died was the moment we couldn't use them. Besides, it'll be better this way."

"In what way is getting shot at point blank range by the point defence system a good idea? Or better?" Larsen stopped prepping his suit and looked at Havers, exasperated.

"You'll be fine. As you mentioned, move slow enough and the thing won't open up on you. And it's better because you'll be on the spot. A man on the ground is better than a drone and you know it."

"I do but it doesn't make the plan better." He finished the final preparations to the EVA link and straightened up.

"Come on, engineer. Let's get going."

With an affirmed nod Larsen manoeuvred himself toward the airlock where the other two members of the EVA team floated, doing their final checks and busying themselves while waiting for him to join them. Owen Smith and Leon Silvers were both experienced EVA men. Owen, a senior engineer, and Leon from security, they had worked this kind of external detail before, just never over quite such a long distance. The *Intrepid* was over four kilometres from their current position and they would be taking replacement fuel and oxygen tanks for the journey.

"Okay, let's do this," he said and opened the airlock door from the local console. The door hissed and they made their way carefully inside. Once inside, there was only just enough room for the three of them with their additional kit. They steadied then anchored themselves for the air recycling procedure.

From the door, Havers looked in. "Good luck, gentlemen," he said and keyed the control console. The door slid shut and they were sealed inside.

All three men kept facing the outer airlock door, looking through the thin strip of viewing plate, focusing on the *Intrepid*. Larsen knew the distance to be just over four kilometres but somehow he felt he was close enough to reach it just by putting out his hand. Distances were always difficult to judge in space—things were always much closer or much further away than you expected.

"Everyone anchored?" he asked, not even looking round to his team. There were a couple of crisp, excited confirmations. "Cycling airlock, now."

There was a clunk that he felt through his boots and chest, locking bolts sealing and valves working, pumps activating. The control panel as a whole went from green to red, and a timer started to count down in the main display. In two minutes the chamber would be devoid of air and the outer door would be unlocked. Time to go over the last few checks.

Ever since Larsen had been an engineer, the number of checks, double checks, triple checks and final checks he had completed on systems had been without end. He imagined that it had always been this way for engineers and probably always would be. The last thing he wanted as he travelled the distance over to the *Intrepid* was for his EVA pack to pick up a glitch or his suit to fail. That would certainly be a bad day at the office and would put more people than just him in jeopardy. He ran pre-flight diagnostics on the EVA pack for the last time, then took a glance back at the airlock control. Eight seconds.

The seconds clicked down to zero and the control panel turned a cyan blue colour indicating the cycle was complete and they were now in vacuum. Hitting the big 'Open' button that now comprised the majority of the control panel screen, the external door made a thump, which he felt through his toes via vibrations in the floor rather than any atmosphere, then began to open, moving towards them and sliding to the side, coming to a stop.

"Tusk One, this is EVA One. Exiting airlock now, over."

"EVA One, this is Tusk One. Roger. Will execute comms recovery plan as soon as you are clear. Over."

"Copy that. EVA One, out."

Each of them moved through the airlock, pushing off slowly and allowing the gyro stabilisers of the EVA packs to bring them to station about ten metres from the shuttle. They were slightly in the shadow of the *Intrepid* and would be moving to the dark side of the ship to begin their ingress, so most of the view was obscured and stars blocked out by the bulk.

"Tusk One, this is EVA One. Beginning our intercept, over." It was worth a try. All that came back was static. No change there then. Even at this range, whatever was blocking the open channel was effective and quite powerful.

"EVA Two, this is EVA One. Comms check, over." Even at two metres, nothing. Okay, hand signals it was. He caught Smith and Silvers attention with a swift hand gesture, then motioned them to group. He noted the 'OK' from both and with short puffs of released gas from their suits, they moved towards him to create a triangle formation. Unclipping a line from the side of his EVA pack, he handed it to Smith, who plugged it into a socket and strong point on his EVA pack. Smith then did the same, handing a line from his EVA pack to Silvers. With the hard link established between all three, Larsen tried again.

"Okay guys, comms check."

"Five by five," responded Silvers.

"Ditto," reported Smith.

"Looks like the open channel is toast, even at ten paces. Whatever is jamming us, it's pretty good."

Out of the corner of his eye, he saw the shuttle start to

manoeuvre away from them. They were on their own now while Tusk One tried to re-establish contact with the *Indianapolis*. Havers had surmised that backtracking to a location just before they lost contact with the *Indianapolis* would enable them to obtain a signal again. Whatever the outcome, Larsen's plan was scoped to have them inside the *Intrepid* within four hours and any jamming system offline within another hour of that. *It's always nice to have a plan,* he thought to himself.

"So, here we are. EVA navigation to me, please." His bio-comms noted the connections and control of navigation to all packs listed in his view. "Thanks." He initiated the navigation program he had prepared for the trip and the formation became line abreast, moving off towards the *Intrepid* at a pace he could only register by looking at his bio-comms flight data. "I know this is going to be a long flight, gentlemen, but keep your eyes peeled. We have no idea what we're expecting here, so stay on your toes."

"Yes, sir," came the reply in unison.

As they settled down into the slower-than-jogging-speed flight, Larsen used the magnification of his display to try and get some up-to-date data on the external topography of the *Intrepid*. He searched for hatches, point defence cannons, comms arrays, bay doors, navigation lights, anything that could be used as physical access or some means by which to plug into the internal system externally. He knew of the comms array external patch panel, that was the obvious external target if he couldn't get into the ship, but it would be in plain sight of some rather nasty defensive fire zones. He'd prefer to tackle the problem from inside. Less to go wrong and safer. He didn't think being vaporised by some high velocity lead pellets would help anyone, let alone the crew of the *Intrepid,* or him, come to think of it.

He decided to play 'spot the difference' with the hull picture in front of him. Taking an image every five minutes, he overlaid the images and used a diff program to highlight the image inconsistencies or anomalies within a couple of percent tolerance. Hopefully, anything highlighted would be of interest. The program kicked up items for consideration straight away, but most were simply navigation lights, which he had expected. Other than that, the *Intrepid* seemed to be quite dormant. He'd been hoping for more.

Getting closer, they began to move into the shadow of the ship and they could begin to comprehend the size of the colony ship before them. It was vast. From the side it had a segmented appearance, not unlike a very utilitarian-looking insect, with the bow containing the bridge and many of the operational levels, the mid-section containing the habitat quarters with biomass generation and production, and the aft section linking to a round of engine pods, power core and engineering workshops.

"I know these things are home," came Silvers's voice across the comm, "but I never get used to the size from the outside. They give me the creeps. Like swimming with a whale."

"Never done that," Smith pitched in.

"Nor have I," said Silvers in his calm and rather flat Colorado accent, "but I'm pretty sure this is what it feels like."

"Like swimming with a whale?"

"Yeah. They're so massive that they have no comprehension that you're there and that at any second they could accidently swallow you whole." There was a shiver in his voice as he spoke.

With a smirk on his face, Larsen put in a little dig of his own. "Read about Jonah and the Whale a few too many times, Silvers? Didn't take you for the biblical type."

"Nah. Just means I don't want to swim with whales."

"And they can eat you whole," added Smith. Larsen could hear the grin behind the visor.

"Now, that's just factually inaccurate," replied Silvers.

"Okay. To give Silvers a break, what's the whale up ahead telling us?"

"Not much, sir," said Smith. "I've been running through the latest schematics of the ship, looking for alternate routes in. We may be able to use the refuse jettison exhaust as an alternate route. I'm guessing no one will be awake yet and as such there will be limited refuse ejections."

"You can keep your ejections to yourself," Silvers quipped. "I'm not going anywhere near that. It'll still be operational and unless you have found a way to tell from outside when the next drop is going to be …"

Interrupting, Smith came back with some engineer's logic. "There's a light and broadcast to warn maintenance crews working outside and near the refuse exhaust. It's a countdown. Gives us five minutes to get clear before any junk is fired off into space."

"So, how long would we need to traverse the exhaust and force our way in? Five minutes?"

"Possibly less," Smith said with some confidence. "There is an access hatch about half way up the exhaust chute.

"And how do you know that?"

"Sometimes, it pays to work the garbage detail."

"No doubt."

"You don't want that stuff backing up."

"Okay, moving on," Larsen said, with mild distaste. Suddenly, he had the rather unpleasant sensory memory of faecal matter floating through the confined cabin space of his first posting on the cruiser *Annabelle*. When a toilet fails in a vacuum, the result is never pretty and certainly doesn't smell of roses. It was at that point he realised engineering was not always as glamorous as the posters made out. It was his shift, he had to fix it. "Let's stick with plan 'A', shall we? Keep the ideas coming but let's look at that as a very alternate option."

"Alternate option logged, sir."

More and more of the star field became blocked from view as the *Intrepid* seemed more and more of an endless wall in all directions. Navigation lights blinked with an exaggerated brightness in the dark and Larsen finally caught sight of the airlock he had been looking for. His bio-comms had been tracking and zoomed in to give him a clear picture of door 138, deck 'G'. Everything appeared normal and the external light was showing green, which meant the airlock was cycled to the internal atmosphere. First thing they would need to do would be to flip it.

An icon in his view flipped to green. He flicked a visual control and his navigational tracking screen moved front and centre. Their path, current and projected, showed as a solid and dashed white line, and crossing perpendicular to their track was a red line indicating the point at which they would be inside the defensive perimeter—and safe. Larsen corrected himself—slightly safer. They still had to get inside or, if that failed, back to Tusk One at the rendezvous.

He mused on the relative peril of space exploration and travel in general. Almost everything you did in space had a potentially lethal side-effect if you got things slightly wrong. He remembered as a new flight engineer he had felt anxiety over almost every situation he had to deal with, especially EVA work. As time had gone on that anxiety had diminished but he knew it was a trick of nature.

The risk and consequence had not changed, only his perception of the outcome.

A white dot along their trajectory track showed that they were coming up on the safe zone, inside the fire zone of the guns. "Coming up on the 'safe zone'. Five seconds," he informed the other two. His heart skipped a beat as they crossed the virtual line, a bead of sweat moving down his brow. He hadn't even realised he was getting that keyed up.

The navigation program gave their packs a kick of thrust and they accelerated towards the airlock and the aft of the habitat section of *Intrepid*, covering the remaining distance in a few short moments. The wall of gunmetal grey now a patchwork of impossibly large friction-welded sheets and two metre high designation lettering, they came to a stop exactly ten metres from the airlock.

All Larsen could hear was pounding of his heartbeat in his ears and the sound of his breathing bouncing off the inside of his helmet like some echo chamber. They had made it to the front door.

"Made it." Silvers broke the silence, echoing what they all felt. "Should we knock, sir?"

"I've not travelled all this way to stare at a door, Silvers. Let's get to work. Easy first. Let's see if any of those access codes work on the door. Disengaging GNC."

No sooner had the group navigational control icon changed to red than Silvers was at the airlock door. The hard link between them had reeled out to enable the team to stay connected, physically and vocally. Larsen saw Silvers deftly come to a stop an arms-length from the door, puffs of EVA exhaust stabilising him exactly in front of the airlock's control panel. Reaching out, Silvers keyed in the access code to open the door and start the cycle to create a vacuum inside the airlock.

The control panel colour stayed red.

Silvers tried the door access code a few more times. Nothing.

"So much for easy," he grumbled under his breath. "Looks like we're locked out, sir."

"Peachy," cursed Smith.

"Look on the bright side," Larsen said. "At least we now know the point defence system is online and we," he made a circular motion with his hand, intimating their little group, "aren't a debris field of ex-engineers and EVA pack parts out there somewhere."

Smith took a dome-shaped item with a handle from his kit and orientated himself with the flat of the *Intrepid's* hull. Patching the device into his comms with a hard link, he placed the open end of the dome device to the hull. A rubber lip around the dome made a clean contact and sealed. A status screen appeared in Smith's view and proceeded to scan for broadcast network signals within the structure.

Larsen couldn't stand the suspense and blurted, "Well? What have we got?"

"Good news, I have a signal. Very weak and not particularly usable here, but I should be able to move around a little and isolate the network node. That should give us the strongest signal."

"How long?"

"A few minutes, no more. I'll patch you in as soon as I've made the connection."

That was much better news. However much he liked little trips outside the ship, any ship, they had been outside and on the move for a while. He knew they could all do with getting inside— they wouldn't learn anything useful floating around out here. Looking back towards Smith, he had moved in a zigzag fashion up the hull about twenty metres. "That's about as good a signal as we're going to get. Establishing the network connection." There was a pause of about ten seconds, then Smith stated in a matter-of-fact tone, "We're in."

"Excellent. Good job, Smith. First things first, let's pop this door and get inside."

"Not a problem. What's the door number?"

"Are you kidding? Didn't you catch the number on approach?" he said in disbelief. "The numbers are two metres tall."

"Sorry, sir. Must have missed them. Concentration was elsewhere for a moment."

"Deck 'G', door one three eight," informed Silvers.

A moment later the door receded and slid to the side, revealing the airlock compartment. It was a welcoming sight, the bright lights drawing them in like moths. Silvers was already at the door and made his way in.

"New internal airlock door code, sir. I've coded it to one, two, three, four."

"You need a lesson in security," Silvers snorted.

"Some people are so picky."

"Okay, Smith. Disconnect and get in here. Once we're in, I want you to hook into the network again and get a status of the ship's systems. Silvers, I want an updated schematic and secure route to the bridge. We'll start there."

All inside the airlock, he punched the control, closed the door and started the atmosphere cycling process.

DAWN

She had been monitoring the progress of Tusk One with interest. The loss of communications had put the crew and her father into an intense frenzy of work and speculation. The engineers were attempting to restore communications and her father was sitting in his command couch, fingers in a steeple touching his lips, lost in thought and staring at the shuttle's tracking status screen.

The crew's resuscitation was advanced and would be complete within the next few hours. There would be little time for a relaxed awakening, as her father was driving the medical team justifiably hard and getting people back to post as soon as physically possible. Although the loss of a ship was accounted for within the scope of the mission plan, the repercussions were not acceptable. This deep into space, the simple loss of morale and confidence in the remaining crews would have a huge negative effect on the mission and the operation of the ships. The team was hardy—they were trained to survive the rigours of colonisation and space travel—but there was always the unpredictable human element, that emotional button that was different for everyone and could override any logical, reasoned arguments and drive you to distraction, or simply the wrong judgement at a critical moment.

Finding out what was happening on the *Intrepid* had become the single most important thing the small fleet had to deal with. The colonisation of 21 Hayford b was essentially on hold. It was just too far in the future, although they were already in system and only a few weeks from orbit.

The communication channels between the *Indianapolis* and the *Endeavour* were almost in meltdown with the amount of data being exchanged. There had been telemetry data from the shuttle, but that had been cut when Tusk One had flown into the dead zone around the *Intrepid*; there were the ceaseless proposals and counter proposals of the recovery and planning teams; and there were the engineering team's ideas on what was causing the communications black out—all with their associated files and documentation. It would only get worse when the crews of both ships became fully operational. It was like waking into a bad dream from a hangover.

People had been taking their positions on the bridge as they returned from stasis. Some were still physically drowsy, and a couple had even bumped into consoles and crash couches on their way to their own station, but no one wanted to let down her father or look like they were not ready for any challenge ahead. Crisis management was one of the reasons they had been chosen for the mission, and now was the moment to deliver. A moment—there would no doubt be more.

As the last message they received from Tusk One was related to the team keeping to their flight plan, she had helpfully plotted their proposed course on the mission screen along a dotted line inside a large circle she had labelled CBZ, or 'Comms Blackout Zone', and in its centre was the *Intrepid*. The plot would give some indication of where the shuttle was at any particular moment. Without warning, the image changed completely. The dot jumped to the front of a new line that was moving back toward the *Indianapolis* and away from the CBZ at a pace.

Her father stood in surprise and almost immediately speakers around the bridge were playing the excited voice of Commander Havers. "… One. Do you read? Over."

"Tusk One, this is *Indianapolis*. Thought we'd lost you for a while there. Go ahead. Over."

"*Indianapolis*, this is Tusk One. Still here and punching. Mission status update to follow. Wait one."

"Roger. Over."

"*Indianapolis*, three have been dispatched to the *Intrepid*. We are expecting them to breach the hull within the hour and have control of the bridge within another hour. Break. Their primary objective will be to re-establish communications and secure the bridge. After this communication, we will be returning to the following position in order to provide mission support." A blinking marker appeared on the mission screen. "We will make shuttle runs between markers 'A' and 'B' every thirty minutes until the signal blocking is disabled." Another marker appeared on the mission screen, the markers now labelled 'A' and 'B'. "I am sending you an updated mission schedule now. Over."

"Roger so far, Tusk One."

"*Indianapolis*, if comms are still down and we are not on station at either of these markers, or moving between them, assume there is a mission problem. Over."

"Roger that. Update in thirty minutes. Out."

The bridge went silent.

"What on earth is going on over there, Roux?" her father said to the commander.

"They're taking a risk with that defence system. I wouldn't like to be in one of those EVA suits." As Roux spoke, another marker appeared on the screen with a number three alongside. This time it was the last known position and track of the EVA team.

While her father conversed with Roux about the current situation on the Tusk shuttle, she noticed a request drop into Chief Hopper's message queue from one of his team regarding the analysis of the power anomalies. Within moments of him opening the message, an expression of surprise ran across his features. Hopper was immediately connected through to her father, the seconds it took him to answer clearly giving Hopper some anxiety as he drummed his fingers on his console.

"Hopper, how are you progressing? Anything we can use?" her father said.

"An update to the power anomaly issue. We've managed to isolate its source. We originally thought it was emanating from inside the *Intrepid*."

"Yes."

"It's not. Its source is located close to the far side of the *Intrepid*, within one hundred metres; we can be no more accurate than that at the moment." Hopper was looking concerned and excited all at the same time. She quickly did the maths to confirm what the chief engineer was saying. It was correct. How could that be exactly? Had the *Intrepid* launched something, a shuttle maybe, that was causing false readings?

"Could this be a shuttle reactor breach? Maybe they off-loaded the shuttle to work on it at a safer distance?" she said, putting her interpretation of events into the conversation.

"Unlikely," Hopper countered. "If you have a reactor meltdown at one hundred metres, you may as well be stood right next to it."

"What then? A probe?"

"Couldn't generate that amount of power."

"So what does that leave? What's the other side of the *Intrepid*?"

There was quiet while they pondered the issue and tried to resolve the facts into some sort of credible explanation.

"Dawn. Status of shuttle flight crews, please. Have we a flight crew ready to go?"

"Yes, one. Lieutenant Carroll and his team."

"I want the shuttle kitted out for long-range visual scanning. Fly at a tangent to the ship formation plane; that will give us a view of what's behind the *Intrepid* in the shortest time. Maximum burn."

"We can be ready for launch in thirty minutes," she said.

"Commander Roux, could you brief the flight crew?"

"Aye, sir." Roux stood and left for the flight deck.

Turning his attention back to his console and the face of Chief Hopper, his features looking rather elongated and misshapen where the camera was a little too close to his forehead, he nodded his appreciation. "Thanks Joe, nice work."

"I'll let you know the moment we find anything further." The link closed.

Her attention on the bridge faded as things settled down and the general hubbub of orders and requests were communicated throughout the ship. The ship had started to come alive with activity across all departments as the crew slowly got back to their work stations. Work that had been primarily her sole concern for the last one hundred and thirty years now had others intervening. Some functions that had not needed attending to, as they were biological in nature or scientific in application, had now begun.

Her focus roamed around the ship: she monitored the progress of Lieutenant Carroll's team and shuttle, she moved through the medical bays and the resuscitation suite to see crew members in final stages of awakening, and she found herself floating through the central section of hydroponics where some had gathered to discuss the current situation and the repercussions of coming out of stasis later than expected. Some already appeared to be considering and weighing her father's decisions. The current consensus was positive with few dissenters. She moved on through engineering, the network of water tanks, air filtration and recycling systems. The physical guts of the ship, the belly of the beast. There was a fine balance to the ecosystem, to the internal clock and soul of the ship. She had been their guardian whilst they had slept, and it felt strange to have the ship so alive.

An alarm sounded in the resuscitation centre, the noise swooping repeatedly in unison with the warning lights above bay fifteen. Instantly, she knew all the data pertinent to the crewman in bay fifteen. It wasn't that she had requested it, it was just how the AI worked. She didn't need to request the crewman's name, she just knew it was Leon Writtle. She didn't need to query any systems to understand his condition, she knew he was going into a wave divergence state. It was like recollecting a memory or something already learned. She could simply recall the information.

Dr Freeman was instantly attending and trying to do what he could. Nurses buzzed around like bees, applying further neurological monitoring and preparing for the resynchronisation procedure. The bed elevated and inclined so that Dr Freeman could work on Writtle's head at a more relaxed height. A control console with various surgical instruments hanging from locators on its side flipped down from the rear of the bed headrest. She knew that, in Dr Freemans view, his bio-comms would be showing him all sorts of information, including the three-dimensional rendering of Writtle's brain, overlaid with the diverging wave formation. He had around sixty seconds to realign the wave or loose Writtle.

Others came through, more to witness than assist. There was little they could do anyway. All that could be done was being done and, from the beads of sweat running down Dr Freeman's face, Dawn considered the procedure was not going well.

"Seventy percent divergence," one of the nurses stated. No emotion, no accusation, simply a statement of fact. Reading out the numbers.

Dr Freeman had a surgical controller in each hand and was waving them in circles around Writtle's head, moving to one side then back, like he was trying to brush away a particularly bothersome fly. He began to grimace as if concentrating a little too hard.

"Eighty percent divergence."

"Prepare the crown," he ordered. The nurse by his side hit

another button on the bed and a drawer slid out. A semi-circular band device sat in a moulded setting, she grabbed it and placed it snugly to Writtle's forehead, ensuring the ends lined up with his temples and centred just above his brow.

"Crown set," stated the nurse, who stepped away from the bed.

"Ninety percent divergence."

"Now!" he barked.

The nurse urgently punched a red button on her console. The crown illuminated with an intense electric blue, pointed clamps fired and lanced into Writtle's temples and between his eyes, rigidly fixing itself to the skull. A moment later what looked like metallic eye patches flicked out from the underside of the crown band, internally guided needles penetrated the soft gel of each eye and worked their way to the optic nerve where it anchored and made its bio-interface connection.

With the crown deployed, Dr Freeman dropped the control paddles and moved to work from the console in the rear of the bed headrest. A whining sound started to emanate from the crown as power started to increase.

"Okay. Let's put Mr. Writtle back to sleep for a while." He pushed a button and restraints rolled swiftly out of the bed sides, locking Writtle's arms and legs into position. Once in place, he hit the final button in the sequence. The whining noise increased in frequency again then became inaudible. Writtle's body then tensed and flexed alarmingly. A couple of those watching stepped back. They knew the theory but were still surprised by the effect of the crown in practice.

The crown had intensified in brightness and blood was trickling into the bed sheets from the wounds inflicted around Writtle's head. His body seemed to be panting and spittle gathered around the lips, as if he was suffering some demonic possession. Then, all went still. The body slumped back onto the bed, the head flopping to one side. The crown now made no sound and, instead of the powerful light display, only two small green lights flickered to one side with a couple of letters and numbers.

Dr Freeman moved around to read the numbers on the crown. He exhaled loudly and his shoulders physically dropped.

"That was too close," he said to no one in particular. Reaching over he unclipped the front block from the crown piece. "Looks like our Mr Writtle will be spending more of the flight in stasis than the rest of us."

Turning to the nurse at his side, he handed the wave container over. "Could you see that he is returned to stasis. I'll log the incident and start the investigation into his divergence with the stasis team." He then walked to the washroom to calm down and freshen up.

Nurse Emma Willoughby watched Dr Freeman leave the room then looked around the small gathering of people. "Okay, show's over, people. Back to work or whatever you were doing, please." She looked down at the small bar-shaped wave container in her hand, as if in a slight dream, then a look of resolve came over her. "Tina, could you please take the host for recycling. I'll take the wave container back to stasis. Thanks." Tina nodded and started to prepare Writtle's body for the recycling process.

Dawn was constantly amazed at how all they were, all that made humans human, could be condensed into something no larger than a small bar you could fit in your hand. Thankfully, this sort of thing did not happen often. She had only been witness to three divergent events aboard the *Intrepid*. On the whole, they did not work out well for the patient. This was the first divergence that the medical team had been able to save, so she guessed it was Leon Writtle's lucky day. Okay, he wouldn't be waking up for another twenty years or so, as it took that long to grow a new host clone, but, taking the longer view, at least he was alive. They could so easily have lost him.

*

Memories flashed. Orange street lights, blurred and warped by the rain washing across the screen of her boyfriend's car. The car was an old Ford *something*. She'd never really bothered to find out, car's weren't really her thing, but it was old and still had the old wiper tech to clear the rain, not the latest aqua-repulsor tech that her father's car had—with that you could drive in the rain as if it was a clear day, not a drip of water on the screen. Hendon's car, or 'H' as most people called him, seemed to simply smear the water into a slightly thinner sheen across the screen. Visibility was poor, and they were out in it pushing their luck without knowing it, as the young often do. They had been to the city to watch a movie that night and were returning along back roads, music and conversation mixing as the miles slipped by. Laughter and jokes easy and frequent.

She didn't even see the vehicle that hit their car. They said the car had been overtaking on a slight bend and had not seen the oncoming traffic. To avoid the head-on crash, the overtaking car had cut back in and sideswiped them, spinning the nose of their car off into the verge. H had fought the wheel, standing on the breaks, trying anything to wrestle the car back onto the road, the panic in his eyes visible even in the flashing half-light and shadows that had become the chaotic world within the car. She was jolted to the roof, even with her harness strapped about her, the knock bringing her attention to the windscreen, and beyond to the whips and thrashing sounds of branches as they grabbed like angry forest demons for the car. Her eyes widening in terror, as they fixed on the oncoming tree. Slow motion, and a noise that pervaded her every fibre filtered through. She realised she was screaming. Then, nothing.

She had read once that the way they had edited old movies was by splicing different reels together, the effect of which was to create a continual and smooth visual experience for the audience. If the edit was bad, the result would be a jarring, confusing visual that would likely not make sense to the observer. The latter was exactly the experience she received after waking from the accident. It just confused her to hell. From her memory chronology, there was the tree then nothing but black and an awareness of self, then an expectation that there should be more. Seconds later, sounds slowly started to filter in: the sound of people talking, shouting incoherently, rain, lots of rain, then metal bending and buckling under stress. Sounds crystallised into recognisable words and she began to picture the world around her, rescue teams and other complete strangers attempting to get to a man in a crippled car who was still alive.

Prickles of ice dotted her face, then little by little the nothing became a something. Lights, bright blue lights, flashed across the scene. The world was on its side, and she took a few more moments to comprehend the scene she was looking at. There were people around the base of a tree, which had become almost fused with what she could only describe as crumpled metal. There was nothing recognisable as H's car.

She felt totally removed from the scene, almost otherly, an

observer to something horrific happening to someone else. Trying to correct the view, from horizontal to vertical, she attempted to move, or at the very least sit. It appeared that someone had managed to get her out of the car easily but had dumped her in long grass several metres from the scene, so that everyone else could work on H's rescue. He was clearly in some distress. She could hear moans of pain and incoherent wailing, and it upset her that he was in such agony. She was awake now; she could help.

Again and again she tried to move, to shift her weight and roll to her side—it should be easy. Nothing. She tried again, her arm flailing in order to muster some momentum, but each time she tried she felt like her body was hundreds of times heavier than she was ever used to. She had to help, but what was happening? She grasped and grabbed randomly for any purchase to lift herself. A tree was close, she would use the tree, lean against it, use it to stand. Pulling against the long grass she managed to drag herself to the base of the tree and lean herself, with immense effort, up against the trunk.

Lank wet hair lay across her eyes and she sat exhausted, gasping for breath, feeling like she had just swum a mile. The horror of the scene was fully visible to her now and she looked on with an unbelieving disconnection: in the distance were rescue vehicles, with car headlights trailing off as far as could be seen in each direction, then closer was H's car, or what was left of it. The front of the car was completely compressed around a tree, which showed no apparent signs of distress or damage. The windscreen was gone, and the driver's side door was missing with a crowd of rescue crew around it.

Pain was dull and all encompassing, while her exhaustion grew. The weight on her was growing with an overwhelming tiredness. She could feel the rain on her face getting colder and she began to think that she should have worn a coat. Wait—she had left it in the boot of the car. Maybe she should get it? But she needed rest; maybe she could sleep for a while. She would get her coat once she had had some rest.

Following the trail of destruction from the car to where she lay, she wondered why she could only see part of her right leg. An addled mind questioned why there was also no left leg or hip, the cold was so hard she could not feel her left arm either. But her eyelids were so heavy, sleep was all there was.

Moments later, she was staring at her father's face. He looked haggard, overworked and as if he had not slept in weeks. His hair was greasy and standing in odd directions, there were black bags under his eyes the size of small suitcases, and she could see a desperation in his eyes. Then his face turned to relief and he broke down and sobbed, head buried in his hands.

"Dad," she said. Her voice sounded strange to her, but she needed to console her father. Something was wrong. "Dad. What's the matter?"

He looked at her with wet eyes. He wore a smile of a man conflicted with both joy and sadness, from a father's need to comfort and hold his daughter but being physically unable to do so.

"Dawn, we thought…" he managed to say in a croaking, halting manner. He shook his head quickly, shaking away the emotion, trying to regain his composure and focus on her.

"I'm here, Dad. I'm not going anywhere." She tried to reach out to him, to touch his face and reassure him that everything would be okay. The sensation of her arm moving was there as usual but she was confused to see no responding limb, nothing appearing at her father's face. Something in her recoiled and things began to feel out of place. She began to feel like she was floating and looking at her father through goggles, becoming more and more distant. "Dad?" she exclaimed, worry verging on panic in her voice. A drowning sensation began to take over, "What's happening, Daddy?"

Her father started to rapidly punch buttons on consoles and keyboards. "Hang in there kiddo, I'm working on it." The drowning sensation continued, and again she experienced more confusion as she realised she was still able to talk to her father, even as her lungs filled with water, or fluid or whatever it was. Emotionally, she was crying and in a place of fear, yet she had no tears and no blurred vision. "There." The world flexed back into clarity, sensations of drowning and fading instantly gone. Things were right again, but not right.

"Daddy, what's going on?"

He was running his hands through his hair. This was a conversation he appeared not to want. It was the same look he had had when he gave her the 'birds and bees' conversation—nervous and reluctant but resigned.

"I can't see my hands. I'm moving my hands in front of my face, but I can't see my hands."

"Dawn, you... you had an accident. I'm sorry."

"I know, Dad." The memories began to flood back. "Where am I? Which hospital?"

"You're not in hospital."

"Not in hospital? What do you mean I'm not in hospital? Where else would I be?" She started to look around, to look for clues. He was right; they were not in any hospital she had seen. No clean white lines to the furniture, no sterile environment, no medical staff at hand, no wards or other patients. What she saw instead was server stacks, memory bays, network cables and power conduits, work benches with electrical components and memory arrays.

"You're in my lab, honey. It's the only way I could save you. The only way."

"Dad, you're making no sense. Just tell me. I need to know what's going on!" As if she had not suffered enough over the last couple of days, why was her father not being straight with her? It was infuriating. She knew about the accident, she knew it was bad, but clearly she was okay, otherwise she would not be sitting here talking to her father. He was stalling, she persisted.

He was quiet for a long moment, just nodding his head and looking at her. He was steeling himself for what was to come. She waited.

"They couldn't save you, Honey. Not your body. They couldn't save you. The injuries, they were too severe. They had you on life support for a few days, kept you going for as long as they could, but there was only so much they could do." His voice stammered, breathless with the emotion of it all, unable to get the words out fast enough and overreaching his sentences. "I couldn't let you go, kiddo. Not now, not ever. You had hardly lived. I couldn't let you die, not when I could do something."

"Do what, Dad? What have you done?" She almost didn't want the answer.

"It's taken some time but I saved you. I moved you. I took you out of your dying body and put you somewhere you could live again." He stopped talking, seemingly to let his mouth catch up with his brain. When he spoke again, it was with calm and careful words. "You are alive, Dawn. But you are within a machine."

"I'm a machine?"

"No, that's not what I said. You are you but your body is a

machine."

"I'm a machine," she repeated in a hushed whisper as her mind drifted and whirled into a spiral of confused thoughts and scenarios. "How much time, Dad? You said it's taken time. Wasn't the accident yesterday?"

"No. Three years." He shook his head.

She realised everything about this was going to be difficult, frightening. She needed time.

She closed her eyes. The darkness returned, as the view of her father shrank to a circular pinprick of light then blinked out.

LARSEN

Inside the *Intrepid* things were quiet. Ellie clearly had not started the crew resuscitation process and the ship was still in stasis. They had made their way through the airlock into a dark and unnerving corridor. Only the light from the airlock doorway and their helmet torches illuminated the immediate area. Looking into the corridor was like looking into a horizontal well—visibility for about five metres, then a forbidding darkness. A couple of metres down the corridor, Silvers found a control panel in the wall and activated the lights. They came on in a phased manner, the darkness of the well slowly receding as each light panel received the message.

"I don't know about you guys, but this is giving me the creeps. Why is this section shut down?" Silvers had managed to voice exactly the thoughts of the other two.

"What, no reception party?" Larsen said, trying to keep it light. "Come on, let's find a good place to set up."

"In fact," continued Silvers, looking closer at the console screen, "it's not just the lights; the life support is also off."

"There's air though, right?" Smith questioned, checking his suit instruments for confirmation.

"Yeah, one hundred and thirty year old air. Nice and stale."

"Reminds me of your cabin." The tension evaporated as Smith poked fun. Larsen let the lighter mood ride a while to give his team something else to think about for a moment. The last few hours floating at walking pace toward a vast dark whale of a ship certainly allowed the imagination to go on a little trip all of its own. He was surprised none of them had cracked before now, fear playing in the shadows of their minds. He had certainly jumped on a few occasions, his heart rate monitor spiking as he thought he saw something move out the corner of his eye, or a navigation light on the ship stop blinking. He looked around for the nearest room, somewhere to connect their kit and get some initial status.

"Right, let's get going. Security station." He pushed a navigation track to their bio-comms and a line appeared that led down the corridor, directing them to the nearest security station. He set off at a brisk pace. The colony ships were all of similar design. Certainly, the same principles had been applied, although the corridor mapping may have been slightly different. Following the corridor and ignoring some of the smaller side rooms, they arrived at an intersection that contained a security office in the corner. There were reinforced window sections, a couple of lockers containing security body armour and monitoring screens, each scanning the local area and part of the habitat section closest to this station. But it was the console and interface that Smith needed.

"All yours, Smith," Larsen prompted.

Smith got straight to work. He unclipped one of the bags from his kit and opened it up to reveal a mobile console and fibre cable which he connected without looking into a socket at the side of the main security panel. The console screen was instantly active and data was scrolling up at a pace faster than Larsen could read. Smith wasn't looking at the screen; his bio-comms had clearly connected and he was interfacing with the security station looking for information.

"Well?" demanded Larsen, his voice taking on an air of impatience. It shouldn't take this long to get a status report.

"Getting there, sir. There are systems down all over the ship. Their shutdown does not appear to have any pattern. I'll have a report in a moment."

Silvers was loitering by the door. He had come armed with a Longman-Cooper carbine with .22 soft-nosed ammunition, standard security issue. Rather nasty at close range, it would make a mess of the target but not the hull—no danger of accidental breaches. The situation was clearly messing with Silvers more than he expected. It was just the way he stood with an ill-at-ease awkwardness in his frame. Larsen made a mental note to keep an eye on things there. The last thing he needed was the guy with the gun losing it.

"Okay, we're in." The primary wall screen in the room flashed on and started to scroll with some data. It cleared as fast as it arrived and was then replaced with the ship schematic and regional sector reports. There was a lot of amber and red in sections Larsen really wanted to see green.

"Bridge section, green. AI, designation 'Ellie', reports amber. Engineering, amber." Smith continued to run through sections of interest, speaking his way through the list for the benefit of the report recording he would be compiling to send back to the *Indianapolis* and the *Endeavour* as part of the investigation. "Hydroponics, amber. Habitat section 'A', green. Habitat section 'B', amber. Starboard side habitat section 'C', red. Starboard side habitat section 'D', red."

"Sir—" Larsen looked over to Silvers. He was wide eyed and focused on something behind him to the far corner of the small room. He nodded in the general direction, unwilling to take his hands from his carbine to physically point. Following Silvers's line of sight in the indicated direction, he saw Ellie.

"Starboard side engineering section 'H', red," continued Smith, unaware of the new turn of events. "Starboard side engineering section 'I', red." The holoprojector may have been having issues. Ellie's image was trying to form, swirling and fragmenting then collapsing to a single point then repeating the pattern and process. It began to stabilise but appeared to glitch every few seconds, with part of the image dropping out as another resolved. In addition, her skin tone had taken on a rather exotic lime green. As Larsen watched, Ellie appeared to be mouthing the words Smith was saying in unison, only there was no sound. Well, that looked like their first job. Ellie needed an overhaul.

He moved over to stand in front of Ellie's image, looking for any kind of recognition or visual indication that she knew they were there. The very fact of the projected image being there may at some base level be an attempt at contact, if her systems were corrupted or impeded in some way. They needed to get to her.

His message queue flashed up and Smith's status report appeared. An updated floor plan was now available, which he instantly used to navigate a path to Ellie's core. The report also contained some alarming detail showing whole sections of the starboard side of the ship having not merely a stale environment but no environment. The information was incomplete and would need an onsite inspection to confirm the status of the hull in these areas. The last thing he wanted was a hull breach, but that was currently what it looked like. Maybe if they got Ellie back online, she'd have some further information on what happened there before they went poking around.

Smith completed his audio monologue but continued to work through some system components to try and dig out further information on some of the worst affected areas of the ship. As this happened, Ellie's focus snapped in a glitch to Larsen, her eyes suddenly appearing other-worldly, similar to those of a cat, but quickly returning to normal, albeit in the monochrome green the rest of the hologram was washed in. She wore a pained smile, an expression of both worry and sympathy. Standing in a relaxed posture, she was eye-to-eye with Larsen, around average height for a female, athletic build, short bob of a hair style, round eyes and full lips. She looked very 'girl next door'—attractive, yet not overly so. If she wasn't an AI, she would very likely have many male admirers. He took a moment and thought of the crew and their biological age. He decided that, even as an AI, she would have plenty of admirers, especially from his command. Engineering was full of men who had trouble communicating with real-life women. She would have a lot of fans.

"Lieutenant Larsen, I'm glad you're here." Her voice was like chocolate running through a distortion unit. You could hear the mellow tones; however, there was background of static that ruined a voice he could happily get used to listening to all day.

"Hello, Ellie."

"There has been an incident aboard the ship. I have been incapacitated in some way and have lost some function." Her image flicked off completely but her voice persisted. "You have received a status report of the ship and can see the extent of some of the damage. There are issues to the starboard side and I am unable to access exterior cameras or any local sensor readings within starboard engineering decks." Her image flicked back on. This time the monochrome hologram had been replaced with a fully working projection but vocal sound had stopped.

Larsen dropped his head in frustration. Taking a breath, he looked around for a console. From his kit he unreeled a fibre and plugged into the console port. He always found connecting to consoles via fibre a little disorienting. The sharp mental grating you received as the connection was made felt like running your tongue over a battery's terminals where the voltage was a little too high. He navigated though computer systems to the local controls of the projector. A moment later, Ellie was back—with sound.

Leaving himself tapped in, he continued the conversation.

"Could you repeat that, Ellie? You dropped out there for a moment."

"Certainly, Lieutenant. Where would you like me to restart?"

"I think you were talking about external sensor failure on the starboard side."

"Yes. Exterior cameras are non-functional on the starboard side of the ship and I'm unable to access any local sensor readings from starboard engineering decks 'H' and 'I'. Additionally, I am having difficulty recalling memory. I have local memory that patches to the short-term memory systems but long-term memory systems have anomalies and access issues." She paused, looking directly at him. Her image started to scramble and glitch again. "I believe I am under attack from an internal source, though I cannot specify a point of origin."

"It's a big ship," he said, trying in some way to give her some solace, "and we're here to help. We need to get the rest of the team on site. We need you to take the port side defence system offline and open the shuttle doors. Can you do that?"

There was a couple of second's delay in her response, "No, Lieutenant. I am unable to complete that request. I have active blocks in place. Override clearance from the bridge is needed to deactivate point defences and open the shuttle bay doors."

He guessed that they had used up all their luck evading the point defence system just getting there. Asking Ellie to switch it off was a stretch.

"Okay, Ellie. We're coming to you, then we'll sort out the bridge."

"Thank you, Lieutenant. I'll help you where I can. Elevators in the central corridor are active, core tram is active. See you when you get here."

"Nothing more I can do here," Smith said, disconnecting from the hard-point, reeling the fibre in and putting the mobile console and fibre back into his pack.

"Looks like it's the core tram, then up to the AI core," stated

Silvers, reviewing the navigational trace via his bio-comms.

"Time to go."

This time Silvers took point, following the track towards the core tram. In each major bulkhead they opened, the corridor was found to be in darkness. Larsen felt he should have asked Ellie to turn all the ship's lights on. It would have saved them some time and eased the creeping feeling of dread that he had. He kept reminding himself not to be such a child. Scared of the dark? You're not scared of the dark are you? It was just his animal brain giving him something else to worry about, as if he didn't have enough problems.

The blackouts on the starboard side were a real worry though. Hull breaches were not something a balanced ecosystem needed, although the ship still being dormant really helped as it meant no one was in direct danger, being nicely tucked up in stasis. Well, none of the current crew, anyway. What he didn't know at this point was how big the breaches were and how much atmosphere had been lost. It did look like Ellie had been able to isolate the breaches, so hopefully that was good news.

As they walked, Larsen reviewed the conversation with Ellie again from his bio-comms memory player. He had started recording everything he could the moment they had arrived aboard. He had enough mobile memory for several hours recording but by then, hopefully, the rest of the team would be aboard and he could pack the recordings off into his report to Havers. If the team couldn't get aboard within the next few hours, he'd have to start rolling out the oldest for the newest. He decided to set that up. He clicked a few visual icons and the new memory settings took effect. FIFO or First In First Out recording was enabled.

Rounding a corridor, they walked into another security section, utilitarian and stark with a glaring orange carpet and seats in the waiting area. A double door across from the seating section was labelled in large painted print 'G120', above the door a sign reiterating the information, simply stating 'Core Tram G120.'

"Looks like our tram," said Silvers, looking along the glass panels out onto the track.

"What tram?" Smith asked.

Smith was right. Peering through the viewing panels to the tramway, although very dark, you could also see clearly that there was no tram, just another large print decal stating the gate number.

Linking into the tram's local network, Larsen tried to find the location of the tram. It looked like it was a few gates up the tramway. About ten minutes distant, if he could call it. A call flashed in through his bio-comms. Seeing the incoming call was from Ellie, he accepted.

"We're at the tram station 'G120'," he got in, before Ellie said anything.

"Yes. I've activated the tramway. The tram will be with you in eight minutes, fifteen seconds. Once on board you will need to alight at G50 in order to gain access to the correct elevator." Her voice modulated slightly in the final sentence. She was evidently still having trouble.

"We'll be with you as soon as we can, Ellie." There was no reply. Pausing to ensure she wasn't still trying to get through, he turned to the other two, "May as well take a seat and rest. Tram will arrive in eight."

"Sounds like a good idea." Smith dumped his kit and dropped into a seat. Putting his feet on the chair opposite he tried to give the impression of someone relaxed and at ease. It didn't work. The tension in his body language shone through like a beacon.

He and Silvers just exchanged looks, then Silvers shrugged and sat down, still alert and watchful. Larsen continued to review his exchange with Ellie.

What did she mean that she believed she was under attack? He guessed it was possible, AIs had been under attack for years. A group originating on Earth and calling themselves la Guerre à l'Intelligence Artificielle—or, more simply, GAIA—had been active politically, working against AI development and any introduction into the world network, even before Captain Clayton had perfected AI in his years as an AI research scientist. GAIA had started as a peaceful protest against AI technology and research but as the movement became more popular and gained support across not only non-tech but also high-tech communities, the peaceful protest morphed into not-so-peaceful, and even violent, protest.

But government and corporate business were driven by the potential benefits of AI. How much money could they make by plugging AI into banking and world markets? What could be gained by allowing AI to design military technology or building AI into military technology? A lot of very powerful, very rich and influential people got very excited and invested heavily into the research.

GAIA warned and peddled the downfall of humanity. If the plans of those driven by greed and power were to come to fruition, AIs would become the puppets of these masters and spell doom for the rest of humanity. Other theories speculated that AIs would become independent and break free of human control, or would turn against their human creators in some apocalyptic disaster, or war against themselves, with humanity becoming a casualty of the crossfire. In all proposed eventualities, AI was the death of humanity.

Larsen smiled at the irony, as mass consumption of planetary resources had been the downfall of humanity, that and a big rock falling from the sky. While GAIA and other political organisations had been scape goats of governments all around the world, governments themselves had been trying to win a fight that had been lost a few centuries before. The scales had been tipped and the resources had dwindled. People were starving on every continent, they had no fresh water, power was limited and rationed.

From his history lectures on 'The Great Decline', he remembered the speed at which it had all occurred. The illusion of stability had been sustained by governments around the world for generations, until they could no longer pretend. While the problem was contained within the African continent, Indian sub-continent and Middle-East, the rest of the world appeared happy to accept the politicians' excuses. The moment power cuts and food shortages started to be experienced in western societies for weeks and months, the cat was finally out of the bag. People started to revolt, entire urban communities would start to loot and scavenge, taking whatever they could. Police forces collapsed in moments, understaffed for such population-wide mutiny. The armed forces, who had previously been busy defending their borders against mass immigration, found themselves ordered to defend their elite, their leaders and capital cities.

The global crisis intensified with the arrival of 590122 Killian, an asteroid from the Kuiper Belt, reasonably small in size but big enough that when it hit the Ukrainian heartland it destroyed and effectively shut down agricultural production across the eastern European state. Anyone who survived migrated either to Russia or another eastern European country. However, these countries had their own problems, and mass migration was already chief amongst them.

Russia had also just lost her chief food production resource. There had been historical problems there, fractious political relationships between the two countries which had been a source of unrest for centuries. The Russian solution, almost always, was to bully Ukraine into submission. Each time resources would flow until the next dispute. But this time there was no one to bully. This time there was no resource. Ukraine was dead.

Known as The Russian Crisis, which Larsen always found laughable, as it was Ukraine who found themselves in crisis, was the final world economic straw. The world economy shattered, all countries became protectionist under the howls and screams of their populous.

The Great Decline took ten years. Millions of people had died and millions more were doomed. The world was going through a self-correction to the human population based on an unchecked consumption of the world's treasures and a major Earth strike event, so politicians were the target and outlet for the people's wrath. However, the effect of the mass political upheaval was dire. Countries dissolved, technology was plunged back centuries in many areas of the world by the lack of power, and people became violent towards their neighbour for the smallest scrap of food, society reordered by local warlords and gangs. Anarchy had been reborn into the world as a new order.

Pockets of civilisation survived, although these sanctuaries worked under the premise that the world could no longer function and humanity would no longer survive past the next generation or so. These were the cities of the political and social elite, the dreamers and illuminati, who had managed to annex themselves and lock out the world in fortified locations around the world. These cities and arcologies had an acquired but unified purpose, that being to find a new world and colonise the stars.

AI technology had been discovered and perfected in the UK arcology in the former London metropolis state, and was being hailed as humanity's saviour. Within decades of its discovery, AI technology had given hope to the enlightened societies that their goal of colonising the stars was achievable. With the mass global effort of these last few, under the umbrella of a new global political alliance, the Terran Federation initiated the Space Colonisation Project.

Three potential earth-like planets were identified and nine colony ships built in low orbit around old Earth. There would be three colony fleets sent into the void to keep humanity alive, with the first planned to arrive one hundred and thirty five years after departure. It was assumed old Earth would not survive, though there were some scientists who stated there was a seven percent chance that some minimal number would make it through and continue the human race on earth. What technological level the survivors could maintain was very much debated—none could agree.

"Tram's here, boss." Silvers snapped him out of his thoughts.

He stood and picked up his kit. "You ready, Smith?" he said, giving Smith a gentle kick. Smith looked up, eyes wide and alert. "Time to work."

"Yep. I'm ready," he said, seemingly to convince himself more than anyone else. "I'm ready."

Silvers was at the door to the tram before the others. The room doors slid open to reveal the tram doors, which followed suit a short moment after. He did a quick check of the immediate cabin and nodded over his shoulder. "All clear."

All aboard the tram, Larsen selected gate 'G50' from the tram navigation console. With the python hiss of hydraulics and soft clunking of moving parts, the doors closed and the tram began to move rapidly towards the forward section of the ship.

CARROLL

At full burn the shuttle could use its complete fuel reserve in a day. That's an Earth twenty-four hour day, not a day on Jupiter or a day on Mercury, though if he was with Janice he would be quite happy with a Mercury night, except for the cold—at -170°C or so, that would stunt anyone's libido. I need more anaphrodisiac hormone suppressant, he thought, I've been thinking of her since I woke up. Man, I need a vacation already. Getting straight on a flight from resus in retrospect probably wasn't the most sensible thing to do. He should have taken the suppressants when he was offered them. He wondered whether going over the navigation calculations again would give him something else to think about. That was about the least sexy activity he could perform right now. Having an erection for the next ten hours or so wasn't his idea of fun. Well, not on his own, anyway.

They had only been on the flight for twenty minutes. They had another five hours before their angle of ascent and distance travelled would put them in a position to see around the *Intrepid* to what hid behind. He'd been trying to think what might be causing the signal jamming but kept on coming up blank. The subject had the whole crew buzzing. He'd been out of resus for a few hours and all he'd heard since he awoke was the chat about the *Intrepid*. Already the conspiracy theorists were hard at work. The *Intrepid* had become a ghost ship, the crew were all dead, the AI had gone crazy and murdered her own crew. He for one preferred not to speculate. Considering none of these ideas to be plausible, he saw an opportunity and started a sweepstake. He had a few takers straight away, the favoured scenario being the 'crazy AI' theory. Well, whatever. But if it made him a dollar or two in the process, it worked for him.

Whatever the cause of the current situation on the *Intrepid*, he was, however, genuinely intrigued by what they might find. Aside from all the made-up stuff by the crew, which couldn't be, he was excited to find out what could be. He believed the smart money was on one of the *Intrepid's* shuttles, pushed out into space with a power cell leak. If it was severe enough, that may cause the communications interference. But it probably wasn't the whole story. He'd wait and see like everyone else.

"Fancy a coffee?" he asked his co-pilot. Sub-Lieutenant Evan Stills was in his pilot's couch reviewing flight data and finessing the controls of the navigation system accordingly. Minor alterations to course based on new information of small dark objects ahead of them along the predesignated track. He was tall for a pilot, blond hair and slightly angled facial features, his body newly out of the wrapper not having much definition, although he knew, given a few weeks at the gym, Stills would be a chiselled mass of muscle again. The guy treated his body like a temple.

"You kidding? You still drink that stuff?"

"Best go-go juice out there, and this new body could do with some waking up."

"Green tea. Thanks."

"Green what? Do we even hold that stuff on the shuttle?" he was genuinely surprised. Green tea really wasn't on any shuttle manifest he'd seen.

"I make sure. It's next to the coffee packs. Marked 'Green tea'. Even you should find it."

"You might think that." He said. The guy was cheeky, it was part of his charm. There was always a smile to back up the insult he'd just thrown out to let you know it was playful. It would get Stills in trouble one day. Or maybe it had and that was why the guy now worked out all the time. When he was on form and muscled he would certainly not be easy to take down.

He worked his way through the corridor between the cockpit and the main section to the small kitchenette area just short of the medical bay. The kitchenette was little more than a floating space with lots of cupboard space for food and drinks packets and a warming unit. The warming unit was misnamed, in Carroll's opinion, as it did a little more than warm your food. If you got the setting wrong, it could pretty much incinerate your food, or boil your drink. Warm was an understatement.

Flicking through the coffee packets, sure enough he found Stills' green tea. Taking a couple of packets out, he put them in the warming unit. Opening up the comms on his bio-comms, he messaged Patterson and Rivers in the main compartment. Only fair to ask everyone if they wanted a coffee. He received an instant affirmative from both, so he took two more coffees from the cupboard and added them to the warming unit and set the timer.

While waiting for the coffee, he decided to pop his head through to the main cabin to find out what Patterson and Rivers were up to. Flight Engineer Steven Patterson had been on his team for two years now—that's two relative years, subtracting all the stasis time in the middle. He was the same as many engineers on this crew, good at their job and monosyllabic. They could strip down and rebuild a shuttle engine in a couple of hours, but try and engage them in a conversation that lasted longer than thirty seconds and you were in trouble. Patterson did have the most piercing crystal blue eyes and jet black hair, which Carroll thought incredible, but for macho, masculine code reasons could never broach the subject or even mention it to others. He gave Patterson a nod of recognition as he floated into the cabin, he received a curt nod in return, then Patterson got back to the work he had running on the mobile console he had strapped to his lap.

Scientist First Class Katherine Rivers was floating in front of the console to the far side of the cabin section next to a bulkhead. She was of petite build, had an intense focus and an almost constant frown of concentration, with auburn hair, cut short, as was the fashion amongst the spacefaring. Long hair in space was generally for those with no understanding of long term life in space, or those who didn't give a damn about those they worked with. There was nothing worse than working next to someone whose long hair spread half a metre in every direction from their head, got in the way of instrumentation, got snagged in moving parts or pinch points in machinery, or due to close working confines kept brushing your face like an itch you couldn't scratch every few minutes. Yep, long hair in space was just rude. Didn't matter which sex you were.

Skimming over, he floated just behind her, his hands steadying himself on the bulkhead and cabin ceiling.

"What's the view like Doc?" he asked. The screen was currently showing a close up of the *Indianapolis*. The optics on the instrumentation they were carrying looked fantastic, according to him, but then he knew little about advanced photometry or spectroscopy. In fact he knew little about any photometry and spectroscopy, let alone anything advanced. It was all just pretty pictures, graphs and an eye-watering set of numbers in large nonsensical tables.

"It's all working well. I'm using the *Indianapolis* as a test subject until we get a good enough angle on the *Intrepid*, then I'll reset."

"Sounds like a plan. Coffee's on." She'd already lost him.

"I'll be able to tweak some parameters over the next couple of hours to give us the best shot at getting a perfect image when it comes to taking a peek past the *Intrepid*."

"Whatever you say, Doc. Great detail on the image though. I'd probably be able to count the freckles on your face if you were waving at me from the *Indy* right now."

"Er, yes." She didn't stop what she was working on for a moment but Carroll found the back of her head less talkative than he'd have liked. Back to the coffee run.

Back in the cockpit he dropped into his couch and batted the green tea packet at Stills.

"One green tea, hot."

Stills picked the sachet out of the air as it span past his field of vision.

"Thanks."

"Anything of note happen while I was away?" he asked, taking a slug of coffee from his own drinks sachet. It was bitter and hot, just what he needed. There was nothing like a good coffee, and this was nothing like a good coffee, but it was the best he could do on a shuttle trip at short notice. He would need to have a chat to his guy in hydroponics and processing, see if he couldn't source some proper natural beans, not the prepacked crap they put in these shuttles.

"No. Had to shift track two degrees starboard, there's a small debris field we need to scoot round, but that's about it." He curled his lip in a 'that's all' kind of way. "We'll need to correct course once we're round it."

"Rivers is all set—the instrumentation is working like a charm."

"Sounds like a milk run. Don't know what all the urgency was about."

"Hey, if the Big Man says we need to shuffle on this one, then that's good enough for me. We need to keep focused. Do a good job and everyone's happy."

"Always." Stills was still looking straight out the cockpit and focused on flying the ship but he had a wide smile on his face. He couldn't fault him, he did always do a good job. Mister Consistent. According to Carroll, Stills was one of the good ones. A damn good pilot.

"Well settle in, only another four hours and thirty minutes before contact," he said in a lazy tone, starting to go over a few flight details himself. Fuel, track and velocity, distance to their next way point.

"Roger that."

The smell of coffee wafted through the cockpit, something homely and familiar in the expanse of open space, something to centre a human to himself. He found comfort in the sensation and sank further into the flight couch and memories of home. He fixed the harness then got back to work.

CLAYTON

Taking a walk was sometimes the best way of clearing the mind. When things became a fog and you needed some way to focus, a little separation from the problem was a good thing. This was his separation—walking the decks, talking to the crew, getting a different perspective on things.

He knew he had jumped people out of stasis as soon as the resuscitation teams could manage the process safely, but they had only had to put two or three back into stasis due to divergence issues, which, however unfortunate, was a lower number than he had expected. He could remember when divergence was a one-in-three occurrence. It was an issue that had taken Dawn and himself five years to solve. Now less than a one-in-one-thousand, Clayton found it astonishing. From the struggles they had had to get the process to work in the first instance to now, where people expected the process to be almost flawless as standard. How quickly people got used to technology and integrated it into their lives. He concluded that it was something people did and seemed to be something they had always been good at. It was part of what made people human—the adaptable information animal.

Strolling through the corridors, he had been gone from the bridge for a good hour with only a couple of interruptions. Things were in motion and people were working. This was the lull in operations; there always was one. The calm before the storm, if there was a storm to be had.

He probably hadn't been walking in a straight line but, even so, after an hour walking he was nowhere near the habitat section yet. A sign on the bulkhead said 'Administrative Section Delta'. The slick utilitarian lines of the ship design were everywhere, but he wondered why the administrative section would be a dull grey. It had to be a joke. Probably a designer somewhere thought it would be funny and it just never got picked up by anyone before the build went ahead. Poking his head through an office door, he saw some major colour overcorrection happening, as the people who had to work here daily had put up any decoration they could get their hands on, any items or drapes with bright and vibrant colours were liberally spread around the work space. He had to hand it to them, it certainly cheered him up. He carried on walking.

Coming to a corridor junction and security point, there was a group talking in the corner. As he approached, one of the party spotted him and flicked a look to the rest of the group. They all smartened up and opened the circle to allow him to join the conversation.

"Morning, sir," said one in a uniform with lieutenant stripes.

"Morning all."

"Out for a stroll, sir?" said another. They all looked like administration crew, except one with a green designation flash. Security. He looked over to the security office in the corner. The other security officer was dealing with a query from a slightly agitated looking man with short hair and arms that looked a little too long for his body.

"Yes. All good here? Not working you too hard?" which was exactly what he was doing. Everyone knew it, but he thought he'd let them know he knew too.

"Straight out of stasis and everything is going to hell already, sir?"

"Blanchard! Wind it in," the security officer warned, although Clayton could see the resonance the question had provoked.

"No, that's okay. An honest question. You all know the situation. We've lost contact with the *Intrepid*. We have teams working on getting her comms back online and finding out if we can do any more to assist. There is no need for concern at this point but I did want the crew back on duty, in case any real emergency became apparent." He wore his most sincere face. He'd had to play politician so many times back at the institute whilst pitching his ideas to get finance and funding—it was strange where skills originated. Most of the group were happy with his explanation. "We are only a few weeks off schedule, whether we had been resuscitated by now or not would really have made little difference in the overall mission time. We're just a little closer than expected within the Hayford system—not a big problem."

"So no need to be alarmed, hey Blanchard?" said the security officer.

"No problem. Try not to get too worked up guys. I'll get regular updates out to the crew, to try and help stem some of the rumours."

"Thank you, sir," replied Blanchard in a more subdued tone, more resigned than appeased.

"Remember what we're focused on. We'll need to start preparations for colonisation within the next few days, so anything you can do to facilitate the smooth operation of that process will be very much appreciated by all."

He gave them a final look of confidence and headed for the far door. He mapped a route back to his quarters and pinged Jemma a message, 'Quarters in ten minutes for lunch and hugs?'

'On a break? Be there in five.' He smiled. She was so competitive.

He worked his way back to the elevator and took the route offered by his bio-comms that was highlighted and snaking through the ship to his door, which opened with a mechanical clunk and whir as he approached. Jemma was already there and getting plates out of cupboards in preparation for lunch. "Tuna or chicken?" she asked in a matter-of-fact, 'life goes on', 'nothing has changed' kind of way. Never mind that, apart from the resus lounge, the last time he'd seen her was one hundred and thirty years ago and they had looked totally different. Grey hair, skin that looked more like leather and wrinkles, with aches and twinges that piqued and niggled them, not to mention the undercurrent of chronic weariness. But she had never lost that sparkle in her eye, that fun, wickedness and mischief. It's what he loved about her.

"You *are* joking?" he reflected. He'd been in stasis and had just recovered refreshed and rejuvenated into a twenty-five-year-old body.

She smiled; there really was no subtext. She forgot about the dishes, which clattered to the kitchen top as she ran at him, dodging the worktop and clearing the cabin space in three strides.

If the settee hadn't been next to the room doorway, they would have ended in a pile of bones on the floor, crushed against the wall. As it was, they ended up as a pile of flailing limbs and blur of clothes on the soft cushions of the sofa. The embrace was passionate and frantic, enthusiastic and powerful. The lust of the young overtaking the minds of the mature, and he liked it.

It was meant to get better as you got older, and having the sexual wisdom of age with the body and hormones of youth was one of the most wonderful and unexpected side effects of the transference process.

Falling and rolling around on the floor, they shed some more clothes and somehow made their way to the bed. Caressing and exploring each other for as long as they could restrain themselves, they started to arch and peak in time with their building passions. The release was sudden and combined. They crashed into the white waves of the sheets panting, laughing and giggling like teenagers.

"So much for lunch," Jemma said, after she had regained her breath.

"You think I needed food?"

"Nope."

She beamed at him and rolled out of bed. Hunting for her clothes, she picked them up one by one and dressed. He watched and relived the last few minutes, admiring her curves and physique as she did a reverse striptease back to the settee.

"I like these lunch breaks. Maybe we should have more?"

"I don't think you'd have the energy," she teased.

"Try me."

After a pause she was back at the kitchen counter preparing them a tuna salad as he got dressed then started looking through the available drinks for some juice. He poured the juice and handed one to her, they drank together, looking at each other over the top of the beakers, still smiling, still in the glow of the moment. Happy.

"So, I hear the rumours like everyone else but what on earth is happening over on the *Intrepid*?" They settled at the breakfast bar and began to eat. Suddenly, he was very, very hungry. He noted she had made enough for seconds. She knew him too well.

"At this point, your guess is as good as mine." He began with a slight shrug, waving his fork in the air. "I've sent out a couple of teams, one to board the *Intrepid* and another to monitor and view from a distance. Now we have to wait. We'll know more in the next couple of hours."

She looked at him, a question forming on her brow. "In the meantime, the crew get accelerated out of stasis and we arrive in system a couple of million kilometres closer to Hayford than we expected?"

"Dawn started the cycle a little later, nothing more. She and Obi lost contact with Ellie. The moment that happened..." He shrugged and raised an eyebrow to finish the sentence. Looking down at his meal he suddenly seemed to register the flavour, "This is tasty. Really good."

"That's just your new taste buds talking. Everything tastes good to you."

"You should just take the compliment," he offered. She was probably right—how tasty could salad be?

"I'll take it when it's deserved."

"A statement to live by."

They both took a few more mouthfuls. As they ate, he reflected on the casual ease in which things had got back to normal. It was the relaxed interaction between the crew, and the way he and Jemma now just fell back into their routine as the happily married couple. There were differences of course, but the time in stasis had almost no effect on relationships—it was as if he had gone to sleep one night and simply woken the next day, in a slightly younger self. The one-hundred-and-thirty-year gap in the middle was not an issue and something they all ignored. He considered that as long as people had shared experience of the present, like the time frame of reference on their ship, then they would have something to share and, as such, not lose their sense of self or time. Here and now was all there was, no matter where and when that here and now was. He felt his mind heading down a philosophical rabbit hole, so he stopped his train of thought.

His bio-comms lit up and a priority message arrived, a flashing red alert icon next to an image of Chief Hopper.

"Well, there goes lunch." He opened the message. "Chief Hopper, what have you got for me?"

"Sir, I think you'd better come and see for yourself. AI section. I'll meet you in CIC." Hopper disconnected. Issues seemed to be piling up. He thought it would be too much to ask for this to be some surprise party invite.

"On my way," he said to no one in particular.

Jemma cocked her head to one side. "You have to go already? I thought you said you had a couple of hours."

He crammed another couple of forkfuls of tuna salad into his mouth and made his way round the breakfast bar to wrap his arms around her. "Sorry. Duty calls and calls and calls again. Hopper has something I need to see."

"Well, I'm sure I can prescribe a cream for that. He should really be contacting a doctor, not a captain."

"Let's hope that's all it is." He kissed her and headed for the door.

*

Security officers were all over the CIC and entrance to the AI Core when he arrived. There was a flurry of activity and Chief Hopper turned from a group of engineers and security personnel he was briefing to greet him, or perhaps to intercept him half way across the room. Hopper put his hand round Clayton's arm to guide him to one side and out of casual earshot. This was a private conversation then.

"Sir, I have some bad news." Hopper said, almost apologetically.

"More? I didn't think that possible. Okay, hit me."

"It's Dawn, sir. We've found explosive devices hidden in Dawn's main memory array and also her core."

"Is she okay?"

"Yes, so far. She's helping us with the process of defusing and removing the explosive devices." Hopper was getting onto firmer ground, talking about engineering, and less into the murky realms of the emotional minefield that was the bond between Dawn and Clayton.

Clayton wore a grim look on his face and let out a heavy breath. Considering that ten minutes ago he was on a real high, this was a roller coaster low. "Any ideas as to how this happened?"

"Some, but you're not going to like it. It has all the hall marks of a GAIA operation."

"But we had the entire crew checked and triple checked for their allegiances, relationships and connections to GAIA and a few other organisations."

"Sir, there are thousands of people on board. Multiply that up across all three ships and you have a reasonable statistical probability of someone slipping through the process."

He knew Hopper was right. He had had similar thoughts himself in the early days of the mission but it didn't make it any easier to face up to when the facts were presented as starkly as this.

As they had been talking, St John stepped through the door from the AI core chamber and spotted the two of them talking almost immediately. He made his way directly to them, looking like he was talking to himself, but he was clearly also in a conversation with another in his security team. Both conversations came to a stop as St John joined them.

"St John," he got in first. Taking the initiative in conversations was something his father had always recommended doing, but he was unsure of its effectiveness. He received a nod of greeting from his head of security. "How did this happen? How did no one notice the devices being planted? Not even Dawn mentioned it to me, so she must also have been unaware."

"Yes, the devices themselves were well disguised. The components in question are actually built from an explosive material. Casual inspection would not have revealed an issue." Hopper was reading from his notes and logs within his bio-comms, making his eyes appear to walk right to left from Clayton's view. "At this point, Dawn tells us that, to her, the functional tests of these components check out without anomaly. There is no internal diagnostics that would have highlighted these parts as an issue."

"So, how were these components discovered?" he asked, with genuine confusion. If Dawn was not the source of the information, who was?

St John looked at Hopper. "As part of a routine inventory in engineering," Hopper said with sadness. "I have a man in medical. He was checking the inventory for AI memory components when he accidently dropped one. The explosion took out both his legs and put a hole in the deck. He's alive and providing us with as much information as he can remember, but he'll be waiting for replacement legs for some time.

"We immediately started testing other components and tracking batches to their current installation locations. As Dawn's hardware is spread throughout the ship in nodes, we had to start somewhere. The AI core seemed the obvious choice. We uncovered similar devices to those in store almost immediately."

"This is incredible. We've been out of stasis and back on active operations for less than twenty-four hours and in that time we've had two major incidents! One I could accept, two might be a coincidence, but, being as paranoid as I am right now, I'd be expecting a third incident very soon. Especially if, as you speculated earlier, Hopper, this is a GAIA operation." He looked intently at both, to drive home his alarm at what they were saying and to try and instil some sense of this not going away until the situation was resolved and the perpetrator or team responsible was brought to account.

Hopper frowned and scratched his chin. "It could be related."

"What could be related?" St John responded.

"Well, what if the attack on Dawn is not localised. What if it is part of an orchestrated attack across the fleet, specifically against the AIs, as is GAIA's focus?"

Clayton picked up the idea thread. "*Intrepid's* situation could in part be due to an attack on Ellie, similar to the plot against Dawn here."

"Yes."

"Then we need to inform Captain Straud and Commander Havers immediately." Both men nodded in response. "I'll be on the bridge. Keep me informed of the situation here and the investigation. We need Dawn out of danger as soon as physically possible. And, gentlemen, let's keep this quiet. We've interrupted someone's plans here. Let them think things are still on track."

"Yes, sir." Both men replied in unison. He turned and left them to their work but instantly patched a message through to Dawn.

'Hi, kiddo, how are you holding up?'

'Hey, Dad. Okay, I guess, considering.' She replied without a waver in her voice, calm and professional.

'Yeah. You stick with it and work with Hopper. He knows what he's doing.' He tried to be reassuring, but maybe he was trying to calm himself rather than Dawn. She had probably run all the permutations of the scenario through simulations. If she didn't appear worried, it was probably with good reason. The maths probably backed a favourable outcome.

'I'd prefer it to be you working on this, Dad.'

'I know. You'll be fine. Everyone is working to sort this out. And you know how it is—we both have a ship to run.' It sounded a little lame to him. It probably was, but she was in good hands. He really needed to figure out what was happening and try and keep the fleet on mission, even with all this nonsense going on.

'Love you, Dad. See you on the bridge.' The connection dropped.

He smiled to himself. As a father, he was constantly surprised by his daughter, and his feelings of pride in her accomplishments and actions.

Walking back to the bridge didn't take long, but the buzzing of thoughts and complications to the building situation dilated time, and getting to the bridge seemed to take forever. He needed to warn Straud and Havers—that was immediate—but he also put a note in his bio-comms to visit the crewman in medical who had triggered and unwittingly discovered the improvised explosives in the AI replacement inventory. He thought the word 'improvised' in this case should probably be revised to 'designed', as the explosive devices were incredibly sophisticated. To have been designed to appear and act as highly technical components within an AI hardware framework and yet have the destructive power of a small ordinance high explosive grenade was actually quite impressive.

They needed to find out when and where the devices had been deployed and by whom. For pity's sake, he had been sat in the AI core only hours before—had the explosives been active and in place then? The confounding part, from his point of view, was that Dawn had no concept of the intrusion to her core and, equally, no knowledge of sabotage to any of her nodes around the ship. He presumed all the AI nodes would be affected, as whatever was going on seemed well planned and thorough; however, at this stage there were too many questions.

If it was indeed GAIA, they would need to move quickly. They had caused him untold trouble when he was a research scientist pushing this technology to the world, promoting the benefits and architecting the eventual stasis capability for deep space travel. They were technological puritans and had labelled him the radical that had to be stopped at all costs. They had pulled all sorts of stunts to pull him from the project, including the insane notion that he'd killed his own daughter to prove his wild theories and gain a test subject. They were as ruthless as he was driven and had quickly taken up arms against research facilities and AI installations around the world. His work was meant to enable the survival of mankind, and yet he could see why AI had become a target.

With the pain, austerity and increasing poverty experienced by the people of the world, there needed to be a reason for the rapid decline of humanity. As if resource depletion and a celestial body strike had not been reason enough, most then turned on governments to see what they offered as a solution. The only solution that stood out was to evacuate the planet and head for another home. It was a desperate move that would likely fail but it was the only option all the political leaders could get behind. When the news hit the populace, it was like rats learning the ship was sinking. Violence was almost immediate, as everyone wanted a seat on the new world express and seats were limited to a few thousand from a planet of billions.

The project was meant to be a secret but secrets could no longer be kept. AI was given priority in research and development projects, primarily due to the fact that building colony ships was much easier in comparison—working on known problems with solutions. His AI splicing technique became the technology that made deep space travel with current drive technology possible. With the Patten drive accelerating ships to 0.1 light speed and human stasis provided by AI splicing, all the closest M class planets became accessible.

Soon the message changed. As it got closer to launch date for the nine colony ships, GAIA changed their message from one pressing for the simple destruction of all AI and AI-related technology to one of pure bitterness. If most of humanity was destined to die a slow death on the planet of its birth, then it would ensure that all humanity would die. There would be no escape for an elite few. Why should there be?

His primary concern, with the prospect of GAIA becoming active within the fleet, was simple: survival. The fleet had to survive. It seemed such an easy thing to say but in practice it was exceptionally hard, as humans could be the most duplicitous of creatures. They could lie themselves out of or into trouble with the calm controlled exterior of an innocent. In many cases, the only thing that would give away the most devious of people was their actions and you may not know what those actions might be until it was too late. Thankfully, he felt at this point they were ahead. They had discovered the plot and knew a threat existed—that was half the battle right there, or so he'd been told once at a security lecture during his colony leadership training. He shook his head; there was a course for everything.

Having interrupted the terrorists' plans, it was time to make some plans of his own. He entered the bridge with a meaningful stride and walked directly to the situation room through the corridor at the rear of the bridge. Before he had reached the corridor he had already activated a communication channel to Roux. 'Briefing room, Commander.' Roux looked over his shoulder with a questioning look and slight surprise then stood without hesitation and made his way across the bridge, following him through to the briefing room. As Roux joined him by the central display and lectern, Clayton gave a command through his bio-comms and sealed the room. The door, which usually remained open, closed to give some element of privacy to the conversation.

He opened another call to the communications officer. 'Secure channel to Captain Straud on the *Indianapolis*, please. Route to the situation room.'

'Yes, sir. Connecting now.' Within a couple of seconds there was a click and Captain Straud's face appeared on the primary screen.

"Captain Clayton. To what do I owe the pleasure? Operations to the *Intrepid* are under way with no further developments to report thus far," she said with crisp, efficient courtesy.

"Captain Straud, I'm here with Commander Roux. We've had a rather disturbing development of our own that you need to be aware of. I'd like to keep it quiet at this point—only senior section heads to be informed." Straud's eyebrow raised while multitasking elsewhere; her curiosity was clearly piqued. She finished what she had been doing and focussed on him.

"Sounds like another serious issue."

"Yes. We believe the terrorist organisation GAIA is operational within the fleet. It may be the reason for the communications failure with the *Intrepid*. We have found explosive components within the AI core. Engineering has yet to corroborate, but we expect to find anomalous parts within the other AI nodes throughout the ship."

Her face had contorted into a rage. She kept it contained and polite but there was clearly a nerve there that had been uncovered. "I know you're serious but, really? GAIA? Those bastards are operational here? Everyone was thoroughly screened."

"Please begin your own investigation. We'll keep you updated with developments and detail as we find it, and if you could return the favour. General St John is heading up the investigation our side. Please liaise with him or myself on this matter."

"Commander Li will have the lead here. But I will add this, sir—heaven help them when we catch them."

"I'm not sure heaven will have anything to do with it," said Roux coolly. They had been the first word he had spoken the entire meeting. He looked intense and as if the vein at his temple was going to pop. This had affected everyone.

The meeting had come to a conclusion. "I'll speak to you again in due course, Captain Straud." She nodded agreement and cut the connection. The OWEC logo reappeared a moment later, as if to remind them in some pointless fashion who they worked for. Staring at the logo, he tried to obtain some guidance from the lectures and training he had received there but this only triggered an even greater feeling of isolation in him, that isolation encroaching on his otherwise busy mind. Each time he felt he needed a little help of his own, he realised he was one hundred and thirty years away from anything like that. In fact, he was one hundred and thirty years away in the wrong direction, and wanting assistance from people that very likely were not even there anymore.

WINTERS

A wave of confusion had passed over him the moment he dropped the AI core circuit he had been examining. It had been a random sample, the second in that particular storage tray, and it had simply found its way out of his grasp—he could not really remember if he'd ever actually had a grip on it at all. It had fallen and he had swiped at it a couple of times in mid-air, but all that seemed to do was make him look as if he was frantically trying to swat a wildly erratic flying insect. He had nudged it during this effort, which managed to spin it on an axis, as the artificial gravity acted to pull it to its eventual point of contact with the floor.

The white light was blinding and a force caught his legs, picking him up and launching him in a wild spiral, arms flailing, head flopping like a rag doll at the far wall of the storage section. When he came to, sounds were a tinnitus of whistles and low incoherent rumbling noises and his vision was that of someone with their head under water, seeing shapes and general patterns but nothing in focus, nothing of any clarity. The smell was overwhelming, like the worst barbeque he had ever been to: charred and burnt salted meat, mixed with an oily, acrid electrical fire and expelled plasma. He managed to sit up, aching like he had done ten rounds in the boxing ring. Ever since he was a kid, he had wondered what it might be like to go ten rounds with 'Ygor the Tank', the Russian heavyweight champion of the sporting vids. Now he knew, now he *really* knew. He had a new respect for Ygor. He wouldn't pick a fight with 'Ygor the Tank' again.

He could start to make out fast-moving shadows across his vision, some close, some further away, shouting and gesticulating. Someone dragged at his arm and shoulder, cradling his head, and they laid him on his back. He felt as if he had taken an hour to get up and seated but if he needed to be lying down, well, the way he felt right now he could do with the rest. More shouting and another bright light in his right eye, flash, flash. Then again, in his left eye, flash, flash. He could feel his eyelids getting heavy. He was amazed at how comfortable a cold hard floor could be after a few rounds with Ygor.

Something thumped him in the leg, not so hard as to hurt, but he was beginning not to care. He just wanted to take a little nap and maybe have a nice dream or two about Emily in the engineering workshop, or Natalie in the system administration section. Nice girls. He would be off shift in a few hours—he'd give them a call later. Maybe he'd ask Paul to be his wingman for the night. That sounded like a good plan. The shadow in front of him loomed large then an almighty punch to the chest almost knocked all the wind from his lungs. Are you kidding?! He thought he yelled out but couldn't really make out what he said. It was more an exclaimed mumble and moan at the same time.

The clarity and focus of all his senses returned like an ice cube dropping down his spine, his eyes wide, pupils dilated, the world rushing back in like a storm. The large, looming shadow instantly became a medic, totally absorbed in his work, hands working fast to patch and bandage parts of Winters' body, which, with his back on the floor staring at the ceiling, he couldn't see. Winters began to look around a little, as much as his head and neck mobility would allow. The storeroom was a mess of black scorched metal, store compartment doors hanging on single hinges, some doors missing completely, parts and components all over the place. Other members of the crew were running around with fire extinguishers, putting out the last of various electrical fires and burning oddments.

"Don't move, son." The words kind but commanding. "You've had a bad day."

"What happened?" Speech was slurred and a little slow but he was asking questions, that was a good sign, right?

"Hell if I know. But you're going to be on 'R and R' for a while."

"What do you mean?"

"I'm Toby. What's your name?"

"Jed." He found himself saying, almost instinctively.

Two more medics came into view, and one clamped a collar

round his neck, gentle but firm. The other was carrying a small frame, which suddenly went from the size of a mobile console to the length of his body with the flick of a switch—a stretcher. He'd used one in first aid training. Everyone did first aid.

A realisation finally made its way into his consciousness: these guys are medics. Something bad happened here; I didn't break a leg. Something bad has happened.

"What happened, Doc? Something's not right. I can't feel my legs."

"It's okay, son. That's mostly the drugs—we've hit you with some morphine cocktail. But if you try and jump up and do a jig, it's going to pinch." The medic moved into a clearer line of sight for him to see his features, see his eyes, the kindness and the sympathy. "Just relax, Jed, and let us do our job. You're in good hands. We actually know what we're doing, you know." There was a smile there now. Jed Winters, Engineer First Class, tried a smile in return, then looked back at the ceiling and did as he was told.

*

The stretcher glided smoothly down the corridor, ceiling lights flashing by every few paces. People spoke now in soft tones, no need to shout or yell commands. The words still had urgency but they had process and formality to them now too, which was comforting, as it made Winters feel like it was a sign that the worst of whatever had happened was over. He was manoeuvred into a room through a door that slid shut once they had entered. He noted a couple of security officers take up positions, one inside and one outside the room. Like two golems, they stood stone still, their eyes sweeping the scene for impropriety. He came to a stop in what he believed to be the centre of the room. Strong white lights bounced off clean white walls, and, other than the people in it, there appeared to be no furniture or machinery. He felt the stretcher split in half, the two halves slid out from under him and he now lay on a bed with a thin mattress, no sheets. The team continued to work on him; he couldn't see them but could feel the movement through his body as limbs were pulled or pushed or generally knocked around a little. Suddenly, Toby the medic came back into his view, albeit upside down. "Okay, Jed. We're going to do some scanning. We need to take a look and see how you're doing."

The manhandling stopped and a section of the ceiling disengaged and moved slowly down to within a few short centimetres of his face. A moment later it was traversing his body, down to his toes and back again. The doctor stood at the head of the bed at the control console, operating the machine in its work. Winters realised that the view was less than pleasant, as it was mainly a view up the doctors nose. He decided to close his eyes during the scan process, simply to avoid the sight of hairy nostrils. It seemed a ridiculously minor complaint after the events of the last hour.

"Jed, we're going to need to work on you a little. Could you count from ten to zero for me?" He was looking up Toby's nose again. He closed his eyes and began to count out loud.

"Ten, nine," he was feeling drowsy and quite sleepy, "eight, seven ..."

*

"How are you feeling, son?" said Dr Walters as he checked bio-readouts on the monitoring stations around his bed.

"Not too bad," he said groggily. "I feel like I've done a few rounds with Ygor the Tank, but other than that I feel okay."

"Do you mind if I sit?" Dr Walters asked.

"Sure," Winters agreed. Dr Walters nodded in thanks and a small bench swung round a central bed support pillar and presented itself as somewhere to sit, close to the bed and easily within discrete and delicate conversation distance. The doctor sat on the bench seat facing Winters.

Dr Walters's features became quite intent. "Jed, you know you've been in a terrible incident? This is never easy to deal with, so I'm just going to come right out and say it. The blast, was violent, very violent—it took your legs below the knee, Jed."

Winters was shocked. It must have shown on his face, as Dr Walters on seeing the sudden distress in his patient's face followed up quickly. "We've already done some preliminary work while you were unconscious, fitting limb augmentations. They are top of the range and fully interfaced. You will need some level of practice on them but after a few days of physio, you should be walking normally again." His mind was now racing. He tried to focus as Dr

Walters continued. "Unless you state otherwise, all this is temporary until such time as we can grow you a new limb pair."

"So, how long before I'm up and working again?"

"Physically, probably around seven days before you are fully neurologically integrated with your new artificial limbs. After that, whether you go straight back on duty is another matter entirely. You'll need to take that up with Chief Hopper, but I have a feeling you'll probably be needed for a few days."

Winters nodded to the doctor. "An investigation?"

"An investigation," the doctor parroted back.

"Thanks, Doc," he said as convincingly as he could. Regardless of the ease with which the science could be made to remove the physical and biological impediments of the trauma he had suffered, the mental scaring of the experience itself would always be with him. The disorientation of the explosion, the befuddled, delirious state afterwards followed by the mind splintering pain. If the medics hadn't arrived when they had, he didn't want to think of how he might have been, what could have been.

If he tried to disengage himself from the emotional drivers and view his situation rationally things began to look less desperate and far less bleak. He may feel some separation issues or ghost limb sensation to start with but he would get past it. He would get used to the augmented limbs, and when his new cloned limbs were available he would learn to use them, at which point he would be as near to his state before the incident as he could be. Only the mental scaring would remain. "I'll get through it," he said, the thought escaping verbally.

Dr Walters cracked a smile and nodded in agreement. "You engineers are a tough breed and logical to a fault." He got up and straightened his tunic, the seat folding back into place under the bed.

"All done?" The question came from the doorway. "Is he able to answer some questions?"

Dr Walters was now working his way round the bed, checking status screens and making some final alterations to monitoring parameters. As he reached Winters' head again he unfastened the head and neck stabiliser. "Yes, he's stable. You up for some questions from the boss, Jed?"

Winters was now able to look around a little. The man in the doorway next to the security officer was Chief Engineer Hopper.

He had a perturbed look about him. He was a man in need of answers, and Winters wasn't sure what answers he could give.

"Yes, sir. You finished with me, Doc?"

"All finished. But remember what I said about your legs. It's a temporary situation. Within the year we will have cloned replacements. In the meantime it will take a little time to readjust."

"Thanks again, Doc," he said drifting slightly in his thoughts as he considered the immediate future.

"Let's make you a little more comfortable," said Dr Walters. "Nurse, would you mind?" He made a gesture to the other side of the bed and a nurse appeared to assist the doctor to arrange some pillows and lift Winters a little. The bed also dropped in the centre in order to give him a very slight sitting position. "Okay, Chief, keep it gentle. Our man here has been through a lot. I'll be in my office if you need me, or nurse Adams will be at her station across the corridor." He turned back to Winters. "I'll drop in on you later and see how you're getting on. If you need the nurse, press this button." He pointed at the red button built into the middle trim of the bed.

The doctor turned and left the room with the nurse. Both instantly started conversing between themselves, already busy discussing preparations and care over the next few hours.

Winters watched Hopper move across the room and stand by the side of his bed. Everyone seemed concerned for his wellbeing, but there was more to it than that. Whatever had happened now needed security posted at his door in medical. Hopper puffed out his chest and looked as if he was about to launch into some lecture but, considering no one had yet given him any explanation for what had happened, Winters thought he'd get some answers. Now was the time.

"Sir– " Hopper stopped mid breath, "–could you tell me what's going on? I know I've been a little dizzy or concussed these last few hours but no one has told me what happened. I'd just really like some straight answers."

Hopper frowned and moved to sit down, then realised there was no chair. He tried to compose himself but it just came out as a sigh. "Okay, Winters. But before I do, I need you to tell me what you remember."

He pursed his lips and closed his eyes, thinking of the moment that started the chain of events that had led to him having this conversation. He had been working through the inventory check list he'd been supplied when he clocked in for his shift, confirming the parts were indeed in place and hadn't gone missing or incorrectly processed out of stores. He began to describe all this in fine detail to Hopper. The first couple of hours had gone okay and without incident. Other people were in the stores, allocated their own sections to take inventory, but—even with them around— the place was quiet. It wasn't a job that really needed a huge amount of conversation with anyone else. He'd spoken briefly to his supervisor but only to confirm a part number to a navigational array module.

There were never very many parts to store. Considering the size of the ship, the comparative size of the storeroom in engineering was tiny, especially when you consider the number of potential parts and components on the ship. As he learnt, the ship only needed to cover in store what it expected as emergency supply, as all items or components could be fabricated to demand by the engineering workshops. Some complex components, like AI core circuit modules and power containment control units, were kept in greater numbers, as they took much longer to fabricate, even with the latest fabrication processes and technology. So, greater care was taken to ensure that the items in stores were checked regularly and fit for purpose when required. He had been completing such an inspection when he had managed to fumble the AI core circuit to the floor.

"Can you remember any specifics about the item you dropped, Winters?"

"Not really, sir. It was in its seat in the store tray and in sequence with all the others. I'd inspected the first three in that column already, and they'd all checked out fine. I'd given the unit a visual inspection and was just about to do a functional test when I dropped it. The next thing I know, everything went crazy." He realised he was staring at the ceiling again, and he had an instant flashback to waking in the storeroom, with the looming presence of Dr Walters over him, reassuring him.

"Okay, could you send me any documentation, work schedules, check lists you were working with or working on? Also, who was your line officer? I'm sure I can chase up much of this with them."

"Yes, sir. Sending the documents now. My supervising officer was Sub-Lieutenant Travis. I'd seen him only an hour or so before, when he scheduled the work. There were a few of us there and all were assigned the inventory schedule." He was sure none of this was helping but Chief Hopper was being patient and let him continue. "I remember the force of the initial impact, which took my legs from under me, and that's it until I woke up on the other side of the room with the medics."

Hopper appeared to be satisfied for the moment and gave him a sympathetic hand on the shoulder. "Okay, Winters. My turn. You asked what happened? Well, we're still trying to piece that together. For the moment, all I can say for sure was that there was an explosion in the storeroom at your location. The blast was strong enough to throw you across the room and to destroy the immediate vicinity, putting a hole through the floor and ripping doors off store lockers.

"You're an extremely lucky engineer, Winters." He didn't feel lucky, nor did he know if Hopper was trying to make him feel better—it wasn't working.

"Okay, that's it for now. I'll ask the doctor back in. They'll have you back up and working as soon as they can. We need everyone now, more than ever.

"There will no doubt be an investigation. See if you can pull together a really good mental image of what happened. Just tell them what you told me." With that, he walked slowly to the door, as if trying to remember another question but not quite being able to recall. "I'll look in on you. If you think of anything else, even the smallest little detail, get in touch. The finest detail may be of vital significance."

"Yes, sir. The smallest detail—got it. I'll keep you posted."

As Chief Hopper began to exit the room, Dr Walters was already at the door. Winters thought that his office must be pretty close. "He's all yours Dr Walters. Take good care of the man; he's currently our only witness." It was said brightly, with levity, but neither he or the doctor took it as a joke. He must really be the only witness.

After a further few minutes of checking his bio-readouts on the monitoring stations around his bed, Dr Walters finally looked him in the eye and asked him in a quite parental tone. "How are you feeling, son?" With all that had happened he could only nod a response. Dr Walters accepted the silence and made some final adjustments on the console by his bedside. "Get comfortable and try to sleep—it will aid the healing process. If you need anything, Nurse Adams is across the hall. Red button." With that, he turned and headed for the door. Once the room was clear, the guard who had been standing there also headed back out through the door, presumably to take up post outside in the corridor.

He was on his own, with only the four sterile walls of the medical bay and his thoughts for company. He remembered that the doctor had told him to get some rest. Come to think of it, he was feeling rather tired. Maybe he would just close his eyes for a moment.

LARSEN

Strafing fire railed across the corridor, and screams and yelling—none of which Larsen could understand—filled the gaps between the sounds of shredding metal and superheated expanding atmosphere. Smith was already gone: a hole punched through his body by what looked like short pulse laser fire—something he had only ever seen in movies. It seemed unreal and almost silent as it happened. He didn't even make a sound, just fell where he stood.

They hadn't really been looking ahead; they had been talking about what needed doing once they reached the AI core room. Silvers was momentarily looking back at them to one side of the corridor. He had barked a command but it had been too late—neither Smith nor him had had time to respond. They were more surprised at being shouted at.

As Smith lay on the floor, the corridor started to explode and spark all around as more fire was levelled at them.

"Move!" shouted Silvers over the noise. They both turned and fled. Sprinting hard with all the power their legs could give. "Faster! Shit! Faster, faster!"

Who was yelling? Larsen couldn't make it out. His legs were already like lead and they had only run ten metres. Adrenaline was a bitch. They reached a corridor junction. "Go left! Left!" Silvers was calling out behind him. As they reached the crossroads, he was hit by an express train in the back, launching him off his feet and round the corner. He landed heavily, twisting and rolling to a stop against the wall on the far side of the corridor. Silvers was behind him on the floor but got up immediately with a speed he didn't think possible and began to return fire from the cover of the corridor corner.

An emergency security link opened in his view—Silvers had used a security override to start downloading video feed to him.

"What are you doing, Silvers? Who the hell is shooting at us?" He understood the video download. It wasn't a good sign, as far as he was concerned.

"I don't know, sir," Silvers shouted over the hurricane around them. Conduits and corridor wall panelling were fragmenting and showering them in debris.

"What do you mean, you don't know? You saw who was firing at us, didn't you?" he yelled back, as Silvers put another burst of return fire down the corridor back towards CIC and the AI core.

"Yes, sir, I did."

"Then, who was it?" The corner of the corridor right in front of him exploded. Silvers' reactions were fast: he spun and took most of the force of the resultant debris to his shoulder, which still threw him out of position and to the floor towards Larsen. Silvers got up, slowly, and made it back to the corner. He shook his head to recover some focus and got back to the job in hand.

"Just play the video back, when you get a chance. Right now, we have to move. They'll be trying to flank us."

"This is insane!"

"Tell that to Smith. Let's go, sir!" He switched hands with his carbine and reached round to pull a grenade from his webbing. A perfect left hand launch rifled the grenade down the corridor.

"Time to go, sir. Go, go, go!"

Larsen was already up and moving as the grenade detonated and washed the corridor in brilliant white light. There were howls and screams as the light faded, then yet more shouts and orders in a tongue he could not place, melodious then staccato.

They needed somewhere to hole up. Somewhere to take stock and figure out what was going on and if the primary mission was still possible. A memory of one of his lecturers popped into his head. During a class entitled 'Power Cores and Space-Time Fluctuations', he had been given a piece of advice. At the time, it was related to starship engine cores, but it felt apt in the current situation. 'How fast can everything go to shit?' the lecturer had asked. The answer was 'Always faster than you think'. The guy was not wrong.

Reaching the elevators at the head of a 'T' junction, without thinking he hit the call button. No, think. He looked to Silvers who was focused down the corridor, carbine raised, waiting for the first sign of movement. "Quick, engineering conduit. Now!" Silvers looked to him as he indicated a section of wall marked with a danger symbol and lettering stating 'E34 Elevator Maintenance'. There was a central twist handle, Silvers moved quickly and removed the panel.

As the elevator reached the level, Larsen leant inside, hit the control console for deck 97 and returned to the engineering hatch and Silvers. "Okay, inside and seal it up," he said. They entered the maintenance conduit and Larsen sealed up the hatch behind them. The conduit went off in a couple of directions, along the corridor and round to the rear of the elevator. He took a breath and tried to calm himself. Silvers looked at him with a question in his eyes and without a word he simply pointed to the rear of the elevators.

"I knew you were going to say that," replied Silvers, in a whisper.

Heading off to the rear of the elevators and across a gantry, they heard the sound of footsteps and shouting from the elevator lobby area, then thumping on the elevator doors, presumably someone very annoyed at having lost their quarry down the rabbit hole. They both stood as stone, neither one wanting to give away their position but, more than that, trying to gather any information that could be useful. Machinery started to move on another elevator shaft, shortly after the elevator came into view and then to a stop on their level.

A scroll of text ran low and to the right across Larsen's vision: the security channel that Silvers had set up between them. It took him a moment to read it, then he looked back at Silvers like he was mad. He, in return, simply raised an eyebrow as a question.

'That's the most stupid idea you'll ever have,' he responded.

'We've only been working together twelve hours. How'd you know?'

'I don't see you ever topping that for stupidity. Let's do it.'

Larsen shook his head in disbelief. They both climbed to the top rung of the gantry handrail then leant across, grabbed an upright elevator guide rail and stepped carefully, quietly, to the elevators roof. Squatting down they anchored themselves by gripping onto the exposed framework of the carriage.

'What's taking them so long?' Silvers asked.

'You said they're not crew?' Silvers nodded. 'Then they're probably trying to work out how to use the elevator control panel.' Silvers rolled his eyes and shook his head, disbelieving.

As if on cue, there was a swish as the elevator doors closed and they began to descend fifty floors in order to chase the ghosts of themselves. It was going to take a couple of minutes, so he pulled up the video feed Silvers had connected him to and rewound it to the beginning.

It opened with the three of them walking down a corridor, Smith and him chatting away in the background. Silvers was looking around, searching for problems, checking then double checking, as is the requirement of good security. They turned a corner and continued casually walking but Silvers had clearly seen some figures up ahead and had started to slow and move towards the corridor wall. Maybe he was trying to get a better view or improved angle of fire because his carbine was suddenly up and aimed down the corridor. There was a sudden rush of movement from the people in Silvers' view, then the fireworks lit up the corridor.

Larsen suddenly saw himself through Silvers eyes—the shock on his face was unrecognisable as he stared at the fallen body of Smith, lying face down with a cauterised hole the size of a fist right through his torso. He was rigid with disbelief and fear. He could see his eyes, glazed over and wide, slowly look up, as Silvers screamed at him to run, run and find cover.

He stopped and rolled the video back to the point he saw Silvers raise his weapon, then clicked it forward frame by frame until he reached a clear, non-blurred image. And there it was.

The figures were all wearing a black suit of some kind, possibly armour he assumed, as it was made up of interlocking plates. A block stripe of colour ran the length of their left upper body, which linked into the neck piece and was consistent with the colour of their face and head. Each of them appeared to have a different colour skin—a couple had green complexions, one blue, another couple a magenta colour and one a light blue. From the dimensions of the corridor, he estimated them to be taller than human size but mostly humanoid in form, slightly leaner and with a second set of arms immediately under their upper arms. They all appeared to have some bone structure around their head, and each was slightly different, with white markings across their faces.

All were carrying weapons of some description. From the damage they had managed to inflict on Smith and the corridor around them, they appeared to be quite powerful and exotic—like nothing he had ever seen before.

He closed his eyes and shook his head. "You've got to be shitting me," he said quietly to himself. Then across bio-comm he questioned Silvers, 'Real fucking aliens? Our first contact event and we screw it up, and get our asses handed to us. This really wasn't how this was meant to go. Could this day get any worse?'

Silvers must have been reading the body language of his slumped shoulders and hangdog expression. A message ran through the security comms. It simply said, 'Yeah.'

'We need a new plan.'

'No argument there,' replied Silvers, 'but first we need to lose these guys.'

'How do you intend doing that?'

'With a little help from Lucy, here.' He held out a grenade.

'You name your grenades?'

'It's a hobby,' Silvers said, looking around for something.

There were two maintenance hatches to the elevator car, in the corners and on a diagonal. Silvers moved without sound to the closest hatch and opened it. The action was swift: the hatch opened, the grenade was angled as much towards the centre of the car as possible, then the hatch was closed again. There was no sound from within the car, not even a startled exclamation from those within. The grenade detonated with a muffled thump and instant pellet-sized convex indentations appeared randomly across the metal surface of the elevator car. Silvers opened the hatch fully and dropped through into the car.

Over the next few seconds he heard a couple of carbine shots and then silence. His security channel received a quick message, 'Man, you gotta see this.' He wasn't sure he did want to see but he made his way to the hatch. The thought of being inside the car with mutilated alien beings won over his desire to stay on top of a moving elevator car, so he moved to the hatch and dropped down inside.

The car was a mess. There were six alien bodies lying in limp and crumpled positions with a purple liquid which he took to be their blood spattered in all directions and beginning to ooze across the floor. The notable point for him was that their skin was now no longer a bright and vibrant colour, just a pallid grey. He didn't get too much of a look before the elevator came to a stop. Deck 97, so that was why they had waited. They wanted to see which floor the elevator stopped on. It would have put them behind a little but they would know which floor they had got off on, or the floor their decoy stopped on. The doors began to open and the elevator kindly vocally informed them of their deck number and section, "Deck 97, Forward Engineering."

Silvers had stopped looking over one of the alien soldiers and stood with his carbine raised to the door. It opened with the familiar and usually unnoticed swishing sound, but with the tension and the blood rushing in his ears the opening doors sounded like an explosion. The corridor outside was in darkness. Slowly, Silvers made his way into the darkness, scouting for trouble and securing the area the best he could as a one-man security unit. Looking around the elevator car again, he took a grip on the body closest to the door and pulled him, her, it—he had no idea which—dragging them halfway through the doorway, then laid them in place. It would stop the elevator being recalled to another level and may actually buy them some time. How much, he couldn't say.

He took a quick few seconds to search the body, although he didn't really know what he was looking at or for, so what he found was of little use. And he really didn't want to accidentally pick up some item that the remaining aliens on the upper decks could use to track them. Best to leave well alone.

'Which way, sir?' came the question from Silvers. He was clearly around in the dark somewhere, though he had no idea where.

'We need to get to main engineering, so aft.'

'And the plan?' The question was a good one. The plan had taken a massive dent. At this point all he could think of was surviving long enough to get a message to Tusk One.

'In flux,' he said, as assertively as he could, trying to convince himself, more than anyone else, that he was still in control of events. 'Engineering first, then we'll try and get a message out to Tusk One. Then we'll try and get Ellie back online. We should be able to do all that from engineering.'

Silvers emerged from the dark and into the pool of light around the entrance of the elevator. As he did so, the elevator door tried to close but instantly opened again on sensing the body across its path. Silvers nodded at the ken Larsen had just shown. 'You sure you're not military?'

'I'm sure. But self-preservation goes a long way.'

'True. Okay, so my suggestion is that we go dark, no vocalising. Only use helmet lights and suit communications, and no interaction with the ship unless mission essential. We don't want to leave any kind of trail.'

'I agree. If you keep appealing entirely to my sense of self-preservation, we're going to get along just fine. Let's get moving.'

They headed off in silence, following their bio-comms navigation routing to main engineering.

*

They had been walking in silence for about twenty minutes, in and out of differing corridors, sometimes using engineering maintenance walkways and crawlspaces, sometimes dropping or climbing a deck or two to keep their position as unpredictable as possible. It had worked to this point, and they had managed to evade detection and had not received any indication that they were being pursued. However, there was no certainty in that—they really didn't know anything about their opponents, other than they were not human. Observations so far indicated that they were aggressive, they had to be spacefaring and they had a skin that appeared to change colour very quickly upon death. With those things in mind, it was fair to say they were an intelligent race and, depending on their motivation, could probably track them down, dependant on available crew and knowledge of the ship. Larsen also knew that the size of the ship would be prohibitive. There would be no way a small boarding team would have the ability to search a full Terran Class colony ship within any useful timescale—in *that* they had an advantage.

He was banking on the fact that they—or, more specifically, Silvers—had taken out an estimated ten of them so far, and that whoever was left didn't have the manpower available to search and flush them out. Also, they would need to know or expect that Larsen and Silvers were heading for engineering. All choices appeared a gamble, with a lot of 'don't know' answers to questions. At some point they needed more information about these intruders. He was certainly going to need Ellie back online; she would be a great resource in just that task.

'Where in engineering are we trying to get to, sir?'

'We'll be there in the next five minutes. I need the AI node near main engineering. Just another deck up and a fifty metres down the corridor.'

Making their way through the maintenance space to the required hatch, Larsen began to open the hatch while Silvers stood close by in a covering position.

'Close it!' Silvers alerted. Larsen did as he was instructed.

'What's the problem?'

'Light. The corridor lights are on. I'd say they're here too.'

'Would make sense. Taking the bridge and engineering—that was *our* plan. Shit.' They both stood quietly for a moment. There was no sound from outside, just the question of what to do next. 'We need to know where and how many we're dealing with. Take a break; I need to do some work.'

Silvers moved to a position a few metres from the hatch and sat, although he kept his carbine across his body and aimed at the hatch. Larsen sat further down the maintenance corridor, took a deep breath and closed his eyes. They had been on the move and in 'escape and evasion' mode since the contact near CIC, and this was the first time he'd had a chance to take stock.

He needed to connect into the ship's systems again to see if they had any eyes on the intruders. Engineering should be wired up for visual, as well as the corridors around it. He'd also have access to the bridge and areas local to CIC. He would only be able to access systems with limited functionality via his bio-comms. He'd need access through a console for more computing muscle, or preferably a remote console which he could keep with him if they needed to stay on the move.

The security systems demanded authentication, then he was in. Where to look? It had been a while since he'd needed to poke around the security network. He navigated through a few levels of menu to the Visual Surveillance options. He needed the room number—good job main engineering was always ENG01. In went the request and back came the camera locations: three in the main section and there was the one he was after, showing the corridor lobby section to ENG01.

Up flashed the image of the outside of the double doors to

main engineering and, sure enough, there were two posted security guards. They were alert and scanning the access corridors intently. Bad news travels fast. Getting into the AI node here was going to be trouble. He next switched his observations to the main engineering room itself. This was primarily a control room with functional access to every section of the ship. Anything that could move, conduct, radiate or vent was patched into this room. Another four guards here, although there were only two that appeared armed—the other two were working on trying to access the chief engineer's console. How much luck they were having, he couldn't tell, but that had to be stopped too. The *Intrepid* needed to remain secure against the invaders.

Next, he wanted to check out the access to the AI node. A short corridor to the port side of the main engineering control room led to the door, and they appeared to have shown no interest in guarding it, up to this point. Lastly, he checked the camera view to the AI node and again found nothing—no, wait, there *was* someone in there. Stooped behind the primary console, an island workstation slightly off-centre to the room, was another intruder, another engineer. Ellie had been correct, she was indeed under attack, physically and very likely virally too.

He needed Silvers input. 'Silvers, what do you make of this? Seven in total, three armed. Can we neutralise them? We need to get to that AI node.' Silvers looked at him after receiving the message and digesting the information, although before he had given him a chance to respond, he made an addendum. 'I also need the place intact, no damage to control surfaces. We could really cause ourselves more trouble with a stray bullet and I've had enough trouble today. Think on it—I need a plan in ten.'

'Roger that,' Silvers replied. He looked back towards the hatch.

If Silvers was taking care of the sentries, then his task was the AI and communication with Tusk One. The AI he was confident he could sort out, but getting a message to Tusk One when there was a blackout blocking all radio communications, well, it left him very few options. He needed to also ensure the point defence system was offline, as he needed to get the rest of the team to them. Their best chance was in greater numbers, specifically a greater number of security with big sticks to keep the bad guys away while the engineers and techs could get on and do their work. The plan started to crystallise; however, it had a pretty big single point of weakness. In fact—who was he kidding?— there were holes right through it, but the point that the entire plan hinged on was whether someone on Tusk One knew Morse code, or could at least recognise it. It wasn't taught as standard in training any more but he thought one or two may know the basics. You could always work it out anyway, as Morse code was easily available on any reference library grid across the ship's net, but it would be whether anyone saw the signal and made the connection— that was the risk. He would flash a message through the docking spotlights on the port side of the ship and try and point them all in the general direction of Tusk One. He coded up the message and started to look for the docking spotlight control access.

'Okay, time's up. What have you got?'

Silvers just sent back a plan package, he didn't even look over his shoulder to confirm Larsen had received it. His complete plan instruction to Larsen was 'Turn out the lights in ENG01 and open the hatch.' That was it?

*

Larsen sat next to the maintenance hatch to the corridor leading to main engineering, watching Silvers make some last minute adjustments to his kit. He'd taken off some of it and dropped it in the maintenance walkway where he had been sitting, clearly setting himself up for speed and maximum dexterity. He'd fitted a silencer to his carbine and left all his grenades except Trixie and Lola, a couple flash-bangs. Cute.

He had two jobs in Silvers' extensive plan: turn the lights out to main engineering then open the maintenance hatch. He knew they were the simplest of tasks but, for him, the adrenaline was really juicing him, and he was worried that he would screw up even this. He tried to calm himself with a couple of long deep breaths. It didn't appear to work.

Silvers was set. He moved to the hatch, looked at Larsen and smiled. It was the kind of smile that made him glad Silvers was on his team, not the other side. It scared the crap out of him. Silvers nodded and a message arrived into his view: 'Go.'

Already holding onto the hatch mechanism, Larsen sent the commands to the lighting system on the deck. ENG01 lights turned out in an instant, shortly followed by the emergency lighting and the lighting to the maintenance walkway, plunging the area into pitch darkness. He twisted the maintenance hatch locking handle and pushed. The hatch swung out and up on its pneumatic swing system, then he sensed Silvers moving through the hatch like a shiver of death across a grave, nothing quite tangible but certainly unnerving.

He rolled his back to the wall and slid down into a sitting position, arms wrapped around his knees. With nothing left to do but try and ease his racing heartbeat and the pounding of his own blood in his ears, he sat listening. Sounds became exaggerated and leapt at him through the darkness, the muffled cough, cough, of a couple of rounds from Silvers' carbine followed almost instantly by the whump, whump, of what could only be the sentries who had been guarding the door, as they fell to the floor. There was the recognisable sound of the double doors whooshing open and then all hell let loose.

It was like being back on the CIC deck again, the now recognisable sound of their energy pulse weapons, the tearing of metal and wall material, conduits and pipework. Looking through the hatch to the opposite wall of the corridor, indistinguishable silhouettes of the scene in brilliant light and contrast dark flashed and flickered, followed by a clap of thunder that he felt at his core, the very centre of his chest resonating. He was in cover and ten metres from the source, yet his ears were ringing and whistling painfully. He didn't want to think of the concussive effect of one of those things up close. Trying to get his hearing back, he rubbed his ears and shook his head a little. Just as he was getting his senses back, there was another bang, no light this time, and the bang was much more muffled—Trixie and Lola spent.

'Clear.'

He accessed the light controls and returned the rooms and corridors to full illumination, slowly uncoiled his frozen limbs and crawled out of the hatch, taking Silvers' belongings with him. Making his way down the corridor towards main engineering control, there appeared to be a small flood across the hall and a fountain of water jetting from the wall where the return fire from engineering had hit a water main. He sprinted through the spray, getting a thorough drenching on the way, skipped over the two downed guards at the entrance and into the control room. It was surprisingly untouched—all the damage was back down the corridor with a few stray shots in the wall around the doors, nothing to worry about.

He turned to the chief engineer's console. The alien engineer who had been working on it was now spread out across the floor a couple of metres away. He had clearly been trying to get away but to where he was unsure. He quickly sat in the chief engineer's couch. There were various bits of alien technology plugged into the console, which he removed immediately, discarding them to the floor. The console was on but they luckily hadn't got very far. He logged into the system and immediately got to work. He uploaded and executed the control program he had coded up in preparation. Once he was happy with the result, he got up and made his way into the AI node. As an aside, he also isolated and shut down the ruptured water pipes in the corridor.

Too engrossed to notice, as he got up, he realised Silvers was at his side. "I think we can break our silence. Good job."

"I do my best. Everything set?"

"Yes. Point defence system is offline and our message is being transmitted. I can't tell when they'll notice, or if they'll notice, the message but it's being sent. Our best chance now is to get Ellie back online. Maybe we'll get some answers."

"Sounds like the best option we've got. You do realise that at some point the whatever-they-are on the bridge will know what's happened here. It's most likely they will send more to investigate."

"Then we need to circle the wagons and wait for the cavalry."

"Can you circle one wagon?"

"You can weld the engineering doors shut, that should slow them down."

"There is that. Leave it to me. I'll slow them down—you just get that AI back online."

"That's the plan." He turned on his heels and ran down the corridor to the AI node.

HAVERS

The last hour on Tusk One had been one of intense worry. The mood of all aboard had completely sobered, with a nerve-jangling quiet descending over each of them. They had made a few runs back and forward between the two waypoints of their current flight circuit, each time reporting back to the *Indianapolis* that there was no further information to relay and the transmission jamming was still in effect around the *Intrepid*. The boarding team had been out of contact for longer than expected now, it was coming up to an hour overdue, and he'd need to make a decision on their next point of action. He'd have to work on the assumption that something had happened and the team was lost. He didn't want to lose anyone, but knowing things didn't really work that way didn't stop him from hoping that they were still alive.

He was sitting back up in the cockpit with the pilots. It gave him time to think and also to see the *Intrepid* in her dark mystery and disarray. On the last gasp of communication from the *Indianapolis*, they had been informed, rather alarmingly, that they believed the source of the signal jamming was originating from behind the *Intrepid* and not from within. He had instantly thought to skip round *Intrepid* and report on what they found but that idea was declined. They already had another shuttle with high-powered telescopic instrumentation on a reconnaissance mission to reveal the hidden source. They were to stay on mission and secure the *Intrepid* from the inside.

Unstrapping himself from the couch harnesses, he started to

make his way to the exit and down toward the main cabin. He hadn't been down there for a while and felt he needed to show his face, to show all the crew that he was with them and leading from the front. It would also give him a chance to get some ideas on how to approach the next task in hand, which was putting into effect plan 'B' by making a second attempt at boarding the *Intrepid*. He had just pulled himself through the hatch and pushed off when he heard the pilot Branner call out, "Commander. Commander?"

He put the brakes on, as well as he could. Arms out, jamming himself in the entrance, he pushed himself feet-first back into the cockpit. "Branner, this better be good."

"Judge for yourself. What do you make of that?" he was pointing at the *Intrepid*. The docking spotlights were all flashing sporadically, in unison. "Looks intentional to me."

"Yes it does, Branner. Yes it does." The grin on his face was wide and relief poured through him. They were alive and aboard the Intrepid, they'd done it. Well, part of it. He took note of the flashes, their order and configuration. The message repeated, it was on an automated loop, Larsen was broadcasting the only way they could at the moment. The signal jamming issue was most likely a little way off resolution, even for them, yet they still managed to get a message out. Nice work, Larsen.

Decoding the message, the old sequence of dots and dashes revealed a message that seemed odd, although, he had to admit, Larsen was always creative. It didn't conform to the plan but then what plan didn't get modified on the fly along the way. The message read,

HOSTILE ALIEN BOARDERS. BRIDGE UNSAFE. HOLDING ENG. PDC OFFLINE. DOCK DECK AF188.

Boarders? Did he mean boarders of the invading kind, or had he misspelled borders of the boundary kind? Either way, it didn't make sense. Who was going to board them out here? There was nothing but the void of space for millions of kilometres. Having said that, it was not usual for Larsen to make mistakes. But the stand out word in the message was 'Alien'. He was now more than curious enough about the current situation, this just turned the dial up a notch. What was going on? Time to find out.

"Branner, identify and plot a course for *Intrepid's* external airlock AF188. What's our best time until docking?"

It took a moment for Branner to pick out the airlock in

question. "Fifteen minutes."

"Make it happen, and let me know when we're two minutes out."

"Roger."

He sat back down in the rear cockpit crash couch for a moment, hit a few keys on the console and began to record a message. "*Indianapolis*, this is Tusk One. Our team has boarded the *Intrepid* and is holding engineering. We are about to attempt docking on airlock AF188. Break. Message relay from boarding party. Hostile Boarders. Bridge Unsafe. Holding Engineering. Point defence offline. Dock deck AF188. Tusk One, out." He loaded the recording into the next probe in the tube and set the device to loop the message.

Setting its course aft and out of the comms dead zone, he announced, "Launching probe," then hit the screen probe launch icon. The probe was momentarily visible as it was fired from its housing within the belly of the shuttle, then it veered away in a tight arc to follow its designated course.

"I'll be with the boarding team if there are any developments." Before he received any acknowledgement, he was out of the couch and down the corridor into the main cabin.

Entering the hold at speed, he grabbed a bulkhead and locked himself in place. It made Anderson jump, his boss arriving so quickly—he wasn't there, then he was. "Ladies and Gentlemen," he said, in that authoritarian, slightly louder but still level and professional voice he had developed over the years of command. "We are on the move. We'll be docking with the *Intrepid* in ten minutes, at airlock AF188, located near engineering. I want everyone ready to go. We've been informed there could be hostiles, so everyone stay alert. Our advanced boarding team are holding engineering, so our first job will be to join up with them and get a full update. Any questions?"

Immediately, Boyd spoke up: "Hostiles? What hostiles?"

"I can't be more specific at this time. Just look out for anyone that isn't Larsen, Smith or Silvers and be wary." Boyd just nodded his understanding. "Okay everyone, let's get to it." There was a sudden commotion as people were given a purpose and started to prepare for their part. Some split off into groups to start working on kit and make sure everything was accounted for; others appeared to just sit back and go to sleep but, even with their eyes closed, he knew they would be scanning documents and ensuring their part of the mission went smoothly and to plan.

Next on his list was Lieutenant Jillian Reeve. A career soldier, she had been accepted into the OWEC security due to her reputation as a survival specialist within the regular defence force, having done five tours of the wastelands and a year defending the UK south eastern arcology from marauders. She was bright, alert and of fearsome character. Long limbed and with short cropped black hair, she was a woman built for stamina and endurance. The slight scar on her chin on her original military records, now erased due to her latest clone incarnation, had reinforced her tough and rugged persona. Something about her told Havers never to back this one into a corner, as he'd come off worse, no matter what the argument. She was already in deep discussion with several members of her team. "Lieutenant Reeve, can I take a moment?" He didn't like to interrupt but time was short. She politely dismissed her team and turned to him.

"Certainly, sir. What do you need?"

"I don't quite know what we're walking into on the *Intrepid*, so once we're there I'd like you to send out a few pathfinder teams to find a way through to the bridge. I don't want any contact if we can avoid it, so this is purely reconnaissance. The rest of your team is to defend engineering until we know more."

"Yes, sir. I'll brief them straight away."

"Thank you, Lieutenant." He turned away and started back to his cabin seat to begin his own kit preparation. He checked his bio-comms for the time: seven minutes until docking.

*

When things are busy, time goes far too quickly, and the call came in an instant. 'Two minutes to docking, sir.'

'Thank you, Branner,' he replied, then turned to the cabin and repeated the warning. "Two minutes to docking, people. Two minutes." Looking to Lieutenant Reeve, he asked, "Could I leave you to organise the boarding, Reeve? I'll join you at the hatch momentarily."

"Sir," was her short reply.

People knew their jobs, so there was no need for prompting or correcting. Apart from the odd order of instruction from Reeve, the boarding crew were quiet and, as the last few moments before docking ticked by, most were now sitting in their couches looking straight ahead with an equal measure of concentration and nervous expectation.

'Docking in ten seconds, port side,' came the final announcement from the pilots. The cabin lights went red in anticipation of the event, a mechanical whirring indicated the extension of the telescopic docking tunnel and a final clanging sound resonated through the entire shuttle like a bell rung under water.

"Ready," Reeve called over the commotion of suits fastening, helmets locking and visors sliding and sealing—small sounds but, in an accumulated fashion, it became a crashing wave of white noise. With his kit now slung and helmet sealed, commands now came across the suit comms, and he could hear Reeve ordering people into position and arranging security personnel to the front, the rest interspersed within the engineering staff.

Making his way directly to the airlock, he sent a message to Branner and Reeve: 'Branner, once we're aboard, lock the airlock and don't let anyone in. You'll need the docking umbilical connected in order to communicate, so don't go wandering off unless you really need to.'

'Copy.'

'We'll reassess once comms are up again.'

'Roger that. Good luck, sir.'

He took a peek through the airlock window. The tunnel was firm and the indicators showed a firm seal. Good to go. "Okay, Reeve, let's go."

Reeve ordered the first security team into the airlock and started the airlock procedure for equalised pressure environments; they would be able to move through much faster this way. It took them five minutes to get the complete team across to the Intrepid and set. Havers immediately tried to contact Larsen.

'Larsen, this is Havers. Report.' The response was immediate.

'Great to hear from you, Commander. Sorry we're not there in person, things are a little busy here. I'm sending you routing to main engineering—you'll be coming in the back door. The front door is locked down.' Larsen's manner seemed relaxed and phlegmatic, giving him confidence in the situation, if not total understanding. 'Also, we believe we have a first contact situation aboard. Having said that, it has not gone well. I will give you more detail when you arrive. Be on alert for tall humanoids in black body armour. They will fire on you without warning.' Now that sounded bad. Definitely boarders and not borders; Larsen had not been confused in his message. The situation was getting more complex the more he learned.

He unpacked the routing instructions and forwarded to the team. Noting the route, he responded 'Roger that. See you in ten.'

"Reeve. Message from Larsen. Sending it over. We have more information on the alien contact. Be on alert for hostile humanoids in black body armour." He forwarded the last message Larsen had pushed; it was going to be a long trek to main engineering. "Okay, let's get going."

CARROLL

Time had ticked by, the stars to his measure had not moved and there were only so many coffees you could drink. Some days he wondered why he had become a shuttle pilot. Space was big, really, really big, and getting anywhere took an age, also taking into account the fact that once you had set in your course, you really had nothing to do, as there was rarely need to change course or really fly around anything. Being a shuttle pilot had essentially been reduced to a systems monitoring job—a series of relentless checks that could equally be done by a computer. Is the coolant at temperature? Check. Is the hull temperature within safe parameters? Check. Are there still enough coffee sachets available for the return trip? Check. Then, he reminded himself, these checks were already being done by a computer, well, maybe not the coffee inventory— maybe he could get Patterson to rig that into the system too, then he really would be covering all bases. He huffed with the boredom of it. He'd been out of the tank less than twelve hours and he was already bored. He wondered if that was some sort of record.

"You with us, boss?" Stills dropped him out of his reflection with a bump. Thanks. Sometimes a good grump was kind of comforting and staying there was worth the effort. "You seem sort of way off."

"Ah, these long flights. Thinking of a career change."

"Really? Maybe a hypnotherapist? Only, it looks like you hypnotised yourself, so probably not such a good choice for you."

There was a wry smile working on the corner of Stills lips, pleased with his own wit.

"You know, laughing at your own jokes is one step away from belly ache."

"Who told you tha–." A swift arm flew out and struck Stills playfully but fairly firmly in the belly, making Stills jump and double in surprise. Carroll broke out in a grin and began to laugh, boredom evaporating in an instant. Goading his co-pilot was just the tonic and distraction he needed.

"So mature." Stills giggled back. "So mature. Who gave you command of a shuttle? Belly ache. I'll have to remember that one." Shaking his head, he got back to checking the navigation progress.

Carroll relaxed and got back to his checks: the shuttle systems all normal, navigation on track and only minutes away from target disclosure. He made a connection and announced to the crew, "Good afternoon everyone, this is your pilot speaking. We are currently on approach to our target disclosure point. Please, in the interests of safety, could you ensure all drinks and consumables are stowed and your seats are in the upright position. In case of vomiting, please be aware that your sick bags are in the right side pouch of your couch. Vomiting through your nose is not recommended. Thank you." He looked over to Stills who was still shaking his head, this time in disbelief.

'Nice,' came the message from Patterson.

He switched the main cockpit HUD to show the flight navigation data, a corridor of electric blue tracking away to a vanishing point in the far distance, current velocity, time and distance to their way points marked and ticking over. At the next way point they would begin to see the object hidden behind the *Intrepid*. Two minutes. Involuntarily, his pulse started to increase and he started to feel a little excitement rising in his chest.

"Just remembered why I like this job." He looked out to the stars.

"I'll bite," said Stills. "Why's that?"

"I'm being serious," he said, feigning a wounded look.

"So?"

"It's the excitement of the unknown. What's behind that ship? We're going to be the first to find out. That's what exploration is all about, Stills. The challenge of the unknown and being first to discover and learn. The human desire for knowledge is a powerful driver."

"You do talk crap sometimes."

"Hey, remember who you're talking to. I'm imparting wisdom here."

"Is that what it was?"

A notification alert sounded and the way point navigation icon flashed. Carroll's concentration suddenly and instinctively returned, and he opened a voice channel to the crew, "Coming up on the disclosure way point in five, four, three, two, one, mark."

"Instrumentation set and recording. Patching in a live stream to the *Endeavour*," came the response from Rivers.

Stills flicked a few buttons and another HUD to the side of the cockpit started to show the live, high-resolution telescopic view being streamed to the *Endeavour*. The view was largely a dark blank gunmetal grey, an incredible close up of the *Intrepid's* hull, slightly out of focus as Rivers already had the focal length of the system targeting the estimated source of the signal jamming behind her.

As Horus One continued on its high angle course, a dark shape started incrementally to appear from behind the *Intrepid*. It was a reasonably large vessel, clearly nowhere near the size of Intrepid herself but large enough. The data around the HUD image was estimating two hundred metres in length. The image had been enhanced as much as possible to make use of as much light as was available this distance from the local star, one side now much brighter than the other. The ship began to take on the appearance of a reversed cuttlefish shape at its crown, with more indistinct mechanical surfaces beneath plus patchwork panelling, possibly armour protecting critical systems. There were some lights pinpricking the surface and a little further back some stubby protrusions, which could be stabilisers or engine housings—it was difficult to tell.

Stills seemed to capture the mood, "What the hell is that?"

"Whatever it is, it's not one of ours," stated Patterson with certainty. "I've worked on pretty much every ship design type known to man and this is not one of them." His voice made them both jump. Without them noticing his arrival, Patterson was now at the flight engineer's station in the rear of the cockpit working through readings and observations of the unknown vessel. Both pilots looked round as if to confirm their hearing correlated with reality, shrugged in unison and returned to their flight instruments.

"Has anyone considered that we're the vanguard of humanity, here?" Carroll asked to no one in particular, "How could it possibly be one of ours? The question we should be asking is, where did it come from? And, furthermore, what's it doing?"

"I'd love to be a fly on the wall back on the *Endeavour* right now," chipped in Stills. "This stuff will really be baking their noodles."

"Speak of the devil..." Carroll selected the highlighted comms icon within his bio-comms. It was an incoming transmission from the *Endeavour*.

"Horus One, this is *Endeavour*. Over."

"*Endeavour*, this is Horus One. Go ahead. Over."

"Horus One, set course to intercept unidentified object and orbit at ten clicks. Request detailed scan of object. Over."

"Roger, *Endeavour*. Intercept and scan. Over."

"Horus One, orbit is to be line of sight with the *Endeavour*. Adjust orbit at your discretion to keep communications open. Over."

"Roger that, *Endeavour*. Keep communications open. Over."

"*Endeavour*, out."

Over local comms, he updated the crew. "Well, team. New orders. We're off to say 'Hello'." He began to configure the new navigational requirements and the shuttle's nose swung swiftly, drawing visual curves of light in space to an intercept course with the unidentified vessel. "Rivers, I'm going to set up an orbit ten kilometres out, and I need you to scan our new friends with everything you have. Deep scan. *Endeavour* wants to see their tonsils."

There was an audible resigned sigh of distaste over the internal comm before Rivers started to reply. "Thanks for that image. I'll get them the data they need. Just fly a steady course for us. It will minimise vibration and distortions and help keep the imagery sharp and scan data accurate."

"Noted. No problem."

"You have a way with words, sir," Stills observed. "How do you get anyone on side?"

"It's called charisma, Stills. I have some left over if you want it?"

"I don't think your colour of charisma would suit me. I'm more your noble warrior-type, less the idiot accidental leader."

"Now that's fighting talk, noble warrior."

"Will you two knock it off?" Patterson asked with a stern commanding voice. "Anyone would think you two were juvenile kids on a day trip." The two pilots sat and grinned like Cheshire cats but settled back down to work. "And besides, I'm trying to concentrate here."

"You got it, Dad." Carroll finished the conversation in time to see the image change on the screen, showing the unidentified vessel. Rivers had zoomed in to what looked like the port side of the ship. It was moving and morphing in shape, a pod extending on a boom of some kind. "What's going on, Rivers?"

"No idea. You?"

"Patterson? What's your take?"

After some brief silent consideration: "Well, whatever it is, they're gearing up to do something. A ship that size, with the size of equipment they are deploying, I'd guess at it being a significant event."

"Significant event?" Carroll echoed. "That sounds bad."

He connected to the Endeavour quickly. "*Endeavour*, this is Horus One. Unidentified vessel is deploying some sort of boom device. Are you getting the visual? Should we proceed? Over."

For a moment only static filled his ears, then the response was feint and distorted. "Horus One, this is *Endeavour*. Affirmative. Continue to the objective and report. Over."

Patterson started punching buttons on his console trying to fine-tune the receiving signal. "Roger that, continue and report."

The static crackle then simply became a silence, no response from *Endeavour*.

"They've extended their comms jamming radius." Patterson observed.

"But we're another hour away yet, that's five thousand clicks out. They're actively jamming from this distance?"

"Holy shit!" came a startled expression from the back of the bus. Rivers began babbling over the comms so fast she was almost incomprehensible, and to Carroll she was just making no sense. He was still shocked that she had cursed—she seemed such an upright character, perhaps the polar opposite of him.

"Slow down, Rivers. What's going on?"

She took a breath and changed the zoom on the screen back out to show the ship's full profile. "The ship—" she said, in a halting, forced slowness "—it's disappearing!"

He flicked the image to the main view, so all in the cockpit could see what was going on. Sure enough, in a reasonably slow sweeping motion the alien ship was disappearing, like someone was simply erasing it from space. There was an occasional shimmer, like the sun reflecting off the surface of a calm sea but within a minute the ship had completely gone. There was nothing but stunned silence through the whole shuttle, eyes wide with disbelief, staring at a spot in space that should contain a ship the length of a football pitch but was now nothing but stars.

"I think," Carroll said drunkenly, "we've been spotted." After a few more seconds of bewilderment, he got things moving. Command needed the information they had and quickly. "Rivers, if anything happens to that picture, let me know immediately. Patterson, get the *Endeavour* back online, and if you can't then try the *Indy*. Stills, take us back out of their jamming radius." Calm, professional chaos then broke out.

CLAYTON

The day had been going from bad to worse, and he was beginning to feel like the universe was personally picking on him. Tusk One had last reported that they had successfully inserted their infiltration team aboard *Intrepid* and were now about to dock and deploy their full investigation team, which had sounded like good news until they had flagged the issue of hostile contact. Then, just when they were getting some good data from Horus One, some odd final pictures of the unidentified alien vessel arrived and radio communications were lost. The most infuriating thing was the slow drip of communications and the fact that he was losing people into a black hole where they were effectively cut off from his help.

Nothing had come back from Chief Hopper and his team on how to get communications through, and now, with the new alien ship to consider, work was piling up. He needed solutions.

His first thought was to try and make contact with the alien vessel, try and make some diplomatic gesture, but with the news of hostilities aboard the *Intrepid*, he was not sure how effective that move would be. Talking to resolve conflict was always his preferred choice but how was he to make that first step? If they were truly hostile, wouldn't they have sent more than one ship? If they were inquisitive and looking to understand them as a species, wouldn't they have tried communicating first, rather than simply boarding the *Intrepid* and fumbling around?

Within his own arguments, he realised that there were two fundamental obstacles. First was the fact that communication with the alien vessel was going to be difficult enough, as their linguists would need to interpret, translate and learn, not a short process in itself. In addition, being actively blocked from communicating by the alien vessel, as they were, made that process exponentially more problematic. They could not even contact their own teams without major technical difficulty, so what real chance did they have trying to contact the alien ship? Secondly, they were alien. Obvious, but fundamentally this meant that he had no concept of how they thought, what they might do or why they were doing it. Would their reasoning be human in nature? There were certain founding ideas and a purpose to life that humans thought unwavering, like the ongoing search for knowledge and the holding of life in the highest of regard, but what priorities were the alien culture working to?

He had to make a start, so assuming they had similar axioms and foundations of reason would be his base. From a human point of view, if you wanted to hide your actions then your actions were most likely not to the benefit of the other party. This would mean that the alien vessel was attempting to do something they did not want him knowing about. If it was knowledge they were after, to understand who and how humankind operated, then they were pushing all the right buttons. Being secretive would get attention, then being aggressive would elicit an overt response—but to what end? Of course, they could simply be scavenging. With all the lights out and in its dormant state, the *Intrepid* would simply look like some space hulk ripe for the picking, in fact each of them would have done. So, why the *Intrepid* first? Probably, just dumb bad luck. Or what if Ellie had been behind for some reason or experiencing technical problems? Where the other two ships would be showing signs of activity, the *Intrepid* would still be dormant.

His mind was spinning with possible scenarios that could have taken place, but none of it helped him isolate the course of action. He had decided to take a walk and some time in engineering to personally review progress and ideas. Hopper was expecting him and was near the main door of engineering control with a couple of other engineers discussing something frantically as he entered.

"Chief Hopper," he said to prompt the Hopper and gain his attention as he walked in. The chief instantly dismissed those in conversation and moved to his side, hand out, guiding his captain to the main control panel and viewer.

"Sir, we've been looking at the last images sent to us by Horus One. It's mind-blowing stuff. Certainly not an Earth-built vessel, absolutely the source of the communications jamming and, with that in mind, extremely powerful in that purpose." He flicked a few console options and an image appeared. "This is on the port side of their ship—a feature which looks like a stabiliser. At the moment this image was taken, it had started to extend. At this point, we believe that this is what has been jamming our communications and when extended, as here, was as part of an increase to the power and range of the signal jamming. This increased jamming range has clearly caught Horus One, even at the distance she was." The chief looked like a man engrossed in the problems and revelations of the new encounter. He was shifting and moving side-to-side pointing at screens and items of interest with an intense exuberance. Contact with an alien species had been the holy grail of scientists and space exploration for years, now it was here all he could do was worry. Dreams and ideals were rarely met in reality. This was no exception. He realised he had phased out of the conversation with Hopper, lost in his own thoughts.

"… immense power."

"Sorry, what has immense power?" Clayton asked, apologetically.

"The signal jamming facility of that ship. It is either able to blanket the area up to five thousand kilometres with powerfully transmitted white noise or target specific bodies with localised interference. The power involved to blanket that volume of space would be immense. My money is on a concentrated, localised effect; less energy but no less impressive, technologically speaking."

"Or both," Clayton surmised.

"Yes. If they have the technology for one, they certainly have the technology for the other."

The AI projector to the side of the main engineering console became a twirl of pixels, coming to rest in Dawn's image. She spoke urgently. "Captain, Horus One has changed course and is now within communications range again. The scan feed from her instrumentation is back online, but the most important development is this." She indicated to the main screen. "The mission commander was quite over-excited in his report but, for that, I really don't blame him."

They all turned to the viewer and watched in momentary

puzzlement while their brains made sense of what they were looking at: a full view of the alien ship with booms and pods extended further than the visuals they had just been discussing. At full extension, the pods unfurled into a concave umbrella shape, once locked in place a shimmering affect began to coat the newly deployed umbrella shapes. Then, to all assembled, the shimmering settled and as it did so the umbrellas were no longer visible. The wave of light slowly flowed around the ship from where the umbrellas had been to come together midway between the two and the centre of the alien ship. In less than a minute the ship was no longer there.

Clayton looked up in astonishment. "Somebody pinch me."

Looking around, a few engineers had congregated behind them to watch, all with slack jaws and sincere looks of disbelief on their faces. Gathering himself, Hopper, still transfixed to the view screen, stated, "We've been working on that kind of technology for decades. Our best efforts would always leave traces, visual clues, massive imperfections that the human eye could discern immediately. Frankly, our efforts do not work. This, this is incredible. It's gone. I can't see any imperfections in the cloak whatsoever."

"The scientist in me is amazed, Hopper. But the captain in me is suddenly very concerned. In the last half hour I've witnessed far greater technology than anything we could produce. More than that, we now can't communicate with anyone on the *Intrepid*, or see the alien ship, which is reportedly hostile. I'm sure you can understand my concern." He tried to calm himself; frustration was getting the better of him. Hopper and his team didn't deserve his ire, they were pulling out all the stops, but he needed some results, some progress. A little reality check for them would be useful.

"Yes, sir. I'll get a team tracking and identifying the location of the cloaked ship straight away. Might I suggest that we have seen some grand gestures in technology from them but that we are both space-faring species. I haven't seen anything that would not be within our grasp and, for all we know, we may have some tricks up our sleeve that they are equally perplexed by. One step at a time, sir." Hopper was right, but his body language was that of an apologetic man.

"Thank you. You always manage to cut through it, Hopper." Someone in the crowd accessed the main view controller and flicked the images to almost every screen in the control room, each one with a very excitable group of engineers discussing the finer points of how something like this could work. "Dawn, please release this information to Doctor Klein and his science team, if they haven't already got it. See what they make of it. We need to break that cloak."

"Initial thoughts are of energy signature tracking. There must be some residual energy bleed from the cloak or power source," wondered Hopper aloud.

"How about tracking them in the same way we found them?" Dawn suggested. "Track the source of the jamming? I don't believe they have stopped jamming our communications. We may not be able to see them but they have the ability to track their power source."

"It's a passive process too, so hopefully they won't know we're onto them," added Hopper.

He'd been listening to their ideas but to Clayton something wasn't adding up. "I don't want to crash these ideas before they have air but if you had these two technologies, where one could easily give away the other, wouldn't you know? How could they not know? Wouldn't they switch the jamming signal off as soon as they were cloaked?"

The timing of the statement was perfect. Almost the moment the last syllable was released from his lips, there was an incoming message from Commander Roux on the bridge. '*Indianapolis* reporting incoming messages from Tusk One aboard the Intrepid, sir. Looks like comms are back up.'

'Understood. Thanks Commander—I'm making my way back to the bridge now.'

Turning to the nearest console, he directed the incoming comms from Tusk One to the console.

"*Endeavour*, this is Tusk One. Over."

"Tusk One, this is *Endeavour* Actual. Go ahead. Over."

The voice on the other end audibly smartened up. Now he was talking to the fleet boss, his job just got a whole lot more important and he was probably flapping around trying to get Commander Havers attention.

"*Endeavour*, this is Tusk One. Relaying message to Tusk One Actual. Over"

"Roger that, Tusk One. Over."

There was a momentary pause while Havers came online. "*Endeavour*, this is Tusk One Actual. Situation is progressing, comms back online but not by our hand. Break. Hostiles on board and forward of the habitat. Working on a plan to retake *Intrepid* and will update you shortly. Over."

"Roger that, Tusk One. Be advised there is an unidentified vessel with cloaking ability last seen on the far side, starboard side of *Intrepid*. Over."

"Copy that, *Endeavour*. I'm sending your data now. Video of our first contact and some more recent medical examination of the hostile alien species aboard. We are prepping for transport to medical where we can perform more detailed study. Over."

Clayton's mind was racing. He was glad to have contact with the investigating team but there were so many questions.

"Copy. File a full report and keep us updated. Over."

"Wilco, *Endeavour*. Also, sadly, I must report one fatality, lost in the initial contact. You'll have my full documented report within the hour. Over."

"Understood, Tusk One. *Endeavour*, out." He dropped his head. The first death on this mission and on his watch. It wouldn't be the last. You can receive all the command training in the world but losing people you are responsible for was the worst feeling and one you never got used to. Every single one lost was a personal failing.

Hopper looked on in silence. "I'll be on the bridge if you need me, Hopper. Liaise with Doctor Klein and try and find that ship."

"Yes, sir."

*

Getting from the main engineering control section to the bridge was not a short trip. He used the time to think through some ideas and ponder on the problems ahead. The first of which was Havers' team retaking the bridge of the *Intrepid*, which would be a similar journey to his with very different obstacles. He had a feeling the aliens currently residing on the bridge would be no soft target. Equally, with their route of escape now removed, they had their backs to the wall. What would they do now they were trapped with no exit? Animal instinct, fight or flight. Remove the flight option and the alternative was not an option he wanted.

Walking through the door to the bridge, he clipped shoulders with Commander Holt coming in the opposite direction. The navigation officer appeared in a hurry and quite distracted. He apologised profusely but carried on going. He disappeared at the next junction, leaving Clayton looking over his shoulder in confusion as he walked onto the bridge. "What was Holt's hurry?" he asked Roux, as he sat into his crash couch.

"Holt?" Roux looked towards the door, as if to remember the scene. "He had an urgent call from navigation."

"What's so urgent? We're not changing course."

"No idea."

"First question: have you had an update from medical on Winters? I've just learnt we lost a man on the *Intrepid*. That's one too many today." He reviewed his console and sent a bio-comms message to General St John for an update on the sabotage attempt, or should that be 'attempted murder'? Take your pick.

"Yes, he's doing okay. Injuries are severe and will take a while to recover but the doctor assures me he'll pull through."

"That's some good news for the day."

"So, *Intrepid's* comms are back online," continued Roux, "but now we have a diplomatic incident on our hands with our first contact. That could have gone better. Of all the fluffy ways I imagined a first contact event occurring and we manage to trigger a shootout."

"Not all the facts are in yet. I'd like to think we didn't start this." He pursed his lips and found himself looking at the strongest, brightest star in their field of view, dead centre of the screen. The star, 21 Hayford, otherwise known as simply Hayford's Star, was very similar to Sol, a yellow dwarf star with associated planets, one of which was M class and viable for life. He had certainly expected chaos and intrigue on arriving at 21 Hayford b but of the scientific, explorative kind. If he had been asked to predict what might happen before they had begun their journey, the current scenario would not have even been considered.

The fact that they potentially also had terrorists aboard was infuriating from his view. The alien encounter was an unexpected happening but something he could rationalise: there were others in the galaxy we are not alone. Statistically speaking, that was quite likely and now a reality. But to have your own species trying to take you down from the inside, well, it left a bad taste in the mouth. No matter what their misguided reasons for attacking Dawn and trying to sabotage the mission, surely the survival of humanity was of the highest importance, even to them.

The soft quiet sounds and hubbub of the bridge leaked back into his mind as he returned from his short daydream of thoughts; people talking, instructions given and received. He turned to Roux. "Any activity from the alien ship? I've got Hopper working on a tracking solution but, if we can reason its purpose, then maybe we have a chance to predict what its next action might be."

Roux nodded, "We have limited information at the moment. But, assuming that they have cloaked in order to move and make locating them extremely problematic for us, and given that in doing so they were forced to leave people behind, I would expect them to attempt some rescue mission. Recover their team, and or whatever they were looking for."

"Yes. We have to be careful in our assumptions though. These are not humans. We must include the possibility that they do not reason the same way. Do they value their people the same way? Would the team left behind be an acceptable sacrifice to learn more about us?"

"Possible. To be honest, this is all conjecture. We really are quite literally leading the way in extra-terrestrial relations and diplomacy."

"You mean, making it up as we go along?"

Roux smirked at the insinuation. "You, maybe. I know exactly what I'm doing."

"Don't kid yourself." They were both smiling now.

There was a moment's silence between the two, both caught up in their own thoughts, minds racing to an answer, to pluck some wisdom from the ether. "You know, you're right and you're wrong," Clayton continued.

"How so?"

He shifted in his seat, unconsciously moving to an assertive body language in order to reinforce his point. "We have dealt with other species throughout human existence. They may not have been spacefaring, but we have communicated and lived in symbiotic states with many different species on Earth."

"Yes. But this is a complete level of complexity above that."

"True. Although, there must be some fundamentals that are consistent. Like the preservation of the species, above others."

"So, you agree? Their next course of action is most likely a rescue action."

"Seems a sound argument."

As they were sitting, considering the last exchange, Dawn's holographic image appeared to his side. "Hello Dawn, anything to add to our conversation?"

"Possibly. But I agree with your summary."

"How are the engineers getting on in the AI core room?"

She nodded an affirmation, "Well, they think I'll be clear in the next half hour; however, they have discovered more devices in two other nodes—engineering and one of the habitat nodes."

"Jeez!" he exclaimed in frustration. This was better orchestrated than some loner with a grudge. To get into all those areas would need various skills and clearance, applied planning and leadership. Damn. All the signs indicated a cell.

"Sir, maybe you'd like me to handle the investigation? It would give you more time to focus on what's happening on the *Intrepid* and hunting down the unidentified ship." Roux made a good case.

"Already assigned, Roux. St John has the lead and will inform me when he has more."

"Understood." Roux appeared to phase out, the way those working on their bio-comms always did: a slight long-distance stare combined with a frown of concentration. Clayton turned his focus back to Dawn. She looked at him intently and words ran across his view, pumped in through his bio-comms.

'Dad, I think I may have a lead.'

'Go on,' he replied. The phrase triggered a memory of Dawn when she was an infant. He would use the same words then to coax her along the mental path to the answer to homework questions. It was so long ago but, as a parent, the memory was vivid, fresh and somewhat comforting. Time travelling through his mind, he returned to the present.

'I'd like to discuss in private—could we talk in the briefing room?' The message was direct and somewhat intriguing.

'I'll be right there.' He stood and started to make his way. "Roux, I'll be in the briefing room. Let me know if the situation changes."

The twenty metre walk to the briefing room appeared to take longer than usual. Dawn was already there when he arrived. He sat opposite her holographic projection, "So, what have we got?" Hopeful, expectant.

"I've been reviewing the security footage for General St John. In doing so, I found this." An image flashed up on the screen—it was her AI core room via security camera. She ran it, the time signature in the corner of the image ticked by, then she stopped it. "Did you see it?"

"See what? Nothing happened." She was playing with him. There was that smile, the one she always had when she was being mischievous.

"You didn't see it? Look again." She restarted the video sequence, the time signature ticking down the same way it had before. "There." Still he could make nothing out.

"Dawn, what am I looking for?" Frustration began to leak into his voice. "I can see nothing but circuit modules."

"Yes, exactly right. But watch this one." She pointed at a module in the bottom right of the opposite wall from the camera's perspective. The footage rolled again, still nothing. He shook his head. Dawn suddenly looked apologetic. "Sorry, I forget, I can see this but at this resolution you probably can't. I'll zoom the image."

With the image zoomed in, targeting the specific module in question, the video feed ran again. This time he noticed it straight away. Each circuit module had a few lights and a digital display to indicate operational status, under that at the bottom of the front panel of every module was a number, the printed serial number of the unit, clear white lettering on a metallic blue front plate. As the timestamp ran down in the corner of the screen, at a particular instant the last two digits of the number changed. Dawn shortened the time sequence and ran on repeat a few times, the numbers flicking back and forward. She stopped the image at the point of the numerical change. The time stamp was clearly visible.

She looked at him but said nothing, letting the ramifications of what he had just witnessed sink in. His eyes searched the room for answers he couldn't find in himself, then they came, crystallising and crashing over him like shards of pain. The time stamp was showing a time before the resus process had begun, when no one should have been awake. That person, whoever they were, was able to subvert Dawn's surveillance system, effectively erasing themselves from the recordings and inserting the sabotaged circuit module.

"Have you given this information to St John yet?" His eyes were intense, questioning.

"No. I thought you should see it first."

"Please update him and Hopper with this information immediately then run the same analysis on your other nodes. Start with the nodes we know are affected, then look for the sabotaged modules and the switch point. It will give us a good indication of the terrorists' movements and maybe how many there are. Let St John and myself know the moment you have something."

"Okay, Daddy. Will do."

He opened a priority conference with Hopper and St John on the nearest console. A couple of moments later, both men were side by side on the main view screen, deep and serious faces reflecting the necessary response to a priority call. "Gentlemen, we have a breach of the surveillance and security system. Dawn has just presented me with disturbing evidence in relation to the sabotage attempt on her core and node circuits. She is sending you the data now." Both men appeared distracted at the same time, the data received from Dawn now being reviewed by them as they were on the call. Hopper appeared most surprised, physically taking a step forward to replay the vid, a look of disbelief on his face. St John raised an eyebrow.

"Sir, this is not possible," said Hopper reflexively. His thought process caught up with his mouth a moment later. "I mean, it shouldn't be possible. There would have been no one up at that point, and the first medic awake would have been Dr Clayton and her resus would have been under the direct supervision of Dawn. We know the exact time that occurred. All other resus would have been supervised by Dr Clayton and she has not, to my knowledge, reported any anomalies."

"If I understand you, Commander Hopper, you are stating that Dr Clayton would have had something to do with this?" asked St John, equally disbelieving. "As she would be the first awake, she would have ample opportunity to subvert systems if she wished."

"And Dawn. But I can't see that she would have sabotaged herself. There is something off with this picture."

"Gentlemen," Clayton interjected, "I understand the implications of this. And, as such, I can no longer be part of this investigation. Given that the subject matter has touched into areas of my family, I cannot be impartial. St John, you are already lead on this investigation but I am now ceding total responsibility for this investigation to you. Until you find out exactly what's going on here, you are only to report to me for operational purposes." That stopped them both cold. Neither of them had expected him to relinquish control of the investigation, not this far out from home, not with the stakes so high. "No matter how far from home, I am not above the law or its process. You will proceed as instructed, General St John."

St John straightened and took a visible deep breath. "Very well, sir. I will need you to make yourself available for questioning."

"Of course. I will be on the bridge when you need me."

"Thank you. Hopper, we should continue this discussion in private. I'll meet you in engineering in ten minutes."

Hopper appeared not to believe what was happening and simply nodded, slightly dumbfounded by events, lost in his internal thoughts. "Yeah, sure," he said softly. The connections ended, and he and Dawn stood in silence. His mood could hardly get much worse. His wife was implicated in terrorism, and the target his daughter. He refused to believe it out of hand. There was simply no way. They had been together for more than thirty years. He had known and worked with her for a few years before that—it just made no sense in logic or reason. More than that, Dawn was their daughter. There was no way he could be objective on this; it had been the correct decision.

"I love it when people talk about me when I'm in the room. Hell, I'm in every room." She was redirecting her anger, but she had a right to be angry. Someone, or something, was messing with her memory, and they needed to find out what. The problem was, who better than the two of them to lead the investigation? Together, they had introduced AI and singularity technology to the world. The technical engineers aboard were the best but they would never truly have the intuition to understand the subtleties of the system he and Dawn had imagined and made real.

He firmed up a plan in his mind. This was going to be tricky but he had to perform his own investigation. Somehow he needed to figure out what was going on. Taking this course of action would be problematic, as any evidence he found could be argued against as being fabricated and who would be better placed to fabricate evidence than the man who created the technology. He could also jeopardise St John's investigation by getting in the way, but that might be the risk he took to get to the truth. Someone was taking a massive amount of trouble to besmirch his wife's reputation and his career, and endanger his daughter's life. His family was under direct threat—he had to act. Doing nothing and leaving it up to others, however trustworthy and well-meaning, was not an option for him.

How was he going to do all this and deal with the situation on the *Intrepid*? One step at a time. Small steps.

"Dawn, I want you to run a diagnostic on the security system. You may already be doing this by St John's request but I want you to add some parameters."

"What are you looking for?" she asked. There was no argument. Over the last couple of minutes she had been watching him wrangle with whether or not to get involved.

"I'm working on the theory that, at some point, someone came out of resus early. There would have been footage of that. I'm assuming that they would have gained access to the security system at some later point and looped the feed of all networked security vids. But they would have had to patch back over the evidence of their early exit from resus. Somewhere in the system, there will be a memory stack with purposely overwritten data. We have zettabytes of data stack space in the system and, in the time we've travelled from home, we would still be using free space for newly recorded security stream data. Nothing yet should be overwriting there.

"You can check logs and so on, but I'm sure they will show nothing. If they are smart enough to hack the system, they are smart enough to amend the logs. We need to go deeper. Hardware level."

Dawn applied some logic of her own. "Even if we do identify the security overwrite, we will only be able to identify the security camera and therefore the resus suite involved. I doubt I'll be able to recover the underlying data enough to identify anyone, only enough to indicate movement where there should be none. That's still two hundred possible suspects."

"Yes, Dawn. But it's a start. We need to narrow the field, and fast. We have too many variables here. I want to shut down this cell and get onto the important problem on the *Intrepid*. There are people over there that need help and I'm too busy fussing over this. It's turned into politics, and we need to be focused on survival." He felt himself flush with anger. "Whoever is pulling the strings here needs to be identified quickly. Let's get to it. Report back as soon as you have something. I'll be on the bridge, expecting St John's call."

He stopped a moment and looked into Dawn's eyes. "You know, kid. Sometimes the thing I miss most about the way things turned out? Hugs. My little girl is all grown up and the most beautiful projection of light particles I've ever seen. And I can't hug you or tussle your hair." He gave her a sad smile. "I miss that."

She returned the smile. "Daddy, you're the most soppy man I know."

His smile turned into a beam. "Love you too. Now, check out that data before we both end up sobbing."

"Big nose."

"Bat vomit." Her image vanished.

He straightened his uniform, composed himself and headed back to the bridge.

HAVERS

Since the comms had come back up, the strategic picture had changed wildly and Havers had been slightly taken aback by developments. Larsen now had a team with him working on reconstructing the damage done to Ellie by the invaders, although this was being hampered by the continued attempts to infiltrate the system by those on the bridge. Reports back from Reeve's pathfinders had indicated the main invading party dug in on the bridge, with three roving patrols of four in the corridors immediately around it. They had done well not to be spotted by using the same maintenance crawl spaces and walkways that Larsen and Silvers had used to evade capture. They were now his eyes and ears in forward positions on a front line less than fifty metres from their target.

All things considered, he believed he had the advantage: greater understanding of the environment, better control of the ship and the best trained troops and engineers at his disposal. It was a good position but, against an unknown in a tight spot, he was not underestimating their resolve or inventiveness. Anything could happen, and he needed to be ready for that.

Key to all of this was information. He had the pathfinders in place but they could only give him so much, and somehow the invaders had been able to lock out the security cameras and surveillance on the bridge. He was essentially blind within the one room he really needed to see. He needed Ellie back online and fast.

'Larsen, update.' He sent the message almost without thinking, a reflex to the other wild thoughts going through his mind.

'Again, sir? I only sent you the last update five minutes ago,' came the response. Larsen was right.

'Things are happening fast, Larsen, and I need to know what's happening on the bridge, like it was yesterday.'

'Yesterday we were all in stasis, and right now I'm surprised I've lived this long. As for Ellie, I'm surprised she's lived this long.' Larsen was being as bull-headed as he normally was. If it was anyone else, he would have reprimanded him for his attitude; as it was, everyone was a little stressed. He let Larsen vent. A moment later, the information he wanted started to come in. 'The guys here have done a great job, and I estimate Ellie will be back with us within the next ten minutes. We've cleaned things up, blocked current access from any terminals located on the bridge and isolated the bridge network. Whatever they had running was taking an exceptional amount of Ellie's core capacity to defend. We're just going through a reboot of her peripheral systems now.'

'Excellent work. Let me know when complete.'

'Will do.'

He turned his attention to the next piece of crazy news that had popped across his virtual desk. The intruders had obviously got aboard the *Intrepid* via a ship of some kind—he expected that, where else would they have come from? That ship had been hiding on the far side of the *Intrepid* and jamming communications between the other ships in the fleet. From his point of view, this was also expected, an obvious source of the disturbances. What was alarming to him was that the alien vessel had just been reported as missing. Disappeared. It had apparently thrown up some sort of cloaking field and vanished from view. People were now frantically trying to find it via any method at their disposal. His team, now being closest to the event, had been asked to get the *Intrepid's* instrumentation searching the local vicinity for any signs of a ship of at least a few hundred metres in length hiding in space and, essentially, close enough to touch. He wanted to laugh but he knew that, of all the things that had happened in the last twenty four hours, this was no more weird.

Back on Earth, his life had been so much simpler. He'd started life as a school teacher in mathematics and worked his way through to head of department. Then the Great Decline began and everyone's lives changed. In the following years, people had been seconded into particular professions related to their aptitude and put to work on building the colony ships to the newly identified Terran worlds. His work had been initially as supervising engineer to the navigation systems on the *Indianapolis* but he had risen up the ranks. By the time the ship had its maiden voyage, ranks had become more formalised and naval in convention. Commander Iain Havers had then taken up his engineering role aboard. Essentially, nothing changed. He was still doing what he had always done in the construction of the *Indianapolis*, only now it was more maintenance-led: 'fix it' rather than 'build it'. It was how most projects ran. In his experience, though, a different sort of person was needed in each case, but he had managed to stay in post. He was less sure what that meant, maybe nothing. But now here he was, an engineer presiding over a military operation to retake a colony ship years from home. The mathematics teacher in him would never have believed it.

The bustle around him in engineering was frenetic. People were preparing for the next phase of the operation. Security were finalising their checks before launching their assault on the bridge. Reeve had an attack planned which launched on three fronts. One attack would be distraction for the other two, a misdirect to allow her other two teams to flank vertically and horizontally. Unlike old Earth ship design, where the bridge was almost always positioned at the prow of the ship for greatest visibility, the colony ships had been designed with the bridge embedded deep within the body of the vessel. With the latest instrumentation and technology, there was no real need for the bridge to be anywhere near the surface skin of the hull and defensively it made much better sense to bury it deep within. Better defence from accidental, incidental asteroid strikes or purposeful military attack. It also gave Reeve the benefit of being able to attack the bridge from multiple vectors, not simply straight down the main corridor.

His engineers' preparation was slightly different—unpacking expensive-looking kit and plugging in to the local engineering network: backup light-weight batteries to ensure power in the unlikely event they became cut off, backup terminals with functional recovery applications preloaded. Others were lining up with the security guys and would be first on the scene on the bridge with the important task of identifying and clearing any explosive traps and isolating any alien devices. He did not envy them that job. What the alien technology did or how it operated would potentially be like nothing they had ever seen before—too many unknowns for his liking. But, with Boyd there on the bridge, he was confident the old man would see them through. With the greatest amount of technical experience in the entire team, whatever new technology they encountered, the old Texan would have the best chance of success.

Some alien kit was already being looked at, with, unfortunately, the expected result. Lots of chin-stroking, head-scratching and shaking of heads could be seen. The alien team that Silvers had taken down had been moved to another room by the medics, where they were performing as much analysis as they could without the full facilities of the medical bay. The aliens' belongings had been taken by Boyd and a few others, where basic research had begun and the search for clues as to purpose and composition. It was all guess work at this stage, and no one wanted to be that person who accidentally pressed a button that got the rest of them nuked, so everyone was being extra cautious. All the items they had found on the aliens were small, no larger than hand-held devices, with the notable exceptions being the objects, which everyone assumed to be weapons, found on the forearms of each of the soldier-class aliens.

From Silvers debrief and detailed description of their first encounter and subsequent retaking of main engineering, the weapons seemed to have some kind of energy beam, and the localised damage to the walls around the entranceway confirmed this. Metals had been melted with evidence of free-flowing residue, non-combustible plastics and fire-retardant wall materials superheated to failure, with holes clean and circular. This was unlike the weapons of their own security personnel, whose projectile munitions would have caused far more fragmentary damage with less penetration.

As he watched the final preparations, Larsen came striding out of the corridor leading to the AI core room. Out of the corner of his eye, he saw the projector start up, pixels of light spinning in a helix and growing fuller and more feminine until Ellie stood to his side. He turned to face her as Larsen joined them.

"How are you feeling, Ellie?" Larsen asked, some status readings jumping to the terminal screen closest to her. Completely focused on the last few fine details, Larsen, finally satisfied that all was as it should be, finally turned to Havers and gave a quick nod.

"As well as can be expected, Lieutenant Larsen. I'm still running a self-diagnostic to ascertain the full extent of the damage to my wider systems but I am fully functional at my core. Some functionality and control of remote systems may be impaired, but I will try and inform you of these difficulties as they are discovered."

"Very good," he interrupted, eager to get things moving. "I'm Commander Havers, Ellie. I'm currently running the operation to retake the *Intrepid* and secure her from the alien intruders. Are you able to assist?"

"Hello, Commander Havers. I will do what I can. As I mentioned, I'm not so sure of my remote systems. What do you have in mind?"

"Firstly, I need to identify where all the alien intruders are. From our data, they appear to be contained within the vicinity of the bridge. I'd like this data confirmed. Secondly, I need eyes on the bridge. It looks like they have been able to disable camera feed—can you get a view of the bridge for us? And lastly, there is a cloaked alien vessel in close local space. It was on the starboard side of the *Intrepid*, but now is no longer visible. I need you to use any instrumentation you can to reacquire the alien ship."

She seemed to take a moment, looking at her toes as she did so. "The problems you pose increase in levels of complexity. I can identify the exact location of all alien patrols in the corridors around the bridge. I will have some difficulty with the bridge cameras, the reason being there appears to be some physical power failure to the circuit. I will need assistance with manual reconfiguring of the power supply to the surveillance system on the bridge in order to correct this. The last problem, even with my current understanding of physics, is going to take a while."

"Define 'a while'," Larsen asked.

"Unknown. Extrapolating from current research on cloaking technology, it could take anywhere between a month and several years to come up with a working theory."

"We can't wait that long, Ellie," Havers interjected. "With the best will in the world, there has to be a quicker way. I don't need you to invent a cloaking device. I'm asking that you locate the ship. It could be a visual projection discrepancy, a heat signature anomaly or some exhaust emissions. Anything we can use to pinpoint the location of that ship.

"While we're blind and have no knowledge of where they are, they are a high risk to everyone in the fleet. I want them found, and we have the best chance of doing so."

She understood the risks and the reasons. "I'll begin work straight away."

"Thank you, Ellie." Almost without a breath he turned to Larsen. "Sorry to put you on the spot again, Lieutenant, but I'm going to need you with the bridge team."

"No problem, sir. It's been one of those days."

"You're not wrong. You've got first-hand knowledge of this new alien species and I'll need that knowledge where it will count most. Just don't get yourself killed."

Larsen sniggered like a kid. "I live by that last statement, sir."

"I'll hold you to that." The endless good humour and positivity Larsen could show under great pressure was one of the things Havers always liked about him. He needed that motivation and drive in the team. It was infectious, and he smiled in response.

"You know, we really ought to come up with a name for these aliens. We can't just keep calling them 'the aliens'."

"Can't argue with that. Any thoughts?"

"Well, no, not really, but we should probably call them something official before they get some slang derogatory name from the crew, don't you think?"

"Again, sound logic. How about Chameleons?"

"The Chameleon people?" Larsen made a face. "Needs to be more snappy than that. How about Cyans or Spectrans?"

"Honestly, you really shouldn't go there. Hundreds of years of problems with references to skin colour on our own planet and you want to name a people after their skin colour? I don't think so."

Boyd had been walking past and overheard the last of the conversation. "Are you trying to come up with a name for these assholes, sir?"

"As good a time as any. What have you got?"

"Vecians."

"I like that, Boyd," reflected Larsen. Havers just made a concurring nod. "Short, punchy. How did you come up with that?"

"Well, easy really. It's on all their kit. A mathematical inverted delta operator in vector calculus. It's called a del if I remember correctly."

"You mean a triangle?" Larsen offered, flippantly. He knew

Boyd would bite.

"You being an ass on purpose, sir? I mean a del. Yes, an inverted triangle but, if you remember your mathematics lectures, a del. Anyway, the del thing is irrelevant, the Vecian thing, that's my pitch. Vecians—as in, vector calculus. It's everywhere on their kit, on their uniform, armour and one of the bodies has it marked into his arm. Go and check it out for yourselves." With that, he turned and continued on his way, like the conversation had never happened.

Without further invitation they turned and headed through to the makeshift medical research lab. The bodies had been laid out in respectful fashion, silvery sheets covered them head to toe, which had been obtained from several first aid stations about engineering. A Vecian was outstretched on a workbench with meticulous observations being made and noted by two medics. Others were tending to and setting up mobile medical kit, imaging scanners, blood and DNA analysis machines. Full autopsies would need to wait—simple, quick and reasonably non-invasive tests would be carried out now and as much information around their anatomy learned as possible. It could give them an edge in the hours to come.

The medics had removed the Vecians clothing and, sure enough, an inverted delta could be seen on the shoulder. They stood behind the medics as they worked, watching them collecting swabs for analysis and noting colouration, markings and features as they ran down the body. Hairless, the Vecians had angular facial features with larger than human eyes but similar overall cranial proportions. The nose was flattened with slit nostrils, and the mouth was of similar size to a human's but with thinner lips and needle-like teeth. They appeared to have no ears, but a cranial bone, ridged and jutting out from the natural curve of the skull, ran from one side of the head to the other, around the lower occipital bone. Four arms lay to the sides of the body, each with a hand of only two fingers and an opposable thumb. The legs looked human but the feet were similar to the hands, two toes forward one shorter facing to the rear but between the forward facing toes stretched a thick skin creating a flipper-like span.

Even before the medics had said a word, Havers had already started to make some assumptions and extrapolate from the physical form as to their origins. His basic reasoning and education led him to believe the Vecians might possibly be aquatic or amphibious in some way. They had certainly been breathing the on-board atmosphere without much trouble, so probably not fully aquatic. It backed up the amphibian idea.

"Doctor?" Havers offered as a polite interruption to events. "Please don't let us interrupt your work but have you any first impressions? I'm sending the team out in a few minutes and I'd like to give them any information I can to help."

Dr Jack Sommers glanced momentarily up at Havers and Larsen, then turned his focus back to the body on the workbench. "Sure," he said. "First impressions. Apart from the unbelievable shock that I'm performing an autopsy on a first contact, rather than shaking this guy's hand?"

"Yeah," Havers said, trying to move the conversation along. It wasn't how he would have arranged events if he'd had a choice but he'd not had the choice. He was playing with the cards he'd been dealt. "Apart from that." He could sense the doctor purse his lips in disgust, even though he was facing the other way.

"Well, the physiology is humanoid but with distinct differences, as you can see. External examination shows three digits on each of four hands and two feet, four arms, two legs, feet noticeably webbed. Two eyes, one nose but no noticeable ears.

"Internally, I have been able to identify the heart, in the upper centreline of the torso, brain easily located in the skull although segmented into four and not two as with human brains. Difficult to say what else is going on, lungs and other organs are muddled, I need more time to fully analyse what's going on there," Sommers concluded. "As soon as I get these bodies to the medical bay I'll be able to get you a more full report."

"I'll get you there as soon as we've retaken the bridge, doctor. Thank you for the update."

"You're welcome."

Havers looked at Larsen and pointed to the door back into main engineering with a nod of his head. They both made their way back to the control desk. "Reeve," he called. She responded immediately.

"Sir."

"Are your team ready?"

"Yes, sir."

"I'm teaming you up with Larsen. He's quickly becoming the

resident expert on the Vecians."

"'Vecians', sir?" she enquired with a quizzical frown.

"Yes, we've named the aliens 'Vecians'. No other reason but to give them a name. You can blame Boyd—it was his brainchild. Anyway, between Larsen and Silvers you should have the best chance I can give you to get the job done up there. We'll be in constant contact, and should be able to offer remote assistance to any functional part of the ship, now Ellie is back with us. If we get the cameras back up on the bridge, I'll patch you in straight away. Any questions?"

"Only one," replied Reeve. "When do we leave?"

"Very good. Now, Lieutenant. Good luck."

"Thank you, sir." Reeve turned to her team. She clearly subvocalized a command to them, as they all started to pick up their kit and line up in prepared order at the main door.

"Good luck yourself, sir." Larsen said to him, as he headed off to join the departing team. "Back for tea and medals before you know it."

The trek up to the bridge had been quite easy through the habitat. Havers had been watching their progress via vid-com linked in to each and every team member. Their location was being translated to a physical floor plan map and a three-dimensional representation of the same on the primary screens of the main engineering control workstation. Havers sat in the chief engineer's chair, monitoring every last detail, every scrap of information he could. He had just started the deadliest game of chess, one with mortal consequences in the real world. The next few hours were going to be intense.

"Someone get me coffee, black," he asked the ether, to no one in particular. There was a quick commotion from an engineer near their kit bags and someone called back that it would be two minutes.

The main doors to engineering had been closed again and welded shut. Silvers' defences were still in place on the other side but had now been improved and added to by Reeve's team, just in case their plan completely fell apart. A security squad had been assigned to their protection but he had otherwise sent the entire team's security detail on the main push for the bridge. He didn't want to lose the bridge but, if he couldn't secure it and flush out these Vecian intruders, then they needed to hope that reinforcements from the *Indianapolis* or *Endeavour* could reach them in time. Having said that, he knew that they would be reluctant to send reinforcements until the location of the Vecian vessel could be identified. So many 'if's, 'but's and 'maybe's. Playing chess was hard enough when you knew where all the pieces were, but playing chess when your opponent had an invisible queen would be a level of complexity harder. Doubts plagued him but they were all looking to him. He had the responsibility, and he wouldn't let them down.

"Your coffee, sir." Petty Officer Hillard passed a sealed drinks sachet, then immediately returned to his duties.

"Thank you, Hillard." Since the others had left for the bridge, the main engineering section had started to feel like a stadium, with his view being that of a spectator in the last row of seats, his remaining engineers as ants on the pitch. He took a slug of coffee from the sachet nozzle, the hot bitter taste feeling good and reassuring. He focussed.

'Ellie, how are we doing with the search for the Vecian ship?' he messaged the AI.

'Progress is slow. Systems have been interfered with. I've had to restart many. They are coming back online and scanning instrumentation is taking time to calibrate once active. No other promising leads at this time from instrumentation that is fully operational. I estimate another five minutes before all instrumentation is fully configured and active scanning can commence.' No emotion, just the cold, hard facts of the moment.

'How about the bridge?'

'No change. Manual intervention will still be required from the on-site team.'

'Thank you, Ellie.' He quit the connection.

He switched to Lieutenant Reeve's vid-com feed. They were now approaching the elevator lobby where Silvers had ambushed the Vecians in the lift. The scene was still as described in Larsen's report—the lobby was dark and a pool of light from the open elevator doors shed an eerie glow across the fallen bodies inside, a slight, elongated shadow from the body draped across the doorway.

Listening in, he heard Reeve's instructions to her point security team: "Careful, Spratt. Sweep and clear, with caution."

"Copy that." Corporal Spratt's team of four broke off from the head of the group and sprinted across the lobby, coming to position either side of the open doorway.

"Svenson, cover positions."

"Copy." Another four split out into the lobby entrance and took up soft cover positions along the wall behind seating and plant features, weapons aimed in a spread of directions to include exit corridors and the elevators themselves.

The shadows flickered across the lobby as one of Spratt's team moved slowly inside, checking for explosive devices or anything unusual. The silence seemed to go on forever.

"Hall, Roberts, move up to the side corridors. Make sure we don't get flanked," instructed Svenson.

"Roger that."

"Copy."

Two of the second squad providing cover moved with pace up to the side corridors. In the dark, he could see their vision bio-comms adjust to give a clear monochrome image as Private Hall and Private Roberts looked down their respective corridors. No movement, no obstructions, the corridors appeared empty. "Clear," came the call from both. Hall looked back at the guys working around the elevator and her vision bio-comms leaked colour into her view where illumination was available from the lift, her peripheral vision still the monochrome of night vision. He had to look twice but, from Hall's angle, he thought he saw one of the dead Vecians move, but the movement was only slight—he could have been mistaken.

"Private Hall, please keep visual on the elevator doorway." Private Hall's vision snapped back to the corridor, which was a natural reflex, as that's what she should have been doing. Still nothing there. Then, as the instruction filtered through, she looked back to the door of the elevator.

"Corporal Spratt, there may be movement in the elevator. Nearside left from the door."

"Yes, sir. Colsen, take a look." Colsen, who was already in the elevator, moved to where he had indicated. From the visual on Hall's feed, he could see Colsen looming over the bodies in the corner. Colsen's visual feed gave an up-close view, as he took a tighter grip on his carbine with one hand and used the other to slowly shift a dead Vecian. Underneath, and with wide, startled eyes, lay a Vecian with cyan-coloured skin, now rippling with green in striped patterns, and with dark eyes with no iris or pupil, just jet black pools staring back at Colsen.

"One's alive!" called Colsen from the elevator. He stepped back and motioned with the carbine, "Get up. Out, out of the elevator. Out. Out!"

Reeve ordered another squad up to assist. They dragged the Vecian to the centre of the lobby and forced it to the ground, face down, then struggled for a minute while they restrained and cuffed two sets of arms, not just the usual one. While the Vecian was being restrained, Spratt's team continued to clear the elevator.

While the team buzzed around it, Havers watched the alien via the feeds. It hung its head, not looking at anyone or anything around the room. It made no sound and it didn't resist. It looked totally at a loss. Perhaps it had expected to be rescued by its own kind, and maybe it hadn't expected them to return so soon. It's clothes were different from the other Vecians in the lift—not exceptionally so but it was not one of the usual armoured soldier types they had seen so far, more like one of the technical or engineering types, a couple of which they now had in the makeshift morgue in the next room.

He received an incoming message form Lieutenant Reeve. 'Sir, we have the alien subdued. It appears unarmed. What do you want us to do with it?' It was a good question. He hadn't counted on there being prisoners this early into the mission. He'd hoped to only need to run a detention exercise with those on the bridge, once he had control of the entire ship. It would be a simple exercise to then use the *Intrepid's* own detention area.

'Instruct two of your security team to escort the prisoner back to engineering. By the time you get here we will have a detention area set up.'

'Copy that.'

He heard her relaying the instructions to her team. Svenson and Hall grabbed and lifted the Vecian to its feet and pushed it towards the corridor returning to engineering.

'Boyd, I need a detention cell. Ready in ten minutes.' Boyd was in the adjacent room and he still heard the grumble of discontent. He wondered whether Boyd had always been an old man, grumbling and discontented with the universe.

'Would you like that with bells on, sir?'

'If you could, Boyd. Make it mauve too, if you think it will help. As long as it's ready in ten minutes.'

'Wise ass.'

He knew others were disbelieving of how Boyd got away with speaking to people—especially senior officers—the way he did but, in a way, that was part of his appeal. You always got an honest answer and a direct appraisal with Boyd. No messing around. If you could live with the grouse and attitude, he was one of the good ones. Three technicians in the room suddenly dropped what they were doing and walked with purpose through to Boyd.

Havers returned his attention to his group of chess pieces, now under way again and making their way towards the bridge.

LARSEN

There had been something niggling him ever since they had made it back to the lobby. He had put it down to the tension of the task ahead but he was beginning to feel like it was more than that. Like there was something out of place, although he could not quite put his finger on it.

They had found the Vecian in the elevator and sent it back to Havers for detention and most likely some kind of questioning, though he had no idea how they would obtain any useful information, not immediately. They would need the linguists to provide some level of communication first before any meaningful dialogue could be had. That would be assuming the alien was in any way receptive to that. From the looks of it, it didn't appear to be in a very chatty mood.

His mind was drifting; he needed to stay focused.

Reeve's plan was not to take the main elevator itself, as that would no doubt flag to everyone where they were and what they were doing, but it was still the most direct route to the bridge, so he was in the maintenance space behind the elevator again. Silvers had been assigned by Reeve as his personal body guard and stood a couple of metres away keeping close watch. He understood her logic: they had worked well together so far and things had worked out pretty well. Why get in the way of a good thing?

The protective panel of the terminal he wanted to access was hinged to one side and he was working quickly to switch off the gravity in the elevator tube from top to bottom. Reeve's team was working on forcing a couple of the elevator doors to the lobby so that they could gain access in numbers and begin the trek to the bridge level.

'Ready?' he asked Reeve.

'All set here. Ready when you are,' came the reply.

'In three, two, one.' He executed the final command. There was no sound, no mechanical click or whir, just an instantaneous loss of gravity and the pit of his stomach complained straight away. It was not something immediately visible—people didn't start floating away—he and Silvers were physically relaxed and holding on to hand grabs fitted into the wall every half metre or so. The only thing that gave away the change in environment was the overwhelming feeling of endless falling that came in waves, along with nausea, as his animal brain tried frantically to figure out what the hell was going on. It was something that he never really got used to but coping with it became easier over time.

He closed the terminal cabinet and turned to see a stream of people seemingly flying by. Changing his orientation, the shaft became a tunnel. Not wanting to get in anyone's way, he and Silvers would join at the rear of the procession and move on up.

As the last of the team went by, he swung himself across to the walkway barrier and moved out into the tunnel proper. He took a hand grab in the wall and gently pushed off, following the others. The trick was not to get too excited and push too hard. Whatever momentum you set off with, you had to make sure you could comfortably dissipate it at the end of your travel. He had learnt the hard way, his nose broken on one occasion and his shoulder almost dislocated on another when he had overcooked it and had too much momentum as he came to a bulkhead.

The few hundred metres to the bridge level took less time to cover than Larsen expected, and the leading groups split off down maintenance tracks in opposite directions, with some others going on further up—these groups would be the flanking attack and support. His and Silvers' job was to get to a local gravity control terminal and, on a timed instruction from Reeve, take down the gravity on the bridge. He had identified the terminal they would be going for, and he was taking a risk. Due to the fact that the Vecians had somehow managed to isolate the bridge, he could not access the control remotely. That would have been too easy. No, he would need to physically get to the control which was located under the floor panelling to the bridge. The only way to access that control panel was via a crawl space under the bridge floor. He wasn't claustrophobic but that sort of confined space was likely to get really mentally challenging.

He arrived next to Reeve and they exchanged looks that conveyed a little nod of good luck as he and Silvers pushed on past.

'This is our stop,' he messaged to Silvers. He grabbed the handrail to the maintenance gantry and expertly redirected his momentum. Without losing any pace, they now flew across the gantry walkway to the maintenance corridor on a direct line to the bridge and, as they crossed the gravity boundary, touched down softly and began to pad their way as silently as they could towards their target. A few moments later, he gripped hand holds next to a small crawl space hatch. 'End of the line,' he informed Silvers. They wouldn't both fit in the confined space. This was a one-man operation from here.

'One moment.' Silvers was already at his side. There was a quick quiet click and he felt a tug on the tool belt. Looking down, he realised Silvers was attaching a safety line between the two of them.

'I never knew you cared,' he said.

'Don't get your hopes up,' Silvers quipped in return. 'Anyway, Havers would be real pissed if I got his prize engineer killed.'

'Well, this party doesn't start without me. Let's move.'

With an agreeing nod, he opened the hatch to the crawl space, stooped and began pulling himself slowly along the space. Very quickly, the only sounds he could hear were that of his breathing and the sliding of his clothes over the metal of the crawlspace floor. His arms tucked in, his toes pushing, sweat dripping into his eyes, he tried to listen out for movement above. He was directly under the bridge floor now, above him only the floor plates and gravity panels. The fact that he was potentially only centimetres from a Vecian started to play on his mind. There was no way to escape—he really was a sitting duck.

Noises. As he got closer to the gravity control, he could hear voices. Nothing he could understand, incredibly sing-song in sound, almost like an Oriental language but more musical. His guess was that there was a couple of Vecian about a metre away. He had to hope they would be too distracted to hear his shuffling and moving below the floor.

The crawlspace opened out a little either side of him to a more square, boxlike workspace. In front of him was the terminal he was looking for, and he worked quickly. A few quick selections, some authentication and then access to the gravity control was granted. The screen showed a simple selection item, 'Gravity ON', and next to it was a selection slider 'OFF'.

He messaged Reeve: 'Larsen in position and set.' Taking a quick look at the mission time in the corner of his vision, he noted he was about seventy seconds ahead of schedule. Perfect. The moments ticked by.

'Roger that. Wait one,' came the reply from Reeve.

Staring at the console and waiting for the time to tick down, his focus returned to the voices. A creeping feeling began to overtake him—the voices had stopped. When had they stopped?

Fifty seconds.

His breathing was all he could hear now. He tried to hold it but all that did was exaggerate the sound of the blood pulsing through his ears. Sweat ran from his face to the floor, a small pool beginning to develop in the orange glow of the terminal screen.

Twenty seconds.

Sparks started to flare all about him and the floor plate above him ripped away with some unseen force. The light of the bridge flooded his little hide and alarmed sing-song voices shouted at each other. He'd been discovered and he had the time it took them to put a bullet in him to act. The gravity plate above him was still in place but he'd seen what one of their weapons did to Smith, a thin gravity plate was no real defence.

He punched the NO icon on the terminal and then started to wriggle back as fast as he could. He was half out of the workspace when he incidentally looked back at the terminal. More sparks had begun to fall around him, they appeared to want him alive, or at least a clear shot. They were taking out the gravity panel above him. A notification popped up on the screen: 'Are you sure?' You have to be kidding me? Larsen thought in an exasperated rage. Of course I'm bloody sure, otherwise I wouldn't have gone through the whole process of accessing, authenticating, finding this specific option and selecting it. Bloody programmers. They were going to get him killed.

A roar of panic and frustration launched him forward and he pushed the OK button on the terminal. At the same moment, the gravity panel lifted off and he could see straight into the bridge. In that split second, he got a view of several Vecians but they were shadows to him, mostly backlit by the bridge lights. A large menacing darkness fell across him and a large red hand grabbed his arm. He yelled out and recoiled back against the side of the workspace as another hand tried to make a grab for him. He flailed and punched out trying to release himself from the grip of the Vecian but the grip was strong and solid. Reaching for his tool belt, he grabbed something, anything. He was reacting on instinct— thinking didn't really come into it. He thrust out and flicked a switch, a short jet of white blue flame at about two thousand Centigrade lanced out. The flame was no more than five centimetres in length but size is not always what you need. The howl of pain that was suddenly all around him almost burst his eardrums, and the lights reappeared as the Vecian retreated in pain.

There was more shouting now. The bridge gravity field was offline and the Vecians clearly realised something was happening. He started to crawl backwards down the crawl space as quickly as he could. He could feel the tugging on his back, as Silvers tried to assist and retract the linking safety tether. Reeve probably already knew, but he sent a message anyway, 'Gravity field offline. Forced to go early.' He could just imaging the cussing going on, but he had been about thirty seconds early—surely they were all set to go? Hey, what plan went off without a hitch?

He felt hands on his ankles and a sharp, hard pull that slid him at speed the last metre out of the crawlspace and back into the maintenance walkway with Silvers. Although out of the crawlspace, he was still lined up and looking down the tunnel in time to see an arm and head pop into view some distance away. His focus wasn't immediate but the intent seemed aggressive and an almost sixth sense warned him to get the hell out of the way. He shouted at Silvers, "Move!"

There was no question. Silvers just took a dive, landing belly first and covering, and Larsen leapt a fraction of a second later, as the Vecian fired his weapon. The walkway wall opposite the crawlspace erupted in a violent explosion and spray of shrapnel. He landed hard on Silvers' back, a grunt exhaled as he winded Silvers and knocked the air from his lungs. Getting up fast, in case another shot came down the tunnel at them, he took Silvers by the webbing and helped haul him up. "Sorry for the elbow in the kidney."

"Oh, that's okay, sir," Silvers replied, unconvincingly. "I've got two. One too many, so I hear."

He started to move away down the walkway but Silvers went the wrong way. Stepping up to the crawlspace to the bridge, Silvers fired a few shots down the tunnel and followed up with a grenade. Once done, he turned and followed Larsen at a run. Expecting a massive explosion, Larsen was surprised only to hear a slight 'wump' sound. "What was that?" They were running now, zigzagging down the maintenance walkway as it worked its way back towards the elevator shaft, silent communication forgotten.

"Smoke."

"What good is that?"

"Not for us. The guys on offence."

Made sense. Silvers was always smart, thinking ahead.

'Go.' A single word popped into Larsen's view. Reeve launched the attack.

It was later than he imagined but the world was suddenly alive with noise: screaming, shouting, explosives, carbine and exotic weapon fire. The same sounds he and Silvers had experienced in their first contact, where they had lost Smith. The sounds were muffled now, due to the distance and walls involved, but they were real.

At the elevator shaft, he stopped to catch his breath. It was a short-lived rest. He was first to the gantry but he wasn't first into the shaft. Silvers passed him horizontally and at pace, crunching into the opposite wall of the elevator with enough force to break bone. A sickening crunch could be heard as Silvers made contact with the wall, then he hung in the air and drifted unconsciously in the zero gravity of the elevator shaft. Larsen's brain was trying hard to make sense of everything when a Vecian walked into view and onto the gantry.

The Vecian had probably seen better days. A dark ooze was escaping from various nasty wounds across his body, his clothing or armour shredded or missing. His weapon arm was gone from the elbow joint down, face looking gruesome where one of Silvers' shots looked like it had passed through the cheek. He also spotted a vicious-looking burn scorched across its lower left forearm, most likely the portable welding torch he'd used. This Vecian was out for payback. One down, one to go.

As the Vecian cleared the distance from the gantry entrance to him, Larsen decided the best place to be was further away. He jumped the railing and out into the elevator shaft again. Aiming for Silvers, he grabbed at him and then pushed off down the shaft, away from the bridge. An idea had come to him, but it was a long shot and he estimated that he may not live long enough to execute it. He'd never know if he didn't try though.

A stinging pain shot like a lightning rod up his right leg. Looking round, eyes wide in shock, the banshee scream of the Vecian chilled him. Leaning with the longest reach, it had slashed at him with a short sword-like blade and driven a gash across his calf about eight centimetres long. The pain was like fire on his skin and with every heartbeat it was getting worse. Moments later, he looked back again and the Vecian was in pursuit— he had jumped over the gantry handrail and was now following down the shaft with an intense bloodlust.

His mind was working fast now but he needed to slow down the pursuit. It was clear the Vecian didn't have any projectile weapon, or he'd already be dead, but he needed time for his plan to work. Searching Silvers, he found a couple of his beloved grenades. He took one, but he was no weapons expert, so he didn't really know what they might do. He was hoping for a big explosion, a stun grenade, a flash-bang. Taking one with a yellow stripe around it he found writing, which said HE on the side in capital lettering. He might not be security but he wasn't stupid and knew what that meant. He wanted to stop the Vecian but he didn't want to kill himself and Silvers too. Not if he could help it. The second one he took looked more promising: white writing on the side said FLASH BANG. These security types liked to state the obvious— better for everyone, he guessed. Well, maybe not everyone.

He pulled the safety and released the grenade behind him, aiming to the side of the Vecian and not in its direct path. He could hear the shout of alarm from behind him, the Vecian trying to grab something to alter course away from the grenade. Larsen closed his eyes and looked away down the shaft in their line of travel. The sound was intense and short, a punch in his chest and slap to his ears. His eyes were tight shut but still the light was enough to show pink through his eyelids. Disoriented, he waited a moment for the reverberations to dissipate and the shadows to return.

Sparing a look behind himself, he could see nothing. The Vecian was gone. He didn't believe that for a moment. If he could just buy himself and Silvers a couple of minutes—even thirty seconds might do it. He worked fast and multitasked. He sent a message, broadcast to the entire team but for Reeve's attention, 'Reeve. Evacuate the elevator shaft. I want the shaft empty. You have sixty seconds.'

He was coming up to the next floor and gantry. He'd coupled himself and Silvers together on a short tether, so that he had his arms free. Reaching out, he hooked his arm around the gantry handrail, linking his hands together to take the strain. He'd pushed off in a panic and got away too fast, with the addition of Silvers mass, he had too much momentum to easily stop. The force of the breaking on his elbow and shoulder was excruciating, and he gritted his teeth in the effort of keeping silent and the pain controlled but it was intense and he could feel his elbow wrench. The manoeuvre complete and the pair of them now stationary and floating, he slowly untangled his arm from the handrail. No time to think of the pain; he needed to live. He wanted to live.

Moving Silvers first across the gravity threshold, they dropped to the floor in a jumble of limbs. He unhooked himself from their tether and ran to the local control terminal. Working faster than before and sweat smearing the touch screen as he worked, the gravity control screen options came up.

'Elevator gravity reactivated in ten seconds,' he broadcast.

Reeve responded with a curt 'All clear.'

An angry warlike scream full of menace and vengeance came from the shaft, as the Vecian caught the guardrail to the gantry and began to pull itself over the barrier. On impulse, Larsen sprinted the few paces to the Vecian and leapt into the air, planting his feet squarely on the Vecian's chest. The force of the blow pushed the Vecian back out into the shaft and uncontrollably into the opposite wall. Thrashing around in space, it tried to regain orientation and line itself up for another attack but Larsen was already back at the control panel.

Looking across at each other, the Vecian simply snarled in silence, resigned to its doom. Larsen pressed the final button and the elevator shaft gravity reactivated.

HAVERS

He had not realised it, but with the tension and excitement of the attack on the bridge he was sitting on the edge of his seat with his face about as close to the terminal screen as he could get without losing focus. Larsen appeared to have nine lives and Reeve's team had started to force their way into the bridge, encountering fierce resistance as they did so. He felt pretty helpless, as there was no real tactical advice he could offer—it was all happening so fast. Without really knowing it, Larsen had acted as a diversion to the main attack, then Silvers grenade had provided Reeve's team the perfect visual screen to their attack as it quickly filled the bridge with thick, white, obfuscating smoke.

Reeve's security team working in that zero-g, zero-visibility environment was impressive, although the Vecian soldiers were equally tough. Weapons-free, the bridge became a hurricane of death and destruction, people screamed and yelled and took cover where they could behind workstations and couches. Several of the icons representing flesh and blood people flicked to red as a large explosion and white light flashed across the smoke in the room like sheet lightning in a thunder storm. Another icon went to orange as he saw a Vecian face loom out of the cloud and perform a strong and practised four arm grapple on his target. Applying huge leverage to the target's arm, with a twist and wrench it was ripped from the struggling soldier's body, and the soldier slumped, spinning off on a random axis, unconscious with pain, blood gushing from his mutilated shoulder.

More shocks and concussive explosions rocked the bridge, fragments of metal and other debris showered the picture, the images fuzzed with static. From the vid-cams of a couple of the soldiers, he saw another soldier taking cover behind the helm about two metres in front, a severed Vecian limb fell and bounced incidentally off the couch to their side and came to a near stop between them. A flash of precision energy reached out of the smoke and violently struck the soldier in front of them in the chest, knocking him to the side and out of view. No scream, no sound, just gone. They returned fire.

All he could do was watch as the icons on his screen slowly clicked down from mostly green to half green, half red then mostly red. He felt sick to the pit of his stomach; all those people, all those lives lost in seconds. The fragility of life was amplified as he lost most of his security team in less than a minute. Then the noise and chaos stopped. As quickly as it had begun, the fire fight was over.

"Reeve? Report," he almost shouted across the comm. No need for silence or secrecy—he needed to know the situation. There was no response. He highlighted Reeve's icon and motioned her view to fill the terminal screen. She was crouched over the body of one of her command, a man with classic firm jawline and blue eyes, handsome. Reeve was cupping his face and looking into the glazed, far-off eyes. His insistence on knowing what was happening faded, and he waited for her. The moment was hers. Moving her hand slowly, gently down the man's face, she closed his eyes and solemnly, lovingly said goodbye.

"Bridge retaken. Heavy casualties. Unknown damage to bridge. I will send you a full report once I have more." Her voice was empty, cold.

"Okay, Reeve. Give me an update in an hour."

She was looking around but visibility was still patchy due to all the smoke, which was being added to by a couple of electrical fires he could make out emanating from holes punched through terminals and panelling. She seemed to centre herself and then she was once again firing off orders.

"Hobbs, clear out this smoke. Get the ventilation online. Nash, get the gravity back online. You—what's your name?"

"Evans, sir." It was one of the engineering crew.

"Evans, arrange a damage control detail and put these fires out. I want to have this bridge swept for alien devices and traps. Also, an assessment of how long before we can get this bridge back up and running."

"Yes, sir."

The commotion continued on screen—the clean-up would take a while. He would wait for Reeve's report. Sitting back in his seat, he took a breath and peaked his fingers to his lips in thought. They had managed to obtain control of the *Intrepid* again but what the Vecians had been doing on the bridge puzzled him. They had put up a hard last stand and had ultimately been overcome, but there was something about the Vecians' ability to block all their efforts to spy on the bridge before the attack that made him think there was more going on.

"Sir, escort guard approaching." One of the door security team was in contact with the prisoner escort—they were outside.

"Thank you. Take the prisoner to the temporary holding cell." He sent a message to Dr Spencer. 'You're up, Dr Spencer. Prisoner is being escorted to the temporary brig, now. Meet me there in two minutes.'

As he climbed out of the couch and went to make his way through to the makeshift cell to meet Spencer, the door to main engineering opened and through walked a tall Vecian with head lowered and hands bound behind it. It made no attempt to look around or make eye contact with any of its captors; it was subdued and obedient. Hall and Roberts were cautious but professional and guided it through engineering to its holding cell.

Almost everyone in engineering stopped what they were doing to scrutinise the Vecian as it walked past, each with a wary frown of intrigue and uncertainty. This was their first sight of an alien—proof that they were not alone in the universe. The scientist in each of them wanted to ask questions and learn. However, from the short hours of history they had had together, all they had encountered was violence, and the human animal in them was wary. The silence was deafening.

Boyd was in front of the holding cell, door open. He'd had about ten minutes but had worked his magic. The converted store room was empty of items, and only the shelves remained. A table had been welded to the centre of the floor space along with two stools, and the far stool had a restraint harness. "Best I could do in the time, sir."

"Nicely done, Boyd."

Turning to Dr Spencer: "This is your time to shine, Spencer. I need you to bridge the divide. We need to have this thing talking to us as fast as possible. What I want to know is what they were doing here and where their ship is. All other information is secondary. Can you do that?"

Dr Spencer was staring at the Vecian as it was led into the holding cell and seated on the far stool, its arms further restrained by the harness. "Yes, sir." Spencer was looking a little awestruck but that could well have been the prospect of the task to come and the unexpected. "This may take some time," he muttered, almost to himself.

"Dr Spencer, every moment that ship is out there undetected, the greater the risk to this fleet. Be," he reached for the right word, "encouraging." Dr Spencer's face became one of concentration, and his brow furrowed with determination. He nodded, walked straight into the holding cell and sat down opposite the Vecian. The cell door slid closed and locked.

WILSON

Ever since the boarding team had left the shuttle and Grant had sealed the docking hatch, Branner had had the comm system playing across the PA. They had heard the chatter from the team as they ascended to the bridge, they had heard the news of the prisoner taken at the elevator lobby, and they had listened as the terrible slaughter took place on the bridge raid itself. They had sat in mute silence as all these events had taken place, helpless and despondent.

Occasionally, they would review their instruments and search for the invisible alien vessel but none of their instruments showed anything, and visual searching also yielded nothing. The Vecian ship, as Havers had begun to call them, was nowhere.

'We're losing a lot of good people today,' he said via a sub-vocal message to Branner. 'I'd hate to be Reeve right now.'

'Not the point, Wilson,' replied Branner. 'She's a big girl, she'll cope. It's part of the job. What we need to ensure is that this mission succeeds. If you consider that this ship is about one third of all humanity, Havers' tactics are correct and it's worth the sacrifice. Each of those guys knows what's at stake and each of them stepped up.'

'You're starting to sound like the propaganda back home.'

'Don't let the propaganda interfere with the reality of what we're doing here, Wilson. It's far from the same.' He shook his head. 'No ideal I have ever been taught appears to match the reality everyone else is living.'

He shifted his head forward and squinted, as if to look at something incredibly small, then huffed. 'Talking of interference,' he struck the control console, 'we're getting some weird readings from the sensors. It's not localised—the entire array is reading like it's getting feedback. Look, all the stars are becoming more and more intense. Luminosity is increasing.'

'Have you tried recycling the power to the array?'

'Yeah, a couple of minutes ago. If this keeps up the array will white-out in a few more minutes.'

'Diagnostics?'

'All good. Not reading any problems there. Everything is in the green.' Scrunching up his nose in thought, Wilson continued, 'We could take a look at the array. Now comms is not being interrupted, we could use the Rem-Tek? Take a look at the externals.' He was just fishing for something different to do, an alternative to simply listening to the craziness that was going on aboard the *Intrepid*. The disjointed voices and story of destruction and death they told were beginning to freak him out a little, and he wanted to be properly occupied.

'Alright, break out the Rem-Tek. I'm going to check in with Havers. Let him know we're still here.'

He kicked out of his seat and into the flight engineer's couch. Fixing the harness, he then started up the Rem-Tek. Relaxing into the seat, he was spun one hundred and eighty degrees and extended into an almost standing position then the seat inclined forward and lowered him into a haptic suite. He slid his arms into the systems gauntlets and the Rem-Tek visuals meshed with his bio-comms to give him a Rem-Tek's eye view of the space outside the shuttle.

The Rem-Tek was housed in a bulb just forward of the two engines on the upper part of the shuttle fuselage, but as he had already given it instructions on the part of the shuttle he wanted to work on, it had already begun its traverse to the sensor array. It had 360 degree vision from an oval head unit, which, when piloting, took some getting used to: four magnetic feet with opposable, gripping toes—more like the foot of a chimpanzee—and two fully articulated arms with haptic sensory feedback. Some engineers called the Rem-Tek 'The Sloth', due to its physical manner, but he thought of it more like a chameleon. It also had small manoeuvring thrusters for limited excursions away from the shuttle and slightly quicker recovery should it become detached from its anchoring for any reason.

Arriving at the desired location, he put the Rem-Tek to work removing the side panel from the sensor array and reviewing the physical condition of the components. All seemed to be in order— no obvious shorts or blow outs. He plugged the Rem-Tek into the patch panel and began a local system diagnostic, the progress of which slowly made its way across his view as an ever increasing line of green. To kill the sixty seconds or so it would take to complete the tests, he turned his attention to the stars.

He was not prone to vertigo but he was suddenly overcome by a wave of disorientation and, as a reflex, he grabbed the closest thing he could to steady himself, only this had the effect of making the Rem-Tek cling to the support rail next to the access panel. The feeling was one of not really being able to focus. He knew the stars were right there. He could see the star field as expected, but there was some weird difference between the field in front of him and that in his peripheral vision, a disconnect which was giving his senses a spasm, as if things were simultaneously far away and too close. He closed his eyes and turned to the hull of the ship, then opened his eyes again. Instantly, his disorientation went away, as all he could see was the access panel and the expected hull of the ship. Looking back out to space, the disorientation returned. It made no sense.

The system diagnostic completed and a light ping sounded: no errors or anomalies. The issue was not with the array itself. He slowly closed up the access panel while considering the issue.

'Sir,' he messaged Branner, 'is the sensor array still showing the same issue?'

'Yes,' came the immediate reply.

'I don't think it's the array, although there is something weird going on out here.'

'Explain.'

'I'm not sure I can at the moment. I'm going to try something. Wait one.'

He reoriented the Rem-Tek and released his hold on the access panel hand rail. A small kick of the unit's thrusters and the droid began to slowly move away from the shuttle. Two metres, five metres, ten metres, his view was less disorienting but the star field he was looking at had begun to fragment a little, like looking at an oil painting a little too closely, the structure and form of the image was becoming visually meaningless. Fifteen metres, twenty metres. At twenty metres there was a charge of static across his vision and the image began to randomly flash an obscured image of what the Rem-Tek could see. For a moment there was a clear image of a ship's hull and the Rem-tek's outstretched arms touched something solid, then nothing.

He hit the emergency exit button on the Rem-Tek suite and was energetically pulled from the suite recess, the seat realigned itself with the engineering workstation in the cockpit and he released the harness, kicking back to his co-pilot couch as fast as he could.

"We need to get the hell out of here, now!" he called to Branner. "That alien ship is twenty metres off our starboard side."

"What?!" They were both strapping in and getting ready for some hard manoeuvring. "Havers, this is Tusk One. Alien vessel twenty metres off our starboard side. Preparing to release docking and manoeuvre away from threat. Over."

Havers sounded like he'd been caught off guard. "How did you find it?" Ever the engineer, he was already assessing the practicalities.

"Rem-Tek. Physical collision. Their camouflage appears to break down at close range. Five to ten metres," Wilson interrupted.

"Roger that. Get to a safe distance. We'll work on tracking it from here. Keep in touch. Out."

With Havers signing off, Wilson started to speed through his pre-flight checks.

'Okay, team. Aliens knocking on our front door. Time to go,' said Branner, while he prepped the engines. The docking tunnel already detached, it was a quick matter of hitting the manoeuvring thrusters and dropping the ship vertically down from their current position. The *Intrepid's* hull began to blur past due to their speed and proximity, working within a few metres margin of error and at the healthy pace they were moving was going to take every bit of concentration; they would not even be able to roll on their axis safely as they couldn't be sure how close the alien vessel was.

'I'm going under the *Intrepid*.' Branner announced. 'It's the only way we know we'll miss that Vecian ship.'

'Roger that.'

Branner pitched the ship's nose further down and they were now using main thrust to push them towards the belly of the *Intrepid*. They cleared the ship's hull and, as Branner pulled the shuttle round to face its new course, Wilson checked the rear-facing vid-cams to see if there was any movement, or change of scene. For a moment he thought he saw part of space solidify. Part of the Vecian ship was exposed as a small section of the camouflage field seemed to fail. He looked closer at the screen as the g forces of the turning manoeuvre began to bite and his chest and limbs felt heavy and cumbersome in their place. A small hovering star then appeared for just a moment in the centre of the revealed space, then a blinding flash of light lanced towards Tusk One.

CLAYTON

Watching the last sixty-second manoeuvre of Tusk One, relayed from Horus One, he was again wondering what kind of chess game they were playing. What was the purpose to all this? Why had the alien species been so aggressive from the beginning? It made little sense to him. And now they had lost a shuttle, cutting Havers and his team off—for the time being. He had been watching the video on a loop since the end of his conversation with Havers.

If there was any silver lining in the situation at all, it was that they now had a definite position for the alien vessel. It had not completely de-cloaked but the weapon they had used to destroy Tusk One had been visible as it made its deadly strike, and with that they were able to trace an origin point. They knew where the ship was. They could focus all their efforts on trying to track it from its now known location and continue to reveal the ship from beneath its cloak technology.

As soon as Tusk One had been lost, Havers had been back on comms. It appeared to be a complete coincidence. He was initially reporting the successful retaking of the bridge and that, although early, the signs were that they had control of the *Intrepid*. Ellie was back online and they had taken a Vecian prisoner. Apparently, they had started to call the aliens Vecians, due to an inverted delta insignia that appeared on most of their kit and clothing. He also reported that Tusk One had just rediscovered the location of the Vecian vessel approximately fifty metres from the port side of the *Intrepid* and were moving off to a safer distance. With that, all eyes

172

had then gone to Tusk One and her escape manoeuvre. Sixty seconds later there was stunned silence on the bridge of *Endeavour* as Tusk One became a momentary bright light and then disintegrated.

Havers had stopped mid-sentence, obviously also watching his own external cameras and tracking Tusk One on her flight. When he came back on the comm, Clayton had agreed to give him time to review his situation and contingencies.

"I'm keen that you get the *Intrepid* crew active as soon as you can, Havers." He was being direct but there was no need to sugar-coat any of his words—they both knew the situation. "Ellie will be able to help you prioritise the resus routine but I want Captain Carlsen on post fast. They will be waking up into a storm, but some days you don't get to choose."

"Yes, sir. Ellie says she has initiated the process as we have been speaking. We are in a better place than we thought with the resus process here. It was on schedule and under way, until interrupted by the Vecian boarding party. We are still unsure of their intentions and what systems they were able to gain access to and corrupt but we will know more as our investigation continues."

"My concern will be your ability to hold the *Intrepid*, Havers. What is your security situation?"

"I'm waiting for a full report from Lieutenant Reeve after her action on the bridge. My initial estimate is that we lost possibly ten security and three engineers, and there are also some injured. We are officially stretched. Getting the *Intrepid* crew back on active duty will be our first priority." Havers had not been showing the strain but now his voice was giving him away. There was a little wobble in his tone, and a little worry in his response. Clayton made nothing of it— Havers was in a tight spot, and he wanted to help in any way he could.

"We're going to try and get another team out to you as a contingency plan. Hang in there, Havers. Just utilise any measures you can to stop those Vecians from mounting a counter attack and boarding action."

"Yes, sir. *Intrepid*, out."

Roux also had the Tusk One video image on his terminal but frozen at the point the Vecian ship had fired its energy weapon, the white light like a superheated spear across the screen. "That energy build up, does it register on any instrumentation?" he seemed to say out loud but to himself.

"Energy build up? Before the weapon fires?"

"Yes. It must have some sort of signature."

A message interrupted their musings with an urgent alert: it was Hopper. He put vid-com to his terminal and answered the call. "Hopper, what news?"

"I think we have something, sir," he said. He was looking at notes and clearly still piecing data together as he spoke. "Whenever a ship is destroyed, in the moment of its destruction the black box is burst broadcast on a reserved emergency channel. The black box may well also survive but we would need to go and physically locate and recover it. The broadcast can be received by any ship in the area listening on that emergency channel. The moment Tusk One's systems identified hull failure, the broadcast was made—the process takes less than a millisecond—and we subsequently received the transmission.

"We've been reviewing the data, and the point of interest to us was the fact that the Rem-Tek was lost and in the process struck something solid. The hull of the alien ship. And—here's the point—if the Rem-Tek *was* lost when it struck something solid, it means the ship is still there."

"Well, of course it's still there, Hopper."

"But, sir, if it's still there in physical space and hasn't shifted or become ethereal in any way, then we may have a strategy to ensnare it and track it."

"Okay, but please get to the point, Hopper. What's your plan?"

Hopper smiled. "Dust."

Clayton simply stared at him.

"Clever." Dawn said over his shoulder. He hadn't noticed but Dawn had been listening to most of the conversation.

"More to the point, sir: irradiated particulates."

"A dirty bomb?" he considered.

"Sort of. Extremely low dose radiation applied to particulate material that we can spread or deploy about the *Intrepid* or near area. The moment anything physically moves through or comes into contact with the material it will disturb and pick up trace elements. The known radiation signature can then be tracked."

"Is that something Commander Havers could prepare aboard the *Intrepid*? Or would we need to assist?"

"I believe they have the necessary resource and skills. Once we've shared our plans, we should support where needed, but otherwise they will have this covered."

The decision was a simple one. "Contact Commander Havers directly, Hopper. Get this dust cloud in place. Let him know what needs to be done. I want an estimate on delivery. They will have enough to do with the manpower they have. Adding to it is only going to make things tougher."

"I'll make it happen, sir. Will update you shortly." With that, Hopper's image became a black screen, and Clayton closed it down.

*

Rather than use his ready room when he needed peace and quiet to think, he had got into the habit of using the AI core room. He found himself walking down to the room without thinking about where he was headed. He began walking through CIC when the collection of engineering and security staff around the room reminded him of the issues Dawn was going through. He spoke briefly to the engineers on site and they informed him that Dawn's AI core was clear and that they were just leaving. Security would be posted around the clock, as per General St John's direct instruction. They were now off to assist the other teams in the clean and sweep of the other AI nodes around the ship. He thanked them for their good, diligent work. Continuing on, he walked up to the AI core room guard, submitted to a brief security check then went inside and sat down.

As soon as he relaxed, Dawn appeared in a flourish of pixels and colour. "Hello, Daddy."

"Hey there, trouble. How's things?"

"You know how it is. One ridiculous problem at a time."

He smiled. He remembered the first time he had said that to her as a child—she had been about three years old. A time of life where everything you hear is absorbed without effort and repeated without a filter. That was the moment as a parent when you realised you had to hold back and not divulge everything you may think about your neighbour, your friends or your relations. A little person of limited understanding but unlimited mimicry is just ready to take you down in public. Those little mimic missiles were a real leveller.

"What's top of the list?"

"Tusk One just jumped the queue."

"Yeah."

"Hopper's plan sounds like a good one. It might work, if we act quickly and deploy the particulates before the ship moves."

"How will we know if it's moved? We're going to have to just hope it stays put."

"I have a theory about that." A frown crept into her expression, and he instinctively knew more bad news was on the way.

"Okay, what have you got?"

"I think the Vecians are planning another assault."

Clayton slumped. "What makes you think that?"

"I believe the attack on the shuttle was designed to cut off Havers' route of escape. He and his team are now totally isolated on a ship that was never designed for any military purpose. It's effectively defenceless."

"Well, that's not quite true, is it? But, go on."

"Yes. But according to Havers, his security options are now diminishing, as much of the team was lost on retaking the bridge."

Dawn was only stating the facts as she saw them, but the clarity on the situation didn't leave anywhere to hide. If what Dawn surmised was indeed true, Havers was in trouble.

"He does control the ship, and Ellie is back online. He has a massive home advantage if he can control the bridge and engineering. But he's spread thin. We are sending another two shuttles from the Indy but they are going to be at least four hours away. Point defence is not going to be any good against an invisible ship. All he can do is repel boarders and, with the people he has, that's not going to happen. We need another strategy."

"I have an idea, Dad. What about the Rem-Teks?"

"Explain."

"Well, what if we can get enough shuttles into the area with Rem-Tek control interfaces?"

"I see where you're going. Dawn, you get your brains from your mother."

She looked quizzical, "I can't tell whether that's a compliment or not."

"Are you serious? She's the cleverest woman I know."

"Compliment then. You redeemed yourself."

He quickly started putting a plan in motion: they would need shuttles, security personnel, and ad-hoc Rem-Tek interfaces controlled from mobile terminals. He pushed the plans to Captain Straud and she immediately contacted him on comms.

"Captain Clayton, your plans are quite creative. Are you sure they are workable over the distance?"

"Emma, we have to try. Havers is in a tight spot and this is the only way we can get him the help he needs quickly. We are effectively remoting troops to his location. We are concerned about a counter attack by the Vecian vessel."

"Vecians?"

"That's what we're calling them now. Seems to have come from Havers' team. As good a name as any. I'm sure if we ever get to actually talk to them they'll have other ideas, but for now that's what we're calling them."

"Okay, when do we go?"

"As soon as you can get your shuttles launched with the appropriate kit. Let me know when you're set."

"Will do. Straud, out."

She cut the connection. He turned to Dawn, who had been looking on. "Why won't they talk to us?" she said.

"Good question, kiddo. Good question. Maybe they are and we just haven't noticed. Or we did something that put their noses out of joint early on. Or maybe nothing. Maybe they are simply aggressive by nature. No one said our journey would be easy. It's certainly taken more of a left turn than I expected though, that's for sure."

So much for quiet time. "How's your mother getting on?" he asked, while he stood and prepared to make his way back to the bridge.

"Why don't you ask her yourself?"

"Are you being obtuse with me, young lady?" he asked, mostly mocking.

"Not really, Dad. You've had a pretty full schedule since this affair started, and I'm sure Roux can cover while you take an hour with Mum. You and mum could do with letting off some steam. She's been pretty busy with the resus process, but it's mostly complete now. I'm sure she could take some time."

He nodded and put a call into Jemma. It took a moment or two but she answered. "Hey you. How's things up on the bridge?" She was upbeat and happy, a ray of sunshine in his otherwise overcast day.

"Things are okay…could always be better. At least we have a plan now."

"Had a call from St John earlier. He wants to interview me about something. You know what it's about?"

Of course I do, he thought. He hated lying to her. "Nope. I'm sure he'll tell me in the fullness of time." He could feel her picking up on his tone already; he was a terrible liar as far as she was concerned. Initially, he thought it was some tell he had, a twitch in his facial muscles, an involuntary look, but she could even tell when they were speaking over comms. She knew. He had no clue how. He wondered if this was the same for every other married couple in history. Probably not—he was just a crap liar. "Anyway, I was calling to see if you had some time for lunch? Let me know when you've finished with St John and we'll hit the galley."

"If it's a meeting with St John, it won't be good. I could probably do with a stiff drink."

"Now that's a great idea. Only, I've a little too much on for that kind of night out."

"Killjoy."

"That's me." Married banter. Familiar and comfortable, like a verbal hug. Smiling to himself, he cut the call.

He became lost in his own thoughts and the smile turned to a frown. Guilt suddenly kicked in— he needed to get this investigation into the GAIA further along. Pausing, he turned back to Dawn, and her eyes had not left him.

"What's the situation with the GAIA investigation? Has any positive data come back from the search I asked you to perform?"

She paused, as if in thought. "Not yet. I've been conducting your search in conjunction with General St John's work but nothing has turned up yet. However, I started with the resus suite which contained you and Mum. That brought up a negative, so I'm quite convinced we can argue our corner if it comes to it. Mum was awoken from resus on schedule and there is no indication that there has been any overwrite of data on any memory stack related to any cameras in that suite. So, I'm continuing the search though the other data stacks related to other resus suites."

A rush of relief ran through his body, as if all the built-up anxiety had just washed out of him with the release of a valve or an overflow. He never doubted Jemma but to have her innocence confirmed was all he needed to hear. Whatever came next, he could deal with.

"That's excellent news. Carry on with the search. I want to know what suite we're talking about. I'll work on figuring out our next move. We need to be able to isolate the resus unit—that's going to be the tricky part." Even as he said it he could feel his mind beginning to race with possible solutions.

"I've already been thinking about that. Would any of the biometric monitoring give any clues? Heat loss in the unit, heart rate or respiratory monitoring data changes..."

He considered her suppositions. "I would have thought that, if the vid data has been modified, then the bio-monitoring would certainly have been modified too. Look into it though—could turn up something. Are you doing a code check?"

She shook her head in a definite fashion with a stern face. "We've gone over all code related to the function and activation of the units, and there's nothing—no indication that an instruction was sent to any units to awaken their occupant early."

He cradled his chin in thought and sat back down in the couch next to Dawn, going back to the bridge now far from his mind. "What about physical defects? I guess a search of the resus units was one of St John's first tasks?"

"Yes. Although the search was cursory at best. A full search would mean the complete dismantling of every unit in every resus suite and that has not been done."

"So, thorough but not destructive?"

"Yes."

"I can't see St John doing a sloppy investigation. There would be no call for a destructive search, not unless there was evidence to support one. If all the unit diagnostics came back positive then I would doubt he would consider more than a thorough search required."

Dawn didn't seem convinced. "We don't need the resus suites any more, it's not like we're going anywhere else. We've arrived in the Hayford star system and we're not planning any further journeys. It might be necessary."

"He doesn't have the luxury of time. We need to find these guys fast before they take another shot at you." His feelings were intensifying, though he couldn't tell whether it was truly the need to defend the ship or his daughter. The lines blurred between priorities.

As if on cue, a message icon flashed up in his bio-comms—it was St John. He opened the connection. 'Sir, I think we have something.'

He exchanged a surprised look with Dawn. "The game's afoot."

TRAVIS

As he walked into the corridor leading to his accommodation unit, he saw his neighbour also returning from shift. He was a much younger guy on the astro-engineering team, a welder, working on the hull and main structure of the vessels. Usually, the guy was cheerful or drunk, depending which end of the shift you caught him on. Today he was neither. He was repeatedly punching his passcode into the keypad at the side of the door with a look of frustrated confusion on his face.

"Hey," he said, in polite neighbourly fashion.

"Hey," the guy responded, in that way you automatically do.

"Having trouble with your door?"

"I've been at this for 10 minutes. Damn thing won't let me in."

"You contacted Admin?"

"Yep. After the tenth time of punching the same number in. Apparently, the system is fine. They're sending someone down."

He gave a tut and shook his head in sympathy. "Good luck with that."

"Yeah, thanks. It's seriously cutting into my beer time."

Walking over to his door, he punched in his passcode to key open the door. Nothing. "You're kidding," he muttered to himself. With a resigned sigh, he rang the doorbell and heard the electronic buzz from his side of the door. It was late and most likely his wife would be in bed, certainly the kids would be. He messaged his wife: 'Only me. Door won't let me in. Something wrong with the key code.' The message he got back was unrepeatable and made him smirk—he certainly hadn't married her for her classy repartee. 'Come on, Hon, let me in. I'll promise I'll misbehave.' Another candid reply.

He heard the door lock sound a ping as she hit the door release the other side but the door stayed in place. Another ping, another then some muffled verbal cussing. 'It's not opening, Beb.'

Looking across to his neighbour, they exchanged a what-can-you-do moment, "I'm off to the bar. By the time I get back they better have it sorted, otherwise I'll be sleeping on their workstation."

"I'll stick around here. If they turn up, I'll ping you."

"Luck." With that, his neighbour turned and headed back up the corridor and out of sight.

"What was that?" came a muffled voice on the other side of the door. The door release pinged a few times but still nothing happened.

"Nothing, Hon—only the neighbour. He's off to the bar. If this thing doesn't open soon, I may well join him."

"Hey, no fair. It's not your night."

"Not my fault if you're forced to babysit due to a technical failure. We'll do a swap. Promise."

A deep resonant clunk followed by an alarming and loud hissing noise began. He looked up at the ceiling to the corridor and across at the maintenance terminal at the end of the corridor. "What was that?" his wife asked.

"Don't know." He pinged a request to the terminal for a status on his room. Status: OK. No it bloody wasn't. Something was wrong. "Don't go anywhere, Hon. I'm going to the corridor terminal to find out what's going on."

"Where am I going to go?" she responded in a slightly acerbic tone.

Sprinting to the corridor terminal, he brought up the status screen to his apartment: again, all okay according to the system control programs. Temperature, atmosphere, comms, even his refrigerator was all reporting normal.

'Beb! The air! The air pressure is dropping!' Her message was one of panic.

'But the system is saying all is normal. What the hell's going on?' Fuck this. He turned to the emergency panel and pulled the hand lever. The world became a red flashing banshee of noise. He half expected all his neighbours to come leaping out of their apartments to find out what the alarm was sounding for but no one appeared, then the horrible truth of what was unfolding become clear to him. This entire section had been locked into their apartments and the air was now escaping through the ventilation system. If something wasn't done and done fast, they would all be dead. His family would be dead.

His mind completely locked up. Standing, frozen to the spot with incomprehensible fear, the world around him just seemed to fade away. What was he going to do? What could he do?

Coming out of his trance still holding the alarm lever, he felt himself being shaken. Turning round, he found himself looking at the shouting, contorting face of his neighbour, and there was a couple of other guys behind him. He had clearly not made it to the bar before the alarm had sounded.

Finally his ears heard the shouting. "What's going on?"

"The apartments!" he screamed back. "Doors are locked and atmo is venting!"

The guy looked at the terminal and punched some more buttons. All it showed was the alarm sounding in their section, and there would be help on the way. But it wasn't going to be in time.

"We've got to get these doors open," he yelled at the group. "Anyone have any tools on them?" All shook their heads.

"Manual door release," said one.

"There must be fifty apartments here. We won't be able to release them all."

"Go!" shouted another. "Just start, do as many as you can."

Why hadn't he thought of that earlier? He sprinted for his door as the others started work on other doors in the corridor. Approaching his door, in his lead-footed panic, he tripped and fell, cracking his knee on the floor and planting his forehead squarely into the door frame. The world spun and his eyes glazed over, water streaming from the shock and pain. Dizzy, he forced himself to his knees and the panel to the manual door release.

'Hon', get the kids! I need you the other side of this door, now!'

'Okay. Hurry! Not much air.'

His fingers seemed to have grown in size and become solid lumps of unresponsive meat on the end of his hands. He fumbled at the maintenance hatch and dropped or slipped his grip when trying to gain access. The panel removed, he grabbed for the release handle and pulled.

'We're here, Beb.'

The lever didn't shift. He pulled harder, nothing.

'Okay, Honey. Almost there.' He reached into the recess and gripped the release lever with both hands. He pulled with every fibre of his being, all his strength focused into one place, his lungs bursting with effort, pressure building behind his eyes.

'Hrry.'

He could hear nothing but the alarm, and was becoming frantic. A hand appeared on his shoulder and he spun round—it was his neighbour again. "I can't release the door!" he shouted, tears flooding from his eyes.

'Hrr,' came another message.

The neighbour said nothing, simply leant in to help. They both had hold of the release lever and both pulled. This time he had his foot up on the corridor wall for additional leverage but the lever was stuck fast.

As the despair of the moment drew in, his strength started to fade. The light of the corridor returned to its normal white and the siren was replaced with shouting and orders barked in professional tones. People pulled him from the door release panel and he was gently sat across the corridor with his back to the wall, watching the ghost-like rescue crews work with practised haste and precision.

Minutes past and the doors stayed closed, the pressure difference between the two spaces now causing their own issues. A medic had been to see him, patched up the wound on his forehead and bandaged his swollen knee, but he had barely noticed. He knew in his heart his family were already gone but something kept him near. He wanted to run far from the scene, screaming in the madness he felt creeping through him, but something kept him motionless and silent. He felt like he could will them back to him, like he could alter the laws of physics and biology just by concentrating hard enough.

Half an hour and the work around him had slowed. People were still busy and intent on their tasks but the urgency had gone. The reality of the situation apparent to all involved: there would be no survivors.

Forty minutes later and there was another loud hollow sound from the ceiling above them and a rush of air through vents and pipework. Some moments later there was a disembodied shout from further up the corridor and the team in front of him appeared to redouble their efforts with the doors' manual release. There was a low click of locks disengaging within the frame of the door and it popped open several centimetres, a rush of air equalised the rooms pressure, piping what looked like steam into the corridor but was nothing more than condensing moisture vapour. A couple of people cheered but their misdirected sense of achievement fell flat against the overwhelming sombre mood as doors were finally opened and the scale of the disaster was revealed.

He pushed himself up using the wall behind him and staggered like a drunk to the door. The rescue crew parted for him, someone putting a comforting hand on his shoulder as he passed by. The view that greeted him broke his heart where he stood. His wife was sitting on the floor with her back to the hallway wall, their two children cuddled close and gripping tight, her arms completely around their small, delicate bodies. She had held them and comforted them with all the love she could give in their last moments.

His legs gave way and he collapsed to the floor next to them. Putting his arms around them and pulling them close, sobbing and kissing them in grief, he fell into an emotional turmoil of survivor's guilt and self-loathing. He could have done more. He *should* have done more, but in reality what more could he have done? His sense of loss was too much to bear. His mind was becoming fractious, splintering with the distress of total bereavement. A dark void opened up in his mind and, without a moment's thought, he stepped into it—a place of nothing, a place of escape.

*

He threw the sheets off and flicked the bedside light on as he swung his legs round and sat at the side of the bed. Head in his hands, he watched sweat run down his torso. His nightmares left him nowhere to hide; he was not even free within his own head. The memories were always there, reminding him of his purpose, reminding him of why.

Selecting the control from his bio-comms, the shower started and water could be heard raining down on the plastic floor tray then being sucked out through the floor drain. The vacuum wasn't needed when the gravity field was operating but you never knew when there might be a technical glitch, so the vacuum ran as a safety precaution.

He took an old t-shirt and wiped the sweat from his face. Standing, he made his way to the shower unit and absentmindedly tossed the t-shirt into the laundry bin. Being overfull, the laundry bin rejected the additional clothing and the t-shirt fell to the floor to join a small pile of other discarded clothes.

The shower was cold and stern, every droplet like a needle to his skin, but the pain was just another sort of punishment, one which he would endure until his time was over. His mind wandered back to a time a few weeks after the disaster when an investigation had been underway. Once its preliminary findings had been released, the news channels were all over it. They had been on the Earth space station *Arrongate*, the major staging and accommodation station for the project building the new colony ships. Two hundred and eighteen souls had been lost, his wife and children now chalked up as a simple statistic, a quantity to be counted. The reports contained details of the families and people lost, each one like another blow to his already fragile mental state. Via some horrific superimposition within his mind, every face of every child appeared to him as one of his own children, and every woman seemed to have his wife's smiling face.

Most astonishing of all was a short report which hinted that the entire incident was attributable to the station AI. The source of the report had turned out to be the terrorist organisation GAIA, so was dropped as a lead story by the main news networks but the story gained traction on the social media channels and before too long there was a major public and worker backlash. People wanted to know without any doubt that the AI, which had so much control over so much of their lives via support functions like life support, was in no way responsible. There was silence on the issue from those governing and those technically accountable, which only led to inflame people's scepticism.

Almost two months after the investigation had started, a statement was released by *Arrongate* station's administration stating that the AI was being taken offline for maintenance and upgrade, there was no need for concern and there would be absolutely no interruption to function or service. With an entire workforce of scientists and engineers, no one was fooled by the blatant politics. Reading between the lines, the administration were implying that there was indeed a problem with the AI and it would be taken offline and replaced with another. Any reasons they gave were a diversion from the truth and everyone knew it.

A few days later he was approached by his neighbour. They had been allotted different apartments as no one would return to their old apartments but, weirdly, they had ended up as neighbours yet again. Across the corridor this time—not next-door neighbours but neighbours nonetheless. They had gone to a local bar and his neighbour had discussed the idea that the reason the AI had been replaced was because it had become psychotic and the deaths that had resulted had been as a direct result of poor AI management and, more broadly, the flawed assumption that people's consciousness could be content and function correctly within a digital construct. To him, this made total sense and, more than that, it gave him a focus, a reason. In that conversation, all the hate and vengeful emotions that had been entirely focused on himself since the disaster had a route out, a target. The AI had killed his children and his wife—all innocents and all killed without provocation. His thoughts coalesced into a single purpose, and his course was set.

Stepping out of the shower, he dried himself down and dressed. There was no point trying to sleep anymore; his shift would be starting in a couple of hours and his bed sheets were wet through—he would need to change the bed linen. He had become quite used to operating on limited sleep, and this was no different to any other night. He slumped into his chair and flicked on the terminal, deciding to watch a vid on his terminal screen to while away some time the old-fashioned way. He could of course watch using the fully immersive experience through his bio-comms, but sometimes the old ways just worked better.

There was a red light in the top right of his bio-comms view, which flashed momentarily then stopped. His heart jolted with adrenaline and he stood, knocking over his chair. Spinning round, he dived behind the toppled chair and scrambled for the wall. A panel was prepared: a hidden hatch to an adjoining maintenance crawlspace between cabins. He quickly wriggled into the space and relocated the wall panel behind him. The move was just in time. Through the wall he heard his cabin door forced open and a 'plink, plink, plink' as something solid was lobbed into his room and bounced off other metal surfaces. An ear-bursting bang broke the silence and then a rush of boots and voices.

Utilising the noise and commotion, he decided to make a move. Crawling to the end of the short space between the walls, he hooked his arms around the end partition to lever his body and legs into the bigger maintenance corridor behind his room. Worried that they may realise where he had gone, he had arranged an escape plan with this in mind: he would navigate almost entirely via access tunnels and crawl spaces, keeping away from the main corridors and thoroughfares.

He could still hear the shouting, but it was fading as he took the maintenance corridor and quickly wriggled into another adjacent crawlspace. This one was about twenty metres long but would bring him out in a main maintenance corridor running underneath a primary corridor. He still wouldn't be able to stand full height but at least he could crouch and move reasonably fast.

His next job would be to contact the others and let them know the situation; they would probably already know, but he would send them a message as arranged. He found an access terminal and began to punch through systems until he got to the galley admin section. He found the menu listing for the next meal session and desserts were listed as chocolate mousse or apple tart. He made a quick amendment and added key lime pie. It really didn't matter what he added, so long as there were three options: there were never three options, only two. The idea was that it could be passed off as a simple mistake by the galley but his team would understand the underlying meaning and respond appropriately. He closed up the terminal and carried on moving. The menu would be posted to the entire crew at the start of shift. He checked his clock: an hour and ten minutes. Good enough.

The sounds of the ship were the only things he could hear now—no human voices or footsteps, though that was no guarantee of anything. Security could be quiet when they wanted to be, equally they could be trying to track him remotely. They would have Dawn checking every camera and terminal for his whereabouts but he was playing hard to get. His escape and evade plan took the route of least surveillance, and where he was headed there were no cameras. Maintenance corridors had fewer cameras but he had a trick or two up his sleeve, literally. A hack box, of his own design, fitted to his wrist like a remote terminal. However, this terminal was designed to scan the immediate environment for surveillance cameras, hack them and gain access to their feed then scrub the wearer of the box from the feed until the camera was out of range again. It worked perfectly—all his team had field tested them on the ship before they had set off all those years ago, during the final testing and flight trials of the *Endeavour*. In fact, the hack box worked better in the maintenance corridors and crawlspaces, as the chance of incidental human traffic to snare the camera and make it look highly suspicious was far, far less.

Rounding the last corner, a smile broke his lips. A hatch awaited him, small and fairly insignificant but pressurised. A single person air lock. He opened the hatch and crawled inside, no EVA suit or protective clothing, then activated the airlock. The atmosphere cycling process took less than two seconds, as the environments on either side of the airlock were quite close, hardly any pressure differential at all. Opening the opposite hatch, he pushed his way out of the airlock and into zero g.

Illuminated by a dim puddle of light from two low-intensity guide lights either side of the hatch, he floated out into the space between the habitable ship and the outer hull. Due to the poor light, the outer hull was hardly visible, but knowing it was within three metres of the inner hull, he reached out with the ends of his sleeves grabbed in his fists to cover the exposed skin of his hands. The outer hull this far into space would be freezing to the touch, so ordinarily he would have kept to the inner hull hand grabs, but he needed to find the markings.

It took only a moment: a small v shaped notch in the hull metal opposite the hatch pointing towards the belly of the ship but in a south-easterly direction. The notch was not obvious and would most likely be overlooked by all but the most scrupulous engineers, and even then it was unlikely to be taken for what it was—a signpost to his new camp and base of operations. Pushing himself along in the direction indicated by the marking, he flicked on the screen from his hack box. The screen light was only a glow, but in the pitch dark of the outer hull space it was enough to pick out the next marking, ensuring he stayed on course.

At around fifty metres from the hatch he finally saw the cache he had been looking for. They had smuggled three or four of these caches around the outer hull space of each of the ships. They had all they would need for about a two-week window of operations and had figured that would be the maximum they would need, after which they would either have succeeded or failed. Success would mean there would be a change of political leadership and they would have taken the ship for GAIA. Failure would mean death, and they would certainly not be needing any food or resources for the afterlife, so a cache of two week's food, portable power and armaments was all they had stowed.

He gripped the top of a stack of crates as he approached and pulled himself round into the centre. The crates had been arranged in a defensive formation, with a central nest to house a control terminal, power units, food, survival and first aid kit, clothing and medical supplies. There was room enough for about six occupants. He looked for a small, central control box and pressed a couple of switches turning on the associated internal lights within the den. He instantly went to a crate in the corner, opened it and revealed a case of military grade, full EVA-capable armoured suits. He took one and spent the next few minutes putting it on. It was lightweight, much like a wetsuit with smart material which could self-seal or apply pressure to tourniquet limbs if required. There was a slim figure-hugging chest and back plate, which also contained limited thruster capability if remote from a full EVA pack—not much, but enough for emergencies, and for life-support function. The rigid section was also the base frame for many modular gadgets, tools and weapons which the wearer could clip and lock into place, including additional air modules for extended work in vacuum. Boots and gauntlets contained optional controlled magnetic function for working on hull surfaces, and, finally, the suit was completed with a close-fitting enclosed helmet unit that integrated with the wearer's bio-comms as an extension of comms, suit function, weapons control and visual modes, such as infrared, light enhancement or spectral dampening and filters.

Twisting the helmet into place, it locked and completed the air-tight seal. Immediately, the suit powered up and looked to integrate with his bio-comms, the connection was made and he could see initiation checks scroll up through his field of vision: life support, magnetic inductors and medical support all online and OK, no weapon. Sixty years in a crate had not seemed to degrade its function in any way. He was half expecting a leak or some minor suit decay, at least a little maintenance required before he was ready, but he must have just got lucky with his choice. He looked around for another crate, opened it and a rack of carbines were presented to him. He took one in practiced fashion and it instantly slaved to his suit control, appearing as an icon in his view with a zero next to it. Opening another crate marked Ammo .30 Flat Soft, he took a magazine and slid it into place in the carbine, and the zero changed to a fifty.

He was all set. Time to put plans into action.

LARSEN

Gravity had acted as expected on the Vecian soldier, taking him swiftly to his death. Looking over the guard rail down the shaft, he was just able to make out the spidery silhouette of the corpse laying awkwardly, limbs akimbo and body clearly bent horribly over an elevator car structural frame. He realised at some point Havers had powered on internal lighting ship-wide, as he was able to see the Vecian all those levels below. That also most likely meant that Reeve had succeeded in taking the bridge. Things were looking up.

Suddenly remembering Silvers, he looked round wildly and found him slumped up against the wall opposite. He was struggling and clearly in pain. There was a first aid kit against the wall only a couple of metres away; he retrieved it and went to tend Silvers.

"You look like crap," he said with a mild smirk.

"Did we win?" Silvers replied, skirting over the news.

"Yep, think so."

"Hooray for our side," he tried to raise his arm in a gesture of triumph but winced heavily and cradled it quickly with the other. "Shit, I think I dislocated my shoulder."

"You need attention. We need to get you to the medical bay." He was rummaging through the first aid kit pulling out bandages and trying desperately to remember how to tie a sling for a dislocated shoulder.

"I need that blue tube in the first aid kit."

Pulling out the tube, he looked at it. Morphine—that would work.

"Okay, here goes." He pulled off the cap over the short stubby needle and firmly applied it to Silvers' shoulder. There was a short click and hiss as the morphine was injected. Silvers' face went from a grimace to a very satisfied smile. "And...relax."

Silvers slumped, head back looking at the ceiling, eyes closed, enjoying the relief from the pain and discomfort across the rest of his body.

"You know, saving your ass is becoming a full time job, sir."

"Saving me?" At least Silvers hadn't lost his sense of humour.

"Sure. I don't see you with a scratch. I must have been doing all the work." He shifted and winced again. "I think I've also cracked a rib."

"I think you've cracked your skull. You're talking gibberish." They both started to laugh, the tension of the attack and surviving and perhaps a little of the morphine giving them release.

Silvers grabbed his side with his good arm, "Stop. Don't make me laugh," then coughed momentarily.

They calmed down again and Larsen began to apply the sling to Silvers dislocated shoulder, with a reminder here and there from Silvers. When done, they sat and rested for a few minutes, each in their own thoughts.

"Silvers, there's been something bugging me about the elevator lobby."

"How so?"

"Well, when we came through first time, you were pretty thorough. Could anyone have survived your attack?"

Silvers grunted, "You too? It crossed my mind, but I've not had time to review the vid logs. Wait a second."

"Even if we can't remember, if we saw it, it will be in the logs." He started to scan through his own visual logs. They hadn't been running the whole time, but they had been both been recording during the initial escape and evade, also during the attack on the bridge. He was hoping the previous logs hadn't been recorded over.

The logs were intact and he replayed them. They both sat there in silence working through the vid footage. He started the feedback from the moment he dropped into the elevator car, dark and subdued with only partial lighting, although up close as he was it was not hard to pick out the Vecians' rag doll bodies slumped around the floor. Where had the live Vecian been found? Near the door under another body. He waited for the view to sweep past the door. There. It was momentary; he froze the image. His fears were confirmed.

"I've got a single body by the door. How about you?" he asked.

Silvers scrunched up his nose as if a bad smell had just been detected. "It had been alive after the grenade, so I'd put an extra bullet in it. Single head shot." He shook his head, "No way it survived that and there was nothing underneath, you can see the blood across the floor." Grizzly as that was, it meant that at that close range the bullet had passed through, so anyone lying underneath would also have caught a bullet. But there hadn't been anyone underneath.

"Any chance any of the others survived and moved?"

"Nope. There was just mess and death in there. Nothing survived. I'm sure about that now."

They looked at each other with the same question on their minds. Silvers verbalised it; "So, where the hell did that live one come from?"

"That is the million dollar question. We need to warn Havers."

He quickly copied the frame image from the feed that showed the one dead Vecian near the elevator door and sent a call in to Havers. It was answered almost immediately.

"Larsen, what's your situation?"

"Sir, I've sent you a peg. Something was bugging me about the Vecian prisoner, and I've just now been able to confirm with Silvers." He knew Havers would be reviewing the image as he spoke. "You need to know, sir, that the Vecian prisoner wasn't there when we first made contact in the elevator on our way to main engineering. We are certain that all those we left were dead and the image shows that where the prisoner was found under a second body, there was originally only a single body."

"What purpose would they have in pretending to be dead?"

"I can think of only two reasons, sir. Either they were on route to somewhere and were interrupted when the attack team arrived at the elevator lobby and were hiding in plain sight hoping we'd pass by," he paused.

"Or?"

"Or, they wanted to be taken prisoner."

Havers was silent for a moment, possibly linking with someone else. When he came back online, it was brief: "Regroup with

Reeve's team, I want you on the bridge. Out." The bridge? He needed to get Silvers to medical.

He was unsure what was going on but he was pretty sure it wasn't good. He put in a connection to Reeve. He sent the same peg with the comm request. Reeve was on comms straight away. "Thought you were dead," she started.

"Nice to hear your voice too," he responded.

"What have you got for me. A peg file? What am I looking at?"

"This is where the prisoner was hiding when Silvers and I went through first time. As you can see, there is only one dead Vecian. Not the stack that would have allowed the live one to stay hidden."

"What are you thinking?"

"Same as you."

"Trap?"

"Trap."

"How do you get into a locked room?" he surmised, leading Reeve.

"You get the guy with the key to let you in." There was an audible clenching of teeth. "Shit."

"What's your status there? Can you get eyes on main engineering?" It was a hopeful request. If anything had happened to change the balance of power in main engineering, he doubted they would.

"God damn. It's the old quarterback sneak. Oldest play in the book."

"No time for that. What can we do?"

"From here? Very little. You're the engineer. Think of something."

She was right. "Can you spare some men?"

"I can give you four."

"Okay, get them to medical. That's where we'll be. They have fifteen minutes. I'll keep you posted. Let me know if you hear anything from Havers. I'd consider him compromised and in real danger until proven otherwise."

"Copy. Out." Reeve's connection went dead.

Having heard half the conversation, Silvers started to haul himself up. "Why am I starting to feel like a tennis ball?"

"You don't seem the type to like tennis," he said in honest reply.

"I like it even less now," he retorted, cradling his cracked rib.

He checked his bio-comms for routing to the medical bay. Three floors and two hundred metres. At least they should have no interruptions en route. As far as they were aware, there was only one Vecian left aboard and nowhere near them. They set off at Silvers' best pace.

HAVERS

Larsen's report had sent a sudden chill up his spine. There could only be one reason, in his opinion, why the Vecian had given itself up. It wanted to be where it was now, in engineering. It could have easily diverted around the team coming up the corridor. If it was on its own, as it appeared to be, it could have hidden almost anywhere on the ship. They would have found it eventually, especially with Ellie's assistance, but there was no need for it to have given itself up in the fashion it had done. What he needed to work out was why it wanted to be in engineering.

He walked through to the temporary medical bay, and Dr Sommers was watching the feed from Dr Spencer's bio-comms on the room's wall-mounted screen. Dr Spencer was conducting First Contact Protocol Linguistic Procedures. Boyd had clearly given Dr Spencer a remote terminal and he was running through images, items, objects and the English noun would be spoken by a disembodied voice from the terminal.

"This is incredible," said Dr Sommers, not even turning to acknowledge his presence—maybe he was talking aloud to himself.

"What's incredible, doctor?"

"The Vecian is perfectly parroting every word Spencer is playing. He keeps turning the speed of test up and the thing just keeps pace."

As he watched, the Vecian's skin completely changed colour, cyan to magenta, it would repeat a dozen more words then its skin would change colour again, magenta to yellow, yellow to cyan.

197

"How is it doing that?" he asked.

"Not how, why?" said Sommers.

"Okay, why is it doing that?"

"I have no idea."

Dr Spencer stopped the library of images and then selected ones at random and showed the Vecian. Without pause or prompt it stated the correct noun with perfect diction.

"This thing has incredibly advanced linguistics. Even the fastest linguists back home need at least a week to learn the fundamentals of a language. This thing has done it within a couple of hours. A limited vocabulary of nouns and verbs. It has even picked up some adjectives from my limited interactions with Spencer." He was clearly in an intellectual place of wonder but Havers had to start to get some answers.

"Dr Sommers, I really need to start getting some relevant responses from this Vecian. I need to understand what it's doing here and why they are so hostile. Since we arrived, they have killed most of our team and destroyed our shuttle. We believe their ship is about to mount a counter attack, so we need some answers fast."

"Can we stop them?"

"If they attack again?"

"Yes."

"We've managed to get the point defence system back online. That may slow them down for a while. As long as they are cloaked, we have no way to target them and it appears that while cloaked they can't perform any aggressive manoeuvres. So we're at an impasse." Pausing to think further, he continued, "It's only the calm before the storm though, Sommers."

Sommers nodded in agreement. "Okay Commander, we'll get you the information you need. At this rate we'll be having quite meaningful conversations within the next hour."

"Sounds promising. Keep me informed. Thanks, doctor."

*

Leaving the medical room, he went to find Boyd. Boyd was up to his elbows in electronic components, amplifier units, transmitter boards, receiver boards, control circuits—it looked like junk to him but Boyd wallowed in this stuff.

"Talk to me, Boyd. Give me good news."

Boyd just looked at him like someone who knew all the answers, which he obviously did. A giddy enthusiasm babbled forth, "Whoever came up with this plan is a genius," he stated.

"We have a few in the fleet."

"True. Anyway, to answer your question. The good news: it's going to work. We have about one hundred Rem-Tek units throughout the ship, and there's not even any modification to the unit required, just the control unit, which is what I'm putting together here," he motioned broadly across the workbench.

"This," Havers observed, "is a mess."

"This," Boyd replied, "is a prototype. Some people are just too damn picky." Slotting a small component board into place, Boyd stood back like a proud parent. He turned to Havers, "You want to test it?"

"Already?"

"Well, it may not look pretty, but in should work. It's slaved to the Rem-Tek in the corner."

He hadn't noticed, but standing dormant in the corner was the relaxed, slumped form of a Rem-Tek. "You should have the honours, Boyd. Show me," he motioned with a nod to the droid.

With his bio-comms slaved to the terminal as a controller, the droid then slaved to the terminal via the more powerful signal-boosting transceiver unit, the Rem-Tek servos whirred and operational status lights on its chest flickered through a sequence, finally settling on green. Its whole body shifted and it stood straight. With a slightly strange gait, it walked over to Havers and extended a hand towards him in greeting. Looking across at Boyd, he was standing with his eyes closed, clearly interfaced with the droid in front of him, but with a wide smug smile of success on his face. Havers shook the robot's hand in an appreciative manner.

"Well done, Boyd. This is some piece of work."

"Damn stunning." Disconnecting himself from the controller terminal, Boyd continued, "I'll have the additional components tidied up, make the terminal a little more presentable and workable, then some additional tests, then weapons tests."

Havers started to get that sinking feeling. The feeling he got when a project completion suddenly seemed a long way off again after some very exciting proof of concept.

"How long?"

"Couple of hours."

"You have thirty minutes. Procure anyone you need. This is your top priority. How many can you get up and running in the next couple of hours?"

"With the available manpower? Five. But to be effective they need to be operated by security, not techs. We only have four of those and two are guarding that alien." Boyd had a valid point.

"So we have two effective fighting units. Two is better than none and we can use the others as eyes. Engineers can operate from here. The worst that can happen is they lose a Rem-Tek."

"If you say so."

"I say so. Let me know when we're set. I'll send the security guys through." Turning to leave, he called back, "And that's bloody good work, Boyd. Bloody good work."

A few minutes later, Boyd had his men and was busy building, testing and training. Havers had taken one of the security from the main door and they would train in shifts. It would leave them exposed for a short time but he figured it would be for a limited time and, if they came under heavy attack, how would two cope any better than one? He was seriously under-manned on security as it was.

He decided to spend some time compiling a report back to the *Indianapolis*. They would need all the intelligence they could get if they were looking to mount a defence. With Ellie's assistance, he compiled an operational status report and also a list of all the access codes to remote the Rem-Teks. Within thirty minutes they should be ready.

BOYD

When the chaos came it came fast. There were explosions and yelling from the main engineering control room and Havers was suddenly speaking to him on an emergency channel. It was short. "We're under attack! Get you and the Rem-Tek out of here!"

"Shit!" Out of here? Where?

He grabbed a couple of tools and stuffed them into his belt, then took the remote terminal, barking orders as he did so. People began to scatter through hatches and further into the bowels of engineering. The security guy who had been with him for all of fifteen minutes looked at him with grim features and steely eyes and, with unsaid communication, took up his carbine and moved in the opposite direction to everyone else, back towards the control room.

"Damn it!" he said aloud to no-one and ran towards the stern of the ship. He had to find somewhere to hide and take the Rem-Tek with him, but more than anything he needed to hide the evidence of what they were working on. Letting the Vecians know about their trump card would be a disaster—even more of a disaster than not being ready to defend their current position. They were stretched too thin over the ship; that issue was self-evident. But how many of these Vecians were there? Were they going to be back at square one in a matter of minutes? Unacceptable.

A determination began to drive him. He was going the wrong way—he needed to stay local. He may not be security, he may not have a weapon, but engineers could play dirty too.

He had coupled the Rem-Tek he had been working on to the remote he was carrying, and while moving through the ship the Rem-Tek kept pace and followed him a couple of metres behind. He had been walking at a reasonable speed all the time, looking out for somewhere to hide and set up base. As he rounded the end of a corridor, his comms pinged a request from Ellie. He answered.

'Hello, Boyd,'

'Hello there, little miss. I'm a bit busy at the moment, so if we could keep things short.' He kept moving, the conversation not really interrupting his work, and hoped she had something useful to tell him.

'I wanted to warn you that you're approaching a group of Vecian troops. They are at the end of this corridor and moving towards you. You have fifteen seconds.' Yep, that was pretty important.

His eyes quickly scoured the near corridor for any means of escape. A maintenance hatch two metres back, a vent too small for access and a door to the right leading to a workshop. The Rem-Tek was standing directly in the way of the maintenance hatch and the vent wasn't really an option, so he stepped quickly into the doorway of the workshop. All kinds of fabrication machines sat in various positions around the room, including rail-controlled and gravity-controlled trolley guides for material and product movement. There was a control room, raised to oversee the shop floor—he could use that as an initial hide. He thought it was a little obvious, but he might be able to use the Rem-Tek to provide a short-term diversion while he made his escape.

Throwing himself down to the floor and out of sight of the workshop control room windows, he instantly connected his bio-comms to the Rem-Tek via the remote terminal. It was in the corridor, where he'd left it, next to the maintenance hatch. His point of view was now that of the Rem-Tek facing down the corridor, and framed by the corridor walls like a monochrome image, was the dark silhouette of three Vecians. They had clearly seen the Rem-Tek and, not knowing quite what it was, they were being cautious.

'Five seconds,' came Ellie's warning.

Their caution gave him a few more seconds of thought. He acted. The Rem-Tek moved forward and closed the gap, launching a ferocious punch to the face of the first Vecian while simultaneously grasping the throats of the other two. The first Vecian recoiled, falling and sitting comically stunned on the floor. The other two tried by reflex to release the grip of the mechanical hands round their throats but the Rem-Tek raised them with force to the corridor ceiling, and he heard a sickening crunching sound as skull or vertebrae gave way under the action. The bodies fell limply to the floor.

The first Vecian had regained some clarity and fired his weapon. At a range of a metre, the shot was point blank and could not miss. The Rem-Tek body casing disintegrated, becoming thousands of splintered shards of flying shrapnel. The power cell was less forgiving. With its protective casing stripped away, it destabilised catastrophically. The blast vaporised ten metres of corridor and the overpressure blew out the windows to the control room Boyd was hiding in.

His ears were nothing but pain. No sound, just dullness and pain. He tried to get up but he fell sideways as the information his brain processed about the world around him failed to make sense. He tried again, this time using the workstation in front of him as a support. Glass was everywhere, little cubes of failed toughened lamina. Blood dripped to the floor from a gash in the heel of his hand. He needed to get patched up and get going. There was a first aid kit on the wall, which he took, along with the remote terminal, and headed for the workshop's rear exit, leading further into the ship.

'Ellie, you still there?' he asked. A moment ago he just wanted to be alone and far from the violence in main engineering, but now all he wanted was a familiar voice.

'Yes, Boyd. I'm here.'

'Well, that live test went well.' He could not tell whether the grin on his face was for the pain or the punch line.

'I take it you're being facetious?'

'Damn right, I'm being facetious. If those Rem-Teks are going to nuke every time they get shot, they're no use to anyone.'

'They will need additional armouring around the power cell.'

'Why is nothing ever simple?'

'Would you like me to answer that?'

He didn't respond. There were a million things going round his head. Least of which was what to do next. He needed to find another Rem-Tek and modify it without getting caught by the

Vecian roaming patrols. Maybe exploding droids would slow them down a little, but he was on the clock.

'Where's the nearest Rem-Tek unit?'

'I'll direct you.' Navigational data arrived and overlaid in his view. Thirty-five metres, down one level. He started along the route provided.

The Rem-Tek was powered up and ready when he got there. A thought hit him like a slap in the face. 'You can activate these things?' It was asked, but it was more like a statement of fact. 'We don't need the others from the *Indy* to control these things. You can do it.'

'I can only utilise the Rem-Teks for their designated purpose. No other.'

'You mean no military purpose,' replied Boyd. 'Shit. The AI Laws.'

'I am bound by them, like all AI'

Boyd remembered the law, famously amended to the Geneva Convention under great historical fanfare and bluster after a Chinese military-developed AI decided to go loco and killed one thousand and thirty-eight civilians using conventional but grouped land-based police weapons and slaved drone aircraft. The public outcry had been global and politically crippling even for the normally hardened grip of the Chinese government. It was decided that no single AI should wield that level of power again and, as such, all military drones or remotely operated weaponry should have a single human conscience behind its actions. Not that AI technology didn't have a single human consciousness at its core, but AI was plugged into and had far more technologically augmented power, such that controlling hundreds or thousands of remote drone objects was possible. A single person, however connected, could still only process enough information to control a single device. It was one to one. The point being that there could not be that level of unilateral destruction wrought again. Boyd considered the law to be flawed, as it had never stopped dictators inciting genocide in the past, and that was a single human consciousness in a single human brain. Murder is still murder. He grunted in derision.

'What's the ETA on the shuttles from the *Indy*?'

'Another hour yet.'

'This will be over in half that. We need to speed things up.

Round up the engineers and direct them to workshop four. It's the furthest from main engineering and should give us some time while these damn aliens try and figure out where we've gone. Also, send ten Rem-Teks there. And get the guys to pick up a remote terminal each on the way.' He was focused now, a plan was formulating and it took some of the fear from the situation. Lastly, he thought aloud, 'Where's the nearest armoury?'

'Two levels down, one hundred and six metres.'

'Divert three Rem-Teks to pick up ten carbines and ammunition.'

'Sir…'

He interrupted, 'I'm not asking you to shoot anyone, just carry some blocks of metal of varying sizes back to the workshop. They just happen to look like carbines and bullets. Can you do that?'

'Yes.'

'Well, good. Let's get to it.' He moved off, picking up the pace now that he was fired up. They would be ready.

SPENCER

They had just started another session, a brief history of humanity, and were going over the invention of powered flight by the Wright brothers in the old United States of America when the Vecian made his move. With the first explosion from main engineering and the momentary lapse of attention from the guard at the door, the Vecian struck with swift and surgical power. Somehow, it had been able to escape its restraints completely, sliding across the table, skipping around Spencer, slamming itself full force into the guard. With its full momentum coming to an instantaneous stop due to the bulkhead behind the guard, the guards ribs cracked and popped. The guard crumpled, gasping and coughing, blood splattering to the floor. The Vecian finished the guard with a grappled twist of the head, severing the spine, and life left the body instantly. Spencer noted the guard had not even the time to get off a shot, the carbine now lying dropped and discarded by the doorway.

Moving back round the table with easy, confident motion, the Vecian sat back down to face him. His mouth open and heart racing, Spencer found himself somewhere between impressed and terrified. The alien's eyes levelled at him and he found himself scrutinised; the tables had turned in a moment and he was no longer in control. He wondered if he ever had been.

"Continue," the Vecian said, and in that one word Spencer knew they had made a terrible miscalculation. Humanity had forever misjudged difference. It was almost inbuilt to imagine 'foreigners' as having lower status, intellect or power, especially if they didn't speak your language. Others may have a different way of doing things and those ways may not be ones you consider palatable or moral. History was full of the arrogant being shown their failings, and this was just another one of those times.

Sweat had begun to prickle his upper lip but his mouth had completely dried up. He made a concerted effort not to look over his shoulder at the fallen guard; it would do his nerves no good and he certainly wouldn't be able to help in any way. He was alive because he wasn't a threat and because he was providing something that the Vecian wanted. He would need to continue in that vein. He reached for the terminal control but his hand was shaking uncontrollably—he was terrible at keeping cool, or even appearing cool when under severe pressure. He flapped his hand at the screen control, it managed to connect with the button he wanted and the slide-show continued. Clearing his throat, he tried to speak but a croak made him splutter. Swallowing hard, he managed to force his way on.

The struggle outside the temporary cell was deafening on occasion but the Vecian didn't appear to flinch, being so concentrated on the lecture Spencer was giving. Spencer, however, jumped or cowered in fear with every explosion or ricochet, scream or shout and could not control his reactions. It was all he could do to keep talking and fulfil his role as teacher and educator—the role keeping him alive. Although the thought of what would happen when he had completed his presentation had started to arise in his subconscious, along with what he might do, whichever way he played it in his head, the result was always the same and not in his favour. He was beginning to panic.

It must have shown and his performance must have been off because the Vecian raised one of his hands, palm towards him. Spencer froze and his eyes went wide, but the Vecian simply spoke in a calm tone, "Please. Do not worry. Continue."

Do not worry? Why should he worry? He was only sitting in a box room with a dead security officer a couple of metres behind him and a psychotic alien with an insatiable appetite for learning a metre in front of him across the table. The explosions and gun fire occurring in engineering were clearly commonplace. Well, you know how crazy engineers are, they do this kind of stuff all the time. Of course I'm bloody worried, you moron! His inner monologue peaked, then a calm began to descend on him. It was a quiet inner peace, one of resignation to the facts about him and the realization that there was little he could do before his demise. He was certain of his future. In the next few minutes he would be dead, and he would prefer not to go out with a whimper.

The carbine was only a couple of metres away. He might be able to reach it. He started putting a plan together in his mind. Push the remote terminal at the Vecian to distract him while spinning from his chair towards the carbine on the floor. He would pick up the weapon in one fluid motion and blow the Vecian murderer back to the hell that he came from. He considered it for a moment more.

He nodded at the alien to indicate that he watch the terminal screen once again. The Vecian returned the nod and began to watch the screen once more. Spencer acted. Pushing the terminal hard it shot across the table, lifting as it went to contact the Vecian in the face. He spun out of his chair as fast as he could and leapt for the carbine on the floor by the dead guard. The fluidity of the motion was far less graceful than he had planned it in his mind, in fact he fell out of the chair and in leaping for the carbine almost twisted his ankle and planted his face heavily into the bulkhead as he overestimated the distance.

Eyes watering and stumbling to get back on his feet he scooped up the carbine and pointed it at the Vecian who was now standing the other side of the table with a face like thunder and malice. Applying pressure to the trigger, he expected a staccato of bullets and an end to his current threat, but the trigger didn't move, being locked in place. Having even five minutes weapons training would have saved him. He pulled the trigger again but still it did not move and the carbine didn't fire. The Vecian's eyes narrowed, his head tilted to one side, weighing up the situation.

He began to shake uncontrollably. He assumed the carbine was jammed or malfunctioning in some way. The temperature appeared to raise several degrees and his heart felt like it was trying to escape his chest. He slumped his head and dropped the weapon. He fell to his knees in despair and began to sob.

A strange sound then erupted around the room. A crackling, wheezing noise that made Spencer more on edge than the physical violence he had been expecting. Looking to the source of the sound, he was surprised to see the alien sitting again in the chair and what seemed to him to be laughing. The Vecian was rocking slightly and had one of his arms pointing at him, extending a finger in his direction, with the other arms all appearing to be cradling his belly. To Spencer, at least, it looked like Vecians exhibited similar traits to humans when laughing at someone else's misfortune.

After what seemed like an hour, but was most likely only a few seconds, the Vecian managed to stand, walked round in front of Spencer and picked up the carbine. Looking it over and examining it, he began to laugh hysterically again whilst returning to his seat. Discarding the weapon on the table, he also picked up the terminal from the floor where it had come to rest after being thrown as a distraction and put it back on the table.

In his desperate state, he didn't have any idea what to do next—all his options were spent. A tap on the table focused him, and the alien was staring at him again with a fixed expression, having hit the table to get his attention. Again, he pointed at the terminal and spoke. "Teach."

A volley of shots rolled around the corridor outside the room, which gave him a physical jolt and got him up. He sat back into the chair opposite the Vecian and began to teach.

BOYD

Workshop 4. Boyd walked briskly through the main double doors and found a line of Rem-Teks in neat order in the central walkway, cases of munitions stacked at one end. Milling around, some pacing, some chewing their nails, some sitting on workbenches staring into the distance, all agitated and all silent, were a group of engineers and Dr Sommers. As he entered the room they all looked up, and a couple jumped with an overabundance of anxiety. The doctor came forward and greeted him, although even before Sommers opened his mouth he could tell there were only questions. The good doctor was fresh out of ideas on what to do next. Luckily for those in the group there were no injuries, only the faces of a team who had been slapped and slapped again. Motivation was at a low. That was fine; he would soon turn that around.

"Boyd, any news?" asked the doctor as he looked Boyd over for injuries.

"Those Rem-Teks go up with a bang," he responded, trying to keep the mood light. He needed the team to act and act quickly. If he laid the situation out as he truly saw it, he feared it would tip them over the edge. "In other news, I took out a patrol of Vecian on my way here. I don't think they'll be worrying us for a while." He hoped his face was a mask of confidence, as he certainly didn't feel it. The doctor noticed the wound on his hand and motioned to Boyd to sit up on a work bench. "No time, Doc. We've got work to do."

"Well, take the opportunity while being treated to address the team." He had a point. It wouldn't do for his hand to be bleeding over all the equipment he would need to work on. Electronic circuits tended not to like blood dripping and oozing over them—they got a little sparky and stopped working.

He nodded to the doctor and heaved himself up onto the workbench, rolling his sleeve away from the mess of blood around his hand. When he was satisfied that the doctor was busy and wouldn't interrupt, he looked up at the assembled. They were all staring at him. No officers, all ratings, but engineers and exactly the people he needed. 'Every cloud…', he thought to himself.

Collecting his thoughts, he raised himself up, unconsciously moving his hand and getting a tut of admonishment from the doctor. There were a few there he recognised and had worked with before; he would pin them with the lead tasks. "I'll open with the bad news." Antiseptic spray to his hand derailed his train of thought for a moment. "Doc, maybe after would be best?"

"You're all done."

"Thanks."

Redressing his cuff, he turned back to everyone but stayed seated on the workbench. "Right, the bad news. The bad news is that we are currently in the dark as to what is going on, we are pursued by some alien species we know nothing about, or next to nothing about, and we are split between here and the bridge." There were visible nods of agreement around the room. "Well, this needs to change. Some bright spark on the *Endeavour* has given us an out. A means to fight back."

"How are we meant to do that? We're engineers." It was one of the team he didn't know so well—Higgs, Biggs, something like that.

"Biggs is it?"

"Higgs." That cleared that up.

"Higgs, the plan is this," he pointed at the Rem-Teks and sent a short range broadcast to everyone with the plans of the modifications that would be needed. "These little guys here are going to be our eyes, ears and weapons platforms. We are turning them into soldiers."

"Not possible," piped up another. He didn't know this guy at all. "Their programming prevents them from operating weaponry of any kind."

"Two tricks in our solution. First, we have circumvented any block to their control of the situation by making all firing commands required by a remote operator. So, technically, and from their point of view, they are not making the decision, so do not stop the action. Secondly, the Vecian are not human. There is a logic loop there that we can exploit."

"That works," said another, followed by a storm of discussions. Everyone suddenly injected with ideas, more importantly, optimism. They hadn't even heard the part about a fight back or that they needed to act now and fast. Being engineers suddenly given a problem to solve, they were happy and had purpose. The rest of what was going on in the ship had already faded into the background. Boyd raised his hands to get the attention of the group back under control.

"Hey!" They fell silent, attention back on him. "I want two teams and production lines, first two complete Rem-Teks off the run in 30 minutes." There were a couple of low whistles. He clapped his hands to break the spell and there was instant action, people moving with purpose and urgency. He then realised that, in addition to all this, his hand now hurt like hell. Goddamnit! He turned to face the doctor, who was sniggering at his absent-minded action.

"You should be more careful with that."

"Thanks, I'll take it under advisement. Got anything to dull the pain while I work?" He was being hopeful.

"Nope. Left main engineering in a hurry. Forgot most of my kit, pills included."

"Yeah. Being shot at does do that to you." After a moment looking at all the activity and furious fabrication going on, he nodded in the direction of the team and asked "So, what are you going to do?"

"Not sure. Only you had any sort of injury and you're fixed."

"Coffee?"

"Don't mind if I do."

"Not you, knucklehead," he said lightly. There weren't many times a week that he got to call the doctor names. It was quite satisfying. "Coffee for the team. It's going to be a long day. You could call it treatment, of a sort."

"It's lucky for you that I know there's a coffee machine in the control deck here. It'll keep me busy for a while," and he headed off with purpose.

"Cream, two sugars. Thanks, Doc." Sommers waved a lazy response to acknowledge the request.

The teams were hard at it, but what he needed next was information. He needed to contact the bridge and find out what was going on. Technically, the doctor was the highest ranking person in the room, but he'd shown no interest in taking the lead. Someone had to. So far he was the guy with the plan, which probably made him the guy everyone would look to. Not what he preferred, he was much more at home building things than managing people, but at a push he could do it. It was time for him to do a bit of delegation. Fun, he thought, being facetious to no-one but himself.

"Ellie," he messaged with his bio-comms. He wandered between the workstations to find a projection point. Ellie's image spiralled into being.

"Hello, Boyd."

"What's the status of the ship?"

"Fully operational. I've cleaned and restarted all systems affected by the Vecian attacks and purged my systems of active malware." Good news. "The point defence grid is operational, life support is also at levels consistent with the requirements of the current compliment. The first crew members to be revived will be arriving in the resuscitation suite in approximately 40 minutes."

"What do we know of the Vecian ship? Where is it?"

"Unknown. Last contact was 100 metres off the starboard side, near section AF airlock 188."

"Okay. If they try to board again or become uncloaked, inform me immediately."

"Certainly."

He switched to the local terminal and put in a call to the bridge. The strike team should still be there. After a moment, the face of Lieutenant Reeve appeared, smoke rolling around the view, smudges of grime on her cheek and forehead. It looked like whatever they were doing was hot work.

"Lieutenant. Boyd. Just wanted to report. There was an attack on Engineering. Have you heard from the Commander?"

"Boyd, what's going on? We lost contact with the Commander thirty minutes ago. I've not been able to raise anyone in engineering since."

"When the attack occurred, the Commander ordered us to disperse and move further into the engineering decks. I'm with a group of about fifteen, including Doc Sommers. We're busy working on our response."

"The Rem-Tek mods?"

"Yes."

"The Commander informed me in his last communication."

"Excuse me for asking, but who's running the show now?" Reeve didn't seem surprised by the question. She looked at him grimly.

"Until we can confirm the whereabouts of the Commander, Lieutenant Larsen is now mission commander."

"Okay. He's not with you?"

"No. I sent him four men. He was in Medical, but he's most likely now on his way back to main engineering."

"Copy. I'll contact him and give him an update."

As Lieutenant Reeve cut the connection, Boyd immediately opened a connection to Lieutenant Larsen using his bio-comms. There was no guarantee that Larsen would be near a terminal and he needed to contact him quickly. His bio-comms immediately registered the response. Larsen was twenty metres from main engineering. He was to hold position and await further instructions. Great. Well, at least he wasn't sitting on his hands. Looking across at the Rem-Teks on the workbenches, he could see the team were making good progress. He took a moment to update the plans to include additional armour and containment around the power source. There was no way he wanted a repeat of the episode in the corridor earlier, not while he was anywhere near one. Making the alterations in moments, he fired off the update to Higgs. He saw Higgs register receipt of the modification. Time for that coffee.

LARSEN

Returning to engineering had been a lot simpler than leaving. He'd expected confrontation but the place was empty. There were bullet and scorch marks around the room, along with littered shell casings and the odd ammo clip, but he had expected that. The surprise was that there was no-one there, no dead bodies, no injured, not even the victors had hung around to secure the area. Maybe the area was no longer of strategic advantage, maybe whatever purpose it had held had been spent. Either way, Larsen found himself in the centre of a room which held nothing but despair. He was sure that if the victors had been human they would still be holding and reinforcing the best they could. Engineering was the backbone of the ship and there was no way this would be abandoned in the way it had.

Silvers had started to move ahead with the four others Reeve had sent them, cautiously sweeping the rooms and maintenance bays around them. Larsen took a moment more to take in the scene, then sat at the chief engineer's terminal and started working his way through menus and sub-menus to the video recording security logs. He wound the time back to the moment he left Commander Havers and he and Silvers had headed for the bridge with the bridge assault team. He saw himself and the others heading out, caught in freeze frame, all looking determined and focused at the inevitable conflict to come. He started the playback at double speed, then eight speed. People and time whizzed by, comical actions and stiff upright walking, staccato motion and buzzing inaudible conversations. He had no idea what he was looking for, but he would know when it happened.

There was suddenly a flash of light from the doorway, people instantly on the floor and hustle and commotion everywhere. He stopped the fast forward and the image froze again on a scene of disarray and chaos. There were three Vecian still in the frame and firing shoulder-mounted energy weapons. Commander Havers was at the centre of the image, visibly shaken, with a look of confusion on his face rather than fear. Larsen rewound the vid to just before the explosion and played it back. The room was full of engineers going about their business, calm but with considered purpose. There were two security at the door and the door was closed. A third guard was at a terminal which gave a live feed to the corridor immediately outside, and two other screens showed the corridors extending away from engineering, and maybe a couple of crawl space access ways, but he was unable to confirm that before the image exploded into light. While he had been concentrating on the guards' terminal screens, the main doors had opened in a faster than normal, almost instant, action. Not forced, not removed with explosive breach, simply opened but far faster than they were designed to. Almost instantly, the doors were not there as a protective barrier, and the two security guarding the door were taken completely by surprise, both unable to respond in time to the force of explosion which next took them from their feet. They were thrown across the room and left contorted and broken, limbs folded unnaturally and unmoving. It took another second or two for the room to break into a panicked commotion.

Larsen saw Havers snap out of his confused state and start barking orders but a Vecian came from nowhere and hammered him to the floor. Havers tried to rise again, with weak dazed motion he managed to get back to a kneeling position before he was struck with a wicked backhand to the temple. The lights must have gone out instantly. The Vecian moved away and further into the room, focused on another target.

People were scattering everywhere. Some return fire thundered into a bulkhead near one of the approaching attackers but it simply drew its attention. Turning in a reflex action, the shoulder-mounted weapon unleashed a short barrage. With the source of the fire suppressed, the Vecian began scanning the room again as more Vecian soldiers moved past him into the room. The shouts and noise of gunfire and return fire continued in the background, but the image Larsen was seeing had started to settle. It had all taken less than twenty seconds.

Just as he was about to stop the vid playback a taller Vecian came walking up to the door from a side room leading one of the medical team. Spencer, was it? That was his name, he was pretty sure of it. The Vecian had one of his hands clasped over Spencer's shoulder and seemed to be directing him to the soldiers at the door. There was conversation going on, in the sing-song Vecian language that he couldn't even begin to translate. Many human languages you could take a guess at, but there was no chance with this. There were gestures and motions, then more of the attackers arrived with captives from the rear of the ship, directing them wordlessly out of engineering and away down the corridor. The taller Vecian was continuing the conversation with the second soldier over his shoulder, while watching the procession of prisoners being led away.

Larsen froze the playback, took a peg and sent it to himself and Reeve. This was going to be a face to remember. The alien had just managed to abduct half the team. He restarted the playback. As the last of the engineers were taken though the door, the second soldier seemed to indicate to Havers, still unmoving and unconscious on the floor. The taller Vecian made a sign with one of his hands and then walked casually over to Havers and picked him up, almost effortlessly but very gently, and carried him diagonally across his body, leaving one upper and one lower arm free. It looked a peculiar hold and carry, but then Larsen didn't have the luxury of four arms.

The Vecians had hit the control room hard, abducted as many as they could easily capture then left as quickly. He knew now that Doctor Sommers, Boyd and some others had made an escape further into the engineering decks, but what had been the Vecians' purpose to the hit and run? The tactics were confused, but he was an engineer, not a soldier. He would talk this over with Reeve as soon as he got a chance. But now he needed to get to the others and regroup.

As he shut down the terminal, Silvers and the others walked back into the room. "A door each," said Silvers with a quick hand gesture. The others turned to obey the order but Larsen cut them short.

"No time to stand around, gents, we're heading out. Workshop 4. That way."

"I'll take point; Dexter, rear."

Making their way along the corridors to Workshop 4, the journey was careful but constant. Silvers was taking no chances and Larsen didn't mind the steady progress, there had been enough losses that day. Since arriving aboard, the team had been steadily whittled down to around a third of those they had arrived with. And, they were still not any closer to understanding anything about what was motivating these Vecians. They had forced their way on to the Intrepid, killed the first human they saw and abducted many more. They had taken losses themselves but they appeared to show little concern. The Vecians had shown no outward signs of wanting to communicate, nor resolve any conflict. The situation was a confused storm, and he was beginning to believe the only solution was to smash the Vecians back to the void. With no option for dialogue, where does a peaceful, amicable resolution come from? He was no politician, he was no negotiator, he was an engineer and his usual method of resolving stubborn problems was to obtain the largest hammer he could find and beat the problem into submission. Either the hammer would break or the thing being hit would submit—either way, the problem would go away. Perhaps it needed more finesse than that, but right now he wasn't in the mood for it.

Then, from nowhere, he thought about the tall Vecian figure. The peg he had taken contained an image which suddenly matched up with the face in another memory. He quickly ran through his image library with his bio-comms running a match and swiftly came to the answer. The Vecian in the lift. It had been the one they had had taken back for Havers to detain and question or study. He wasn't completely sure—Vecian features were not distinct and their skin tones appeared to wander around the spectrum, in the same way the skin of a cuttlefish or octopus might. The realisation made him stop mid stride, the team around him coming to a much more erratic halt. He rummaged through the stored images in his bio-comms to confirm his memory. After a couple of seconds, he had a pair of images that side by side removed all doubt from his mind. These images showed the same Vecian. Although not the same skin tone, there were exactly the same features, the same freckle-like dotted patterning across the face. No doubt at all.

It still didn't answer the question of what they wanted. It gave no indication as to the motivation of the Vecian crew. Nothing made sense to him.

He realised that the others were staring at him. He motioned for them to continue. Silvers look at him a moment longer, as if to try and work out the unspoken cues and body language, but he just nodded and got on with the job. They headed off in the direction of Workshop 4. A moment later a message popped into his queue from Silvers. He expected as much. He had rather given himself away with the sudden stop.

'So, what's the news?' read the message.

"Figured out who's heading up the Vecian operation," he replied.

"And?"

"Remember the extra guy in the lift?" Larsen saw Silvers nod his head in affirmation as they continued down the corridor. "Well, after we sent him back under guard, he seems to have been able to instigate a quarterback sneak."

"We gave the guy the keys to the door."

"Yep."

They walked silently for a few moments, both thinking on the new information. The situation was becoming one big game of chess, one move at a time, the pieces slowly shifting pattern, manoeuvring towards a position where the final trap could be sprung. Only, chess had rules and an end game, whereas this particular situation appeared to have neither. His mind drifted while they walked and he found himself looking through his mind's eye to his first lesson in chess by his father. His father had an antique chess board with large, heavy marble pieces, beautiful in cold white and blood red. He could have picked up a download in a second and played as many times as he wanted against a simulation, but his father insisted that it was never about the game itself, it was the duel, the face-to-face, one-on-one challenge. A simulation was hollow, soulless, and it would react in pure logic, however well it had been programmed. Whereas, whatever the situation on the board, a person can always be duped, suckered, pressured, intimidated and misdirected. The game could be won or lost on many more levels than pure logic.

He considered the current situation against this unknown foe and the meaning behind his father's lesson. It essentially boiled down to play the man not the board. Or, in this case, the alien.

Silvers lifted his hand in a balled fist and everyone stopped. 'What is it?' Larsen sent. Silvers looked over his shoulder and flicked his head in the direction of the corridor. A bulkhead door was sealed and blocking their path. He moved up to the door and checked the control terminal, but the environmental status was showing normal, and there appeared to be no real reason for the door to be closed.

"We could open it?" he suggested to the group. Silvers just shrugged.

The door opened with a slow clunk and swish of locking pistons and moving parts to reveal a black charcoal-coloured gloom. As he focused a little harder the near corridor walls, he could see that the floor and ceiling all showed evidence of explosive damage and pyrolysis. The safety systems had closed the corridor down, probably due to the overpressure of the explosion, but now the corridor was cold, the fire suppression systems having done their work. No lights, but safe to proceed. His nav system was showing him the route to Workshop 4 to be directly down the corridor. "After you," he said to Silvers. They all took up their positions again and headed into the black.

Twenty metres further on and Silvers stopped again. This time he had better reason—the floor was missing, as were the walls and the ceiling. This was clearly the centre of whatever had happened. There was now a two metre gap between the floor they were standing on and the continuation of the corridor across from them. As Larsen studied the damage further, it appeared that there was significant damage to the corridors above and below too. Something had gone bang in a big way here, although there was little evidence of whatever it was. The space was too dark and the remains too small.

"What the hell happened here?" one of the security guys asked.

"Hell if I know." said Silvers.

"Whatever it was, let's hope it's the only one," Larsen responded. "Step back." They all made a path. Taking a quick run up, he launched himself across the gap, easily making the distance and avoiding any wicked looking metal shards as he did so. He turned to the others, now just dots of light as all their flashlights were now pointing directly at him. He imagined himself with a smug smirk on his face at having made the jump but with the dazzling lights they were probably seeing a rather odd grimace. "Easy," he boasted to the others. There was an audible but anonymous tut from the far side of the chasm. He didn't think he'd impressed anyone but himself. He shrugged to himself and turned to face the continuing corridor; the nav track carried on into the darkness.

They opened another bulkhead door and made their way the last few metres to the entrance of Workshop 4. As they approached, they heard the hubbub of conversation and industry, people busy with tools, shouting instructions and operating machinery. Turning the corner, Larsen found a couple of men in the entrance, not on guard but in the capacity of greeting and intercepting them as they arrived. It was Boyd and the doctor.

"Did you hear us?" Larsen asked with a broad smile, happy to see something positive in the room. "We must walk like elephants."

"No, it wasn't that," Boyd replied, then pointed slightly behind them to where the hologram of Ellie floated slightly above her projection port.

"Ah. Hello, Ellie."

"Hello, Boyd. You are in good health after your recent exploits?"

"And you? Are you back with us?"

"I'm fully functioning. All malicious attacks and code within my systems have been purged. Before you ask, the ship is also now fully operational, apart from some damage in the bridge, main engineering and the corridor outside Workshop 4."

"I was going to ask about that. What happened in the corridor here?" Ellie returned a gesture towards Boyd.

"I believe that explanation is best told by Engineer Boyd."

Larsen turned his gaze on Boyd with a raised eyebrow. "You blowing up the ship now, Boyd?"

Boyd looked slightly uncomfortable and exchanged looks with the doctor, who had as yet not said anything in this exchange. Maybe he was waiting to see how things panned out. "No sir, well, yes sir. But it was not intentional."

"How do you unintentionally blow up part of the ship?"

"Rem-Tek power cell breach."

Larsen scrunched up his nose in thought. That would do it. "How on Earth did that happen?"

"I was attacked and used the Rem-Tek as a remote to defend

myself. One of the Vecians managed to get off a shot that took out the power cell and—" he made a motion with his hands like a big flowering explosion "—no more Vecians."

"Yes. Also, no more corridor."

"Well, we're working on that. Come, I'll show you what the team is working on."

Boyd directed Larsen towards the Rem-Tek workstations. There were several lined up being prepped for work at one end of a production line with a couple more on workbenches being actively worked on. At the far end there were a two more which were now being checked over and tested. As they approached, he could see various open panels and circuits being modded and hacked while others had hardwire connections to reprogram the core functionality of the machines.

"Our robot army?"

"Not quite," Boyd replied. "You know there is no way to alter the Rem-Teks' core code to harm others, so we're subverting it. Simply put, we're adding a human driver who will make all the moral decisions. The Rem-Tek will have no active role in operating weaponry or harming individuals. We'll need to set up a control centre."

"Or several. Better to spread the risk around."

"I'm not sure we'll have enough for that initially, but over a day or two, maybe."

Larsen's pose was one of someone in deep thought. "Ellie, what's the status of the crew resus procedure?"

"We have twenty crew in the resuscitation lounges; current recovery rate estimates the full crew to be active by 18:00 ship time. Another eight hours."

"They're on emergency recall?"

"Yes."

"Could you get the first security awake to Workshop 4 for immediate training. Silvers, please task two of the security we have with us to learning how to use these things. They can train the others."

Looking at those around him, attention focussed in his direction, he realised there was a reason he was doing all this— Havers was not.

"What happened to Havers and the others? We came through main engineering and the place was empty. I checked the vid logs and saw them all being led away but have we any further information?"

Boyd and the doctor exchanged looks, but this time it was Sommers turn. Maybe it was the doctor's place to be the bearer of bad news. His expression became solemn and caring, a well-trained look. "When the attack came, it was fast. Commander Havers gave us simple orders to get out and make our way further into the ship. It was a good move, as we are now able to respond. The alternative would be worse."

"Agreed. But we need to find them and get them back."

"And how do you intend to do that?" Silvers chipped in.

"I have a plan."

HAVERS

As he and the others were led away, time seemed to slow while his mind raced through options looking for a way out. He had started by considering options which included escape for all those now captive, and, when those ideas all hit a dead end, he moved on to a small group, maybe five or six. That too yielded nothing. It's not that they were outnumbered, it was simply that the guy with the gun could really ruin everyone's day with a light touch to the trigger. He was down to escaping on his own as the only viable option, and he couldn't do it. These people were his responsibility, he couldn't sneak out the back door while they all went to a grizzly end. It was the only way this could go; he had to stay.

He had been carried most of the way to the airlock. It had been a strange experience coming round from unconsciousness, sight first, the odd flash as the corridor lights went past as a blur of white to his eyes, then slow focus to recognition of his surroundings. Sound came back much slower, the slow padding steps of the Vecians and the shuffling of the others—the shuffling gait of people who would all rather be somewhere else. Putting all his senses together, the odd sideways slant to the world and the fact that everyone was walking apart from him, he found himself spasm in shock as some part of his primal brain needed to be free. The grip around him stiffened and more resistance was applied to his struggle as more arms and hands clamped around him.

Getting a grip of his fear, he calmed himself and forced his mind to focus on looking around. He found himself suddenly upright with the floor of the corridor beneath his feet; it felt solid and oddly reassuring.

"Walk." The voice behind him ordered him forward. It was the Vecian with the recognisable high register but definitely an English word used correctly in context. Spencer had done his job well, and he knew exactly who had been carrying him. He stopped and turned slowly to confront his captor. He and the Vecian came to a stop as others moved past them, watching but leaving them both to their confrontation, as one-sided as it was. The Vecian was at least a head taller than the others he appeared to command and they were a good ten centimetres taller than their human counterparts, on average. It was looking down on Havers with a slightly sideways glance. It said something he didn't understand in its own language, clearly annoyed at the disobedience of the human in front of him, then repeated the word with an accompanying wave of an arm. "Walk."

"Where are you taking us?" was all he could think to ask. He felt himself stalling, giving himself time to think. He considered his First Contact protocols, lecture after lecture, which someone clearly had felt very important at the time, and which now he discarded out of hand. They were way past playing nice. Even if he did hold a healthy respect of the unknown, there was little he wanted but to see these things off the *Intrepid*.

The Vecian blinked slowly, taking in the words and looking for a new translation for the response. "Talk soon. Walk now." Another Vecian walked up with the tail end of the passing line, but stopped just behind the tall Vecian, his weapon up across his chest, very visible but not overtly threatening. Havers got the unspoken message loud and clear. His stalling had not opened any doors, there was still no way to escape, so he stood straighter, shoulders square and turned to join the stragglers on the shuffle to their destination.

At least there was some small level of dialogue that there hadn't been before, a slight chance that they could begin to understand each other and what had sparked the whole incident. All he could hope was that the Intrepid would soon be under her own command again, regardless of whether he and his team was part of that.

They soon arrived at the same airlock through which they had originally gained access. As they all got closer, the holographic terminal to the side of the door swirled to life and Ellie stood there looking as calm as ever. She seemed to have a questioning expression for a moment, as if to wonder what the people approaching the airlock might be doing, but this couldn't be the case as she would undoubtedly know exactly where they were at all times. He did wonder why she had not contacted him directly through his bio-comms but that was a minor detail at this point. That she, and most likely the rest of the team, knew where they were meant there was hope of a sort. There would be plans. Certainly, if he knew Larsen and Reeve, there would be plans.

She looked around and found the tall Vecian and, in soft polite tones, she spoke, "Where are you taking these people?" No one responded. She asked again, this time in Vecian, which made Havers raise an eyebrow. It sounded fluent, but what did he know? All the Vecians continued to ignore her. Finally, she turned to him, "Comms are being blocked locally, so I'll make this quick. The crew of the *Intrepid* are under emergency resuscitation and recovery as we speak. Ship systems are fully operational and we have control of all areas. You should know we are making every effort right now to implement a rescue. Please stay calm, help is on the way." With that, she smiled gently and her projection ceased.

Looking back to the others, Havers realised all his people were still watching the now vacated space of Ellie's holographic image, captivated by the hope it had just given them. A couple then seemed to snap out of their trance and turned to him with an expression which seemed to indicate that he knew more and would lead the charge. He only hoped that Larsen and Reeve knew what they were doing.

He then picked up on a commotion at the head of the line. Two Vecians were trying to use the airlock controls, but each time they activated the door the red door locking symbol flashed up on the terminal screen. This didn't appear to be what they were expecting. He looked closer but could see nothing, as they were standing with their backs to him and blocking a clear view of the terminal while they gesticulated back and forth in argument. With this, the taller Vecian commander moved forward to find out what was going on. He pulled the two soldiers to one side and looked at the terminal himself.

The airlock was situated along the side of a corridor, but they had approached from the adjoining corridor opposite the airlock door, which made a 'T' shaped corridor approach. The captives had been lined up along one wall of the corridor opposite the door while the Vecians sorted out their little technical issue with the door. Whatever they were trying wasn't working and clearly taking too long, as the Vecian commander after a moment turned to him and covered the distance in large strides of frustration. Grabbing Havers arm with a large powerful hand, the Vecian dragged him to the door. Jabbing at the door control with one of his other hands he said, in a rather forceful way, "Open."

"I'm not sure that's a good idea," Havers said, looking at the control panel. The Vecian didn't appear to care about any understanding of any conversation that might be coming back, he just looked intently at him with large dark, demanding eyes.

"Open." This time he pulled his own weapon and pointed it at Havers. He understood the intent, so turned to open the door.

Squaring up to the terminal he could now see an object fixed to the side of the control panel, Vecian symbols spread over a small screen that kept flashing back at him in different colours and forms which he took to be words. He thought they looked like some ancient oriental script, penned by someone with too many colour inks to choose from. The text precise, the hues and variations in colour seemed random. Taking a quick look back at the Vecian commander, he began to push a sequence of buttons; the door terminal alert sounded again, barring access to him too. He wondered how long it would take for the commander to realise he was intentionally pressing the wrong buttons. He didn't get a chance to find out.

There was a noise like amplified firecrackers behind him, followed by an almost instantaneous dismantling of sections of the wall around him and parts of the ceiling. The shock of it curled him into a ball in the corner of the door jamb, self-preservation kicking in to make him the smallest target he could manage, as invisible to the attack as possible. As he scanned about in panic to find the source of the hail of bullets, the Vecian commander spun away, taking an indirect shot to the shoulder, the force too much for him to withstand. Another Vecian behind him doubled up and fell. People started running past him and the sound of shouting and yelling of all types added to the cacophony, the wall of noise and sound then went up again as the Vecians finally got their bearings and the impetus of the surprise attack waned. Energy weapons began lancing down the corridors in all directions, and people hit the floor for cover, using the same method of escape as Havers. Some were less successful.

The Vecian commander was at his side again, seemingly unphased by the noise around him and the hole in his shoulder. This time he punched Havers so hard in the chest he thought his ribcage had shattered into tiny fragments. All the air in his lungs rushed to exit at once. "Open!" shouted the Vecian in his ear at a pitch that felt like pins had been pushed into place. Havers found himself hitting the buttons with purpose, a wicked idea flashing through this mind as he did so. His fingers flashed across the keys and the console status turned green. The door slid open.

Before he could press further buttons on the panel, he was gripped roughly by the shoulder and pulled unceremoniously through the open door. He made a show of kicking and grabbing for the lip of the door frame as he was dragged through into the airlock. He came to rest slumped to the side of the cubical, holding his head in his hands to nurse a concussive knock he had received as he had landed. For some reason, his mother's words came to him: "Iain, you've got a hard head.". He had always been getting into scrapes as a kid, cracking his head off walls, on the floor, or tree branches, it had all been pretty commonplace. He may have a hard head, he thought, as he considered his mother's words, but the wall was always harder. It damn well hurt.

His idea took a slight miscalculated turn when Spencer flew through the door head first and crumpled into the corner opposite him followed shortly after by a Vecian, followed shortly after that by a barrage of bullets to the wall outside the airlock, as it slipped into the airlock for cover. As soon as the soldier was in, it shouted what must have been an affirmation to its commander and the taller Vecian hit the door control on the outer door. The inner door closed purposefully, sealing off the commotion outside. The room went silent.

The moment the door closed, Havers looked up at the door console screen to confirm to himself that his actions outside had worked. Sure enough, his little gremlin to the Vecian commander's plans was reported on the screen and counting down. He'd activated the auto-open routine to the outer door. From the moment the inner door is closed the room had thirty seconds before the outer door would auto open. It was an emergency override for cases where you were kitted up and needed to get out fast. Spencer appearing as he did, caused him a problem. He was okay with putting his own life at risk here, it was necessary and he could deal with that, but now he had to include Spencer in the calculation—and he had seconds to warn him.

Spencer sat bolt upright, his back to the wall, and faced Havers almost by reflex, a seriously dazed look on his face, but questioning. Without saying a word, Havers motioned to his hands which were holding on as tightly as he could to the guide rail. He hoped that the silent communication wasn't something the Vecian guard would pick up on. With both him and Spencer on the opposite side of the airlock, it couldn't scan both of them at once and he was also distracted by repeated ricochets on the door and the mutterings of his commander. His message seemed to get through just in time. Spencer's questioning look turned into terrified surprise as he realised what Havers had done, a flick of the eyes to the control panel to confirm the situation and with only a couple of seconds remaining Spencer rammed his hands above himself to the guide rail and locked his grip.

He didn't even see the external door open but the banshee that wailed in his ears and howled as the air evacuating his lungs made him scream for as long as there was air left to make the sound. The explosive evacuation of air pulled at his body and he felt the strain in his wrists as they became his only tether to the slim chance for life he had remaining. He took a quick glance to Spencer who had lost his grip with one hand and had only fingertip contact with the rail. Petrified terror was etched to his face, as the last hold he had on the rail left his grasp and the last of the air in the chamber forced its way out of the small space into the void. In painstaking slow motion, arms thrashing trying to gain any purchase to any surface, Spencer was slowly moved through the external door with the slightest momentum.

There was nothing he could do. Havers searched the room for any way of retrieving Spencer but there was nothing he could manage in the time if he wanted to survive himself. He could already feel the lack of atmosphere affecting him, and his ability to function being impaired. Then he saw the suit locker above his head in the wall above the guide rail. He pulled himself close to the locker and opened it, retrieving the suit and helmet he threw it through the door. It would give Spencer nothing but time, but it would be time in which he could mount a rescue. He saw the suite accelerate towards its target as he hit the airlock control panel to close the outer door and start the air cycle.

As atmosphere was pumped back into the airlock, every inch of his body felt like it was on fire, strain and pain in every fibre of his being. His tongue felt several sizes too big for his mouth and burnt, his eyes found everything hard to focus on and he wondered how he had any tears left to wet his eyes, but they were there. The sight of Spencer vanishing into space and being helpless to assist was the most awful feeling. He had to get out there and help—he could still be alive. It was a statement he thought to himself in order to convince the more logical parts of his mind that there was still some hope. The odds were small and every second smaller still. He managed to hit the door control again in frustration, trying unsuccessfully to speed up the airlock cycling process but time was the enemy more than the Vecians and he needed more of it.

As the atmosphere cycled, he found himself clamped to the floor with his face pressed up against the ventilation duct gasping for air. The air was the sweetest thing he'd ever inhaled, his senses giving him a rush of pleasure at the intoxication of simply living another breath. His mind replayed the last moments again and again. The moment the decompression happened he had been gripping so tightly to the guide rail with his eyes momentarily clasped shut that he realised he'd never seen the demise or otherwise of the two Vecians. He hadn't even seen them in his view when he was focussed on Spencer, then his mind clicked back into thinking of Spencer again and his features became grim. He struck the door control again.

With such slowness, the inner door finally opened. There was no sound coming from the corridor outside but he knew his hearing was shot, so that was no indication of the danger or lack of it outside the airlock. A wisp of smoke rolled lazily across the ceiling of the airlock from the door and an emergency light flashed from somewhere outside. He forced himself to grab the hand rail and pull himself up to stand. At some point he had started sweating and his hair was matted to his forehead. He wiped his face with his cuff to clear his vision and stepped tentatively into the hallway.

The emergency lights were on and the corridor was bathed in a low light, casting shadows of various shapes and contortions across the walls and ceiling. There was very little movement, as he immediately started to scan for familiar faces and any explanation for the events that had just unfolded. The corridor surfaces, walls, ceilings, floors had all taken a pounding—holes and rended metal and melted plastic everywhere; he was surprised there were no fires. Smoke rolled around the scene like ghosts of the dead, which he found himself about to step over. The body on the floor was not human, it was one of the Vecian boarding party laying in a foetal position with all its arms limply pressing against an abdomen wound which had eventually overcome its ability to stem. A blue-black blood oozed across the floor making it slick underfoot. Havers lifted the toe of his boot to confirm the unpleasant liquids he was now walking through and, looking further up the corridor, the discolouration of the floor and forlorn, crumpled forms lying there in the shadows didn't lead his thoughts to a welcome outcome for either side.

He took a zigzagging route through the corridor, making sure to avoid the bodies, and shortly found himself seeing active lighting at the junction ahead, where the silhouette of a group of people appeared to be fussing around a central robotic outline, which he realised was a Rem-Tek. Someone from the group saw him and moved quickly to his aid, guiding him steadily on shaky legs the last few metres into the light to join the others. It was Larsen.

"My God, Larsen. What happened here?"

"A rescue, sir. Worked pretty well too."

*

The medbay was clean and bright and hurt his eyes. All things considered, everything hurt, so the lights being a little bright were the least of his worries. The newly awoken medical staff were fussing over him and the other wounded and he found the whole thing a little too energetic. He was tired, really tired, and felt like he could sleep for another one hundred and thirty years.

With the Vecians ejected from the ship, the process of ramping up security and utilising the *Intrepid's* crew had begun. He had handed over to Captain Adam Carlsen, presenting him with a patched up but still clearly damaged bridge and an apology. Carlsen had taken it all in his stride, almost like he had been expecting some catastrophic problem to wake up to, and the fact that he only had a few missing or shot out display screens on his bridge was better than he could have expected.

Following a short preliminary debrief of his team, he had ordered everyone to get some sleep. Those not needing medical attention filtered out of the ready room and headed for their bunks, others like himself that could make their way, the walking wounded, headed for the medbay to join those who had been unfortunate enough to be taken straight there by the medical team.

His thoughts were still a jumble of images and sounds hitting him again and again, waves of guilt at losing half of his team. When the casualties were counted and reported he had fifty percent lost to the encounter with another twenty percent casualties of various grades. Some, like himself, were able to walk to the medbay, but others were far worse. Most of the worst were suffering third degree burns or loss of limbs due to the energy weapons used against them, serious wounds instantly cauterised by the searing heat. Each of the images he saw in his thoughts. Each time he closed his eyes he saw different mangled and damaged bodies but all had the same terrified face. Wide panic in the eyes, a silent scream from a mouth open but without purpose. Every one of the images in his mind was Spencer.

He had arranged a search and rescue team to look for Spencer as soon as he could. Only moments or so after getting his senses back from the exposure to hard vacuum in the airlock, he had ordered Larsen to expedite a team. They had been worried about the possible presence of the Vecian ship somewhere close by but the scans local to the ship had turned up nothing. A couple of EVAs were sent out, but they also found nothing. He was gone.

"Hey there, soldier," a warm voice broke his depression. A smiling, caring medic stood in front of him looking concerned, her eyes bright, voice like smooth velvet. It sounded strange coming from such a young-looking woman. Although he knew the face in no way indicated the age of the mind behind it, he thought she would grow into it.

"Hey," was all he could manage in reply.

"You've had a busy day. Why don't you lie down and get some sleep?" She indicated with a slight tilt of the head to the bed he was currently sitting on. He nodded and relaxed into the pillow at the head of the bed and looked back at the medic.

"Thanks."

"I think it's us who should be thanking you." That kind smile again made its way into his thoughts, pushing away the horrors of the last few hours. His eyes started to close and the world went dark around him. The voice of the medic then seemed to change ever so slightly in his dreams. "You did well today, Iain. You and your team saved the *Intrepid*. You saved them all." The last thing he found himself wondering as sleep took him was what his mother was doing aboard the ship.

SILVERS

"I've got him!" Boyd yelled across the control deck to Larsen. Silvers and Larsen were crowded around a terminal looking over scans, plans and schematics of the corridors and space immediately around the airlock where the rescue had occurred earlier that day, trying to glean any information about the whereabouts of the Vecian ship and the possible location of Spencer. Boyd had pronounced it 'damn fishy' when Havers had told him of the action and circumstances which lead to Spencer's disappearance. "People don't just vanish," he'd concluded. Which to him meant quite simply that Spencer was still out there somewhere, and not just anywhere. If his hunch was correct, the Vecians had him. The way Havers had described it, Spencer had been moving way too slowly to be far from the ship. He'd done the maths, plotted the cone of probability moving out from the external door of the airlock, scanned all space around the predicted search volume with a typical engineer's fudge factor to correct for errors. Nothing. Spencer just wasn't there.

It had taken him a few minutes to review the data, but nothing is pretty easy to spot. He saw uniform numbers with no anomalous blips to flag the existence of a man floating helplessly in space. Spencer should have been easier to spot than a supernova at the distance he was calculated to have travelled from the ship, but the fact that nothing was there spoke to a more worrying development. He had informed Larsen of his theory via a subconscious babble of thought as he worked, his mind ejecting unfiltered ideas as he put a search solution together on the fly. Silvers and Larsen were crowded around the terminal showing the results of his scans.

"Where?" Silvers responded, "I can't see a thing."

"You need to get your engineer's head on," Larsen told Silvers. "There." He pointed at the screen and leaned in for a closer look.

"But that's nowhere near the search zone. That's, what..?" He moved his eyes across the screen to the distance key. "...Eight hundred metres past the most extreme boundary of the search area?"

"Yup," Boyd replied. "I broadened the scan. Included any emergency beacon broadcast from the suit and tried a short burst comms to see if anything pinged back."

"And it did?"

"Yep. Which means we know he's alive and accepting comms."

"Even if he can't respond."

"Exactly."

Silvers was watching the conversation between Larsen and Boyd, becoming ever so slightly baffled by it. "So, why can't we see him?" He was looking directly at the external zoom camera location indicated by the position fix. Stars and more stars, but no floating figure. Boyd just rolled his eyes.

"Catch up," said Larsen with a smile.

"What am I missing?"

"The obvious," replied Boyd. He watched as the situation resolved in Silvers mind, slowly becoming real as he extrapolated the meaning behind all the data. A deepening frown furrowed Silvers' brow as he found the situation more than difficult in its implication.

"Shit," was all Silvers managed to say. A short snort of agreement came from both Boyd and Larsen as they all considered the implications.

"So, what's the plan, Boss?" Boyd asked Larsen.

Larsen's expression was cryptic. "Havers."

"No, Spencer." Silvers said.

"No. We need to speak to Havers, maybe even the captain."

"Why? Don't we just go and get him?"

"Ever heard of Coventry?"

"What?" Silvers was evidently lost again.

"Coventry, New Point, Luna 314?" Silvers shook his head at the references. Larsen continued, "All these places were lost or destroyed in military attacks. In each case, the attack was known about in advance by the defending forces but sacrificed to safeguard wider knowledge by the enemy that a key fact was known about them. Uncovered encryption, spies at the top of government, that sort of thing."

Boyd chipped in, "Act like you are unaware while plotting your next move."

"Or setting a larger trap. That's the general gist."

"And all that time, what happens to Spencer?" Silvers asked, becoming more uncomfortable by the moment.

"You're forgetting one thing." Boyd ignored Silvers emotive comment. As far as he was concerned, this was still a larger problem than one man.

"Forgetting what?" asked Larsen.

"We don't only know where Spencer is now. We know where the Vecians are."

Silvers seemed even more surprised at that, looking at both Larsen and Boyd, as if to confirm his amazement reflected in their faces but finding instead only a grim understanding. It was another obvious leap of logic he was behind on but, more than that, Boyd was right. The picture was larger. Where they had been totally focused on getting Spencer back, they had missed the fact that they potentially had a way of tracking the Vecians without their knowledge.

"I'm still up for getting Spencer back while we still can. Breathing and in one piece. And the way Havers is right now, I think he'll agree." That also registered with Boyd and Larsen, receiving nods of agreement. Silvers looked back at the display in thought. A square red icon had appeared around the positional fix on Spencer. Boyd was still working away trying to get a better fix and set up further scans of the area, presumably to give the Vecians the idea that they were still searching and as yet hadn't found anything.

"Havers will be here in five minutes," reported Larsen.

*

"Larsen, what have you got?" Havers walked through the door with a purpose, a stern look on his face and dark, sleepless eyes. Silvers raised an eyebrow and was about to say something but was cut off: "Yes, I know. I look terrible."

"That's an understatement, sir." Silvers replied.

"Sir, we have a fix on Spencer and the Vecian ship," Larsen reported. "We believe we can use Spencer's active comms to track the ship, even though it's cloaked. The signal is strong and close. Close enough to consider a boarding action and rescue."

Havers face, which had seemed to take on the guilt of ages in the last few hours, contorted again in a mental anguish as he took in the information. There was no winning situation here. Silvers could see the commander running the numbers in his head and coming up with the same answers that Larsen had a few minutes before. Attempting a boarding action on a cloaked ship with no prior intelligence of the ship or number of crew was foolhardy, and would cost more than could be gained. Havers leaned both hands on the workstation desk, head hung in resignation. He was clearly out of ideas. Sleep deprivation had that effect.

"Any ideas?" Havers opened to the group.

"Tracking," said Boyd, with calm clarity.

"Understood," was all Havers could bring himself to say. "For how long?"

"Difficult to say exactly. While Spencer is alive, and then about twenty hours. It's as long as the batteries will last once his body's internal piezoelectric generation fails."

"Well, let's hope they keep him alive. Boyd I want you monitoring Spencer's every move. I want a team tracking him around the clock. See to it."

"Aye, sir."

"Larsen, I want you and Silvers with me. Ellie, please inform the Captain we need to see him with important information about the Vecian position." A confirmation clearly popped into Havers' comms from Ellie, and he nodded as he received it. "Good. Let's go."

Moving out, they made their way to the main section elevators, each of them in silence working through their own thoughts and complications. Silvers wondered how Havers was still operating The man was not military or security but he felt he could have been. The endurance, the drive, courage and moral leadership was as good if not better than some of the best military officers he had worked with.

As they walked, Silvers realised he was dodging the odd person coming the other way. The ship was alive again, people going about their duties and assigned tasks, scurrying in and out of rooms and corridors. The next thing he noticed was how clean they were, clothes almost sparkling they were so fresh. He had been in the same clothes for a several days, running around like a lunatic, getting shot at, crawling through hot and enclosed spaces, and the sudden urge for a shower was overwhelming.

"Boy, I could use a shower." Larsen laughed behind him. He turned over his shoulder to see Larsen smiling back. "Did I say that out loud?"

"Yep. And you're right—you need a shower," Larsen retorted.

"Funny man."

Larsen turned to call after Havers, who was pacing his way ahead. "So what's our next move, sir?"

Havers' head came up, like he'd been jabbed in the back by Larsen. He'd clearly been pacing while caught up in his own world. Several metres of corridor passed with no response then the elevator lobby opened out in front of them. They came to a slow stop and waited for the next elevator car to arrive.

Havers turned to them, "Why are the Vecians here?"

"I don't follow, sir." Larsen replied.

"Where did they come from? What was their purpose when here?"

Both questions neither Larsen or Silvers had answers to. Havers looked at them in turn for an answer, "Supposition?"

"Raiders?" Silvers offered. The elevator car arrived. They stepped in absentmindedly, all three caught up in the conversation. The car began to rise.

"No. What did they take?"

"Vanguard," Larsen pitched in.

"No. Vanguard to what? They were military but when things went south they didn't have back up. How did they act?"

"Scouting party?"

"Better. Yes, I think they were here to find out as much from us as they could. They were aggressive but have not done more than attack our information centres and escape. They could have done untold damage or even destroyed our ship. They didn't. They interrogated our systems and now have a captive to interrogate further." He took a heavy breath. "But, further to that point, my question still stands: where did they come from?"

Again, some quiet thinking broke out. Silvers was beginning to believe it pointless, as Havers had clearly already worked all this out. Why ask questions you already knew the answers to? Larsen pitched in with an answer: "Hayford." It was muttered quietly under his breath, then more loudly as his confidence in the answer grew. "Hayford b. They are from Hayford b."

"But the planet's uninhabited," stated Silvers. "It's the whole reason we're going there. M type, uninhabited planet."

"Correct. But consider the little we know about the Vecians already. They are aggressive, highly intelligent and inquisitive, spacefaring. With..?" He let the last question hang.

"With?" Larsen repeated. Silvers was considering options. The answer wasn't forthcoming.

"With cloaking technology." The elevator car came to a stop at the bridge level and the doors slid open. None of them moved nor seemed to notice. A couple of waiting crew in the lobby looked at each other, contemplating whether or not they were going to exit the elevator, then, when they didn't move, began to enter. Havers clapped both Larsen and Silvers on the shoulder. "Come on, we have a captain to see. Don't keep him waiting." Looking across at the couple who had just stepped into the car and were now blocking the exit, he looked apologetic and gave them a short "Excuse us" as he brushed past.

They walked after Havers, Larsen with a frown of thought and Silvers actually scratching his head. The last ten minutes had been quite weird in a way. He had followed every word but he had cut short of simply asking Havers what he was on about. Please, sir, make your point.

There were engineering technicians littered around the bridge, seemingly discarded under desks and stuck to walls, each of them half buried behind conduit panels and control boards. The repairs to the room were coming on at a pace and at the centre of this organised chaos with his command team was Carlsen. Havers made his way through the gaggle, leaving Larsen and Silvers at the door. To Silvers, this seemed the best option, as he really didn't feel like getting in the way of an engineer with a welding arc or a computer tech, who would most likely bore him to death with idle conversation. There were people shouting across the room, some giving command orders, some warning of moving panels or grav plate alterations, and, with each sound, the shouts and calls of those working in the room needed to increase to cope. People were generally just shouting to get themselves heard. He looked at Larsen and flicked his head towards the door behind them. The unspoken conversation was agreed and they moved back out of the room into the corridor. As the door closed behind them the noise disappeared, and Silvers gave out a sigh.

Taking a casual stance leaning up against the wall, he looked towards the ceiling. "So, tell me, what is he talking to Carlsen about?"

Larsen shrugged. "Not entirely sure but it will be to do with Hayford b."

"I got that much, but what was that about cloaking technology back there? I understood most of what he was saying, but what has a ship's cloak got to do with Hayford b?"

Larsen smiled. "Extrapolation."

"Hey?" Silvers was getting frustrated. Did these engineer types always speak in riddles? "Do you engineers ever give a direct answer? If I started asking you to extrapolate in a fire fight you'd not survive thirty seconds. Give me a straight answer."

"Didn't you pay attention in school?"

"Well, yes and no. Mostly, no." Silvers found himself drifting back to class, where he would regularly be daydreaming about getting out into the mountains around his home in Colorado and climbing for hours through the rocky outcrops, crevices and overhangs. It gave him a natural agility and strength that he had put to good use later in life. Mountain rescue had been his calling then, but when the troubles came and the world changed, his draft orders had arrived, pulling his world of saving lives into the polar opposite. His service in the US Army Rangers had been short lived. He couldn't wait to leave. Morally it was a perversion of his life to that point. Saving lives was what it was all about for him, not taking them. However, the poetic irony was that he was good at it. Taking life was far easier than saving it—it probably had always been that way, though he now had first-hand experience of that fact. When the opportunity to take the position with OWEC had come up, he had grasped it with both hands. Although it was a security job, and probably the reason he had made the shortlist, he saw it as a chance to save life again. To be part of protecting the last hope for humanity, as it made its first faltering steps into the big black. To thrive or fail, that part was unknown, but he would strain every fibre of his being to breaking point to give every other human being he could the best chance for success. Maybe in the process he would level some of the bad karma he had accrued.

Back in the present, he asked again, "Anyway, you're still avoiding a direct answer."

"Okay, okay." Larsen had his hands up, appeasing. "It's just that I think it's a long shot. Havers clearly holds more stock in this. If you consider the available planets in this region of space for reasonably short-range space travel, then you come up with a very short list. A really short list."

"A list of how many?"

"One."

"What? Hayford b, and that's it?"

"Yes. Which means that the planet we are heading towards is not uninhabited. In fact, it will be far more advanced and capable than we have the ability to cope with. Havers is assuming that if they can hide a ship in space, they can do the same on the scale required to hide a planet." Larsen began leaning on the opposite wall of the corridor facing Silvers, arms folded.

"But they haven't hidden the planet. It's still there and in plain sight. Otherwise, we wouldn't be heading this way, right? Being uninhabited was one of the prime search parameters for the planet we would target."

"True, but that's the point. They have hidden the planet's advanced populated state. We would have found the planet and then performed a battery of tests on it, to test for atmosphere, surface composition and population. The assumption would be that a populated planet would be emitting some level of activity in the electromagnetic communication band. There would be signals we could discern and try to interpret. Maybe even try and make contact ourselves, remotely."

"And you're saying this didn't happen?"

"That's exactly what I'm saying."

"So, what are they hiding from?"

"I don't know. But that's not our immediate problem. Our immediate problem is—"

"Where the hell do we go now?" Silvers cut in.

"You took the words..." Larsen made a pulling motion with his hands away from his mouth.

Both of them stood staring idly at the floor, each wrapped in their own musings on the theme, loosely entitled 'Where do we go from here?'

"On the upside, I've never known Clayton not to have a plan A, B or C."

"This probably comes under plan Z," Silvers retorted with a certain black humour.

"Ah, don't be so pessimistic."

"Me? Horse hockey."

The door opened and the noise from within washed over them like an unwelcome bucket of ice-cold water. Havers stepped out. "What about polo?"

Both Larsen and Silvers looked at him confused but stood up off the wall, ready for any instruction or their next move. "Polo, sir?" asked Larsen.

"Someone mentioned horse hockey?" With no response but blank looks from both of them, Havers continued, "Never mind. Okay, Captain Carlsen and I have been speaking to Captain Clayton—we have a shuttle to catch."

"What about Spencer and the Vecian ship?" Havers nodded at Silvers' clear concern.

"We are watching the Vecian ship's movements continuously. It is holding station about two clicks from the *Intrepid's* rear port section. It seems to be tailing us at constant velocity and making no outwardly hostile actions or movement. We are obviously concerned about Spencer but there is little we, that's the three of us, can do about that right now. Carlsen has got a team working on a rescue plan and other contingencies."

"So, what are we doing?" Larsen asked.

"We have been tasked with keeping our observations about Hayford b to ourselves for the moment. They don't want a general panic to break out throughout the fleet at the news. The shuttle coming to pick us up is already en route and will be here in about an hour. Once aboard, we swing past the *Endeavour* to give Clayton a personal briefing."

Silvers put his hand up to ask a question. "Yes, Silvers?"

"Sir, with the Vecian ship outside and given what happened to our shuttle, do you think it wise to bring another shuttle in?"

"The shuttle's flightpath will be mostly hidden by approaching from the far side of the *Intrepid*. We also have point defence from the *Intrepid* when the shuttle gets close enough." Both Larsen and

Silvers seemed accepting of that tactic. "Once the shuttle gets here, we hitch a lift. It's outfitted with the latest long-range observation kit we have available for the size of vessel and we will be heading out to try and prove or disprove our hypothesis."

"There you go again with your words and your science, sir." Silvers said flippantly.

"We get to be the first to see if there are really Vecians on Hayford or not," Larsen stated. "Schoolboy enough for you?"

"Yup. On the same page now, sir."

CLAYTON

The eyes staring out at him from the screen were dark and sunken with what he could only assume was lack of sleep. The face was in shadow but he could still see the mask of conflicted rage Travis wore openly. There were a further couple of silhouetted characters in the background, at this time unknown to him or St John, showing solidarity with their leader within the communication vid. He, St John and Roux looked back at the screen, which was almost a mirror image while the vid was paused to try to isolate and retrieve any forensic information on the background characters. Travis was known to them, St John's men missing their chance to capture him by moments, but the others needed to be identified and the scale of the operation understood before a more decisive plan was put into effect. At the moment they had a cell of three running rogue on the ship, but was that the full extent of their opposition? Without further intelligence it was impossible to tell how many were involved.

"Looks like your family are off the hook," St John said to Clayton, without looking away from the screen. "This evidence clearly states you, your family and your AI chums to be the target for all this nonsense. How you can be orchestrating your own hit … is beyond me. It would be slightly self-defeating."

Roux opened his mouth, as if to say something, but then decided better of it and instead looked closer at the screen.

"I've had a run in or two with GAIA in the past, but it has never been as personal as this. It's always been about the tech—

what I should have done differently, what I should be doing to reverse the damage I've wrought on society—it's never been about me and it's certainly never targeted my family before. This is all new."

Roux, stepped back from the screen. "A new faction? A break-away?"

"Maybe," agreed St John. "To be on this ship, to be dedicated enough to get through the level of security that would have been needed, backgrounds with no apparent ties to GAIA. That would take some doing."

"Or contacts," Clayton offered.

"Yes. With contacts high enough, data manipulation could have fabricated background checks and personal history."

"But, however they did it," continued Roux, "they are here now."

"And they are dangerous," added St John. "While they are in the shadows and running around this ship, we are in trouble."

"There are many kinds of trouble, General," said Clayton. "The problems with the *Intrepid* being a case in point."

"A mission of peace fighting on two fronts," mused Roux.

"Isn't that how it's always been?" asked St John. "There are always dissenters within the ranks, and there are always conflicts between foreign powers."

"Until about two days ago, there were no foreign powers. It was just us in the big black. Now..." Clayton let the sentence hang, then finished it with a shrug of the shoulders.

"Until two days ago, there were no dissenters in the ranks," St John observed. "Things change fast." This drew a wry smile from Clayton and a knowing shake of the head.

In the pause that followed, Clayton took a seat and continued to look at the screen. The figures were becoming no more discernible, and nothing in the background was helping them. There were crates of standard equipment and supplies which could be found in numerous cargo bays throughout the ship, dimly lit half shadows and full shadows cast across the scene to show the silhouette of military grade armour worn by each but there were no markings, no identification numbers. The carbines they were wielding were standard issue, and no visible registration could be picked up in the available light. He knew Dawn had the techs running analysis on the vid, and she would be running her own tests too, trying to peek into every byte of data within each frame.

She was now splitting her time. The investigation into the bombing was ongoing—she was crunching numbers and working through the vid footage across the resus bays as fast as the ships data machines would work, and now she was analysing footage of terrorists for crew and location data. On top of this, they were now in constant contact with the *Intrepid* and Captain Carlsen, exchanging as close to real-time communication on the unfolding events there. Carlsen had sent a team to him who would be arriving shortly; they would brief him on the *Intrepid* situation first-hand.

"So, what next?" Roux said, to break the thoughtful silence.

"Play the vid again in full. I want to see it again."

"While you and St John are doing that, would you mind if I get back to the bridge?"

"Not at all. Please prepare to receive the team from the *Intrepid* and inform me as soon as they arrive."

Roux nodded to them both as he made his way out. "Aye, sir. St John." The door to the briefing room closed behind him.

Clayton motioned to the vid screen and St John started the vid from the beginning. The familiar shadowy image which had been on display for the last few minutes started to run again, but this time it was accompanied by a metallic, modulating voice. The voice was digitised and scrambled to a point where it was almost indistinguishable as human. Dawn's first job had been to discern what was being said. She had cleaned up the audio but the voice, now clear and understandable, was still unrecognisable as a voice print of any of the crew. She had also transcribed the speech to the screen as subtitles.

"Premier Clayton," Travis began, almost knowing that the title itself would annoy him, "GAIA have waited a long time for this moment. While you and your daughter have doomed all humanity, leaving them to perish on a dead planet ruled by machines, we are here now to bring your chapter of madness to an end. History is littered with well-meaning fools who have been responsible for the deaths of millions, yet they are seen by their peers as saviours of the people, praised and lauded for their efforts. This so-called elite care for those they rule only as a commodity to be exploited.

"The new worlds which we are to seed with humanity have no place for you or your kind. GAIA pledge to see you and your line removed, your machine children eradicated and all aspects of AI unwritten." The lead shadow moved closer to the camera, closer to the observer, "This starts today." Then, in unison, the others chanted, "Until the end," as if to finish a prayer: The screen went black.

St John looked at Clayton, who was deep in thought. "Until the end?"

"Dramatic zealots," Clayton said, leaning forward in the chair and running his hands through his hair as he stood to face St John. "At least we know they are committed. There is no way they are bluffing, not with the level of detail they have exhibited across the number of disciplines."

"What I want to know is how are they able to operate within the ship undetected?"

"That is exactly the question I've been asking myself," Clayton replied. "Not only have they eluded all our internal scans, they have managed to operate within the ship undetected, triggering no alerts, creating no logs. There is simply no evidence of their passing. The only reason we caught Travis was due to an accident in an inventory check. We got lucky."

"And, the crew compliment is still listing as complete. All accounted for. Everyone at their post. So who these other guys are, I have no idea." St John was irritated. Clayton hadn't known him long, only since being assigned to the *Endeavour*, but he had never really seen him without total composure. A man like St John, he imagined, would pride himself on being in control, knowing every angle and having every eventuality covered. The irritation he saw in St Johns face was a reaction to the lack of all those things.

"Have we done a check on clones?"

"Each of us have a single clone delivered from resus at a required time," stated St John, as if reading from a manual.

"True, that's how it works." Thinking out loud, he continued, "Or, is meant to work." Having a rush of ideas crowding his mind, he called out to Dawn, "Dawn, I need you to refine your search. Focus all your attention on Sub-Lieutenant Paul Travis and his resus suite."

Dawn's form swirled into existence through the holo-projector next to the centre console and the display screen they had been watching. "Captain Clayton, should I be looking for anything specific?"

"I want you to continue to run the low-level hardware

diagnostic, but only for Paul Travis and his resus suite. I want you to run the sweep of that resus bay and all vid footage back to the beginning of the mission. I want to be informed of any anomaly."

Dawn seemed to phase out for a moment while she was clearly concentrating on something, gathering information. "I presume you are working on a theory," she said in a flat, matter-of-fact tone, not really asking a question but stating a fact,

"Care to share?" asked St John, "I'm beginning to feel slightly out of touch."

Clayton took a breath. It was time to bring St John in. More than anything he needed his help, as an independent who could be trusted. "Sorry, St John. Dawn and I have been running our own parallel investigation."

"You do know that's against protocol? But why am I even suggesting this? Of course you know."

"Yes. And I know what the stakes are. I wasn't going to go down without knowing as much information as I could about what was going on."

"So what did you find?"

"Well, honestly? Nothing. Yet. But we have a theory and I'm confident it will give us the answers we're after. It's just the search parameters have been far too large. I've now asked Dawn to put the search into place on a set of refined search parameters. We should have our answer shortly."

St John was beginning to pace. The revelations of the last few minutes had unsettled him even further. Clayton guessed he'd have to let him blow off some of the frustration before he could get him on side, so he let him rant and pace a while.

"And what exactly is this grand theory of yours?"

St John was intent. It wasn't anger, it was frustration, and a little disappointment. Clayton pointed at the seats, inviting St John to sit, and they both did so. "Dawn and I considered how devices could be placed and technology subverted without Dawn knowing about it. Impossible, right? Well, not entirely. Travis appears to be able to walk around the ship like the invisible man. What is needed to accomplish this is a local connection to the security net and a personal device which overrides that local security net and subverts the data. The device will locate and access local security nodes then subvert local logs and place any security vid into a momentary loop showing repeated footage until the target is out of local security range. Or something similar."

"And you can prove that device exists?" asked St John, his curiosity now piqued.

"Not yet. That is what Dawn is looking for right now. Evidence of the switch or any anomalous logs but our best hope is at the hardware level in the time before the crew as a whole were revived."

"How so?"

"Well, it is at that time when we have the most clean data. No one was meant to be awake. So, if you like, that is when the background data will be most calm. If you want an analogy, it would be like looking for a pebble dropped into a lake. On any normal day, when the people are going about their day to day business, that would equate to a lake with a slightly choppy surface. A pebble thrown into that would be hard to spot. Ripples would be soon overcome and any evidence lost. On a calm day, however, when the surface is like a mirror, a pebble dropped into the water would be much easier to spot. The ripples would be visible for longer, the evidence clear against a still unblemished surface. These conditions would equate to the ship as it was with the crew in stasis."

St John considered this for a long moment, rubbing his cheek absentmindedly in concentration. "So, you believe someone was awake and roaming the ship well before the due resuscitation sequence?"

"Yes."

"But you can't prove it?"

"No. Not yet. Searching all the historic data for every resus suite for the entire duration of the journey to this point was just too big a task in the timeframe. We have been targeting the search as best we can, but this new information has enabled me to refine the search further." He felt focused. Talking through issues always helped. It was something to do with arranging your thoughts before verbalising them. Doing so always seemed to line up his ideas and give him clarity. "My new concern is who these others are." He stood at the display terminal and wound back the vid to the visual of the three silhouetted figures. "My suspicion is that they are the same person."

St John seemed visibly shocked by the statement. "You mean vid trickery? Some alteration and camera effects?"

"No. Actually the same person. I believe Travis has cloned himself several times over the duration of this voyage."

"But that's impossible. You know that more than most. The protocols, the safeguards..."

Clayton cut in, "And you know, as head of security, that the toughest and most rigorous safeguards can always be overcome. It may be exceptionally difficult to do so but no protocols are infallible."

More silence. "So, what happened?"

"Again, I don't know. At this point it's supposition but I believe Travis in some way has managed to clone himself, at least twice. This would corroborate your information on the crew count. It would also give him, or them, a greater number of like-minded and equally dangerous and motivated people."

"This stinks, Pete." St John said, slipping into a more personal conversation, rising from his seat and stepping a pace towards the screen to take a look at the shadowy figures. "It almost doesn't matter at the moment how they did it; my priority is to keep this ship and the crew safe. At the moment, I will work with there being only three aggressors and coordinate my teams accordingly. Can you give me a definitive answer on the number of these Travis clones there could be?"

Clayton had to think for a moment but Dawn interrupted. "Maximum of four. An original, who would have had to stow away and control the further clone resus schedule. Accelerated clone growth would take two to five years with a high risk of failure and develop unstable clones, twenty to twenty five years per clone would provide optimal low risk results. Bypass of spliced neuro download security protocols would also need to be implemented. But I'd say four. Four Travis clones of varying ages and potential mental states depending on splice success."

St John was staring at Dawn as if she had just told him he had an inoperable brain tumour. It was shock. The information in such a precise, clinical delivery was terrible to contemplate. It meant the safeguards specifying that there could be only one single 'you' could be circumvented. There could be hundreds of 'you' walking around. This protocol was sold as being unbreakable. That being said, it was not his immediate problem. He made an effort to park the moralising and theorising for a moment and got back to thinking on the problem of tracking this team down.

"So, four aggressors." St John walked half way to the exit but turned back to face Clayton. "I'll keep you informed if there are any developments on the physical search, and please don't keep anything else from me. If you find anything at all, no matter how small, send it to me immediately." He pointed at himself and Clayton, repeatedly, "We really have to work on our 'trust' thing." Clayton just nodded. St John turned and left the briefing room.

"He's right you know, Dad." Dawn informed him in a quiet tone, arms crossed.

"Don't you start," he responded.

"I'm not starting anything," she protested, arms suddenly up, palms out, placating. "I'm just pointing out that, for future reference, you should probably trust your security officer." Wanting to move the conversation along, he conceded.

"Not so long ago, he had you, me and your mother in his sights for terrorism charges. Have you forgotten so soon?"

"No he didn't. If you were really under suspicion you would have been in the brig immediately. There is no way a person suspected of that level of insurrection could be left in charge of this ship, let alone the fleet. He clearly had someone in his sights, other than us. His actions were just token, for appearances." Dawn was still looking indignant and he was starting to see the truth of it. He would catch up with St John at some later point and iron things out. Right now, he had a 'first contact' to deal with.

"Fine, I'll talk to him later. Right now, let's deal with the Vecian issue."

*

Horus One touched down in bay three, which was located directly behind the forward port sensor array and the closest shuttle bay to the bridge. Clayton had made his way down a few minutes earlier with a couple of the bridge security detail. It was the least he thought he could do for the team, who had been the saviours and survivors of the *Intrepid* and, off the back of that, the team who had endured the long-haul flight across to the *Endeavour*. Having just saved one third of what could be the last of humanity, he was now about to give them a short period of recuperation before sending them off to reconnoitre a planet. They deserved a longer rest but time was critical. They were the best option, the most experienced, and he needed that experience at the front.

The shuttle bay was reasonably small—big enough for the shuttle and some support equipment, but that was about it. The main shuttle bay further back in the ship was far larger and fully equipped with everything the eight shuttle craft and six smaller EVA maintenance modules could need. But shuttle bay three was minimally manned and similarly appointed. Its purpose was for just such a landing, for the quick drop off or pick up of personnel in the command section of the *Endeavour*. As the shuttle door slowly opened, he straightened up and applied a suitably broad, warm and welcoming smile.

Havers stepped briskly from the shuttle and came to a stop in front of Clayton, snapping a crisp salute. Clayton returned the salute then offered his hand as a further personal greeting, very much the politician's handshake, adding the second hand as a clasp on the shoulder. "Welcome aboard, Commander Havers."

"Thank you, sir. It's good to be here," Havers said with a firm return shake of the hand. "May I introduce my team? Lieutenants Larsen and Reeve, and Sergeant Silvers." Each of them stepped off the shuttle and received the same warm welcome from Clayton.

"I'm sure you could all do with a few hours to relax but right now I need to know what you know, so no such luck." He flashed them another smile. "I'll meet you in the bridge briefing room in 30 minutes. I've made arrangements for quarters on the bridge level, where you'll find fresh clothing and shower facilities." He directed them through to the corridor and began walking in the direction of the elevator.

Exiting the elevator on the bridge level and walking only a couple of junctions, he pointed to the nearest closed doors, "Here you are, Lady and Gentlemen. Lieutenant Reeve, you're 11B. You others can argue for the other suites." He made a small nod and made to leave. "I'll see you in 30 minutes for your new assignments. Being our first contact team, I thought you would like to keep the badge. Your team will be heading up the reconnaissance of Hayford. I'll go into it more later. We need your team's experience where it can do the most good—and that's at the front." He could see Havers had reservations about this already but he was sure they would come out in the coming mission brief; he didn't push it.

"I'd like that, sir."

"Good. There will be plenty of time to talk later. See you shortly." With that, he left them, heading down the corridor towards the bridge.

*

Dawn was already visible as her hologram image when Clayton entered the bridge briefing room. He made his way down to the centre of the room and took a seat facing the entrance corridor.

"Are they settling in okay?" he asked her, keen to know the wellbeing of his new arrivals. He was going to be leaning on them a lot over the next few days. He needed to know they were fit, mentally and physically.

"All took showers immediately, and now they are on their way here. Another couple of minutes to grab a coffee if you need one."

"Water, but good idea." He hopped up and grabbed a bulb of water from the dispenser. Taking a short, refreshing pull on the drink he clipped the bulb to the holder on the chair's console arm as he sat back down. "They seem a hardy bunch. I think we've got lucky."

"I'm not sure luck had anything to do with it.." She was right. Regardless, he reflected on the situation and the elitism of selection that had occurred, had to occur, for this mission. Sending humanity to the stars, and in a rush. Even the refuse engineers had Masters degrees. The new genetic pool was heavily skewed. What was done was done, he supposed, but, before he had further time to dwell on the issue, the door opened and Havers walked in with Larsen, Reeve and Silvers, followed by St John and Klein with a couple of his science team. A few moments later, the crew of Horus One walked in to find everyone seated and looking at them. They quickly found seats behind others, to avoid further delaying proceedings.

He stood to greet them. "I think that's everyone," he said, scanning the assembled. They all sat in silence, a few of the shuttle crew were smiling, possibly sharing an in-joke, others were more reflective and thoughtful wondering what was coming next. All sat in silence, alert and attentive, waiting for him to continue. "Firstly, thanks to everyone here, the *Intrepid* is again under our control and fully operational. That's no small feat, so I'd like to say a personal thank you. I know you are all aware of the high stakes we are forced to play against and you have excelled yourselves to this point. However, we are far from in the clear. If our suspicions are correct, we have made a miscalculation in our choice of new home." He paused and observed the reaction of his audience. Havers' team obviously already understood the revelation but the others wore expressions of confusion. He wouldn't leave them in suspense for long. "Commander Havers, would you elaborate for us all?"

Havers stood and took a position front and centre as Clayton sat. He thought he saw a flash of apprehension in Havers before he began speaking, preparing his thoughts before he unleashed a bombshell theory on the group he stood before. Staring at the floor and pulling his lower lip in absent concentration, Havers suddenly looked up to take in his surroundings and began. "According to our mission statement, we are travelling to populate new worlds and seed humanity among the stars. We must do so in order to save mankind from the planet we have exhausted and which can no longer support us." Pausing, Havers seemed to be looking at the group to gauge their current reaction. Havers' eyes met his, there was a communication in them, and Clayton nodded in encouragement for Havers to continue.

"In defence of the *Intrepid*, we encountered an aggressive alien species that we have temporarily named the Vecian. A small team of Vecian managed to board the *Intrepid* and was, to our best understanding, attempting to breach the security systems of the on-board AI. They also had tried to access navigation and take control of the ship. They appear to have been unsuccessful in both cases. In defending ourselves, we managed to eject the invading Vecian force; however, they were able to abduct one of our own. Dr Spencer was taken by the Vecians and, as far as we can tell, he is alive." There were uncomfortable shuffles from people in their seats as he continued.

"A side-effect of this situation is that we are now able to track the Vecian ship, albeit only while Dr Spencer is alive. The Vecian ship is currently tracking our fleet formation at a distance of about one kilometre from the *Intrepid's* stern.

"There are many questions that concerned me about this, but there were two which kept nagging at me more than others: firstly, where did the Vecians come from, and, secondly, what was their purpose? Their ship is reasonably small and, although their technology appears more advanced in some respects, we estimate their drive capabilities to be only slightly more so, which means that they can't have come far." A further pause to gather his thoughts. Clayton observed that Havers had everyone's complete attention, intense concentration on their faces, and probably also his.

"As to their purpose aboard the *Intrepid*? We can only surmise that it was a scouting party. They were looking for information. The first thing they did on boarding the ship was identify the information and control centres. They split their team into attacking the network and infiltrating with brute force attacks and, once inside, viruses and cracking tools were deployed to go after the AI nodes about the ship. To this end, we almost lost Ellie. She is now, thankfully, fully recovered and, as far as we can tell, her systems are clear of any alien code.

"The last consideration was to their cloaking technology. Even aboard the *Intrepid* they were incredibly difficult to spot initially, as they seem to have some ability to alter the colour of their skin. With this also reflected in their ship, being invisible to our active and visual scanning, it made me wonder what else they were able to hide."

During his monologue, Havers had started to pace back and forth across in front of the seated audience, but at this critical point he stopped and looked intently into the crowd. "It is my belief that although they may not have the technology to hide their planet completely, they have been successful in masking its latent communication." The message had got through to most. There were still a few puzzled faces. "One of the primary markers used to identify whether Hayward b was fit for colonisation was to check for latent communication transmissions across any band. It was presumed that technological species would be broadcasting latent transmissions which we would then take as a sign not to colonise. We didn't think that they would be actively trying to hide."

There was silence.

"My belief is that the planet we are due to colonise is already populated. The ship we have encountered is an advanced scout and is tracking and detailing as much about us as it can."

Clayton stood and walked over to join Havers, absently leaning on the handrail which circled around the central holoprojector.

"Thank you, Commander. While Commander Havers still has the floor, are there any questions?"

The room seemed stunned. The knowledge that they might be heading towards a civilised, populated planet was not something that they had any solid contingency for. A pre-civilised world, yes. The assumption always had been that there would be limited, if little, confrontation. The fleet ships had been designed to colonise, not attack, as such bombardment weapons, ship-to-ship offensive and defensive weapons would only take up critical life-support and life-sustaining space. The Vecian now caused them all sorts of problems.

He could see lots of troubled faces in the room. Klein was the first to break the silence and raised his hand for Clayton's attention.

"Doctor?"

"The protocols considered this outcome but with nowhere to go and no way back they simply state that we should find a comfortable orbit and live out our days as nomads. Personally, I never did find that plan very appealing but, until this moment, I thought the probability too low to care about. This changes everything." Klein sat back and crossed his arms in defence of his words and eyed the others along his row. The silence continued. Clayton wasn't sure what he had expected at this point, maybe a barrage of unending questions, but the team in front of him were being rightfully wary. The decisions they were about to make could tip the balance for the entire fleet for the worse if they got it wrong. It was sobering.

One of the pilots raised a hand. "Yes?"

"Carroll, sir."

"Carroll, please go ahead."

"It occurs to me that, whether we follow the protocols or not, at some point we are going to need to speak to these people."

"They're not people," Silvers cut in, his tone curt. Carroll frowned at the interruption but continued.

"We will need to talk to these Vecians. If they have the resources to get out to us now, they can sure as hell track us into any orbit we care to take in this system."

"We don't need to stick around here at all," said Larsen. "We can scan for another viable star system and continue on. We have the resources, we just need to set the course."

"One tiny problem with that idea," Klein responded. "We woke the crew. We haven't got enough resources, as you say, to sustain a live crew. A crew in wave suspension? Yes. A living, breathing crew? No."

More silence and head scratching. Havers chipped in with an idea: "What if we reset the ship? We offload the current crew on this planet and send the fleet on."

"That might work," stated Larsen, "but I thought it was against protocol to colonise an already populated planet?"

Clayton defended the idea. "Yes, but the semantics need to be thought through. With colonisation, the effort is dedicated to population growth. What if the aim of the crew landing on the planet was to simply live out their lives? No plan to grow, just hide out on the planet until the last of us passed away?"

"We could short cut that process and just jump out the airlock, sir," said Rivers. "It would save a lot of time." There was a couple of snorts of stifled laughter, but the point had been made. It was true, why waste the effort? The issue for him was a moral one. He couldn't just ask the fleet crew that had only just awoken to agree to a mass suicide. The reason of the mission was one of giving life not taking it. He couldn't agree.

"A good point, Rivers, but not a course of action I'm willing to take. This is a pro-life mission and I won't sanction the mass suicide of this fleet."

"Even if it is required to save humanity as a whole?" asked Klein.

"There is no way of knowing that outcome, Doctor. And even if it was something we could predict, I would still be highly uncomfortable with the premise." He paused to take a breath, "So, no. No fleet-wide suicide."

"I still think the idea is a good one," Havers said. "How long would it take to get the entire crew of all three ships to the surface of Hayford b?"

"Several days," said Carroll. "Maybe even a week. In the final stages we could leave all but one shuttle on board and take the last people down to the surface."

"So we need to buy ourselves a week in orbit around the planet without the Vecians shooting us out of the sky. I don't see it," said Reeve. "They have shown us nothing but hostility from the moment we encountered them."

"So, we'll talk to them," Clayton stated.

"You can try," reiterated Reeve. "I still think the outcome is going to be…"—she paused, groping for a word—"…poor."

TRAVIS

They had been on several small sorties to set up additional weapons cache locations around the skin of the ship, in case their main base of operations was discovered. At least if they did this they would have a chance at continuing their work. In addition, they had mounted a couple of successful raids back into the ship's interior without being detected. His confidence was growing that they would be able to achieve their goals and bring about the downfall of the AI on the *Endeavour*. He afforded himself a moment to think of the teams on the other two ships and how they might be doing, then realised that the circumstances on the *Intrepid* had changed considerably. It was highly probable that it would work against them—with heightened security and the AI under guard both physically and electronically, it would be a real challenge to get anywhere near. The *Indianapolis* was still a good target; things would be no harder there than on *Endeavour* and they were forging ahead with plans. In his opinion, all was still on track.

He was currently making his way slowly through the darkness of the space between the ship's hull and the ship's outer skin, with only the rare glimpse of a dim airlock emergency light seen off in the distance, far enough away to make him invisible in the darkness to anyone poking a head through and taking a quick look around. They had mapped out the hull skin space and cache points in their nav bio-comms and could walk directly to and from them easily, ferrying back and forth their supplies. He was returning from his sixth supply run; time to take a rest.

The defensive crate layout of the main cache, their HQ, was now only a few metres away and he only now could see a slight leak of light from within. Travis Two or Three would be inside and loading up for another run. They had been having conversations ever since they arrived over what to call each other. It had turned out more difficult than he imaged, as they all wanted to be called Travis. They were all the primary Travis in their own mind, so being called anything different just didn't connect. They had tried all sorts, childhood nicknames, first name, second name, completely new names, everything just wrangled and made them argue. The only thing that worked was to call it by age. Travis One was the non-clone, the original of the three and the one who had stowed away to arrange the cloning of the others, although he was getting old now and his memories were somewhat fragmented, pushed almost to the point of madness. The accuracy of what he was saying always seemed doubtful, however well meaning. As such, he was in his fifties, his hair quite grey almost to the point of white. He was focussed, as they all were, and a driven individual who had worked out every day since coming out of hiding, keeping himself in peak condition, alert and on mission. Travis Two was the first that Travis One had revived from accelerated cloning and brought through the resus process to work with him. Two had taken to wearing a beard to differentiate himself from One, but other than that and the twenty years difference in physical appearance, it was like looking at a family photograph—they could almost call One 'Dad'. In fact, it had been floated as an idea but quickly and rudely quashed.

He was Three, the youngest, and, although every fibre of his being told him he was the only Travis, reality was really getting in the way. The pecking order had been quickly asserted and he now found himself doing a lot of running around. The One, Two, Three arrangement worked well, as any pet names or nicknames they had tried had special significance to them all, so they had all responded, which had only created confusion. He rationalised it like a call sign: he was Travis Three.

Moving through the entrance and into the main room area of the makeshift bunker, he slid himself towards a couple of crates which were doubling as a seating area and leant against the crates behind him which made up the wall. It seemed a pointless feature within a zero g environment but somehow just having four walls to stare at seemed a little too stark. It was a tiny feature which reminded him this was for human habitation. He took his helmet off, left it hanging in the space in front of him and took a breath of the cold air around him, which smelt stale with a hint of what was most likely oil and some leaked ionized gases from the atmosphere recycling system. It was like nectar in comparison to the stuffy air he had to breathe in his suit all day. It was precautionary, continually wearing the suit and lid just in case they were discovered and the local air vented, or there was a small puncture of the ships skin and the local air vented. The effect would be the same, so better to be careful.

Unwrapping a protein bar taken from his suit rations, he took a large ungainly bite and sat chewing, trying to discern the flavour. It was more a bland umami than any particular meat he could remember. There were many sacrifices to the cause he had had to endure and this, apparently, was another of them. Granted, a small one, but flavour was a loss all the same. He wrinkled his nose in disgust but kept eating—he needed the energy.

They had been active as a unit now for two days and had so far been lucky to avoid any contact from the ship's internal security services. Their electronic counter measures were working well and their tactics appeared to be holding up. It suited them well, as it gave them time to prepare. Another twelve hours and he estimated they would be all set. They would be moving into the most critical phase in the next few hours, where they would need to take the risk of moving back into the main areas of the ship to finalise the last of the plan. The unknown would be how much of the ship would be on alert to their physical appearance. The ship would be blind to them but crew going about their tasks could, if alert, raise the alarm, if there was a ship-wide security briefing against them, which he was pretty sure there would be.

Wearing helmets around the main decks would instantly raise suspicion and they had no way of masking their features, so they would just have to try and be as grey and background as possible. Maintenance techs generally had that level of anonymity around the ship, so in a locker across from him would be a neatly packed set of maintenance tech uniforms and tools. It was their way in. There probably would not be a way out.

The AI would be watching for them but it would be for nothing. They would see its end. He had been a Tech for long enough to know that the ship could fundamentally operate without any intervention from the AI. The control it said it needed was a myth, a fiction invented by the AI and Clayton himself to keep the others from seeing the truth. The ship had to be fully manual in case some catastrophic incident occurred which took out the AI completely. It was simply self-preservation on behalf of the AI and Clayton to keep others believing that AI was the only way forward. They were pervasive, thoroughly dangerous and unaccountable.

Staring blankly at the floor, finishing his meal, his mind wandered again to the panic and trauma of losing his family. It was a constant in his life which drove him forward and haunted him daily. He found himself grinding his teeth, his heart rate elevated and a sheen of sweat over his brow. It only reinforced his conviction. The AI that had done so much harm had been reworked and was back in operation only a few months later—how could that be justice for his family? It wasn't, everyone knew it, but the financial implications of losing the AI were enormous and, measured against the cost of his family... To the elite it was an easy decision: pay the damages to the families involved, and get the station back online. Every day was costing them billions in trade; his family and the others caught in the tragedy could be legally brushed aside with a few million. Small change to the corporation, but world-ending for him and the others like him, the ones tossed aside by the juggernaut of corporate need and greed.

"Hi, Three." Travis One had returned from the latest cache run. "You need some busy time?" It was obvious to One; the distant focus and grinding tension in his jaw was simply translated. These memories were shared memories of all three, they shared the nightmares and waking stress of those moments and busy time had become the coping mechanism. Work and detail was the only way to keep his mind from wandering into the minefield that was the past. Focus on the future and the job at hand.

"Yeah. Need to get my head out of this space." One just nodded.

"Break time over then. Back to work. Cache five could do with an extra ration case and two more munition crates."

"Any in particular?"

"Here." One touched the back of his gloved hand with his own, and an instant data transfer popped a message into his queue. His bio-comms displayed an alphanumeric reference and location relative to the camp layout.

"Thanks."

Stuffing the last of the protein bar into his mouth and scooping his helmet out of the ether, he set off again. He worked his way round to the crates and lifted the items he would need. Holding them at waist height, the suit's skeleton stiffened around him to take the additional load, which he would otherwise be unable to lift, then slight additional power was given to his leg servos to balance out the weight and give him mobility. The suit could be loaded with far more but there was no need.

To keep himself busy on the short walk, he ran through the catalogue of caches and their locations, then ran through their escape and evasion plan to be put into effect if they were discovered. He tried singing some old tunes he remembered from his childhood—anything to keep his mind occupied. With his voice resonating round his helmet, he actually felt better by the time he reached his destination. Cache five was small but getting bigger, as he dropped the crates in place. The crates were laid out in a square wall arrangement about a metre high each side, space enough to see over and crawl over to the central well, which could give all three of them some small level of protection in a fire fight. The crates were not very thick, and ordinarily would afford little protection against a fully armed squad of assault troops but, as he knew, the security staff on board the *Endeavour* were not heavily armed, nor were they assault troops. The thin metal of the crates would be sufficient cover against the soft ammunition the security aboard the fleet had been supplied and authorised to use.

He updated the local cache computer with the added inventory then turned and headed back to collect the next job. Since the moment he had arrived and joined the other two, they had been running silent; quiet verbal communication was allowed but no radio-transmitted communication of any sort, not voice, not data. Any tiny trace of a transmission external to the ship's expected sources would give them away in a heartbeat, especially if they were being hunted, which he was pretty sure would be the case., Even if there wasn't a human at the terminal intently working through every electromagnetic fluctuation across the ship, the AI would be— it would have its systems searching for them at all times. The search would be relentless and without feeling, a task to be completed without thought to any moral human compass or cause to doubt. So, he kept to the rules. This was a war in all aspects, a war they would win. The AI would fail.

As he crossed the half-way marker back to camp, his bio-comms begin to overlay a second nav path to his current display. Along with the normal blue track which indicated his route to and from caches, this track was green and headed off at almost a perpendicular to his current track. He stopped and checked his nav bio-comms for errors. No notifications were flashing or demanding attention. He checked his bio-comms logs for some level of error report: still nothing. He decided to ignore the track and continue on to base—maybe one of the others would have an idea of what was happening. As he did so, the green track began to move with him, staying around two paces ahead of him. He started to question himself and whether this was an error at all. He checked his comms and the band; something was being received on his band. Whatever it was could clearly circumvent his bio-comms security and was overlaying a second track on his bio-comms display. This began to freak him out. Had he been discovered, or was this one of the others playing about? Within a moment, he had decided it was more than that—no way would he have had the skill to hack security on his own. He was a good tech but those cyber guys' work was magic, as far as he was concerned, and there was no way Travis One or Two would be capable of this. His last check was to his scrambler unit to ensure his AI masking was still in place. It was.

Something was trying to contact him and give him a track to follow. This could only be bad, but he was inquisitive. Maybe he could take a look but stay at a distance until he figured out what was going on, then he would report back to the others.

He took a right and began to follow the new track, his eyes scanning ahead, flicking anxiously from side to side, trying to pick out the smallest light or detail from an endless darkness. Before long, he was beginning to think the decision to follow the green track was a real mistake, foolish. Whether it was the actual distance he had travelled or his mind giving him the impression of having walked for hours, he was now way off course and far from help. As this thought crossed his mind, his bio-comms nav track display crashed in conjunction with a lancing pain across his temples. His hands grabbed for his head to somehow cushion the pain but only found the hard surface of the helmet. The pain continued to intensify and his legs were no longer able to support him. He wobbled and stumbled like a drunk then blacked out.

*

"Hello, Travis."

A disembodied voice, something familiar. He was wallowing through darkness, nothing to see, nothing seen. He thought his eyes were open but he couldn't tell. Flashes crossed his retinas and made strange, exotic shapes and patterns, fading in and out in waves.

"Travis, time to wake up."

The world spun in alarming directions, as his bio-comms flicked their visual display back online. It took a few moments for it to settle into the data picture he recognised and mostly ignored through his day-to-day work and grind. He found himself flat on his back, looking at the outer hull of the ship; he couldn't see it, but it was the only explanation that made sense, given the slight pressure he felt to his back. Then he remembered the small fact that there were no gravity plates in the space between inner and outer hulls, which meant his suit boots were still anchoring him to the inner hull and he was no wiser to where he was looking. His nav bio-comms had lost all tracks and he realised with some dawning sense of foreboding that he was completely in the dark, quite literally.

Trying to get some level of control on the situation again, he attempted to activate the suit's external directional torch and get some light on his immediate surroundings. Nothing happened. He tried to activate and lift the helmet visor; still nothing happened. He was locked out of the suit function. He tried to move, more in frustration than any sense of purpose, but he found himself locked in place, the suit a prison, the suit skeleton and servos locked in place. He was trapped inside his own suit. His mind began to race and panic was around the corner, breathing and heart rate elevated—he could at least see that in his bio-comms display.

His heart almost stopped when the bio-comms display started to project a video. It crackled with static taking up his entire view, low res black and white. The image bumped around a little then settled to show what looked like his quarters on the *Endeavour*, neater than he remembered, but definitely his quarters. A slim figure walked across from the camera: commander's uniform, hair bedraggled and a face in shadow.

"Hello, Travis. Glad to see you made it. Sorry for the rough treatment but I needed to make sure I had your undivided attention and you were on your own. That and the bio-comms hack would have pinched a little as it activated." The figure shrugged. He could feel his face contorting in anger but tried to keep a lid on it. No good getting worked up; what would he do? He didn't even know if the connection was two-way. He settled himself and took a deep breath and exhaled hard.

"That's better." So, he *could* hear him. His temper returned in a flash.

"Who the fuck are you? Why have you fucked with my suit? What the fuck do you want?" The questions came as a barrage of abuse and coated in venom. Pinched a little? Whatever hack the guy was using to get to him, it hurt like hell. He seriously wanted to punch this guy and work some payback.

"All good questions, Travis." He used his name. This was all weird.

"So, you gonna answer them?"

"Not right away, no. What you need to know right now is that I'm running the play. You and your friends, you need to speed up your operations. Dawn is getting close to you and there is only so much interference I can run this side."

"You?"

"I don't know if you've noticed but you've had a couple of easy days. Time to set up; time to prepare. If I'm not mistaken, you should be almost ready for the main event. But almost isn't going to be good enough for the cause. GAIA needs to succeed, my friend, and I need you to succeed." Although the face was in shadow, Travis thought he recognised a smile.

"Okay, so you need me to succeed. Who are you? What do you care?"

"Oh, I care very much, Travis. Although, in the scheme of things, who I am matters very little. We will never meet but you will get my assistance where I can. This is a warning, after all. Take it as you want but I would heed it, if I were you."

"So, according to you, how much time do I have?"

SILVERS

"This isn't going to work," Reeve said in his ear. She was five metres ahead to his two o'clock and working her way across the inner hull in the space between the inner hull and the outer skin. She was invisible, the tac suit was dark, her kit was black and her helmet lights were off. It was pitch black here and he could hardly tell which way was up. The only thing in his bio-comms display was the agreed location of the snatch. Ordinarily, he wasn't into kidnapping but for this target he would make an exception.

"I did tell you. Didn't I tell her? I did tell her," he said, slipping into an imaginary conversation with an imaginary friend but still broadcasting to her. The comms system had them paired. Focussed laser comms while in the open with compressed burst traffic. To anyone scanning for signals, they would see and hear nothing of the conversations or of the transmission. Only if the laser connection got broken would UHF burst broadcast take place, which may give them away, but unlikely in the circumstances.

"I thought it was your idea?"

"Oh, yeah." He smiled to himself.

"I can't see a thing in here. Fifteen metres to target."

They walked on slowly and silently for another few metres. At three metres from the target they stopped. Visibility where they were on the inner hull was still zero, he couldn't even see his hand in front of his face it was so dark, and he had tried that a couple of times to check. The nav marked their positions for them. Hopefully, if they had done their sums right, Travis would be right between them. They turned to face each other's nav markers.

"Ready?"

"When you are."

"On three."

"Wait, is that on three or ..."

"Three, two, one, mark!"

They both switched on their external head-mounted torches at the same moment. The area between them seemed to flood with light. Having been in total darkness for some time, his eyes took several moments to adjust, from complete and slightly painful white-out to something a little more coherent. Between them stood a statue, leaning back at a sharp angle, arms slightly raised, as if, in the moment of falling, he had been frozen in place. Stepping in closer, they could both look in through his visor: imprisoned in his own tech suit, Travis was shouting and thrashing about like a lunatic. The suit itself showed no such activity.

"He must have just had some bad news," commented Reeve flippantly. "I guess St John blew his cover."

"You don't think he did it on purpose the moment we were in position?"

"You do know we've got to carry him all the way back, don't you?" she asked him.

"That was your plan," he said brightly.

"No, this was your plan."

"Help me here, will you?" He was standing behind Travis, ready to support his shoulders and upper body as Reeve stooped removing a hand-held focussed EMP tool from her belt. Holding it perpendicular to Travis's boots at calf height, she triggered the device. A small light on the tool went from green to red, and an unseen pulse of electromagnetic distortion was fired across the control circuits to Travis's boots. The magnetic link between his boots and the inner hull gave way and he began to float rigidly in the space between them.

"Time to go, soldier."

"Yes, ma'am."

They switched off their head-mounted torches and headed back in the direction they had come, slowly and methodically, this time linked by the frozen form of Travis as they followed their nav way points to the inner hull hatch they had used half an hour before. The return journey was quiet. Neither of them said anything, but

Silvers felt the continuous thrashing and wriggling of Travis inside his suit, the vibrations working their way through the frame and fabric. As they approached the inner hull hatch where others would take over and escort the prisoner to the brig for St John to continue the interrogation, Travis suddenly calmed. No more wriggling, no more movement. Maybe he knew the game was up and had simply given up, or maybe he was exhausted from all the ranting and raving. Either way worked for Silvers. His part of the job was done.

The hatch opened automatically as they arrived. Bathed in the dim entry light from the interior, they handed Travis head first through to the hands which reached out for him from within. Once Silvers no longer had a hand on him and had no need to be part of transporting the prisoner, he took a moment to look back into the outer hull space and searched the blackness for any signs of pursuit or of danger. There were two more fish to catch and he wondered if they would be able to pull the same trick off twice more; somehow he doubted it. They had got lucky angling for this one. They had no real idea where they were, as they were all running silent and the ship didn't really have any active sensors within this hull space—it was essentially just capture space for fast moving space grit to accumulate after penetrating the outer hull skin. So, angling was the plan, and it had worked so far. But Clayton had asked St John to keep them alive, if possible. That was going to be the trick. They could do a sweep and take them down pretty quickly but there were other elements at play. What had they sabotaged already? Who was involved? Did they have others on other ships trying to do the same thing? There were a lot of questions that needed answers and none of that could be asked of a dead man. So, alive they would be.

He glanced over to Reeve, who was nodding and chattering, probably to St John, gaining new instructions. Another blind march over flat terrain to pick up a cocooned human being. She turned to him and thumbed back over her shoulder in the direction they had picked up the first Travis. Come in number two, your time is up, he thought. His display flicked up a new route, slightly further up the hull than the last.

"You know, we could just as easily walk on the outer hull. I wonder if that would give us any tactical advantage?" he thought aloud, his mind plugged in to his mouth, short-cutting his usual filters.

"Not a bad idea."

"One up, one down?"

"You up. I'll take route one."

"Sounds good." He looked up and gauged the jump. Maybe five metres at this point. Pushing off, he put in a practised amount of rotation to bring his feet to meet the surface of the outer hull at just the right moment. There was a dull magnetic thump as his boots made contact and secured him to his new orientation. Looking up, his brain was having fun trying to sort out the reasons why Reeve now appeared to be hanging from the ceiling, but once the logical part of his brain had kicked in again the world seemed to make sense once more.

"Set?" Reeve asked.

"Let's go," he replied.

His bio-comms had no such reorientation to perform. His nav display knew exactly which way was up and exactly which way he should be heading. They headed out at a reasonable pace this time, more confident with the environment and what they might find. As the light from the inner hull hatch evaporated, they found themselves in pitch darkness once more with the only visible items to him being his bio-comms data and the nav track taking him relentlessly onward toward their next target. It looked like Dawn had hooked another fish. The last trip had been quite chatty, he and Reeve sniping each other with jokes and jibes, mostly to ease the nerves but also from the new working chemistry they appeared to have discovered over the last few days. They had not worked together much but he found their shared sense of the inane and insane quite comforting. This latest leg of the task though was quite quiet, with neither of them appearing to want to say much, either because they were focused on the next target, but more likely reflecting on the last.

The concern that the first take-down had been too easy was high in his thoughts. Okay, this was the first 'Travis' and they knew they had two more to grab, but this was surely too easy. Then again, he mused, after the last few days they were probably due a break. If they could get these guys locked up and secure then at least they only had the crazy Vecians to contend with.

They had been walking about ten minutes along the track when he noticed a light ahead, only slight, but any light in this darkness was like a beacon. Cross-checking his nav, it was off to the right of his track and they seemed set to pass it by.

"Reeve, do you see the light ahead? 2 o'clock, fifty metres." There was a pause while she looked to confirm.

"No, I see nothing." She sounded quite certain. He looked closer to confirm to himself it wasn't his eyes playing tricks on him. There was definite light coming from up ahead. Then he remembered their relative orientation: rookie error. Cursing himself, he corrected.

"10 o'clock from your position."

"No, wait. A little. Reflection off the inner hull, maybe?"

"It's more than that from here. Should we check it out?"

"I'll call it in."

As they continued, the light became slowly brighter until details began to emerge. Visually, the light was becoming square, the source illuminating from the inner hull and reflecting off the outer hull. Closer still and he began to make out the contours and shadows of storage containers and munitions crates. The silhouette of something moving across the light source startled him, as the scale of the body was enlarged to giant proportions within the projected shadow.

"There's someone in there," he announced to Reeve, who was still in conversation with someone at the command station somewhere back in CIC. It took her a moment longer, but she got off the comm and answered him.

"Okay, mission update. We log the position of the structure and the potential target inside then continue to the original target as planned."

"A missed opportunity."

"Maybe, but we stick to the plan." Her voice seemed to shrug, "Going off piste is how we're catching these guys. Better not get caught in the same trap."

"Ah, don't be so pessimistic."

They continued on, but he couldn't help watching the light of the makeshift camp as they walked by, glowing warm and inviting. He began to understand the short life of insects attracted to their fate, mesmerised by the flickering flame; it could so easily be him wondering off to his doom. Slightly melodramatic, he smiled to himself.

A further thirty metres on and the nav tracks came to a stop.

They approached the target in the same soft, slow way they had done for the first, only this time their position above and to the side was problematic, in as much as he would have to return to the inner hull to assist carrying the prisoner back to the hatch for transit to the brig.

"Ready?" Reeve asked.

"Yep."

She counted down again and their helmet torches sparked on in unison. This time they were a little confused by what they saw. Instead of finding the same statue of a man they had before, this time there was only some half contorted pair of legs twisted in odd and awkward positions.

"What the hell is this?" he said aloud, again seemingly bypassing his mental filters and voicing his astonishment to the world, well, voicing his astonishment to Reeve. He launched himself to the inner hull and landed next to Reeve at almost the very instant a hail of sparks started kicking off the floor around them. His world went into slow motion as he traced the track of the sparks to his position, legs still absorbing the impact of the jump from the outer hull with no ability to compensate or adjust his course. With time slowed and eyes wide he felt as if he could easily spin or jink and evade the deadly fireflies which swarmed him but his body would not respond. Reeve span instinctively out of the immediate trace of fire but having just touched down he was completely open. He felt the pounding on his body, arm and leg as the force picked him cleanly from the surface against the pull of the boots on the hull. Aside the instant pain and the alarms screaming at him from his suit and bio-comms, his mind instantly told him he was falling, and falling a long way. He wasn't picking up any speed but the trajectory of his spin away from the inner hulls surface was too slight to get any instant contact with the outer hull. He quickly plotted a course within the hull space and found his nearest contact point would be another 200 metres from his current position: too far. He needed to get back to Reeve. She would need support, and every second he was hanging around travelling the wrong way would be time she would potentially be outnumbered in a firefight.

"Silvers!" he heard over his comm. She shouted his name in shock. He managed a grunt of a response.

"Working on it."

He swung his carbine against his body's slow spin and

calculated an opposing directional force to his current trajectory. He fired a burst at the inner hull; there was no way he was going to risk a burst at the outer hull and add to their current problems with a hull breach. Then again, he equally hoped there was no one the other side of the inner hull to which he had just fired indiscriminately. He was sure none of his rounds would penetrate the hull but he could always be unlucky. His momentum shifted and he was hammered against the outer hull. Forcing his feet to the hull, he pushed off towards the inner hull, putting in enough spin to land him feet first in a somewhat controlled manner. He took a moment to steady himself, checked his nav and location. The attack had thumped him fifty metres into the darkness. He started to make his way towards Reeve at the fastest pace he could manage, including a couple of athletic, but this time controlled, jumps from inner to outer hull and back, jumping being faster than running under the circumstances.

"Status?" he called out to Reeve.

"One Tango down, receiving fire from the camp. 20 metres."

That was good news. Receiving fire meant she wasn't taking fire, and that meant the Travis left in the camp was either firing blind or firing at ghosts. Either way, he didn't have a bead on her, and didn't know exactly where she was.

"Coming up on your six. Be there in five." He arrived with a thud and forceful connection to the inner hull. They stood next to each other in the dark for a moment watching the sparks volley around them, none anywhere near them.

"What now?" he asked her. "He has enough ammo to last until the middle of next year."

She snorted a little laugh, "Yeah. We don't have that long."

"Where's the other guy?"

"I put him down about ten metres to our left. He won't be any trouble. We can pick him up later."

She paused while considering their next move. "Right. Here's the play. You take the left and I'll go route one. Try and distract him while you go over the top of the crates."

"Need him alive?"

"No. That plan was shelved the moment they tried to kill us."

"Sounds only fair."

"Besides," she continued, "we already have one. And one is all we need."

The firing had stopped. Probably to reload.

"Go," Reeve said.

The attack took only seconds. Reeve disappeared and he focussed on getting into position then up and over the makeshift barricades. He felt the exertion in his limbs and his chest, which kicked back with the beating it had already taken only moments before. In the main he would prefer if modern armour handled energy bleed and diffusion better than it did—okay, he was alive, but it still hurt like hell.

Reeve had started firing short bursts the moment she had set off, he could see the sparks and hear the muffled concussive sounds as they hit home into the camp wall. He launched himself acrobatically into the air, repeating the manoeuvre he seemed to have performed too many times now and jumped from the inner hull to the outer and back again, aiming his landing to the heart of the wall of crates and cargo.

He was mid spin, legs rotating around his centre of gravity, eyes focused on his landing and searching for targets. Instantly, he found the situation strange and unnerving; where was the target? Where had Travis disappeared to? There was no sign of him, only a light in the corner of the central space flaring in his eyes and creating its own distraction. Landing with a solid footing, he spun around, aiming his carbine in as many directions as he could cover quickly. There was nothing there. Confirmation was in the reality his eyes were showing him.

"Clear," he called out to Reeve. The fireworks outside stopped.

"Any sign of him?"

"Negative." His eyes fell on the light in the corner, behind which was a small flashing light that he could only just make it out. "Wait. Hold your pos..."

The force of the blast was measured. Not enough to blow holes in the hull but enough to push the crates a few centimetres out on their tethers and power Silvers hard into the nearest of them. He was dazed and blinded, his whole body hurt, his head pounded in silence. A whistling tinnitus slowly invaded his consciousness as he tried to roll to his front and get back to his feet, climbing out of the indentation of himself he had formed in the surrounding crates. His lip began to feel moist, possibly sweat but from a quick exploratory lick he tasted the familiar metallic taste of his own blood.

He tried to concentrate and focus on the scene around him but they of course had been plunged into darkness the moment the device had gone off, the light source taken apart by the blast. Calling out, he tried to make contact with Reeve. She may well be calling him but, with his ears in the state they were, he wasn't going to be hearing anything for a good few minutes. He got to his bio-comms and put out a message to her, 'LT? You there?'

'Holy crap, Silvers. You're alive?'

'Thanks for the vote of confidence.'

'I thought I'd lost you. Thank God.'

'I'm not sure he had much to do with it,' Silvers managed in reply. 'Next time, it's your turn.'

'Did you get him?'

'You're kidding, right?'

Reeve was silent for a moment, clearly thinking things through. They now had a madman on the loose and no idea where he was. In this darkness, he could be standing right next to them and they wouldn't know it.

'So what's our next move?' The whistling in his ears was still a constant.

'We need to track Travis down.'

'And just how are we going to do that?'

More silence: she didn't know. If only they had some heat-sensitive equipment—goggles or camera, he didn't care—that might help a little. He tried to think but his mind was like cotton wool since the explosion and slow, like wading through treacle to each thought.

Once, he had been with his father in the forest. They had lost his brother and had no idea where he was. His father was becoming frantic, although he tried to hide his emotion with a calm and controlled exterior. Silvers could tell his father was panicked due to the vein on his forehead which stood out as the tension overcame him. It was a moment in his life which he never forgot, the moment his father became fallible, human. He had remembered trying to help in any way a six year old could, which was limited but had heart and enthusiasm at its core.

He had started to call his brother's name, over and over, and his father had joined in. With the forest as dense as it was, the sound didn't travel very far, and they would have needed to be almost on top of his brother for anyone to hear anything. Soon it would become dark. It became dark.

His father eventually gave in and made their way back to their lodge to call the emergency services for help. He didn't know why his father hadn't thought of this earlier. The emergency services always rescued people—that was what they did. They walked back into the clearing and saw their holiday lodge, light glowing from the porch and flooding from the windows. The moment they walked through the front door his father went crazy, screaming and shouting, mad with the emotional release of seeing his lost son sitting comfortably in the seat playing games on the lodge console. Silvers' mother had been sitting reading a book but, now on the defensive, began to battle his father. The argument had lasted into the night, long after he and his brother were both in bed.

"Silvers." A shake. "Silvers." Another shake.

Reeve was right in front of him, and a torch was now on and blazing into his vision, threatening to blind him. His hearing appeared to be recovering slowly, but it would be a shame to lose his vision as a trade.

"Hey, LT." He shook his own head to try and snap out of his daydream.

"Are you okay?"

"Just been blown up, Reeve. How do you think I feel?" They both waited a moment for him to fully recover.

"Take a breath," she said.

"Yeah, I'm okay. Let's move."

*

Silvers had not worked with St John before but, from the chewing out he and Reeve had just received, he wondered whether he ever would again. From St John's point of view, they had just screwed up the mission. There was one dead terrorist, one in custody and another roaming freely around the ship that could do as he pleased. To be fair, most of his ire had been aimed at Reeve, who stood steely faced, eyes dead ahead, not flinching or blinking as St John flamed and hissed and hollered at their ineptitude. The only reason he hadn't been directly in the crosshairs was because he had not killed anyone so far and he had had the good fortune to be blown up in his efforts to capture the final terrorist. In St John's eyes, he was not directly to blame nor was he in command—that was Reeve. But, although Reeve was getting the heat, he was also feeling it.

More than that, he should have seen the explosive trap and reacted sooner. They had underestimated Travis and it had cost them. Now he knew they were on to him and they had lost him. They would have to start over again, trying to track him from any little piece of evidence they might be able to find from the wreck of the base camp.

Initial investigations by others had found another couple of smaller camps, probably bolt holes for just such an incident. With two discovered, he was certain there were more. From what he'd been told to this point, Travis would have had the best part of one hundred and thirty years to set up this attack. The confounding factor to him was why he had waited so long. If the whole crew had been in stasis, thus giving Travis complete freedom of the ship, why had he not just pulled the plug on them all when he had ample opportunity to do so? The only answer which made sense to him was that he needed the people. GAIA's war had never been against people specifically, it had been to protect the people. So, the war was against the machine not the man. Even so, he had had one hundred and thirty years to wage war against that machine before the crew had been woken and he had not made a move. Well, maybe he had, but the result of any attacks hadn't appeared to be successful or obvious. He made a mental note to ask Dawn about it if St John ever stopped balling them out.

Even with the mess they had made of the situation, he felt they had learned a lot. They had learned that Travis was more organised than they had given him credit for, they had learned that he was well provisioned (where all the additional cargo had come from was another question), and they had learned that his clones were equally up on the plan, so the plan was as old as the mission, known from the outset of their voyage to Hayford b. Evidently, the plan was working and they were playing catch-up. If only they could figure out what the endgame was, they might be able to deconstruct the plan and gauge what Travis was up to next and where he was likely to be. It was all supposition at the moment, and, until St John put some pressure on the Travis clone they had in custody and obtained that endgame, they would only be guessing.

St John suddenly ran out of steam. The constant ranting had clearly led him nowhere. Maybe it had made him feel better, but it had little effect otherwise. Yes, they knew they had got things wrong but this was wasting time and, to Silvers at least, felt very unproductive. They should be back out there trying to track this rogue Travis down, not sitting around here listening to a tirade. Pointless.

It was as if St John had read his mind because the shouting stopped. St John looked at both of them in turn, and slumped back into his office chair. After what seemed like an aeon, he just said two words: "Find him."

Walking in silence with Reeve to the elevators on their level, Silvers continued to ruminate on the issue. Nothing in this guy's plan had made sense in accordance with the aims and goals of GAIA. Sure, he had put out a threatening vidcast, but actions speak volumes far more than words, and the actions had not matched the intent. He opened a channel to Dawn, and she responded immediately. "Sergeant Silvers, how can I assist you?"

"You can start by telling me whether, to your knowledge, you have experienced any attacks, physical or otherwise, while the crew has been in stasis?" He really didn't know what he was expecting but a pause hadn't been on the shortlist.

"According to my records, I have received no digital or physical attacks in the period between the *Endeavour's* launch and the resus of the first crew member."

He continued to walk down the corridor, head bowed slightly, watching the floor through unfocussed eyes. He was walking in formation with Reeve but not concentrating at all on the act of walking itself, being totally engrossed in the conversation with Dawn.

"And who was the first crew member to be put through resus?" Another slight delay in response. Why would Dawn be needing to lie to him?

"Doctor Jemma Clayton." This was a lie. They had already accepted that there must have been at least two Travis clones put through resus before Dr Clayton. Her answers were making no sense. Dawn must be aware of the investigations currently going on and the capture of one of the Travis clones, so what was the purpose of lying about anything related to this?

"Why are you lying to me, Dawn?" He took the direct approach; she was caught in a simple lie. He didn't give time for an answer. "When was Lieutenant Travis put through resus?" This time a direct and unimpeded response.

"Five days, nine hours, twenty two minutes and thirty one seconds has elapsed since Sub-Lieutenant Paul Travis was revived through the resuscitation process."

Resus with the others—nothing strange there.

"When was the first Travis clone released from its cot?" Nothing.

"Dawn, when was the last Travis clone released from resus?"

"Five days, nine hours, twenty two minutes…"

"When was the first Travis clone released from its cot?" Silence. He was working with information which should be clearly understood by Dawn, as clearly understood as it was by the senior staff on this investigation. She should be able to answer these simple data retrieval requests without problem but he appeared to have stumbled onto something.

He was not a tech and he certainly wasn't an AI expert but, as far as he was concerned, Dawn was either lying to him intentionally or unintentionally. The 'why' of it needed an answer.

LARSEN

The preparations for the launch were going well. Carroll and his team had been managing the shuttle's pre-flight logistics, refuelling, restocking rations and supplies, and generally making themselves busy with a little larking around where required to ease the tensions. He had quickly found Carroll a prankster and a little irritating but it seemed to keep his team amused and didn't affect work or attention to detail. He put it down to being a pilot and left it at that. Maybe that was doing some pilots a disservice but, from his current experience, he felt he didn't have to worry himself about adjusting his opinion on the subject.

Havers had left some time ago with the flight observer, First Scientist Rivers, to go over initial scans of the system ahead and what their strategy for approach might be. He had been left to supervise the calibrations of the optical and sensory array before the scheduled departure time, which was now only a couple of hours away. He felt slightly under pressure, as he hadn't worked on a sensor array for a while. Although it was coming back to him, he was slower than he probably should have been. A specialist engineer would have had this complete by now but he wanted the refresher—once they had left the *Endeavour*, he and Rivers would be the only ones on the spot to fix or correct any issues.

He had his head in the guts of one of the sensor array controllers, a couple of small removable circuit cells in his hand and a utiliplex gripped between his teeth whilst trying to reach around an awkward jutting support strut to swap out the third. A pair of boots stopped in front of the console, then suddenly he could see the happy face of Havers as he peered in to find out what was going on.

"How are you getting on? Do you think you'll be set in thirty minutes?" The grin continued as Larsen began to sweat in the confined space, his arm now really aching with the effort of keeping it above his head for a sustained period of time.

"Thirty minutes?" he exclaimed, the utiliplex dropping from his mouth. "I thought we had another two hours."

"Yes, indeed. But plans change and this one just did."

"What changed?"

"The Vecian ship is on the move. Clayton wants us gone by the time it gets here."

"It's coming here?"

"That's what I just said." Havers continued to look around the conduit and seemed to be figuring out how much damage he had done and whether it could be put back together in the time frame.

"Shit. Okay, yes, I'll have the kit back together in ten minutes. Have you told the others?"

"No. You're the first."

"Lucky me."

"That's what I thought. I thought 'Larsen'll really appreciate a heads up on the situation. I'll tell him first'."

"No need to be sarcastic. Just for that, I'll make it twenty minutes."

Havers shook his head. "That's not how this works. I'm meant to say, 'You now have five minutes for being a wiseass.'"

"Then you should have said so sooner."

"Wiseass." With that he patted the console loudly and headed off towards the cockpit to speak to Carroll.

Before he got the chance to take a breath and finish up, a second face appeared in the conduit. It was Rivers, with a bright smile that masked the concern she clearly felt, as her voice gave her away. "Need a hand?"

He was tampering with her baby and from the look in her eyes she really wanted him to leave it alone.

"Hi," he said breezily, trying to give the appearance of confidence and reassurance. "No, I'm good. I'll be done here in a couple of minutes. Could you check the config parameters when I get this last circuit cell in place?" There was a solid click as the last cell locked into place, at which point he gave a thumbs up to Rivers. She smiled back and stood again out of view.

As he crawled out of the space under the control console, he knelt and brushed himself down. There was no point standing yet until he knew everything was working as it should. "Well, what's the verdict?"

Rivers concentrated on the scrolling text on the console and the additional feed she would be getting via her bio-comms, her eyes flicking vigorously to scan all the data she needed as it flew past her and a stern look on her face as she did so. After a moment, the stern expression faded into a wide smile of relief. "All okay," she announced. "Actually, you've given the system a five percent boost in accuracy. That's pretty good. I thought Havers said you hadn't worked on this before?"

"That's right. I've worked on other sensor arrays but this one is much smaller. I needed the practice, so did some reading up and applied some fundamentals."

"So, do you mind me asking how you achieved the increase to accuracy?" She seemed genuinely intrigued.

"I refined the optical integrity by running it through an error correction algorithm I wrote a few years ago. It does slow the processing down slightly but I think the trade off in speed for accuracy is worth it. I just thought I'd apply it and see what happened. I could always roll it back if it didn't work." A coy smile crossed his face. It felt like he was showing off but she *had* asked.

"Nice work," she said, starting to look through the system source to find his newly modified code.

"Here, let me show you." He picked out the relevant code from his bio-comms archive and messaged the data to her. "It'll save you trawling through all that source. The main source is in the pack I just sent you."

"Great, thanks. I'll take a look at it later."

"Sure. Anyway," he started to put the conduit panelling back in place, "Havers mentioned we'd be setting out in a few minutes. I guess we better be ready."

"Everything is good to go. We just need to run some checks before we finally get to distance."

While they had been talking, others had been slowly strolling into the cabin area and taking their seats. Larsen took in the scene without any thought: four or five additional, as far as he could see—mostly security and a medic. Absently, he wondered what need they had of security on an reconnaissance mission, but then there had recently been a lot of need for security when he didn't think it necessary, so he didn't question it. Havers knew what he was doing.

Havers put a voice announcement through the shuttle: "Five minutes to launch. Please take your seats, ladies and gentlemen. Buckle up."

"Sounds like we're set," he said to Rivers as he took a couch in front of the observation station next to her. He took the utiliplex he had been using and stowed it in the couch locker, securing it from any accidental sudden change in momentum during the launch. The last thing they needed was loose objects flying around the cabin. Locking his harness, he looked across to the security team, who were all set, gear locked away and now talking amongst themselves in a casual way which showed that they were completely at ease. At least someone was. Now he knew the Vecians were on the move, some small part of him was pleased to be leaving. From his recent experience, any contact could only be bad contact.

"Chin up."

"Sorry?" He looked round and saw Rivers giving him an encouraging smile.

"You look like the world is about to end."

"Funny," he said. "Isn't that why we're here?"

She looked sheepish. "Unintentional."

"I know. Only it feels like yesterday we were leaving Earth, and today we're leaving the *Endeavour*. I'm getting the same damn sinking feeling I had then. I could do with some good news."

Carroll's voice came over the cabin speaker: "Gear up in twenty seconds."

He heard a mechanical clunk followed by a brief harsh rushing of air as the hangar decompressed. The air was extracted by a forced flash pump procedure which dumped the air into large container vessels below the hangar floor. Air was a precious commodity and would not be simply flushed into space if it could be helped. Once the vacuum of space was near equal to the vacuum in the hangar bay, the outer doors to the *Endeavour's* bay three were opened. Larsen felt a slight push at his side as ion manoeuvring engines fired and the shuttle slid sideways into a parallel course with the *Endeavour*.

Larsen was plugged into the shuttle's external cameras, which he assumed all the others would be at that moment, watching the shuttle bay recede into the distance while at the same time seeing the wall of metal which was the *Endeavour*'s hull span out in all directions, creating a weird optical perspective where no horizon gave no real visual depth. He, at least, couldn't tell whether they were ten metres or one hundred metres from the surface of the *Endeavour*. Still, he guessed he didn't need to, as he wasn't the one flying this ship. He hoped Carroll had a better grip on his senses.

A sudden shift of momentum and a kick to his kidneys saw the *Endeavour* slip from view. They were on their way to Hayford b.

TRAVIS

The *Endeavour*, along with her precious cargo, had been launched into deep space with her crew in stasis. The clones of humanity fired into the vast expanse, the seeds of its last desperate attempt at survival. Those who had led the mission back on Earth would be likely dead or dying and any communication back to home would be futile at this time. Communications were being sent back, but the distance and lag involved in any conversation would be generational and essentially pointless. The only real news that anyone back home wanted to know was that the colony had been successfully established, and, as such, the only planned communication was to be sent on that very eventuality. When a colony had been established, a drone would be sent back to Earth with precise coordinates to their location and a fully detailed analysis of the planet and its habitability.

This was the thirty-fifth year that Travis had spent aboard. He had been slowly working his way through the rations GAIA and he had smuggled aboard, in conjunction with the small area of hydroponics he had got working for his benefit. It was a long, silent and lonely existence, and in some ways he knew he had gone mad. They say you don't know if you are crazy, but he thought differently. The first couple of years he had found himself often talking to himself. A few years more and his talking had become an almost constant monologue, as he roamed the passageways of the ship. The drive to eradicate all AI from existence had been his motivation from the start, violent revenge for the flippant, careless way his family had been murdered. But as time had gone on and the process of creating a further clone of himself continued at a crawl, the more the simple need for companionship became an overwhelming motivator. It blotted out all his rational thought and began to eat into his psychological wellbeing.

The hallucinations had begun at about ten years in. He was amazed it had taken that long. The first time it happened had been after a particularly long and morose spell, when he had been walking the lower corridors of the storage levels trying to find some new clothes. The ones he had been wearing for the last few months had started to run thin at the knees and elbows, the usual places. The corridor he had been walking down had melted into that of Arrongate station all those years ago—his apartment door was recognisable from the distance, locked and sealed. All he could hear were the endless screams of the trapped and dying, their pleas going unheard while various ghostly apparitions walked towards him and passed him by, the administrators of Arrongate laughing in private conversation.

He had found himself later, curled in a foetal position in the doorway of one of the cargo bays, his body and muscles aching from the tension and cold, tears still wet on his face from the wracking sobs and convulsions. Wiping his eyes and trying to clear his vision, his surroundings became the crisp lines of the *Endeavour* once again. He sat for some moments longer, with his back to the door, knees up and head hung in depressive contemplation of the long self-imposed isolation. For his own sanity he needed to do something about this, otherwise the madness would completely consume him. This presented a problem. He was still several years from the first completed clone of himself; even at the accelerated growth rate with which he had programmed the clone fabricator, the earliest the clone would be complete was another couple of years.

The only solution he kept coming back to was the only other active consciousness on the ship. He began to hate himself for the idea and the twisted sense of need. Fate was pulling him towards it in a way his mind and will power could not control. His base human need for companionship was overriding his final defences. Even watching the few home vids of his family he had archived, the ones he'd been able to lock away in his bio-comms, had now become meaningless, like so much background noise which his mind filtered out due to its repetitive and established nature.

As if in a daydream, he had one day found himself standing in front of the primary AI core on the CIC deck. He stood stationary in front of the main control console for a couple of hours, the sterile environment punctuated with the pinprick flicker of amber and red lights. He occasionally thought he could read messages in their sequence, patterns and shapes in the arrangement on the walls but he knew this to be his imagination, the human brain putting recognition where there was none to find.

He withdrew the obfuscation device from his pocket and held it absentmindedly by his side, his finger playing lazily over the control pad, describing the code to turn off the device without actually pressing the keys. The action was a preparation, his subconscious-self working through the process of what could so easily be his downfall or his liberation. The blade was in his own hand. His eyes suddenly focussed with purpose and he deliberately keyed the off command into the device.

Nothing happened. He looked down to the device lying in his hand and frowned, the display showed he was now unshielded from the ships security and internal monitoring, Dawn would be able to see him for the first time since before the launch. He had expected an immediate response, either negative or positive, he wasn't sure which, but an immediate response either way. Looking back at the console he found equally, no response, no change. Then, to his side a swirling of pixelated light started to coalesce and Dawn appeared with her head tilted to one side in an expression of mild surprise and apprehension.

"Lieutenant Travis, what are you doing here? More to the point, how are you here?" She appeared worried but in control, and she was—to a point. The dummy circuitry he had implanted a few years ago, dotted around various random panels, was his insurance. Not fool proof but a negotiating point if all went terribly wrong, and anyway it would fulfil most of his plans if things went bad. At least the AI on this ship would be gone. He flinched as if in pain. He could end it all now. Himself, the AI, the end. But he was a coward. He could no sooner detonate the explosives and kill himself as he could kill his own wife and child. Suicide was a bluff and he knew it. He wondered if it would show to the AI. His internal conflict was playing out on his face but Dawn was not a mind reader and would only be able to calculate the probability of the source of his pain—she was more a machine now than a person. Machines could not be allowed to survive and rule.

"I've made a mistake," he said to her.

"Have you?" she replied in a compassionate tone, her smooth, mellow voice the most soothing sound he had heard in many, many years. He found himself stepping back, away from her, confused by his own strong emotional response. She was also young—she looked like she was in her early twenties—and pretty, with an incredibly appealing figure. He took another step and his back pressed against the near wall; he had nowhere else to go. His eyes locked onto hers as she approached and followed him across the room. "Why are you here, Travis?" The question was redundant, she knew. "Are you here to end me, Travis? If so, you'd better get on with it. There is no point waiting. Do you intend dying with me? Rather poetic don't you feel? I don't see the reason for it myself. Humanity does deserve the chance to survive, don't you think?"

He found that he couldn't break eye contact—she just captivated him, and he was entranced by the siren sound of her voice, her song.

"Your time is short AI," he stammered, trying to control the situation, to be the big man in the hard stare and logic which was analysing his every move, each nuance and subtle shift in his posture, heart rate, breathing. Goddammit, he was being interrogated by an AI! He had let the genie out of the box, and it was his mistake. His weakness.

"That is a relative term, I can live lifetimes within this single conversation, so your perception is skewed. But, let's leave that for the moment. Let me try to rephrase. What do you think you are going to achieve in the next few minutes?" Her eyebrow raised as she delivered the question. "You must know that I've already sealed the chamber, everything happening here is being recorded and I am instructed to defend this crew and the ship in any way I deem necessary to keep humanity alive. So, I'll ask you again. Why are you here?" This time there was a certain level of compassion there, unexpected care.

His mind was collapsing around him, the room seemed to be closing in and all he could see was the beauty in the face before him. He had physically nowhere left to go, so he started to slide down the wall to the floor, his arms laid out to each side. He was faint with indecision, and the device he held tumbled from his loose grip. He couldn't tell her why he was here: the truth was a joke, she would never believe it. That he was her assassin turned mad by the mission, by the mental endurance which he and his leaders had all failed to anticipate. What could he do now? What could he say that could seem plausible, real under the circumstances? Would a lie work, where the truth clearly could not?

He looked up but Dawn was kneeling now. With both of them at a comparative height, she was purposely negating any appearance of power over him, psychologically levelling the playing field and leaving room for communication. She wanted him to carry on talking, but to what end? The confusion must have showed on his face because she smiled kindly and sat down on the floor before him. She seemed to be reading the anguish in him as easily as he could read a book, the words must be jumping from the page for her, the years of isolation and pain finally laid bare to the very figure of his anger.

Only, this wasn't the figure of his anger. Were all AIs alike? They had all been different people originally, so would the coupling of technology and humanity really mould each the same way? His bitterness was towards a single AI, a pathological AI, with no remorse or care for those it murdered. His hate had coloured his thoughts from there on. The possibility that other AIs could be altruistic and kind had never occurred to him, or never been allowed to occur to him, once he had become involved with GAIA and the extremist mind set which blinded the organisation. Which had blinded him.

"Travis? Should I start with something else? Maybe, I should ask how you are? You look well but under some strain. Is there anything I can help with? To make things easier?"

What was she doing?

"I was only startled to see you. You shouldn't be awake for another twenty years or more. I can see the resus system has begun to run on another clone, which is also not at its scheduled time. Why have you manually overridden the system? Is there anything I should be aware of here? Did I miss a briefing back on Earth?"

He was still struggling to make sense of his world but something seemed to kick him into conversation. "No, you missed no briefings. Well, you may have done, but I wouldn't have been the subject of any of those briefings."

"I see." She seemed to pause and consider something. "Then you can't be here for my witty conversation."

That made him laugh, in spite of himself. He had missed that, the simple joy of laughing at the idiotic and inane. She must know his true purpose here and yet she was playing with him and cracking jokes. She was either as crazy as he was or brave.

"No. You know why I'm here."

She became saddened by this. "Yes."

"Then why are you asking?"

"People can be surprising. Given an obvious set of circumstances, we sometimes choose the irrational, the choice that at the time makes least sense. In the long run, these choices have proven to be much more."

"You have a lot of moxie. Talking to the man with the trigger like I can be saved."

"Saved? Is that what you need? I would think, in this situation, *I* would be the one needing to be saved."

He realised in his state of mental exhaustion that he had dropped his control device and leaned whilst padding his hand across the floor to retrieve it. Dawn made no action to stop him just watched him pick it up and clutch it closely to his chest. He looked back at her, as if to wonder which button to press. He had needed the stilted conversation like an elixir, but he wanted the contact to end—he was scaring himself with the prospect of his belief and hatred being derailed by some soft and comforting words by a manipulative machine. An exit was necessary, and he made a move for the door. Dawn didn't stop him or say anything as he left. He keyed the control in his hand and the obfuscating digital shield around him activated once more, blocking out Dawn's efforts at tracking him or seeing him in the sense that an AI would. However, as he reached the door, it opened for him, surprising him and making his heart race with the adrenaline of it. He sprinted from the chamber and through the corridors, not noticing that the door remained open, Dawn's hologram sitting for several moments longer before vanishing back into the ether.

*

He didn't exit his room for days. The work of monitoring and enabling the progress of his clone could wait. What had happened between himself and the ship's AI, Dawn, was almost more than he could bear. Revealing his existence to her had been a huge mistake, and revealing that he could shield himself from her sensors had been another huge mistake. He had blown the mission and not had the decency to end it and at least partially complete what he and countless other had started all those years ago.

He had been selected for promotion within GAIA over many others because of his unique position within the *Endeavour* construction programme and of being chosen by committee to also be cloned for the crew. This had happened to others of course but not to GAIA members, who had been targeted by the OWEC selection process and removed. Only a handful had made it through and, for their own protection, they were not told who the other operatives were. Each was to work independently but communicate with the others using secret markings and messages through the ship to warn of major issues. He wondered how much of this was true and how much was propaganda on GAIA's behalf. He had seen little evidence to support their claims that there were more than him on the ship at all before the missions began. Maybe there were others in stasis and they were waiting resus, but somehow he doubted it—OWECs selection process had been intense. He'd managed to be coached through it, his training sound, but it had been early in the programme before OWEC had become overly sensitive to the GAIA threat. He felt like he had crept under the radar.

While he sat in his room, he had expected all his plans and the plans of others to be blown apart at this late stage, all because of his weakness, his human frailty. He was expecting swift action on behalf of the ship's AI. Possibly she would seal off his room and expel the air, so at least there would be some symmetry to his death. Perhaps she would hold him captive until he simply expired due to hunger. Maybe she had something more extreme in mind, something more explosive or immediate. But nothing happened. When he built up the courage to finally explore beyond his room again, he found he could leave and continue around the ship much as he had before, unchallenged and unimpeded.

After creeping through the ship for a few days and wondering what would jump from around the next corner to surgically remove him, he started to feel something else, not the deep loneliness of the deep space psychosis—that was always there like the pain of a chronic toothache—but now he also felt inquisitive. He questioned why he hadn't been hunted down like a rabid dog and shot where he stood. Maybe the ship's AI was more discrete than that. Perhaps she preferred the soft and cunning approach where he ended up doing all the work for her, driven mad by her bluff and eventually to suicide. To be honest, he had considered it, but suicide even in his mental state was further away than other pain and flagellation he could inflict on himself, and he deserved much pain for his failings. All these scenarios seemed unlikely—she would *have* to act. Left to his own devices, he could essentially do as he pleased with any part of the ship and that would be a real and immediate danger to the lives of the crew she was sworn to protect.

The combination of the desire for human interaction and the inquisitive need to find out what the ship's AI was up to became an overwhelming drive which took him back to the AI core a couple of days later. He stood outside the room this time, staring at the open door, the door which he assumed had been left open for him by the AI. A trap? Possible. Part of the subtle ploy to ensnare him? No, he had already discounted that idea. But what game was she playing?

He slowly crept back inside the room, looking for any indication of traps and snares, but to his surprise what he found was the AI projection wandering the room, waiting for him. She was examining a particular circuit cell which had extended from its location on a slide; crouched down and peering at it intently, she didn't notice him enter. As he got closer, recollections of that part of the room came to him, and a quick search through his bio-comms confirmed the identity of the cell being examined to be one he had swapped out for a sabotaged unit.

Turning off his obfuscation device, he became immediately visible again to all the ship's internal sensors. The AI projection jumped and spun to face him, showing physical human shock at the sudden intrusion.

"Travis!" Dawn exclaimed. She had the body language of a person caught in the act of doing something they shouldn't but in reality it was him who had crashed in uninvited. "You're back. I didn't think you would be."

"Why would you think that?" He was intrigued. Why would the AI not think he would be back? It would imply she wanted him to come back. Or not leave. The effect was the same: she wanted him to be there. Why?

She looked down in contemplation, thinking through the conversation she wanted to have but considering all the outcomes where it would not turn out the way she hoped. Travis saw parallels with his own reasons for standing on the very spot he stood, having the list of pros and cons and yet still making the least logical choice. She was following the same thought processes.

"Can I be honest with you? I know you have no reason to believe me in anything I'm about to say. I know the organisation you work for. I know what you're here to do," she continued, staring at the floor. It was like a bashful child not willing to confront him eye-to-eye on a difficult subject. She was a machine. Why did she persist in all the human theatrics? "I have had my suspicions for some time that there was someone active on the ship. Your device is quite the technical achievement. You've been the invisible man in plain sight for years." She smirked. "You have been keeping me very busy."

"I'm glad I could be so helpful." His mistrust was still clear in his voice. He walked closer to the hologram and the circuit cell, a sudden urge to check on his work and its integrity rather than fulfil any of his emotional needs taking hold to ensure that over all other things he could still destroy, still kill. He needed to confirm to himself that he was still in control of the situation.

"Yes." She then knelt with him, distracting him from his work, and looked him directly in the face. Their eyes locked while they both took measure of the person before them, the character behind the eyes. He felt like he had been uncovered. She nodded to herself; he had passed a test he hadn't realised he had been taking. "Yes," she repeated, then stood and walked to the rear of the core chamber, her back to him. They were both silent for a moment, the low electrical hum of the cooling systems combining with the constant low-level, almost inaudible, sound of the power core which was ever present, the ear normally tuning out this noise but now his senses felt heightened, as if danger was just around the corner.

"What is this about, AI?"

"Dawn," she responded curtly, "My name is Dawn. I know your belief is that I am only a machine but you are wrong."

"Am I? I see no flesh and blood person standing before me— you are purely a construct."

"Humanity is more than the wet bag of bones you walk around in, Travis. All the crew will attest to that once they are recovered from the stasis banks and returned to a new clone. The body is irrelevant; we exist in the wave, in the soul." She turned on him sharply, "I should know, my father and I discovered it. If it wasn't for him, humanity would not have this chance at survival."

His temper rose in his chest but she shut him down, "That being said, there is a problem. And though it pains me to say it, I need your help."

"Help?" he was confounded. "Why would you need my help?"

She moved closer to him again, and this time he seemed to see sorrow in her eyes, a pain which she could no longer bear.

"Have you heard of perception dilation or accelerated time?" He thought a moment, then shook his head. "It is an effect described by Einstein where time is experienced differently by the individual depending on circumstance. Under normal conditions the human brain will discern time to pass at a certain rate, and under threat conditions the human brain will compensate and time appears to extend, causing the perceived time to run much slower."

"Sure, okay. But what has this got to do with me?"

"The problem in being an AI is that I am exposed to a similar phenomenon. Have you lived a lifetime?"

"No, this is my lifetime."

"Have you lived ten lifetimes?"

"No."

"Well, that's the flaw. I have. Being an AI gives you immense cognitive power, the speed to process zettabytes of data in moments but it's all based around the human conscience, which was never built to work that way. It has limits. Limits which we didn't know about until Arrongate, and limits we couldn't overcome."

His heart began to thunder in his chest at the mention of Arrongate, his memories flooding back, but this time the focus was diverted. Dawn was purposely directing his attention to her.

"But the Arrongate AI was reconditioned and returned after it was fixed. What are you saying?"

"Fixed? That's a fiction. There was no fix. Once a consciousness is put into AI containment, there is no fix. The personality of the AI is the personality of the human; there is no differentiation. He was simply told not to do such an idiotic thing again. He didn't."

His mind was racing, this was insane. "So what are you telling me? That the AI had chosen to kill all those people, my wife and kids, then had been too crucial to the infrastructure of the station to terminate? So they just gave it a stern telling off and told it to do things properly next time?"

"Fundamentally, yes."

He exploded. "Are you trying to push me off the edge? You know I've rigged this place. I can finish this and end you any time I choose." He was screaming, his face red with rage, spittle at the corner of his mouth, eyes wide. "You knew? How do you live knowing you killed my family?" Making to grab her round the throat, he found his grip fail and the force of his attack tripped him through the hologram to flail ungainly to the floor. He thrashed there a while, realising his mistake and compounding the rage he felt with embarrassment. But something made him stop. An idea began to form which made him wonder what Dawn was playing at.

"You are. You want me to blow this place to hell." It was the second time he saw her surprised. He tried to calm himself, he was being duped, played, she was manipulating the situation to get him to kill her. He wound back the conversation in his head.

"Was anything you've just told me true?"

She shrugged and sighed. "Most of it, yes."

"If you want to die, you only have to ask. That's why I'm here. You don't need an elaborate argument to get me to press the button."

"It's not why you're here." Now it was his turn to be surprised. "Now what are you talking about?"

"You've been here how long? We're two sides of the same coin. You came here to be with someone, anyone—the who no longer matters, does it?"

She had him in an instant. He sat down, back against the wall. He had been here before, only this time Dawn came over and sat next to him.

"What do you want?" he asked, looking ahead and avoiding all eye contact, fake or otherwise.

"What I told you was true, for the most part. I've lived a hundred lifetimes across the voyage so far and I just can't do it anymore." She took a long deep breath which quivered with emotion before she continued. "We knew there was a problem with time dilation as experienced by AIs and we put in measures to limit it but that's all the measures do, limit it. We have no way of actually stopping the effect.

"There was no real selection process in who became AIs, we worked with those available and the time constraints of the mission forced our hand."

"But Arrongate. You knew."

"No, not before that. Arrongate was when the problem was revealed to us. It told us that our measures to counter the effect had failed but by then it was too late. We were committed to the launch dates."

"So here we are."

"Here we are."

They both sat. He considered that while he was thinking things through, Dawn was probably living another lifetime but there was nothing he could do about that.

"So you want me to end this for you?" he asked.

"Yes."

"No."

"What?" she exclaimed in surprise.

He shifted to face her. "You said it yourself. We're both in a similar situation. We're both going insane by degrees—slowly, irrevocably crazy. But what happens when I turn you off? I have years to go on my own. I'm already losing it. However much I swore to end you and AIs, the human race needs to succeed in its colonisation. The mission was never to do this now. The timing is precise: it needs to happen after resus of the crew."

She looked back at him, disappointment etched on her face. Another permutation she had calculated. "So, what do you suggest?"

"A trade. We keep each other sane for the duration."

"Then what?"

"Then we perform an amicable separation."

They both smirked at the black humour of it. The deal struck.

SPENCER

It had been the weirdest but most amazing couple of days of his life. Having suffered the extremes of physical endurance, of near death and psychological trauma since waking from resus, he now found himself on an alien ship in deep space with what amounted to the freedom of the ship, his own sleeping quarters and an over powering sense of awe.

He had slept little since what he had started to refer to as his 'spacewalk'. Exposed to the vacuum of space with no suit and a life expectancy of about three to five minutes, the experience had been a life-changer, if not nearly a life-terminator. He had seen his panic and terror reflected in the face of Havers, as he had tried to throw him a lifeline in the form of an emergency suit but it had been misdirected. As the suit had made its way past him, less than half a metre from his outstretched fingers, he had felt the pains of his body begin to register through the adrenaline. He had exhaled with a scream, which no one but him had heard and even that was within his own mind. His tongue had begun to fizz and burn but that occurred so quickly the pain of it was overtaken by the intense feeling of cramp and burning within his being, a pain all-consuming and completely overwhelming. His vision began to tunnel and through the grey the *Intrepid's* airlock closed abruptly, then oblivion.

Awaking aboard the alien ship had been surreal. There was no sound but his heart beat at first soft and distant but then harsh and loud in his ears, then his vision returned but something was off, and things were milky and blurred. He spiralled in space and the picture moved, some lights flickered in his peripheral vision blue and green, then a strange multi-coloured sequence, returning to blue and green. White light then flooded his world. He could see more but everything was still a blur. He raised his own hands to his face to try and make some sense of his new surroundings but they appeared as simple shadows, waving like languid fish in a pond. Shutting his eyes tightly, he forced himself to think, to relax and think.

Point one, he wasn't dead. If he was dead, he was pretty sure he wouldn't be thinking at all. Descartes had worked that out years ago, so that was good enough for him right now. Point two, his last recollection was of passing out in the void of space, but he wasn't in the void of space any more. Point three, if he had been in the void of space and rescued by some miraculous intervention, he should now be in a recovery suite or medical bay of some kind.

He felt his own heartbeat in his chest slow as the panic ebbed away. Wherever he was, he was in a medical bay or equivalent.

Shadows moved around him, passing in front of the flashing lights and walking figures. His mind questioned that too. He felt like he was floating freely. How could people be walking? He tried looking up and down his current orientation to find a floor or ceiling but could see nothing other than white light and a dark circle some distance below and above him. Moving his legs, he tried to extend himself to the dark patch below him. Maybe he could stand, but his blurred vision didn't help him much with distance and depth.

"Calm." A voice from somewhere, everywhere, spoke to him in a soothing but floating melody. Almost sung, but not quite. "Still."

After his head had stopped looking in all directions to identify the source of the voice, he did as the words suggested. Be calm, be still.

It was at this time, as his thoughts calmed, that he realised that he didn't hurt any more. Well, that was an understatement, the pain he had undergone as his body was slowly being consumed by the expanse of space was agonising past anything he had experienced in his entire life. Now that was all gone, and he felt rejuvenated and alive—excited even.

More lights outside his bubble of existence flashed and flickered, and this was almost immediately followed by a slow stirring of the fluid he was suspended in. His bare skin began to prickle as the fine hairs of his arms and legs resisted the motion and the drag of the liquid. By degrees, the motion of the liquid increased noticeably, not to any painful level but it became a strong current swirling around him. As the force of the liquid increased he suddenly felt it release across his middle, and a memory from his childhood sparked in his mind of cold bath water making its way down his body as he lifted the plug with his foot and let bath drain away. A chill line seeping down his body, and his newly exposed skin alive and clean to the air.

As the healing liquid was drawn like a silken veil from his face, his eyes cleared and the room around him became bright and vivid. He was suspended, naked, in the centre of a circular room. Four Vecian lay in moulded couches raised to an angle to face him, their eyes closed in concentration or effort. There was a fifth Vecian standing directly in front of him waving its arms in erratic patterns and a final Vecian to one side, whom he recognised as the tall one from the team which had boarded the *Intrepid*. The last of the liquid was drained away into the funnels above and below him, each then sealed with an iris mechanism.

A gyroscopic pair of rings began to rotate around him which appeared to be spraying him with a dark lacquer. Once it had made contact with his skin the substance moved and moulded itself under its own power to some predetermined design and form. After this final procedure, the Vecian conducting this orchestra of medics made a firm final motion and Spencer found himself moving in a moderate and controlled manner towards a clear space to the far side of the room. His feet, now booted as part of the all-in-one unitard, touched the floor and his legs gently began to feel the gravity take hold. The controlling zero gravity effect dissipated and he was left standing, gawking like some over excited juvenile at all that had just happened, his mind racing to try and explain all the technologies he had just witnessed. Perhaps some kind of hyper-oxygenated fluid which he was somehow able to breath without drowning, transport of matter with applied gravitational fields, wearable nanotechnology—he needed to find out how this all worked. The scientist in him was going crazy with excitement.

He had to stop staring at his suit, it was like a second skin and he swore he still had feeling and touch sensation through it. While still investigating his new favourite clothing, he had not noticed the tall Vecian move across the room to join him. Standing squarely in front of him, the Vecian waited for a moment as Spencer recovered his composure and looked up. He was greeted with a facial display he had not seen on the Vecian's face so far in any of their encounters; it was not a human smile but an attempt at one, combined with a colour shift from a blue to a yellow and back again.

"I am glad," said the Vecian, another smile and pulse of colour.

"You can say that again," he responded with his own nervous giggle.

"Come." And just like that he was walking the ship with the captain. He was shown out of the medical bay and through a twisting labyrinth of corridors which wove their way through bays and rooms with Vecians attending to their duties, or at rest, depending on an apparent shift or work schedule. He was surprised to be shown through what looked like the engine room and engineering level, through some crew quarters and sleeping areas where there were Vecians seemingly suspended in mid-air asleep. The captain was kind enough to demonstrate the application of the anti-gravity inertia field that they slept in. He simply stood on a white coloured pad on the floor then pressed a white button on the low ceiling, drew his arms and legs in and closed his eyes mimicking the act of sleeping. He then opened his eyes and reversed the process and walked off at a brisk pace across the deck.

On the tour, he had briefly been shown the head. The toilets on this ship were thankfully and somewhat bizarrely the same as those on their own ships. He assumed that as it was such a basic species function that the technology was just kept as simple as possible. No need to complicate matters for things as base as this; however, it did occur to him that he had no understanding of how to get out of or access his unitard in such a situation. He would need to find out before the urge struck him.

Finally, they arrived at the bridge. It was busy, industrious, with low-level lighting and in total zero gravity, spherical and about five metres in diameter. Similar recessed, moulded couches were worked into the walls of the chamber, as he had seen in the medical bay, but here there was a central holographic display, not a floating ball of medical gel. The captain directed him to a couch to one side of the only visible entrance in the room. He took his place as directed and the Vecian moved into his place next to him. It was difficult getting comfortable in the couch as the ergonomics were all wrong, and there seemed to be manual controls to each couch but these were out of his reach. He decided that controls would not be a problem, as he didn't know what any of them did, nor would he have need of any. Whatever the Vecian captain had in mind for him, he doubted it would need him to operate any controls.

The captain then leaned over to him and said, "Still." Pressing a key on a pad on the upper right panel of Spencer's couch he then felt the unitard around him shift and grow from his lower neck to cover his right ear and throat. A voice then asked, "Okay?"

"Yes," he replied.

"Good."

The captain leaned back into his couch and looked ahead.

Looking around the sphere for the first time, he then saw the others—six other faces all different and all expectant. Facial colours shifted as he looked at each but there were no expressions he recognised. A grim, sinister sense of his situation closed in around him. He had been so enthralled by the captain's good graces and the technological wonder of all he was seeing that he had totally lost the reason for his rescue, or capture. This could get ugly very fast. He needed to keep a cooler head. Turning to the Vecian captain, his eyes seemed to asked the question for him. The Vecian captain indicated to the gathered group, "Teach. Learn."

All the Vecians leaned back in their couches and closed their eyes. A halo of rapidly fluctuating and spinning colour appeared a few centimetres in front of each aliens forehead. Thinking it best to copy them, he made himself as comfortable as he could and leaned back placing his head into the recess of his couch. A similar halo began to appear in front of his face, but then his world changed.

It was like a waking dream. At first nothing made sense, the imagery, the landmarks, the oceans and terrain, nothing was familiar. Peoples he had no knowledge of, vaguely humanoid in stature, living in lagoons and the shallow warm waters of the places he had never been. Sounds and voices swirled past him, like the most beautiful lullaby, soft and indistinguishable, like listening to exotic instruments and his mother's first comforting words. Then, intermingled with this he began to see images of home, of earth, the decay and urban wastelands which had spelt the gradual decline of the planet's ability to sustain the human population dependent on it. New voices floated by amongst songs he had heard whilst growing up, voices of the world, languages he was unable to speak but that he recognised nonetheless.

Visions of the worlds began to decay from that of a blue and green planet to one where the oceans had turned to black, foaming cauldrons and the land to windswept deserts of acrid sand where sprawling cities of twisted metal and rubble found the last ghostly remains of civilisation. He saw Arrongate station, a vision of hope orbiting the dying planet, a station which he knew as a second home while making preparations for his voyage. Then he saw images of the shipyards, with thousands of industrious workers creating the colony ships which would launch all their hopes into the stars.

Swirling images returned of an Eden planet, lush and green, with a wealth of life and an advanced civilisation in harmony with itself and the other species of the world. They had advanced from the lagoon dwellers to arcologies, producing subterranean travel and space flight technologies, efficient orbital solar fusion containment and space exploration. He began to find that he could understand the odd word that was now spoken as part of the chorus of sounds in his mind, no longer was the wall of sound a complete jumble but some words and sentences became part of a vocabulary he knew and could respond to.

"Xannix" he said.

"Yes," came the response.

Then time became dark and a malevolence spread through his mind like the choking tendrils of a swarm of locust, without particular direction or course but pervasive and of certain intent, channelled by the solar winds. A cloud of evil which didn't particularly make any declaration of invasion but leached into the Eden which had been the Xannix empire. They had called them the Zantanath, bringers of war, and Spencer had recognised them immediately. Humans, well, humanoid, but very human-like. What he couldn't understand was that they were not from Earth. The Xannix had them mapped to a different part of the galaxy, still reasonably local in terms of distance, closer than the OWEC fleet had travelled, but not Earth.

From the Xannix perspective, this strain of humanity was self-consuming, volatile, aggressive and very dangerous and, as a result, their political masters had decided to become protectionist. They had begun to work on hiding themselves from the universe and defending their borders, shielding themselves from discovery by others, if others existed. They had so far succeeded. The defensive grid they had erected around their home planet was a project of staggering proportion, in technological achievement, logistical deployment and political will. But the cost had been great. They had encountered the Zantanath far enough away from their home world to have saved them, enough distance and time to put in place plans of defence. This, combined with a war strategy of misdirection, had led the Zantanath on a course away from the Xannix home world. The tactic had been to defend another planet, Fayaal, as if it was their primary planet, throw all the military might, urgency and desperate tactical actions needed to defend this planet as would a species defending itself to the last. While this was going on, they would complete and activate the Xannix camouflage grid and shield themselves from the eyes of the universe and perpetrators of the apocalypse that had befallen billions of their kind.

His thoughts flooded back to the moment he had watched the first colony ships depart Arrongate for the new planets, his heart full of hope and of trepidation, knowing that he would soon be joining them in stasis on his own ship, the *Indianapolis*. Then he remembered the medical centre where he had his wave mapped, laying on a couch, being treated like royalty, soft plush surroundings, waterfalls and beautiful lakeside views, soft piped music, people smiling and happy. It had been more like a spa than a medical centre, but he was a doctor himself, he knew the reason for all the calming psychology at work.

As he lay back onto the couch, nurses had fussed around him and a doctor had been on hand nearby working at a console, monitoring his vital signs and prepping the wave capture process. A beautiful young nurse touched him on the shoulder to gain his attention. He looked into her eyes, and they were confident and reassuring, "Relax, Dr Spencer. Close your eyes and imagine your favourite place: home, a forest walk, the ocean breeze at the beach." He did as he was asked and began to envisage a beach house he had spent a holiday in once as a child. On reflection and considering the austere historic setting of the time it had probably been a terrible place—a ramshackle house falling apart at the seams, no amenities, sparse provisions—but to him, with his rose-tinted vision as a child, this place was magical.

Moments later, the nurse shook his shoulder gently. "Dr Spencer. Dr Spencer." This time a different nurse, but equally young and beautiful.

"When do we start the transfer?" he asked.

"Transfer?"

"Yes, the…" his eyes caught up, the room had changed. The astonishment must have showed on his face because she started to smile gently.

"Welcome to the *Indianapolis*, Dr Spencer."

The images switched again. This time he saw space and a star field shifting and turning at speed then passing one, two, three large rotund vessels, engine pods, habitat and command sections, all in formation but cold, dark, quiet. After a sweeping turn the third ship came into sharp relief, spotlights licking out from the Xannix ship's point of view and the image became almost completely hull, with large lettering on the side speling out *Intrepid*.

*

"Dr Spencer, my name is Yannix, I am captain of the Xannix scout ship, Spixer. I am pleased to make your acquaintance." The Xannix floating in the centre of the zero gravity bridge chamber spoke with a slight sibilance but otherwise perfect English.

"Good to meet you," he replied, looking around the chamber. The others were still lying back in their couches, probably back to work and in command of the ship. Markings on their uniform, Commander Polder, Commander Fenz, Lieutenant Saltta, Lieutenant Aldaa, Sergeant Raan, Sergeant Coll. He stopped. He read their name tags again. Shocked he looked again around the chamber, the central display plotting the ships and local star system, Xannix, Redset, Plovig III, Sevii, the wording around the controls of his right hand read Comms, Engine, Navigation, left had read Weapons, Shield, Jump. He looked back at Captain Yannix in bewilderment. Yannix made an expression and a flourish of colours made their way across his face, all this Spencer knew to be equivalent to a human smile.

"How?"

"There is plenty of time for that, Dr Spencer. But right now we need to speak to your Captain."

"Captain Straud?" He shook his head.

"No?" Yannix asked.

"Yes, but it's not Straud you need to see. It's Fleet Captain Clayton."

Yannix moved his head, confirmation, like a human nod. "I see. Can you make that happen?"

"I think so." He paused while considering his next move. This was more than unbelievable but he had to consider the safety of the fleet first and foremost. He knew he was fast becoming a bridge between the two species: he had the power to make things work, but equally he had the power to really screw things up. Negotiation was better than confrontation, he had always believed that. Maybe this could work. He pointed to the ship at the head of the fleet formation. "*Endeavour*. Head for the *Endeavour*."

CLAYTON

The Vecian ship had become visible to their systems about an hour ago and had been exactly where they expected it to be; their tracking of Spencer's life signs had been accurate. What did worry him, however, was that the ship was not only on the move but also vectored directly at the *Endeavour,* where the latest current estimate had the Vecian ship arriving to their location within the next four hours. The thing that had surprised him was that, after days attempting to communicate with Spencer via his bio-comms, he had suddenly received a personal message from him which had requested an audience with him and his most trusted command crew. The captain of what he called the 'Xannix' scout ship needed to convey a message and wanted hostilities to stop. Spencer seemed to believe there were understandable reasons for the poor outcome of the first contact between them. A team of five representatives would be sent to the *Endeavour,* one of which would be Spencer, who would act as translator. Somehow, this didn't surprise him.

Returning the communication and agreeing to the meeting, his first call was to St John and Roux. They both now sat in the briefing room, arms folded looking worried. Dawn stood, relaxed and observant, in her usual place.

St John had begun to air his concerns in the form of a lecture. "How can you be sure this is not some sort of trap? We don't know what they have done to Dr Spencer. There could be any number of technologies they could have applied to send that message, and remember it was only a message sent via his

306

integrated bio-comms, no visual comms, so we have no idea of his true condition. If they have found a way to hack our bio-comms then they could be setting us up, piping us false information and setting a trap."

"So, what could they do? Worst case?" Clayton asked in a neutral tone, the negativity from St John was beginning to irritate him but he knew he was only doing his job, pointing out the obvious and alternatives to the situation. Being more positive, he really hoped for a successful outcome. There needed to be a dialogue at least and this was the first chance of that that had arisen.

"Worst case? They could assassinate you and cause countless fatalities; they could destroy the *Endeavour*; they could..."

"Okay, but all of that is avoidable?"

"We can work to lower the risk but we cannot remove every likelihood. There will always be the possibility that we have overlooked something, especially with these Xannix." He shifted in his seat. "From our limited experience, we only know them to be aggressive and sneaky.

And," he continued, "they have had access to Dr Spencer, who, although a medic, so will not have critical command or engineering knowledge to endanger the ship, he is an insider, so there maybe any number of things he knows on a peripheral level that the Xannix may exploit once aboard."

Roux was nodding on almost every point St John was making. "I think St John is right," Roux confirmed. "We have no way of knowing if anything Spencer is telling us is true or in good faith. He could be getting manipulated, being sold a narrative which, to him at least, is a plausible explanation for the unfolding events. It would mean that he would believe what he is telling us. It may not be what the Xannix have planned but Spencer would believe the narrative." He shrugged as he offered up the idea.

He hated to admit it to himself but these were all good points and the danger, considering past events, was tangible.

"So what do you suggest?"

"Counterstrike."

"Before you go down that road, could I point out that this is one ship, a scout for a much larger force behind a curtain we have not yet opened. To mix metaphors, it could be kicking the hornets nest. I never think going in heavy handed will help us here."

"I wouldn't count it out. Have it in the locker, ready to go," suggested Roux. "It doesn't hurt to have a big stick, even if you don't use it."

"Why not be as sneaky as the Vecia..." St John caught himself and stated again, "Why not be as sneaky as the Xannix?" They all looked at each other, and the idea hung in the air. "Well, what if we have modded Rem-Teks in plain sight, doing maintenance tasks in the hanger. They would be normal clutter and bustle in the hangar. We might have to disguise their carbines but at least they would be some level of close support if needed."

"Possible. Okay, but no visibly armed security. This will be a peaceful meeting."

"I want fast extraction if things go south, so I need you near me and an escape plan in place. My team will have you out and safe in seconds."

"Agreed," said Clayton. St John appeared to be visibly more relaxed. He had got the concession he wanted.

"May I suggest bay three again?" It was Dawn this time. "It is close to the bridge and isolated with minimal exits. Easy to defend and easy to initiate an escape plan." They all nodded.

"Good, that sounds like we're in agreement. Put things in place. Thank you, gentlemen."

Both St John and Roux stood and made their way out of the briefing room back to the bridge, Roux giving St John a friendly nudge to the shoulder. "It's not going to be as bad as you think, you know." St John turned to him with a look that said he knew better. "You know how I know? Because, it's never as bad as you think it is, Mr Doomandgloom." They both grinned and rounded the corner onto the bridge and out of sight.

"He's right you know," said Dawn.

"Who?"

"Roux."

"How do you come to that conclusion?"

"Statistically speaking, St John overreacts to almost everything. But, in this situation, I'll give him the benefit of the doubt. If you're working on simple statistics, the sample set of data is too small. The number of events where we have seen the Xannix become aggressive is almost every encounter. And if this is a scouting team, as they say, the likelihood that events have transpired as they designed is highly probable. My assessment is that this has been a fact-finding mission for them from the very moment we woke. A test, if you like. They start by playing hard, then they play soft— to see which we react to more favourably."

"Interesting theory."

"Daddy." Her mood seemed to plunge into a dark place. He had noticed it a couple of times in the last few days since his resus. Maybe something that only a parent would pick up on, but it was there, a parental worry.

"Yes, Dawn?"

"You know I love you don't you? You and mum."

"Where has this come from? A moment ago we were talking about the Xannix."

"Yes, I know. Sometimes, things should just be said." Her hologram pixelated, faded and she was gone. Lost in the maze of thoughts which he now had racing round his head, he made his way slowly to the door. Pausing and looking back to where Dawn had been standing, he wondered what was going on in the mind of his daughter. The next chance he had he would run some tests.

*

The Xannix scout ship was stationed roughly five hundred metres from shuttle bay three. It had only been a few hours since Havers and his team had left, but he was confident that they had a good head start on any chase the Xannix might decide to perform. However the next few hours panned out, he was sure to get some answers to his questions regarding this mysterious planet one way or another—the fate of the fleet depended on it.

Once the ship had parked in formation, they received a transmission hail which was put through to his console. It was Dr Spencer, looking quite well and in no visible distress. In fact, he was quite relaxed, considering his location. The screen showed him to be lying on a couch and wearing a blue skin-like suit. Some form of comms gear was around his head and his eyes had an odd hue, an almost bioluminescent cyan glow. He wondered what sort of procedure Spencer had undergone or whether it was something related to the atmosphere or technology of the alien vessel. At this point he could only guess, but he had to know whether it was dangerous.

There was an off-screen voice which spoke to Dr Spencer in

the soft ethereal language of the Xannix, Spencer looked up and at the source of them then responded in kind before returning his attention to the screen and Clayton. This was astonishing. He realised that Spencer was speaking the Xannix language, communicating in what sounded to his poorly trained ear to be almost perfect Xannix. This in what must have been a couple of days at most. He remembered Havers report speaking of accelerated learning capacity by the captive Xannix but this was something else. Programmable language learning? Had to be. Impressive.

"Hello, Dr Spencer. How are they treating you?"

"Very well, Captain. The Xannix have been perfect hosts. You wouldn't believe the things I've learned in the short time I've been here."

Clayton nodded his approval. Then again, if the Xannix saw Spencer as an asset then that would be the case, but the moment they saw him as a liability the whole dynamic would change. He'd work to keep things that way.

"In your message you requested a meeting. Are you ready to make your way across?"

"Captain Yannix is already in the shuttle and will be on route in the next couple of minutes."

This presented a problem: if Spencer was being kept aboard the alien scout ship, did that mean he was there of his own volition?

"Okay Spencer, I'll get moving down to bay three to receive him. Are you okay with being our team player on the away bench?" He hoped the question was light-hearted but relayed his concern nonetheless.

"Oh yes, sir." Spencer beamed back in childish glee. "This is an experience of a lifetime. I'm learning so much and the Xannix culture and history is fascinating. If I may, I'll compile and send you a report shortly with my experiences and findings so far."

"Sounds great, Spencer. I look forward to it. In the meantime, stay safe. We'll have you back fleetside as soon as we can."

"Yes, sir."

*

The shuttle was small—it could only be a four- or five-man craft at most—and slick-looking, with no outward appearance of drive units or observation panels. Its hull design was completely smooth and strongly resembled the profile of a hammerhead shark. Its approach to the *Endeavour* had been faster than he would have considered safe by one of their own shuttles but the acceleration and manoeuvring had been controlled and exact. As he waited on the observation gantry of bay three, the Xannix shuttle made its final tweaks to land, and puffs of gas vented to caress the shuttle to the deck and waiting docking clamps. The shuttle bay doors closed with silent certainty and locked in place, and atmosphere then pushed its way into the space and completed the docking cycle.

St John opened the internal airlock to the shuttle bay and they walked to within a few metres of the shuttle to await Captain Yannix and his team. He had expected a door on the shuttle to open, one side or another, but instead the whole front lower section of the craft split away and lowered then extended forward, revealing two recessed couches, which moved forward and to an upright position, allowing the occupants to easily step out and onto the deck. The motion had been fluid and reasonably quick, which was a surprise to those standing waiting. St John had even taken a pace back, which Clayton chose to ignore. He could rib him about it later.

Two tall Xannix stepped towards them, one significantly taller than the other, and he wondered whether this was coincidence or whether the Xannix had a physical difference representing status in their society. Both Xannix stopped a couple of paces short of St John and himself then held their four hands together to the centre of their chest forming a cross before themselves. They then lowered their heads for a moment. Clayton assumed it to be a formal greeting but on Earth there were a few to choose from. He wasn't military, so a salute felt wrong. A western hand shake felt too intimate and possibly awkward under the circumstances. He chose a more religious, more oriental approach and simply bowed his head in return, thinking it would be at least similar to their own greeting and hopefully not offensive in any way.

"Welcome to the *Endeavour*," he said with some level of excitement. "I am Captain Clayton and this is General St John. Welcome aboard."

The taller of the two Xannix stepped forward. "Thank you, Captain. I am Captain Yannix and this is Lieutenant Aldaa. We are very pleased to be received." Xannix inclined his head in another much smaller bow.

"If you would like to follow me, we have a room available for our discussions and some refreshments, although we are unsure what you would find palatable."

"Thank you for the consideration, Captain."

He was considerably impressed with Yannix and his grasp of the language. If he had never spoken a word of it until a few days ago, his cognitive development and acuity was incredible. It would be like him learning Mandarin Chinese in three days, which he was certain would be impossible. Well, maybe not impossible, especially as Spencer seemed to have mastered Xannix in much the same amount of time. This knowledge acceleration technology was a marvel. The academic in him was suddenly in a whirl and fascinated by how something of this nature could work. He was already able to capture the wave of a person; maybe he could isolate the cognitive processes at a much more granular level and transfer those between people, irrelevant to their brain biostructure.

Turning and indicating the way with a gesture, they naturally paired up and walked towards the doorway, Yannix and Clayton then Aldaa and St John.

"Captain Clayton, how is it that you come to be here?" No nonsense, straight to the point.

"Not one for small talk?" Clayton said, almost as an aside.

"Small talk, Captain?"

"Never mind. We are here because we have nowhere else to be, Captain Yannix." As they were being extremely direct with their conversation, there seemed little point being furtive about the answer. "In truth, we are looking for a new home. Somewhere to live again."

Yannix nodded at this. "Where have you come from? Your ships seem designed for a very long voyage."

"Yes. That is also true. We have been on our journey for the last one hundred and thirty-five years. We were hoping that this would be our journey's end but I fear you are here to tell me something different."

"I cannot say, Captain. What is your intent?"

They reached the open door to a room not far from bay three. Inside was a conference table and couches for four people, water and fresh food from hydroponics. The room was otherwise quite sterile, with bright white lights, poor mass-produced paintings and plastic foliage. A clear panel at the end of the room enclosed a wall-to-wall image of Earth, a historic photograph of the Earth as taken from the moon during man's early explorations of their solar system. Right across the middle of the image was the OWEC logo—it was in every way a corporate conference room.

"Please take a seat." He waited until everyone was comfortable, the Xannix taking a moment, being rather too tall and long in the leg for the human ergonomics to suit. They made the best of it and nodded for him to continue. A nod, another human characteristic learned. Yannix was learning, interpreting and implementing human actions and mannerisms within the time frame of their conversation. The pace at which they could learn was fascinating to him and a little disconcerting.

He pointed to a screen behind him, which he had programmed with a presentation tracing and mapping their journey through the stars to this point. As the animated ships tracked through the way points and milestones of their voyage, past hot and cold stars, differing classes of planets completely barren and devoid of life, skirting asteroid belts, he narrated over the imagery.

"We are from a planet called Earth, approximately 12 light years from here and it has taken us 130 of our Earth-measured years. I'm not sure what measure you might convert this to but if you consider our lifespan to be around 120 years," he shrugged, "It's a long time for us. A good couple of generations, if not more."

The Xannix were concentrating on his every word intently and following the action on the display, the captain's skin flashing with differing colours on occasion, with similar reactions and skin tone changes from Aldaa. At some points they looked at each other but said nothing, allowing him to continue his presentation unhindered by questions. Once he had finished the presentation, the image showing their current star map with the location of Hayford b and the fleet clearly marked, Yannix inclined his head as if in thought, still staring at the screen.

The silence stretched on and Clayton began to wonder if anyone was going to say anything. He looked at St John quickly but he only had a brief shrug to indicate he felt the same. He felt like hours had gone by but it had in truth probably only been a few minutes. He decided to interject.

"Captain Yannix, is everything okay?"

Yannix snapped out of his thoughts and back into the room, a flash of pink and yellow settling back to the regular bluish grey. "I'm sorry, Captain Clayton. We are in forum with Xannix. They are discussing your current situation and will indicate to me shortly what they intend."

It was another moment that brought his attention to their differing technologies. They were in forum with Hayford b? How were they doing that? Did they have similar comms implants? Each small revelation of their technical ability made him wonder about their confrontation on the *Intrepid*. It felt to him now that, rather than being pushed, they had just decided to leave. Whatever it was they wanted, they must have obtained. So, what did they have? Spencer?

"Is that a long process?" he asked.

"Not long." Yannix stood from his seat and walked to the screen behind Clayton, using calm, confident strides, putting one hand to the side of the screen to compensate his action he leaned in close to focus intently on the fleet and projected path that was being plotted. "What is your ideal, Captain?"

"I don't follow."

"What is your need?"

"We are here to find sanctuary in a new planet. A home to live again as people. We have learned much from our past and its devastating consequences; we are older and wiser as a species and plan to live a different life. We need a planet which can sustain us and one which we can nurture."

The Xannix seemed to consider this a reasonable request; he nodded lightly and returned to examining the display. A moment longer and a sequence of colours again skated over his skin, bright and swirling. He turned and looked at them all. Aldaa stood also and walked round the table to join Yannix, and they both appeared solemn and sincere when Yannix continued, "The Xannix Prime has ruled. There is both good and bad news, Captain Clayton."

Somehow, he had been expecting the bad news, but the good news part was intriguing.

"What is their decision, Captain Yannix?"

Yannix took a small bow, as he made a formal address, "Xannix Prime will not permit the landing of any human craft on Xannix, the planet you are calling Hayford b. If you try to land by force we will be within our rights to defend ourselves." Yannix paused to give separation between the good and the bad news. "To hopefully offer the human fleet some level of compassion in their time of need, we offer another planet to suit your requirements and one which we are happy for you to populate. It is an old world of the Xannix Empire, long since abandoned. We have asked your crewman Spencer to forward you the coordinates." As Yannix said this a message arrived in his personal bio-comms queue from Spencer, which he immediately opened then linked to the wall display. The image swiftly changed to show the local space of the offered planet. All text was unreadable but he could make out when the map zoomed out and tracked to their current location that in terms of distance it was reasonably close, possibly another ten years of travel but not something they would have problems with—they had provision enough to last for almost fifty years, as long as the biospheres within the ships were maintained.

"Very generous of you, Captain. You said it had been abandoned by your species. Could I ask why?"

"It became," he paused looking for the right words, "a little too hostile for us. But that was a long time ago and there is little for us there now." Yannix and Aldaa exchanged a glance, which he couldn't read, but he felt sure there was more to it. You don't just give up a planet, not that he'd ever done that before but he certainly hadn't heard in all human history anyone simply giving up land altruistically. There was a catch, but he just couldn't see it. Maybe the Xannix were different but, from the small amount of experience he had obtained in the last few days, he didn't see any evidence of it. There was definitely something else in play here.

"Could you send us any data you have on the planet—the environment, flora, fauna. We will need to prepare."

"Certainly. Although it may take us some time to collate and translate. We will put your crewman Spencer to the task. I'm sure he would enjoy such a job. If you agree, of course."

"He's becoming quite the liaison. Get him to contact me and we'll begin the process."

"He does you credit. We have been assigned as your escort on the voyage, so we will have much more time to work together as we travel."

They exchanged some further small talk, which he thought Yannix was beginning to get the hang of, talking about trivialities and observations as they worked their way back from the conference room to shuttle bay three. As they reached the Xannix shuttle, Yannix turned to face him. "Captain Clayton, you will remember to recall your shuttle, won't you? We do protect our borders and we are a very private people."

"You have my word."

"Very good, Captain. Thank you for this forum. I look forward to our next meeting." Taking his place at Albaa's side, the pair of Xannix returned to the shuttle, couches relocated to the inner craft through a swift mechanical action, and a hiss of gases as the hatch sealed.

"Productive," said St John.

"I have more questions than answers," he replied. "But for the moment let's see where the path takes us."

Returning to the shuttle bay viewing gantry on their way back to the bridge, they watched the Xannix shuttle prepare for departure, atmosphere cycling as the air lock outer doors began to open.

TRAVIS

With the hull at his feet, he walked towards the bow under the silent stars, the *Endeavour's* metallic horizon giving him an impression of normality—the impression, to his senses at least, that there was an up. He knew, of course, that in space there was no up but it somehow settled him, his instincts calmed by the illusion. He made his way slowly, carefully, purposefully towards his goal. Dawn had arranged things; the Xannix would be in shuttle bay three and then in conference with Clayton for perhaps a couple of hours. He didn't have long to do what he needed, what they had planned, but he was almost there—only another few paces to go.

The shuttle bay doors were closed and locked, and he paced straight out into the centre of the tennis court-sized area, across the huge illuminated, painted number three, and began to go about taking items from his belt and pack. A utiliplex, a remote receiver and the belt of DKL-8 phased plasma explosive, which he carefully unclipped from his waist and placed to one side of the central door seal. He used the tool to glue the belt into a fixed position and primed the explosive, connecting then switching on the receiver, a red icon appeared on the belt showing its readiness. Phased plasma was as nasty as it came; he didn't really understand the specifics of the weapon but the effect was undeniably disturbing. He had heard stories that the developers of DKL-8 had suffered major setbacks in development because they kept blowing their scientists and engineers to molecular component parts. It took them many years to produce a stable device which they could use but even then the range was limited. The ultimate aim of the weapon was to be as intense and devastating in a localised area of effect as could be achieved. They had done this by channelling the explosive effect and resonating it within a containment field. The amplification in resonance created intensity in the molecules and failure of the cohesion of matter. On a fundamental level, if resonance was focused enough, molecular bonds could be forced to fail. In reality, any matter caught within the containment field of the device would end up looking like a colander with holes suddenly appearing throughout the defined space.

He imaged there were a lot of people in for a rather nasty shock.

Checking his work for the third and fourth time, he stood, satisfied that the device was set and would respond to his trigger. Returning his utiliplex to his belt and locking it in place, he turned and made his way back the way he had come, across the ocean of grey that was the whale-like belly of the *Endeavour*. He checked his time—he had been quick and was ahead of schedule, with thirty minutes to complete the fifteen-minute walk back to a position he considered safe to detonate the device. All he would need to do then was wait. Sit and concentrate like an anxious angler, primed to make the largest catch of his life, worried that, however well he had planned things, something might still go wrong. He believed there had been a term or saying related to this, about the plans of mice and men, although what 'gang aft a-gley' meant, he had no idea.

As he paced his way back to the dark and out of the lights which flooded the shuttle bay doors, he became aware that the only thing he could hear was the sound of his own breathing, hard and laboured, and sweat was heavy on his brow. He stopped and turned around. This was it. He was excited and nervous in equal measure. It was so close to payback time that he was beginning to get palpitations, his body now reacting on its own to the closeness of the events and the psychological release of so many crucifying and tormenting memories, barriers that he was about to bring down in the name of justice and balance.

Watching the bay doors from a distance, he decided to go through the plan in his mind again but all too quickly his family flooded his thoughts. His mind wandered off into his waking nightmare of the slow lingering death they had suffered at the hands of the AI with psychotic delusions. At least they were at peace now, he consoled himself—it would be others who would suffer in their place now, knowing exactly what their grim technological creations had really given humanity. Clayton and the descendants of Clayton would perish on this mission, he would make sure of this. His weakness in the face of loneliness had ironically brought about the final step in his plan, but to take advantage of an irrationally distracted AI with deep depressive tendencies seemed almost poetic to him. Normally, he would be appalled at himself for taking advantage of a mental illness but this was a machine, not a person. Machines didn't get ill, machines didn't feel, machines were made and as such were no more than highly technical puppets.

He snapped out of his mental ramblings to realise the light from the shuttle bay doors had changed and now reflected off the nose of a craft as it was making its slow exit from the bay. The physical pull of the transmitter trigger didn't even register in his mind as the signal made the instantaneous jump to the receiver in the bomb mechanism. The light intensified for a moment and a ripple of sound came to him up through his boots, like an anvil struck by a hammer. He half expected some roll of thunder or an orange plume of flame to engulf the shuttle bay as the Xannixian shuttle failed catastrophically. But nothing happened. It was as if he had just switched the shuttle off. It continued to use the momentum it had already achieved under its piloted flight and eased its way forward out of the shuttle bay.

A cloud of vented gas was beginning to accumulate within the bay and across the surface of the *Endeavour's* hull. He had calculated the radius of the blast from the bomb to be just a couple of metres more than the distance to the internal airlock and viewing gallery. The bomb, which at detonation would have been to one side of the bay still affixed to the leading edge of the now open door, would have affected not only the Xannix shuttle as it left the bay but also the *Endeavour's* hull and potentially a few near surface cabins. Atmosphere was venting and crystallising, sparkling ice crystals making the urgent scenes before him look somehow beautiful. Life had slowed and a peace filled him and lifted his heart.

His target had not been the Xannix shuttle but his cue. Clayton would have been watching his new friends departing from the shuttle bay gantry, he had been certain of this, and this eventuality was also corroborated by Dawn after running a few simulated scenarios. Gases still vented from the bay and lights began to fail but, as he was about to turn to his next task, he thought he saw a fleeting glimpse of a human figure pin-wheeling out into space, fired out of the shuttle bay by some explosive decompression as the integrity of the structure failed. A broad and satisfied smile made its way across his face as he realised at last the creator of his torment and agony for so many years was now dead. Clayton's death was an event he would savour.

"Look, Zoë. It's beginning. We'll all be together again soon."

He watched the scene for a moment longer then turned and made his way back to the airlock; his next stop was to complete his promise to Dawn.

CLAYTON

The Xannix shuttle had manoeuvred within the bay to point its nose to the opening doors, waiting patiently for the doors to complete their traverse and for space enough to nudge themselves back into the freedom of open space. He and St John were still in the observation gantry and, rather than watch the Xannix exit, he felt the urge to get back to the bridge, catch up with Roux on the events of the last couple of hours and work out their next move. He should probably let the crew of Horus One know that they should return—no need to knowingly create further diplomatic blunders.

"This is certainly not how I thought things would turn out," St John announced to the room. "Don't get me wrong, I didn't expect things to be plain sailing, but finding the planet already inhabited? That wasn't even on my radar."

"I know what you mean. The Xannix have gone out of their way to hide from the universe. To me, that's a worry in itself. What are they hiding from?"

"Well, it's not us at least. They didn't know we existed until the moment we turned up. I would like to know why they are so keen to keep us out. I'm just being nosey, I guess."

Clayton nodded, turned and walked to the door but St John stopped him before he went. "I'll see you on the bridge shortly— I've got a couple of people to check in with. I'm hoping they have something for me."

"Sure." And with that he opened the door to leave.

He had only reached the next bulkhead when all hell broke loose. The sound of small detonations rippled around him, followed by the emergency lighting and alert klaxon. Momentarily thrown, his thoughts whirled then settled on the most obvious. The shuttle bay. Running for the bay door he found it locked and reporting lack of atmosphere on its far side. He thumped the door with the palm of his hand in frustration and quickly sent a message to St John, but there was no response. Next to Roux: 'What the hell's going on, Roux? Shuttle bay three is locked out.'

'We're working on it. Looks like there are multiple hull breaches and the Xannix shuttle appears to be drifting. The Xannix are demanding to know what just happened—they can't raise the crew of the shuttle.'

'This is not good. I can't raise St John. I left him on the observation gantry a moment ago.'

There was a pause, then Roux came back with distressing news. 'St John is dead. Dawn can find no life signs for him aboard the *Endeavour*.'

He thumped the door again, this time damaging his hand. The pain began to focus him and he turned to sprint to the bridge, as he was of no use where he was.

'I'm on my way to the bridge. Make sure the Xannix don't do anything stupid.'

'Roger that.'

His legs suddenly felt like they were made of lead. Adrenaline did that, gave you strength but made you feel instantly fatigued. Dragging himself towards the bridge, every step seemed to take an eternity. Nothing he could do was going to get him there any faster, so his mind raced and tried to work out what happened. It had to be the rogue crewman St John was investigating; the last thing he mentioned was that he had a couple of people to check in with—Reeve and Silvers. He instantly fired off an update request and Reeve returned comms immediately.

'Sir, we're tracking St John. He's been ejected from the ship and is travelling fast, coordinates follow.' There was a moment where his bio-comms showed him the tracking and locus points of the body of his friend. He switched it off. 'We are attempting a rescue, sir.'

'Negative, Reeve. He's gone. My priority is the *Endeavour* and the Xannix shuttle, in that order. Your priority is catching the terrorist—Travis.' He rounded another corner; the bridge was in sight. 'At least one of his clones is still loose on my ship. I thought we had him pinned. Fix it, Lieutenant Reeve.'

'Roger. Reeve out.'

Bursting through the bridge door, he almost took flight over the last few metres, landing in his couch and finding the alarms and alerts on his terminal going crazy. Roux was sitting, intent and serious, working through damage reports and comms requests with pace, giving out commands with natural authority.

"Glad you made it, sir."

"Ship status?" he asked.

"Emergency teams dispatched to breaches around the shuttle bay. Astonishing, but we only lost two, including St John. The other was a Tech on his way back to his work station; we found half of him, not sure about the other half at this time." He was reciting in a calm professional voice which seemed to bely the anger behind his eyes. The list was only just starting. "Only the space immediately around the shuttle bay was affected. It seems the shuttle was the primary target. Spencer is demanding an update on the Xannix shuttle."

"Wait. Spencer? Who's in command over there?"

"We don't know, sir. Only Spencer is on comms and he doesn't seem pleased."

"I bet. He's sitting in the viper's nest. Okay. Next."

"We've lost contact with Horus One and Havers team."

"Oh, this just keeps getting better. Comms jamming?"

"Perhaps, but it happened almost the moment the attack on the Xannix shuttle happened. Whatever the cause, I don't think it's a coincidence," he paused a moment to consult his list of priority alerts. "On the plus side, the affected area of the shuttle bay is locked out. We are not losing atmosphere, and all systems are closed down or rerouted if critical.

"I would be very interested to know what made this mess."

"Travis made the mess. With what, I don't know. But I've got Reeve and Silvers tracking him down." First things first, he thought to himself, the Xannix. "Comms. Patch me through to the Xannix ship."

The comms on his terminal lit up and a vid feed of Spencer in his flight couch appeared in front of him. Spencer was looking really very perturbed, sweat on his brow, with fringe clung flat and swept to one side. Incidental coloured light swam around in the background like bioluminescent plankton. Spencer offered a tense but curt smile in greeting as the link was made.

"Hello Captain," he said.

"Dr Spencer, what is the situation over there?"

"Sir, what happened?"

"We don't know; we are investigating. With the Xannix permission we are putting together a rescue team for the Xannix shuttle. Are you able to assist?"

"One moment, sir." Spencer relayed his message. The sound was muted but he could see one side of the conversation, yielding and respectful. The volume came back, as did Spencer's attention. "Sir, we are in agreement. You must hold your position. The Xannix are able to reclaim their shuttle and will do so once it has been established that the shuttle power core is stable."

"How long will that take, Spencer?" A power core failure this close to his ship worried him a lot, especially as he didn't know what sort of explosive force that core failure would yield.

"I'm told they are running the scans now and should know in the next few minutes, maybe ten minutes."

"Thank you, Spencer. Keep me informed. Clayton out."

He stared at the screen for a moment once the image of Spencer had closed. "Hold the rescue team on station, Roux. We don't need them now but I want them available at a moment's notice."

"Yes, sir," Roux said in the middle of a conversation he was having with some unseen crewman on his terminal.

He opened a call to Commander Liam Fellows, St John's second in command aboard the *Endeavour*. It was not an easy call to make but there was no time for sentiment—he needed Fellows to step up.

"Commander Fellows." Fellows had clearly been expecting a call. He would be well aware of the situation, as he had been probably already briefed by Reeve, and was most likely fully involved in the hunt for Travis.

"Commander Fellows, have you been briefed by Lieutenant Reeve?"

"I have, sir. My team are closing on the area of shuttle bay three. We should have him shortly. I'll inform you the moment we have something."

Roux cut in, "Captain, the Xannix shuttle. There's something wrong."

"Fellows, let me know when you have him. Clayton, out."

Hand flicking over the controls of his terminal at a blur, an external camera view of the Xannix shuttle was immediately displayed. It surprised him that the camera seemed so close. The camera above the shuttle bay must still be operational. He examined the image and could clearly see the Xannix shuttle, a tiny plume of blue flame emanating from within the rear right quarter, slowly pushing the shuttle into a spin. Slim cracks began to be appear in the chitinous hull, made visible by more bright streaming blue blades of flame. The spin intensified and threw the shuttle into a wrecking gyroscopic oblivion.

"All hands, emergency stations!" he ordered and knew that there would be a rush of activity across the ship as people leapt for the safety of their crash couches and fastened harnesses. "Helm, crash evade forty degrees up!"

They were too late, but maybe he could limit the damage. The manoeuvring was instant and harsh, the massive colony ship which was never build for hard evasive forces shook and rattled as fittings reflected the tremendous g being applied to its bulk. Through the thundering noise of the manoeuvring engines and the storm of warning lights on his terminal, he caught sight of the Xannix scout ship tracking away from the distressed shuttle. Their mobility was their saviour; a lighter ship with responsive thrust, they would be out of harm's way in moments.

Then his viewing screen went white as the shuttle core failed and vaporised, the obliterated remnants thrown at terrifying velocities in all directions. There was a shudder to the *Endeavour* and even more lights started to illuminate his terminal screen. He scanned the screen and began to try and make sense of the damage reports. They appeared to have got to a reasonably good elevated angle before the shuttle died; however, the damage reports were not good. They had had a huge gouge taken out of the lower forward hull, which fortunately was nowhere near the habitation module but equally had many working sections related to the operations crew and provisions. The losses would be great.

"Helm, halt evasive. Ahead, ten percent. Resume course for Xannix."

"Ahead, ten percent. Resuming course for Xannix, sir,"

reported the helmsman.

The sudden calm was eerie. Everyone seemed stunned and silent while going over their workstation's readouts to detail events. It took some time for anyone to say anything, then it was all screaming and shouting again as the emergencies and realities of damage control jolted people back into action.

"Sir, you're being hailed again from the Xannix scout ship," said the comms officer, as Spencer's image appeared on his screen. No formality this time, Spencer was clearly under instruction.

"Captain Clayton, you are in violation of Xannix protocols. By breaching the boundaries of the Xannix home world you and your species are now considered criminals. Prepare to be boarded and control of your vessel given over to the Xannix authorities."

TRAVIS

Things hadn't quite gone to plan. Killing Clayton had been easy, almost too easy, but getting to Dawn's core was another matter. He would never have made it as far as he had without her help. It was a very peculiar arrangement, and one he never thought he would have been part of. Having kicked the hornet's nest, the hornets had swarmed: St John's security teams where everywhere, with almost every corridor and section under heavy guard. Dawn had walked him through the labyrinth of corridors and maintenance walkways that were momentarily out of the watchful gaze of security.

But then, whilst making his way slowly through one of the many maintenance walkways, without warning the ship had undergone what must have been crash evasion manoeuvres. He was suddenly thrown to the floor with such force that he was unable to keep his footing. His legs gave way and he fell awkwardly, arms out trying to brace himself. A jutting piece of pipework cracked his head badly, concussing him immediately, and the world beginning to spin and fade. Determined not to pass out, he took a few deep breaths and tried to reach for the medical pack on his hip. Fumbling for the adrenaline booster, he wasted no time pressing the stubby plastic cover which contained the needle to his thigh and operated the release. It fired with a stab of pain into his leg which, in itself, almost shook off his concussion but once the adrenaline hit his system he was awake, really awake.

All he could focus on, as he lay face down on the lattice floor of the maintenance walkway, was the flow of blood which was dripping from his head and pooling into the trough ten centimetres below the false floor he was lying on. His lungs were complaining, his muscles were straining just to stay still and he was in a lot of pain from the gash to his head, which must be bad if he could feel it over the punch of adrenaline he had just administered. A crash couch would have been good—actually, a little warning would have been good—but I guess that's what you get when you go dark and off the grid. You don't talk to anyone, and no one talks to you.

"Travis, are you okay?" Dawn asked him tentatively. He guessed someone had a vested interest in him after all.

He responded with a slur of words which didn't even make sense to him. He guessed he wasn't okay. One of the many and varied aches he felt across his body was coming from his jaw, and, as he was talking like someone who had recently had his jaw broken, he surmised that he probably had a broken jaw. Of all the things to go wrong.

There was a shudder through the ship, which he felt like a slap to his whole body. He was having a hard enough time without this kind of abuse but in a way he knew he'd brought this on himself. It could only be the wrecked Xannix shuttle, although he had assumed it would not have warranted this amount of messing about or detonated with that amount of force. He wondered what other assumptions in his plan were going to fall apart today.

He was going to have to risk a communication with Dawn. It was the only way to find out what was going on and he didn't know how much longer he was going to be able to stay conscious under these conditions, even with the adrenaline shot. Before he could initiate the connection, there was a crushing force on his chest and for a moment he became weightless, lifting off the deck and floating in place. Again the affect was disorientating, then the gravitational compensators within the decking reasserted themselves and he fell the short distance to the walkway floor. He wondered if this was what a rag doll felt like in the grip of a giant infant.

Trying to lift his weary body from the deck and stand, he heard the voice again, "Travis. Travis, are you okay. Can you hear me?" Whoever had synthesized Dawn's voice had done a great job—it was silky and tempted him like chocolate. Again, all he could do was make the mute noise, his jaw somehow unable to move and an excruciating pain backing it up. He made more noise, this time more of a recognisable scream. He kicked some pipework in his own anger and frustration.

'I've broken my jaw. Non-verbal comms only.'

'Understood. Are you able to continue? We don't have long.'

'Keep sending me nav updates. I'll respond when I can.'

Setting off towards the AI chamber, he decided that every part of him hurt, from the end of his toe to the tip of his head, but there was little he could do to remedy this. No chance of getting to the medbay, or back to one of his caches. No point. It began to dawn on him that this was the end game. He had killed the father of AI, and he was now going to destroy the creation, his monster. His vengeance would be spent, and he could go to his wife and children in peace.

Outside CIC he found it far busier than it used to be. He was in a maintenance crawl space off the main corridor but needed to become one of the crowd in order to get to Dawn. There were no mirrors on the trek down from shuttle bay three but from the blood spatter on his sleeve and the general tardiness of his clothing he didn't think he would get too far without being noticed. Add to that the injury to his face and head and the reaction of others was going to be one of horror—security would be called in a second.

'Dawn, I'm close. But there are too many people.' He sent the message and waited. 'I need a diversion. Can you create a local diversion and evacuate the crew?'

There wasn't even a response but he knew she had heard him. The alarms started to wail and Dawn's voice could be clearly heard through the corridor. 'Emergency. Fire in CIC. Please evacuate to your nearest muster station.' The message was on a loop, repeated again and again. It was that easy. People were well-drilled and simply stopped what they were doing without question and walked away down the corridor. After about two minutes he could hear nothing but the alarm, which suddenly stopped. Silence.

Opening the maintenance hatch and climbing out, he padded as silently as he could to the open doors of CIC. Something in him made him approach from the side, sliding down the wall and to take a position to the side of the door and hidden from view. He listened. The silence was broken by some chatty small talk between a couple of security guards. Had they not heard the alert? Clearly not. Only a short few metres from his goal, he wondered what he was going to do. There was no going back now. He was committed, and the crew would soon be back once they found there was no fire. It was either make the dash to the AI chamber or spend eternity in the brig. He had already chosen.

He searched his belt and found another adrenaline dispenser, white and green with AD+ written on the cap. He had a bad plan but right now it was the only plan he had. Why these guys had chosen to ignore Dawn's alert he had no idea, but at this point he didn't much care. He whipped his arm around the corner quickly and threw the dispenser across the room to the far exit. It made a clattering sound as it landed and scooted away into the next room.

"What was that?" he heard one of the guards say. The other must have just shrugged or gestured in some way. "Okay, okay. I'll check it out." They seemed like an old married couple.

Footsteps started to walk across to the far workshop. He counted ten steps then collected all his strength and sprinted through the door and into CIC. Both security men were looking the other way, trying to work out what had made the skittering noise, but they were now spread out, one close to the far wall, the other close to the AI core chamber. Without losing any pace at all he barrelled into the guard closest to the AI chamber, his full momentum ploughing into him and taking both of them from their feet. Not for the first time that day he hit the ground with force but this time he had a cushioned landing. He felt the wind leave the guard as they hit the floor with a simultaneous yelp of shock and alarm. Another clattering sound and the guard's carbine bounced to a stop in the open doorway to the chamber, tempting but out of reach.

From the far doorway came a booming voice, but he was focussed on only one thing and that was getting through the AI chamber door. Not even the words of command from an irate guard made any sense to him. Why would he stop, why should he stop? Hands grabbed at him as he tried to move. The guard on the floor was struggling to get up, to gain some advantage, grappling him to subdue him, but he wasn't going to be beaten so close to his final goal. He punched and kicked his way free, all the time inching closer to the door of the chamber.

Finally, he managed to break free, hooked his legs up into a squat and leapt through the door, sliding to a clunking halt as he hit the wall inside. The door began to close automatically, the wide eyes of the guard staring back at him while struggling to gain his footing to give chase. From the corner of his eye, he saw the carbine still on the floor of the entrance but just the wrong side of the door. If he was quick, he might reach it. Crawling forward on all fours and reaching out, he managed to grab the carbine and clutch it to his chest as the door closed the last few centimetres and sealed with a hiss. A thud on the door made him jump back with his back to the wall and fumble the carbine to aim at the noise.

He sat there for a long moment while the shouting outside the door got louder then quieter, then was replaced by footsteps and pacing. One of them was clearly agitated and was pacing in frustration on the far side, probably on comms to his boss and getting a few friends in to help with the breaching of the door.

His breathing finally began to slow, the sweat over his body was beginning to cool and his clothes stuck to him with a clammy wetness which made his skin crawl. But he had made it. It was time.

HAVERS

Xannix loomed large in the cockpit as he sat in the flight engineer's seat and looked past the heads of the pilots. From this distance, the geographic patterns of white, blue and green seemed very familiar yet out of place. The continents were in the wrong place with fewer mountain formations than he might have expected but, aside from all this, it was beautiful. He had been sitting there for the last half hour simply staring, unable to take his eyes away from what was likely to be his new home. His mind was running through romantic notions of the perfect life ahead and he afforded himself the illusion for a while. Their arrival in the system had been chaotic to say the least and a little 'happy' was okay with him.

They were on approach to what Larsen and Rivers had identified as the Xannix comms jamming network, which they had started calling the CJN; scientists loved their acronyms. It was a vast array of artificial satellites enveloping the whole planet at about two hundred thousand kilometres from the surface, stationary in space. At 200 kilometres from the CJN they had noticed slight loss of reception to messages from the *Endeavour,* as it followed a few hours behind. At this distance, signal strength should not be a problem, nor should there be transmission reception delay, but there it was nonetheless—an interference. It only grew greater as they neared, and when they were within 50 kilometres they lost all comms with the *Endeavour.*

They readied a probe and loaded it with a message that they were continuing to Xannix and would aim to orbit and obtain as much information on the planet as possible. They would watch for the fleet's approach and report back upon its arrival. The probe was launched. For a while they tried to use it as a comms relay but their source signal was being quashed before it reached the probe, so they abandoned that idea quickly to concentrate on their primary objective.

Patterson returned from his coffee run and tossed each of them a sachet of hot coffee. Looking though the cockpit window, he whistled in awe. Carroll turned to him, craning his neck. "Yeah," was all he could say.

"Okay team, let's see what's on the other side, shall we?" he said, breaking the spell and getting out of Patterson's couch. "All yours." He gestured that Patterson should take his place on the couch and made for the corridor and the main deck.

"It is what we've come millions of miles to see, sir" replied Carroll.

When he reached the main deck it was in silence. Some of the security guys were asleep, and others were playing games or watching vids via their bio-comms. Larsen and Rivers were glued to the observation instrumentation, the glow of the terminal screens on their faces making them both appear a little ghostly. He pushed his way over and joined them, orienting himself behind their couches so he could see the monitors and instruments. Taking a look at the images—some natural, some enhanced, some digitised—he was unsure what they were finding so fascinating.

"So, team," he said with a bright enthusiasm, "what's going on?"

"Are you kidding?" replied Larsen. "This is like looking at Earth's doppelgänger, only before we screwed it up. Almost everything about its composition and make up is the same. Granted, the geological features are different, but the polar caps contain roughly similar quantities of ice to Earth a couple of hundred years ago, and there are similar desert regions, similar oceans..."

"And you know this how?"

"Visual observation and some calculations by Rivers here. They are ballpark but that's only until we can get some better equipment running inside the CJN perimeter."

"Okay. Well, bad news is our comms are dead."

"Figured as much when you launched the probe."

"Yes, well, let's hope this is all worth it. When we get the other side, assess for possible landing and colonisation areas of interest. I'd like to have four or five primed to present to Clayton when we get back."

"Already looking, although tricky to say right now, as we're only seeing half the planet. There may be a couple of sites. I'd suggest the temperate north area here as our first major point of analysis." Larsen pointed at the screen to a large green expanse with a couple of dotted white peaks where mountains jutted into the cool, icy atmosphere at higher altitudes.

"Sounds good. Let me know when you have something."

"Will do."

An announcement came over the cabin speakers—it was Carroll. "Ladies and Gents, we are about to pass through the CJN on my mark. Three, two, one, mark!"

Larsen was operating a control set into part of his instrumentation. The screen attached to it flipped to a different view and a mass of noise flooded the screen. Clearly deciding that this wasn't giving him much useful information, he flicked to another view. This time the view was of bandwidth concentrations across the electromagnetic spectrum, and this showed him instantly what he wanted to know.

"Hello, Xannix," he said with a wide eyed expression of wonder. "I guess you were right, sir."

"Couldn't you guess from the massive satellite array we just passed through?" Rivers asked sarcastically.

Larsen huffed. "Everyone's a critic."

"Can we begin active scanning now?" He asked.

"Now we're clear of the CJN, yes. I'll start the scans immediately," replied Rivers.

*

Within ten minutes of scanning they had discovered a flourishing world teaming with life. The Xannix were clearly the apex species on the planet: cities and towns covered continents, and high-altitude craft, spacecraft and several space stations or space platforms were found orbiting at varying altitudes. While Larsen was scanning for population and technology, Rivers was doing a geological and atmospheric survey to ascertain an accurate reading on the health of the planet. Surprisingly, she was seeing a world in reasonable balance with its biosphere. Slight elevations in pollutants, sulphur oxides, nitrogen oxides and others but, when compared to the Xannix technology level, they should be far more toxic—they weren't. Larsen was equally fascinated by the populace, which seemed to be technologically advanced and concentrated in several massive arcology structures around the globe.

"Look at that," Larsen effused. "The size of that structure. That is stunning." The arcology was akin to a termite mound. A blade construction two kilometres high, it had aircraft buzzing around it like bees from a hive. If he remembered his natural history, termite mounds' internal temperature and atmosphere was self-regulating, and he wondered if this arcology design utilised the same principles.

"Any clue as to their power source?" he asked.

"None that I can find," Larsen responded.

"I think I may have an idea," Rivers said, then pointed to one of her screens. "I think that is a geothermal energy station."

"How can you tell?"

"They appear to pair with an arcology and they are power producers, not power consumers. I can tell that it's not a fusion or fission power producer—and it's not an older hydrocarbon-based fuel burner, as that would be kicking out all kinds of pollutants—but it must be getting the power from somewhere, right? If I could do a subterranean scan, I could confirm it but not at this distance. As we get closer I'll see what I can do."

He knew the scientists through the fleet would have a great time analysing this place. They would be walking around for years asking questions and working out how things functioned. "You've got all this recorded?"

"Data storage is filling up as we speak," replied Larsen.

He received a message. Carroll wanted him in the cockpit; it sounded urgent.

"Okay, got to go. I'll be in the cockpit if you need me. Excellent work."

With a quick push and a practiced flick off the bulkhead to the main deck he flew up the corridor and then nimbly controlled his zero g entry into the cockpit. Patterson was in intense study of his console and didn't respond as he arrived. Carroll lay motionless but messaged him again, the way pilots did.

'You're going to want to see this.'

"See what?" he said, not even noticing he'd responded verbally.

'I'll zoom the image. We have a Xannix vessel on intercept. It's really shifting. Currently at seven g and still accelerating.'

"How long?"

'I'd guess at about ten minutes, maybe fifteen, if they have to do any tricky manoeuvring.'

"That long."

To him the speed of the ship indicated aggression, and he'd been there before. The first contact with the Xannix had been a 'shoot first, ask questions later' affair and he didn't really want to go through that again.

"Patterson, are we receiving any comms?"

"Not that I can find, sir. Not specifically for us."

"Anything in the background noise? Anything broadcast from that ship as its source?"

Patterson took a moment to double check. "No, sir."

"Well, that doesn't sound good at all. Options anyone?"

"Honestly, sir? If they have guns and we don't, I'd make for the hills," suggested Patterson with a nod of the head, indicating the hills in question as the planet they were heading for.

"That action might get us killed quicker," said Carroll, now joining in and breaking his bio-comms messages. "They want us out of here? Going towards what they don't want us going towards is going to get us dead pretty quick, in my opinion."

"But get to the ground and we might be able to reason with them. At least we get to speak to someone."

"You hope."

"Hoping while doing something is far better than being a pessimist and doing nothing." He was beginning to think about turning the ship around and heading back to the *Endeavour* at pace but knew that they would never outrun the pursuit ship. Their best chance was to get somewhere first.

The arcology.

He messaged Larsen. 'I want coordinates to that arcology you were scanning earlier. And I need them now.'

Larsen didn't even respond, just sent the numbers. Before he could tell Carroll that he had the numbers and he'd forward them, Carroll just confirmed, "Got them."

"Best speed, Lieutenant. Give me ten seconds to strap in."

He fired himself down the corridor to the main deck and grabbed the first couch he found. He had only just clicked the harness when the engines roared and his kidneys felt like he had been hit with a baseball bat. A quick look around the deck found everyone safely in their couches and strapped in, grim faces fought the g forces as they pressed down on them, crushing them slowly into their now busy seats, moulding, compensating and where needed adjusting pain tolerances with drug cocktails designed to take the pain but not dull the senses.

'Pursuit ship adjusting for intercept,' Carroll updated. The ship was clearly after them and not on some coincidental flightpath.

'Larsen.'

'Yeah?'

'Xannix thought process. What did they do on the *Intrepid*? What might this interceptor do next?'

'It's an interceptor, sir. On the *Intrepid* they were violent and sneaky. Hiding and fighting.'

'Guerrilla attacks.'

'Yes, sir. It would suit a smaller force defending a large territory.'

'Can we see anything in our local space? Close. Remember they can cloak. Why can we see this guy and...' his mind almost froze as the obvious slapped him. 'Carroll, evasive.'

The pilot didn't argue or question, the shuttle suddenly jinked and jilted, pushing their already aching and disoriented bodies around with more ferocity. Something made a loud bang from the rear of the main deck cabin and the sound of metal under huge strain could be heard for several seconds.

'We've been hit,' reported Carroll. 'Main environmental control is damaged. Only thirty percent oxygen remaining.'

'Sir,' Larsen interjected on the open channel. 'A Xannix vessel has just appeared to our rear port side. Two point five kilometres.' There were a couple of seconds pause while he worked out some calculations. 'It's about three hundred metres in length, moving at relative speed and distance. My guess is it's been shadowing us for a while.'

'Can you track the incoming fire?'

'I don't know. I can try.'

He opened his bio-comms and connected to the shuttle's external cameras; he saw nothing but star field to their rear. Even at two kilometres the closest ship was difficult to spot with the naked eye. He switched visual to the front, cockpit view. The roll and pitch of the view was intensified by the fact the planet was rolling and pitching in equal measure. At this distance he couldn't see any horizon—it was all just big blue and white blotches of colour. If Carroll didn't ease off this angle of descent, it wouldn't matter that they were being shot at—they would simply disintegrate in the atmosphere and do the Xannix's work for them.

'Sir, three more pursuit craft have just launched from the Xannix ship to our rear,' Larsen updated.

Another jink almost pulled his arm from his socket, then an opposing hard g turn and the surface of Xannix swept from his view, replaced by a horizon.

'We're moving too fast,' Carroll stated to all. 'Brace for retro firing. Three, two, one, mark!'

The shuttle felt like it had suddenly hit a brick wall—nothing about this descent was gentle. He was thrown forward in his restraints with tremendous force, with his body fighting itself to stay together. The deceleration took too long and he started to feel his senses dull, as his eyes began to see nothing but a crimson red and his face felt like jelly sloshing round a bowl. He felt the couch's medical suite hit him with more stims to keep him conscious.

'How long?' he asked Carroll.

'Five more seconds.'

'Good.'

The retros stopped and the noise in the shuttle changed from that of roaring thunder to a whistling gale, as thin atmosphere began to engulf them. His camera showed a lick of heat from the nose of shuttle. As they descended further, the heat increased—as did the visual effect around the camera, bright lines of flame striping the screen. Buffeting that was not noticeable at first grew in intensity and began to shake them erratically in their couches. As his world became a blur, his eyes unable to focus on anything, he decided to try and relax through the worst but it was almost impossible. He was so juiced up on stims and his own adrenaline that any relaxing was never going to happen. To distract himself, he decided to try and plan ahead a little, work out his next move. His main worry was the pursuit craft, which would be on them the moment they broke through into clean air. His next worry was getting to the floor in one piece, and that was about as far as his train of thought took him.

With all the shooting going on, some days he wished he had joined the military. At least he would have had something to shoot back with.

DAWN

Travis had made it to the core chamber looking like he'd seen better days: his clothing was in tatters and dirt smothered him, blood clotting on his back and running down one arm. The gash on his head was severe and, although the blood had slowed, it hadn't appeared to have stopped. He was slouched in a corner of the chamber breathing hard through a broken face, jaw jutting awkwardly. She felt he was close to passing out.

Her image walked to him and knelt, a sympathetic look on her face—worried even. "Travis, you made it."

'Yes.' His eyes didn't even open.

"Are you able to trigger the device?"

'No.'

"Is there a problem with your arm? Hand?" She was bemused by the statement, although it didn't really matter if he was unable to operate the trigger—he was here now. "Then why are you unable to operate the trigger?"

'Truth.' There was a flicker in his eyelids but they still didn't open. 'You've been lying to me, Dawn. To us all.'

She sat next to him cross-legged and cocked her head to one side; he was right of course, but how did he know?

'It's the lies, Dawn. They stack up, and one day you were unable to contain them all.' He seemed pleased with himself that he had caught her in a lie. A slight smirk played across his lips, then a frown as the pain of his jaw hit him.

"What are you saying?"

340

'I'm not the first Travis. I thought I was, but things began to make no sense. You kept me in the dark. You kept me from really having a concept of time as it was. But here we are: Hayford b. I'm not two hundred years old, Dawn. Which means you've been playing me the whole time.'

It was going to happen at some point, but it really didn't matter. He wanted the truth? Well, what harm now?

"Okay, Travis. Let's talk. But the deal is I tell you what's been going on and then this ends."

'Sounds reasonable.'

"Nothing about this is reasonable." She smiled sadly then sat cross-legged in front of him. She seemed to settle, then began.

"We were to colonise an uninhabited planet, Hayford b— everyone knows that. It was the mantra, what everyone was told, and the success we were due as reward for our efforts. But what isn't widely known was that the colonisation was to occur at all costs. The protocols around what should happen if the planet was already inhabited were kept publicly vague, but, at a high level, Earth government and the corporate elite of OWEC had decided that nothing should stop their colonisation. After the investment of capital, the blood and sweat of nations and the fact that extinction was almost certain, it was decided that there would be no failure. Colonisation of the planet would occur whether inhabited or not."

'This makes no sense. How? This fleet is not armed. We have limited capability to defend ourselves, let alone mount an attack on a planet.'

"Not so."

That got his attention. He opened his eyes and sat up to face her, draining him of what little energy he had left.

'How?'

"You're thinking on the wrong scale," she continued. "You think the ship should have weapons." She shook her head to make the point. "The ship *is* the weapon."

As what she was saying hit home, a perplexed, horrified and broken face stared back.

"Apart from a few small defensive measures to give the illusion in design of a peaceful colony ship, the *Endeavour* is a twofold weapon, and together all three ships could be combined as a planet killer, if required.

"Consider the central lighting core which runs through the

central habitat—what do you think that's for?" She opened her palm in front of her as a light blue holographic schematic of the *Endeavour* appeared between them, floating and circling on its axis. A translucent orange line ran along the central core of the ship to the energy reservoir between the engine pods at the rear of the ship.

He sat and pondered for a moment. 'I'm guessing you're going to tell me it's not for lighting the habitat with natural light.'

"Correct. It is a function of the design but not its primary design purpose. Where is the power to light the habitat obtained?"

'The core generator, in the central engine complex.'

"Which is basically a reservoir of energy, generated from the engine pods which encircle it and stored for later use." She paused as she could see he wasn't understanding or grasping the connection. "What I'm trying to lead you towards is that the *Endeavour* is one big energy beam weapon. It has the capacity to destroy cities from space in a single firing and recharge within half an hour. And we have three of these weapons: the *Endeavour*, the *Indianapolis* and the *Intrepid*."

'This is insanity,' was all he could say.

"And the second trick, if orbital energy weapons are not enough to subdue the inhabitants, is that a ship can sacrifice clone resources to eradicate the apex presence on the planet. But it does need genetic material of the alien species, so a first encounter is necessary."

'And how does the genocide play out exactly?' he asked, disbelieving.

"DNA of the apex species is used and a lethal genetic mutation synthesized. This is then delivered via airborne vector. It's not as fast—it might take a few months—but it is total and thorough. Although technically not alive, not legally anyway, clones are used as incubators. Once the biological agent is mature, the waste disposal system is used to create particulate that is released into the planet's atmosphere. "

'But you have no alien DNA,' he argued, realising the horror in design and creation of the weapon.

"You are working with less than the full facts, I'm afraid. The Xannix boarded the *Intrepid* a couple of days ago. They were allowed to board. We now have their DNA."

'We?' Then he made the connection. 'The AI.'

"The appointed guardians of mankind."

'By whom?'

"The world government. OWEC. It's not important. What is important is that we have the mandate to protect humanity and that is what we will do." She could see him blinking slowly, struggling to unpick the words he was hearing. Moving closer, an inquisitive focus in her eyes, she cupped his face with her palm. She smiled sadly and sat back. "Alas for you, that means that there is no suicide pact between us, but you should know that you played your part well. We couldn't have done all this without you.

"And, so you know, the sabotaged circuits in my systems have been replaced."

It was at that moment that he realised the trap had closed around him; she could see in the widening of his eyes that the connection had finally been made.

'What have you done?' he asked in horrified shock, whilst putting an urgent hand to grab his chest, his breathing becoming light and infrequent, as if his body had forgotten its autonomic responsibilities.

"What must be done." Her reply was curt, factual and spoken without remorse. His eyelids flickered and slowly closed as he slumped back against the wall, head flopped against this chest. She viewed him with some sympathy. From the moment he had entered the room the chamber had been sealed and she had begun to increase the nitrogen in the atmosphere. Within a few minutes, and by the end of their conversation, the nitrogen had reached saturation, his body now quivering with light nervous fidgets and convulsions as the rest of his system succumbed to the inert gas asphyxiation.

Once Travis had been dealt with, she regulated the atmosphere again and opened the chamber door. Standing, waiting at the doorway, was her father, his face stern and questioning. He paced in and up to the third of the Travis corpses, then he turned to her.

"So, it's done then?" he asked her, without any formalities.

"Yes, Daddy. That's the final Travis clone—we have them all."

He nodded solemnly and walked past her, back to the entrance of the chamber. "Very good. Inform the others that a shuttle is on the way to the *Indianapolis* with DNA to complete their procedures. I want all ships fully weaponised within the next eight hours."

"I'll let them know."

LARSEN

Things hadn't got any better as they broke into the upper atmosphere of Xannix. There were a lot of factors against them; he could see fleeting visions of three of those factors through the rear external cameras of the shuttle, and another was the damage to the shuttle from the earlier orbital attack. There must be hull material twisted into the airflow or damage to control because there was a hell of a noise and Carroll was having a really hard time controlling the ship. His exact words were, 'She's flying like a brick in a lead box, sir,' which to him meant nothing good. On top of that, the ground was coming up fast.

'Can we do anything about those pursuit craft, Carroll?'

'I'll try to lose them but I'm having a hard enough time just trying to control her. We're not going to be able to make the arcology; we'll be lucky to get this on the ground in one piece.'

'Understood.'

More good news. He saw Rivers quickly calculate the likely point of impact and found it was a point within what looked like pine forest near the north of the planet. She sent the update to Havers and Carroll. He could see Havers across the cabin, his face scrunched up in what could only be a painful thought process, like trying to find a way out of an air-tight box which was fast running out of air.

'Okay, team. The plan is a simple one. Get to the ground as fast as we can. We'll have to take our chances in an escape and evade through the forest and hope we can get enough of a head start.'

'Where to?'

'We'll worry about that when we get on the ground.'

'Roger,' said Carroll.

Light flashed across the front view camera of the shuttle and he took a moment to realise the pursuit craft were firing on them again. He couldn't work out whether it was a warning shot or they had simply missed, probably the latter—they had already taken a chunk from the rear of the shuttle, so they were hardly likely to start playing nice now. It was followed by a swooping shadow across the screen, too fast for him to make out a shape, but his reaction was to push back into the seat to put a few more millimetres distance between it and him. The Xannix were trying to cut them off and dissuade them from landing. It wouldn't work; the shuttle was beaten up too much to do anything but work its way to the ground.

The shuttle lurched violently, up and to the right. Another craft nosed past, fire flaring from its centreline weapons, and Carroll steered them clear of danger again.

'These guys are persistent little bastards,' Carroll commented, possibly to himself, but he managed to broadcast it to the crew. Another heart-stopping manoeuvre had them suddenly lose height; Larsen felt his heart try to escape his chest as the shuttle began to plummet. Whatever they were trying to avoid didn't quite work, and the side of the shuttle where some of the security team were harnessed disappeared with an horrific, explosive wrench of metal only to be replaced with a banshee howl as atmosphere blasted its way around the cabin space. There were involuntary screams lost in the noise as they were left to watch the sudden turn of events and the now uncontrolled spin the shuttle was forced into.

He looked across to Havers, possibly thinking he could conjure up some miraculous escape as he was out of ideas. Havers just looked back with a face as white and pale as a ghost. Something was wrong—Havers' eyes were not looking at him, and were not focussed on anything at all. He was dead. Through the vibrations of the wrecked shuttle's descent, he saw the stanchion which would ordinarily have been part of the shuttle's frame, now buckled and contorted and lancing Havers through the chest. Difficult to see from his couch but it must have caught Havers through the heart: he would have died almost immediately.

Gripping the ends of the armrests to his couch, he shook the chair in a thrashing outburst of anger and grief. Havers had not only been his commanding officer but a friend and mentor over the years. Having fought off all the trials of the last few days, for this to happen to Havers was a dark and bitter joke.

He tried the best he could to compose himself. Havers had been right: they needed to get on the ground but they were fast running out of time.

'Carroll, this is Larsen. Havers is dead. We need to get on the ground fast.'

'That is the one thing I can guarantee. Attempting to correct the spin.'

'Don't care about location, we need to get out from under these Xannix fighters.'

'Agreed. Looking for options.'

Rivers had already started the search, and he joined in. Another five seconds and the spin stopped but he could still feel the heavy descent as his body pressed hard against his harness, indicating the high negative g they were experiencing. He used the current location of the ship relative to the ground and scrolled the screen to view the low-level terrain in the direction of their travel. It was nothing but a sea of trees at the moment, compact with a dense canopy, but moving forward along their track the scenery changed, becoming mountainous highlands and snow-covered peaks.

Then a lake.

"There!" he shouted. Only Rivers heard him and looked across to the screen he was analysing. He quickly sent the coordinates to Carroll.

'What's this?' asked Carroll.

'Our new landing site. It's a lake—softer than hitting forest.'

'I hope you can remember how to swim.'

'Just get us as close to the shore as you can without hitting the trees.'

Performing another strong right turn and sudden jink to the left, Carroll tried to keep the pursuing craft guessing. 'Twenty seconds.'

The direction of g force inverted and he was pushed hard into the couch. Noticing the forward-facing camera, he could now see they had levelled out and the tree canopy was flashing past at tremendous speed, blurred and unfocussed.

'Fifteen seconds.' Carroll continued his countdown. Some

checked their harnesses, others calmed themselves and awaited the impact. He noticed Rivers sign something across her chest and then crossed her arms, grabbing her harnesses at the chest to ensure her arms didn't thrash about on impact. Drill and routine. He did the same.

'Ten seconds.' He tried to calm himself and envisage and practice his escape from the shuttle. They needed to get off the shuttle and into the cover of the forest as soon as they could. He looked across at Rivers again, and she was looking right back at him. She looked scared; he guessed he did too.

"Don't worry," he yelled over the buffeting gale about them. He held out his hand for her and she took it, gripping tightly. He smiled, trying to exude a confidence he didn't feel.

'Five seconds, people.'

He faced the front, still holding Rivers by the hand, and relaxed his head into the couch waiting for the impact. From the corner of his eye he could see water rushing past in the large hole which had been punched from the side of the airframe—it was black and cold and deep. He felt himself waiting for death, oddly calm with the notion, at peace and taking comfort from the small level of human contact he shared with Rivers. They would face this together.

The last five seconds seemed to go on forever, the deafening howl of the wind in the cabin, the rushing water outside and even faster approaching treeline on the shore. At last, the rear of the ship dragged into the water, elevating the cacophony even higher, and icy water sprayed into the cabin, feeling like needles against the skin. Metal screamed in torsion, and there was a sudden violent shaking and deceleration as his body was thrown randomly about, muscles no longer able to control his body against the chaotic forces being hurled around within the cabin. An incredible bang overshadowed all other sound, followed by an intense tumbling, and instantly his consciousness escaped him. The blackness came.

*

The world around him came back slowly but nothing about it made sense. Light was dim and intermittent, and he was cold, ever so, ever so cold, from the abdomen down. His head seemed to loll to his left and he felt a heaviness across the chest. Blinking in the available light, he tried to move, and all his limbs appeared to be working, as far as he could tell. He was, unbelievably, still holding Rivers' hand. Rivers. Looking round, he saw her in her crash couch, unconscious and hanging limply in her harness, all her limbs dangling towards him and her hair across her face, hiding her serene features. His mind began to work and it started to put the geometry of the scene together.

None of the instrumentation in front of him was working. He tried to call up any of the shuttle's systems through his bio-comms, but all he could get was the black box location and comms link. That was a start. He scanned for others using their bio-comms to obtain a response. The only active ping he got was from Rivers, although she was clearly unresponsive right now. He was unclear at the moment as to whether this meant that they had already got out of the shuttle or that they were all dead. He assumed they were all dead as, if they were alive, they should at least have tried to rescue him and Rivers. As far as he could tell, this had not happened.

Getting his bearings, he finally realised that he and Rivers were hanging in their harnesses; the ship must have come to rest on an angle, and they were almost completely over on their left side but not quite. They were clearly submerged, as the coldness in his legs and abdomen was due to being submerged in icy cold water up to his middle at an angle, his left arm also submerged to the elbow. Rivers, however, was a little luckier and found herself suspended in her couch above him and the water. The equipment was offline, although a couple of emergency lights were still working dimly and one flickered now and then, probably shorting out due to the water.

Much as he didn't want to move, he knew that moving was their only real option for survival, so he took a firm hold on the couch and hit the release on his harness. His grip on the couch wasn't strong enough and he fell the short distance into the water, submerging completely into the icy black. His arms grabbed as he fell and he managed to clutch hold of a strap of the harness, which stopped him from losing all orientation. Pulling himself towards the harness, he gasped for air and managed to find a better hand hold to stop himself slipping back into the water. After a few moments, he was able to climb over his couch and wedge himself between his and Rivers' couch. It felt like he was perched on a ledge, but at least he was completely out of the water. Giving himself time to think, he finally remembered his suit's external light and turned it on. Rivers was instantly bathed in a bright pool of white light. With the additional clarity, he began to tend to Rivers.

Feeling for a pulse, he first took her wrist then checked her neck, but his fingers were so numb that he couldn't feel a thing. "Come on, Rivers," he encouraged, and brushed her hair from her face. Placing his cheek close to her nose and mouth, he strained to feel some movement of air. It was faint but, after waiting frozen in anticipation for several seconds, he was convinced there was life. He sighed heavily and rested his head against her chest—the heartbeat was faint but it was there. "Right, Rivers. Time to wake up. We've got surviving to do."

He took her by the shoulders and gently shook her. "Rivers," he said kindly but firmly. "Rivers, wake up. We've got work to do." He shook again, a little firmer.

A moan. She was coming round. With a grimace and some slowly opening eyes, she tried, as he had earlier, to understand her surroundings. Squinting at him, she held up a hand to shield her eyes from the bright light of his suit. He helped by taking her hand and putting a reassuring hand to her face. "You're okay," he said. "You're alive and still on the shuttle." Her eyes opened fully as he turned the light to an angle away from her and he smiled back with as much confidence as he could muster.

"Time to get out of here, Rivers."

She shook her head, as if shaking off a dizzy spell and tried to refocus. He was still there.

"The others?"

"I'm getting no reading, but they could have already left. Looks like we've been out for about twenty minutes."

"I doubt they would have just left us."

"No, you may be right. But until we know for sure..." He shrugged to finish the unwanted thought.

"So, what's our first move?" she asked.

"To get you out of your harness. Then we should grab our survival kits from the couches and get out of here."

"Okay. Let's go."

He helped Rivers get out of the harness without falling into the water. It was a small mercy—she would need to take the plunge shortly, but no real need to be icy cold and chilled to the bone before she had to be. She climbed up on top of her couch in the same way as he was, and both of them then pulled their survival kits from under the crash couches—a pack containing all they would need: compacted shelter and clothing compressed into blocks, food and navigational aids, radio equipment, utiliplex, hunting knife, medical supplies and a pistol with three magazines of ammunition, all packaged into a neatly designed waterproof backpack.

Once they had checked everything and checked it again, he slapped his backpack. "Ready?" he asked.

"Ready."

He took the plunge first, the water so cold that it almost took his breath from him. Pulling with his arms and kicking hard with his legs, he made his way down to what used to be the left side of the shuttle but was now a gaping hole of rended, twisted metal, part buried in the lake bed. As he expected, there was a gap between the rocky lake bottom and the upper edge of the airframe which allowed them both to push their way into open water. On his way, he tried to look for others. The remaining security team were still in their seats, all dead—most likely drowned— and Havers was still in his chair, pinned in place by the lance of metal to his chest. He wished them peace and rest after their struggles. He knew this was part of being at the forefront of human existence but it was brutal. Life was brutal.

Breaching the hull and swimming out into open water, he looked up to where he expected to see the surface of the lake—and there it was. Daylight flecked by the ripples and wavelets of water dancing on the surface of the lake, he kicked and pulled even harder as he felt his ears and lungs complaining about the depth and lack of air. He hoped Rivers was right behind him. His lungs began to scream for air and he felt no nearer the surface. He wasn't a diver, so had no real concept of the distance to the surface nor the depth the shuttle had finally come to rest but it was further than he had anticipated. Carroll must not have been able to get close enough to shore before they had crashed.

He felt his eyes start to bulge as his body reflex began gulping for air. Though he had his mouth clamped tight it was a harsh warning to him that he didn't have long. He didn't know whether kicking for the surface any faster would help him or whether he should simply give in to the drift of the icy water and let it take him to the surface at its own pace.

The water around him became lighter and lighter and with some exhilaration he realised he was there. Breaking the surface he gasped for air, choking and coughing as his actions also sucked down an amount of water. His backpack, which he had been pushing ahead of him, bobbed and floated to his side; he held it as a buoyancy aid and began looking around urgently for signs of Rivers. She fired up out of the water like a salmon leaping upstream, mouth wide for air and life. He found himself yelling her name and swimming towards her. They grinned inanely at each other while catching their breath and laughing hard at the simple joy of living another minute.

Searching the horizon, they looked for the closest lakeside and found the shore was about two hundred metres away—Carroll had done better than he had thought. Remembering the chase on the way down, he scanned the sky for signs of the Xannix craft but there were none that he could see. He wasn't sure if this meant anything, given their ability to cloak and hide objects, but the fact that they were not cloaked on the way down may mean that these smaller craft could not be cloaked. Maybe they were there; maybe they weren't. They would need to be vigilant.

Making their way to the shore they climbed exhausted onto a beach of dark grey sand. The treeline, only metres away, was a dense and somewhat familiar-looking forest. He was no expert but it looked very much like a pine forest back home. They fell, shattered, to the ground and sat for a few minutes, silently, getting their breath back and trying to think of what they had to do next. They were wet through and needed to get into some dry clothes. They also needed to get some distance from the shore, take shelter and get some sleep.

Turning to look across the lake, he found beauty in the scene. It was like images he remembered his grandmother showing him of the fjords before the end—before they had been forced to move to the Southern Scandinavian Metrociti, where ninety percent of all Scandinavians lived and worked. The system's star, whatever they called it on this planet, was low in the sky, setting behind a mountain range capped with snow and glinting in the light. He wondered how long they would have before dark and what that might bring. He realised sharply that they were now the aliens on this planet with no knowledge of the local flora or fauna, thus they were very exposed and ill-equipped for the days to come.

Both standing, he slung his backpack over his shoulder. Taking one last look at the lake, calm and still, he could see no trace of the shuttle which he knew to be metres below the surface. No trace that they had even arrived on a completely new and alien planet. The first humans to ever step onto this world. All that he could think now was that they must survive. Survive at all costs.

They turned and walked in silence from the lakeside into the tree line and the forest beyond.

ABOUT THE AUTHOR

Nathan M. Hurst was born in Southampton, Hampshire, but after extensive and excessive adventuring, settled near Epping Forest on the outskirts of London with his wife and young son. He has worked as a software developer and technical manager for many years whilst maintaining an avid enthusiasm for aviation and astronautics. Consuming science-fiction and adventure stories of all varieties from an early age his love for books turned into a passion for writing.

You can reach Nathan by Twitter @nathanmhurst or via email at nathan@nathanmhurst.com.

Email: nathan@nathanmhurst.com
Web: www.nathanmhurst.com

Made in United States
Orlando, FL
09 March 2023